UNSUNG

ALSO BY SHANNON RICHARD

UNSUNG

A Country Roads Novel

SHANNON RICHARD

FOREVER
YOURS

New York   Boston

Copyright © 2015 by Shannon Richard
Cover design by Oceana Garceau
Cover copyright © 2015 by Hachette Book Group, Inc.

Forever Yours
Hachette Book Group
1290 Avenue of the Americas
New York, NY 10104

hachettebookgroup.com
twitter.com/foreverromance

First ebook and print on demand edition: November 2015

Forever Yours is an imprint of Grand Central Publishing.
The Forever Yours name and logo are trademarks of Hachette Book Group, Inc.

The publisher is not responsible for websites (or their content) that are not owned by the publisher.

The Hachette Speakers Bureau provides a wide range of authors for speaking events. To find out more, go to www.hachettespeakersbureau.com or call (866) 376-6591.

ISBN 978-1-4555-6504-7 (ebook edition)
ISBN 978-1-4555-6510-8 (print on demand edition)

To Jessica Lemmon,
It just goes to show that sometimes this weird and wonderful
life knows exactly what it's doing,
especially when it gives me extraordinary friends like you.
Thank you for being a constant sounding board in both this
fictional land of writing and in the real world.

Acknowledgments

I remember the days when friends of mine would read what I wrote and I couldn't be in the same room because I was so terrified of what they thought. Never once did any of them give me anything but support and love in this crazy dream of mine. It's because of their words of encouragement and support that this dream became a reality and these stories have been written.

Thank you to all of my very first Beta readers: Kaitie Hotard, Gloria Berry, Diana Quintero, Katie Crandall, Catie Humphreys, Jenna Robinson, Jennifer Pezzuto, Jennifer Ewing, Kelly Filippini, Marina McCue, Sarah Pennell, Katie Waldow, Tyler Sojourner, Kerrie Alexander, Molly Kane, Heather Seeman, Mike Widener, Chris Widener, Amanda Blanchard, Michelle Blanchard, Ronald Richard, my parents, and to everyone else who ever took the time to read for me. I appreciate you all more than you know.

Then there are all of the lovely Beta readers who I've acquired since then, especially Nikki Rushbrook. You are a wealth of information and insight. Thank you for always offering up your invaluable knowledge. Also, thank you to Amy Lipford for your dry wit and real-time talk.

And finally, thank you to my agent Sarah E. Younger, my editor Megha Parekh, my publicist Julie Paulauski, and everyone at Grand Central Publishing for all of the hard work you do day in and day out.

Forever

Love at first sight was something I'd never seen
but you walked in and became every single one of my dreams
Violet eyes and the lips of a goddess
I knew I'd want more than just one kiss

A day, a week, a month, a year
It would never be enough
I want forever
Forever, honey
Forever with you

A million simple things that aren't so simple at all
Your hand in mine
The taste of your tongue
Your head on my chest
You stealing my heart

A day, a week, a month, a year
It would never be enough
I want forever
Forever, honey
Forever with you

You were something I never knew I always wanted
Something I never knew I always needed
And now that I know, I can't let go
I need forever, honey
Forever with you

UNSUNG

Prologue

Found

The crowd of people in the ballroom of the Brogan-Meyers Hotel was only getting thicker as the minutes passed. The space was packed with men in tuxes and women in designer dresses of varying lengths. Some gowns trailed along the floor, perilously close to getting trampled on, while others had barely enough fabric to cover the women wearing them.

Harper Laurence's dress was somewhere in the middle. The midnight blue fabric clung to every single curve of her body, the neckline dipping just low enough to show her very impressive cleavage without being too immodest. Add to that the fact that it made her violet eyes pop, and looked pretty spectacular with her long black hair if she did say so herself.

Or she would've said so if it had been a few months ago.

She'd grabbed the dress when she'd been packing. It had been a magic dress before tonight and she'd always been able to rock it with every ounce of her confidence.

But said confidence was gone.

Gone. Gone. Gone.

She'd had it before. Before she'd been left by her fiancé. Before she'd taken a trip to Tennessee to get away. Before she'd fallen in love with a stranger.

But was he really a stranger?

No. Not by the end. Not when everything was all said and done. Not when she'd turned tail and ran scared. But he'd broken the rules…and so had she.

The rules had been so simple. Well, *rule* really. There'd just been the one: nothing personal.

But she'd been fooling herself from the moment she'd met him. Everything about their time together had been personal. Every moment she'd spent with him. How was it that she'd fallen faster and harder for him in two days, felt more for him in those hours than she ever had for her ex? How was that even possible?

And now everything was five thousand times more complicated.

What had she been thinking coming here?

Her stomach rolled and she closed her eyes, breathing deeply through her nose and counting her breaths until the nausea subsided to a tolerable level. When she opened her eyes it was to find Mel making her way over, a champagne glass in each hand.

Melanie Hart was one of Harper's best friends and the reason she was at the party in the first place. A party of beyond attractive athletes, celebrities within elbow rubbing distance no matter where she stood, a handful of very important politicians, and even a Nobel Peace Prize winner. But as the Jacksonville Stampede had just won the Stanley Cup, it was a reason to celebrate. A distraction as Mel had put it.

A distraction from Harper's current predicament? Impossible. There wasn't anything that could detract from what was occupying her brain.

Harper raised an eyebrow as Mel passed her a glass.

"It's ginger ale. Maybe that will calm your stomach," Mel said as she brushed one of her short blond curls behind her ear.

"Maybe." Harper nodded, not feeling confident in that prospect at all.

"Come on. Let's go find my husband and the boys before they get into trouble." Mel grabbed Harper's hand and led her across the room. Good thing, too, because the crowd of people was thick and it wouldn't take a lot to get lost among them.

Her eyes caught on a couple in the corner, the woman obviously pregnant and the man resting his hand on her belly as he whispered in her ear, grinning. The sight made her both sad and envious beyond reason.

She tipped the glass of soda back, wishing it were something much stronger. The bubbles popped against her nose and lips as the cold liquid hit her tongue.

Mel's pace slowed and her grip on Harper's hand loosened. Mel was talking and Harper turned her head at the sound of her own name being said.

Her eyes landed on the man directly across from her and she choked on her sip of soda, coughing uncontrollably.

He was here. The *rule-breaking stranger* was standing right in front of her, the green-gold gaze that she knew so well focused on her.

Yup, there was nothing in the world that could calm her stomach now. No more hiding from the reality she was going to have to face head on in this moment. No more running away.

It was Liam. He'd found her.

Chapter One

Love at First Sight

May 8th…six weeks earlier

Sometimes in life, there are moments of grief that are so deep and thick that a person can't possibly see the other side. Moments where it seems impossible that the future could hold something even a fraction better than the past.

And in those moments there was only one thing that could help.

Tequila.

At least that was Harper's philosophy on the matter and how she had every intention of spending the weekend that would've been her wedding. Because really, what else was a person supposed to do when they'd been jilted at the altar?

Okay, maybe not *literally* at the altar…but three months to the altar, and that was close enough by her calculations. Especially as she and her fiancé Brad Nelson had been planning the wedding for seven months.

Seven. Fucking. Months.

Locations had been confirmed, deposits had been paid, save

the dates sent out, and her two-thousand-dollar dream wedding
dress customer ordered to perfection.

Per-fec-tion.

Not that it mattered anymore. The dress had been sold to the
highest bidder on eBay, a whopping five hundred dollars. But
whatever, it was no longer in her apartment staring her down every time she walked by.

Brad had been kind enough to leave everything for Harper to
take care of in the cancellation department. Such a gem. But at
least he'd left Mirabelle, packed up his stuff and taken a job in
Louisiana so she didn't have to worry about running into him at
the grocery store. Because if she did she just might run him over.

Or at the very least clip him with her car.

She'd worked past the grieving stage of things—for the most
part—and now she was just angry about it. Really angry. But it
was hard to move on when just about everyone in her town of
Mirabelle, Florida, knew what had happened.

With a population of a little more than five thousand, there
were very few degrees of separation between anyone. Someone
knew someone who knew someone. And courtesy of the ever-aw-
ful—and Mirabelle's resident gossip hag—Bethelda Grimshaw,
Harper's jilting had been sensationalized to a point that was hard
for anyone to ignore.

Bethelda had once worked for the local newspaper, and when
her human-interest pieces morphed into a nasty tell-all about the
residents' less than savory business, she'd been fired. Now she had
a blog where she spread her poison, and though she changed the
names—which in no way protected the innocent—everyone always knew exactly who she was talking about.

It hadn't even been forty-eight hours when Harper and Brad's breakup hit the blog page, and the story had haunted Harper for the last three months.

THE GRIM TRUTH

DISSED AND DISMISSED

If I've said it once I've said it a thousand times, no one is going to buy the cow if they can get the milk for free. And my words of wisdom have yet again proven true with the case of Voluptuous V. and her hightailing ex-fiancé Human Ken Doll.

Voluptuous V. (or VV for short, which is probably the girl's bra size) was given the old heave-ho. Ho being the operative word here. And I feel bad for the girl, really I do, but what did she expect? Ken was out of her league to begin with.

I mean when it comes right down to it, a civil engineer with three degrees under his belt isn't going to *settle down* or *settle with* a woman whose talents are purely physical. Now I'm not saying that VV used her "massage" skills to seduce him, but I'm not *not* saying it, either.

I would imagine that VV's skills must be extensive, because it took Ken a year and a half to see the light of day. And as soon as he did he packed up his things and headed out for different horizons.

And as to the incident that ignited his speedy getaway? I'm not *exactly* sure what happened to make the man remove his blinders. But what I can tell you is that it happened right after her bridal shower.

Maybe it was the china pattern that set him off, or the color of the bathroom towels, or the idea of waking up in floral sheets next to the same woman for the rest of his life. Who knows?

But what we do know is that come May 9th, VV will not be walking down the aisle to marry the man of her dreams…nor will she be walking down the aisle to marry the man who almost settled for her.

The real kicker? Bethelda's article hadn't been too far from the reality of the "incident." It had in fact been right after Harper's bridal shower. But it hadn't been china, or bedding, or towels that had set him off.

Nope. It had been a potato masher.

They'd been loading up his car with all of the gifts from her shower when he grabbed it out of a bag. He held the utensil in the air, his brow furrowed quizzically.

"What is this?"

To be fair to the guy—something she was in *no way* inclined to be—the shape was odd. A handle connected to a weird metal wave that somewhat resembled a heartbeat on a monitor.

"You use it to mash potatoes."

"Oh." He nodded before he'd put it back in the bag, and that furrowed look on his brow only got more pronounced.

It was a five-minute drive from where the bridal shower had been to Harper's apartment. They hadn't even gone a mile when they were stopped at a red light.

She asked him what he wanted for dinner.

He told her he didn't want to get married.

How did he get from Point A to Point B? Apparently the potato masher made him think about the holidays. Thanksgiving and Christmas with family all gathered around a table, turkey and stuffing and *stupid mashed potatoes* all piled high. He'd pictured it all quite clearly…and Harper hadn't been a part of it.

As they'd never officially moved in together—her mother would've had a fit—it didn't take him very long to get his stuff out of her apartment. He left Mirabelle two weeks later. She might not have to deal with him living in the same town anymore, but she did have to deal with the pity from just about everyone she knew.

And that was why Harper was currently in Nashville, Tennessee, free from her mostly well-intentioned friends and family—complete with hovering/overbearing mother—and their looks of concern. She loved them all dearly, but she just couldn't deal with it. And to be honest it was hard to be around them.

Her friends were all settled and popping out babies like it was their business. And she was happy for them. Really she was. She'd just wanted all of that with Brad. He'd been part of her dream…she just hadn't been part of his.

And that was why tequila was on the agenda for the evening that would've been her rehearsal dinner. She was meeting up with her aunt at the Second Hand Guitar, Harper's go-to bar in Nashville.

Celeste Angelo was not only Harper's favorite aunt—and current sanctuary provider—but she was also a renowned obstetrician who specialized in high-risk pregnancies. Women from all over the United States came to her to save not only their babies' lives, but sometimes their own.

Celeste was the only woman in Harper's life who was happily unmarried. She and her longtime boyfriend Reed were more than satisfied with their separate houses and bank accounts.

Maybe there was something to be said about that.

But she wasn't going to think about any of that tonight. Nope, tonight was about forgetting.

It was a little before ten o'clock when Harper walked into the building. She made her way through the crowd and to the square bar that sat at the back of the room. A couple got up from two seats on the side corner and made their way over to the dance floor where a live band played from the stage. A girl was belting out a fast-paced song while she strummed on her guitar, a guy sang backup and played base, while another guy beat out a steady rhythm on the drums behind them.

The Second Hand Guitar was one of Harper's favorite places to come when she was in Nashville, with its exposed brick walls, hardwood floors, and constant stream of occupants that made people-watching thoroughly entertaining. Not to mention the selection of alcohol was excellent. There were about thirty taps lined up behind the bar, and shelves of more assorted hard liquor than she could count.

It was her second favorite bar after her local watering hole the Sleepy Sheep, owned and run by one of her close friends, Nathanial Shepherd. He was like the alcohol whisperer, could tell someone what they wanted before they even opened their mouth. And his ability would be nice in this moment because Harper wasn't sure what to get. Though tequila was on the agenda for the evening, she figured she and her aunt should start with something lighter.

By the time the bartender made his way over to her, she settled on a mild beer with vanilla and orange undertones and ordered two. The second he turned around to go get the drinks her phone vibrated on the bar in front of her. She grabbed it and looked at the screen to see a message from her aunt, her heart sinking somewhere around her navel as she read.

Emergency surgery on patient. Can't make it. So sorry. I WILL see you tomorrow and we will drink in style and excess my sweet niece. Love you, Cee.

Harper didn't even get a second to process the fact that she was now going to be spending the evening alone when someone came up next to her. She turned to find a guy with unkempt blond hair, a faded flannel shirt over a dirty white tank top, and a neck tattoo that said *Bubba* blocking her view. He was leaning against the bar and looking right at Harper.

Fantastic…not only had she been stood up but she had to deal with this on top of it? Don't get her wrong, she was a fan of tattoos in certain locations, but neck tattoos of this caliber required a special level of *I-ain't-ever-gonna-be-a-functioning-member-of-the-workforce* crazy.

"I was so distracted by that banging body of yours that I ran into that wall over there," he said as he pointed to the wall behind him. "So I'm gonna need that name and number of yours for insurance reasons."

Oh. Dear. God. No. Just no.

"I'm afraid you're going to have to claim a hit and run," a deep voice drawled from behind her.

Harper spun on her stool, her back now to the bar, to find a very different sort of man than Bubba. The sort of man she really wouldn't mind hitting on her in the least bit—if she was ready for that sort of thing…which she so obviously was not.

But ready or not, she could still appreciate his strong jaw covered in day-old stubble, dark brown hair long enough for a woman to run her fingers through and get a little lost in the process, and green-gold eyes that were focused on her.

The bartender returned at that moment, sliding both drinks onto the counter and Sexy 'n Scruffy reached across her, handing the bartender a bill before grabbing both of the beers. He gave one to Harper before he held his up in the air.

"Thanks for ordering, babe." His mouth quirked to the side—flashing the kind of grin that made her thankful for the fact that she was already sitting down—before he brought the glass to his mouth and took a sip. He lowered it a moment later and made a sound of satisfaction that set her imagination on fire, not to mention the way he was looking at her.

Good God, the amount of intensity directed at her should be illegal. When his eyes left hers a moment later she realized she'd been holding her breath. Though she found herself disappointed by the fact that he was no longer looking at her, it was good that she was breathing again.

Sexy 'n Scruffy's eyes were now focused on a spot over her shoulder, presumably at Bubba. She wasn't quite sure as she couldn't pull her gaze away from his face to check. "You should move along now."

"No harm, no foul," Bubba said before he went off to find another victim.

Sexy 'n Scruffy's attention was now back on Harper as he took another sip of beer. "Good choice," he nodded as he slid onto the empty stool next to her.

"Glad you approve of *my* beer that you're drinking."

"Your beer?" He gave her that tilted grin again. "I believe I paid, after saving you from Recently Paroled over there."

"Saved me?"

"Yup, he was about to ask for your social and bank account information."

"That man wasn't going to get anything personal out of me."

"Of that, I have no doubt."

"So what, you want a *thank-you* for saving me?" she asked, raising her eyebrow before she brought her glass to her mouth and took her first sip of beer.

"Nope, no *thank-you* required. Just doing my civic duty. But it would be nice to know your name."

"Oh, so you're just going to start up where Bubba left off?" She set her glass on the bar before she placed both of her elbows on the edge of the wood and leaned her head against her hands.

"Nah," he said as he shook his head. "I just wanted to know so that when I tell this story years from now, people will know the name of the most beautiful woman I've ever met."

Harper threw her head back and laughed. When she looked at him again she couldn't stop the smile that spread across her face. "Wow, that was a line if I've ever heard one."

He shook his head again, leaning in close to her, his intense gaze locked on her eyes. "Oh, you want a line? 'Do you have a map? Because I'm getting lost in your eyes.' *That's* a line. Now as to you being beautiful? *That's* a fact."

She'd be lying if she said those words hadn't made her heart race just a little bit…or a lotta bit.

He pulled back and took another drink of his beer, swallowing as he lowered the glass. "Who was this beer intended for anyway?"

"My aunt. Who just got stuck at work. Life of a doctor though."

"So really I'm just saving it from going to waste and saving *you* from getting hit on by any more guys with neck tats."

"I guess you are." And there was that smile taking over her face again. *What the hell was going on?*

"So what's it going to be? Do I have to share this beer with a nameless stranger?"

"I'm not telling you anything personal, either."

He leaned in close again, a seriousness in his gaze that she somehow *knew* to be sincere. "You don't have to tell me anything you don't want to."

Over the years she'd given out her fair share of fake names, and it was on the tip of her tongue to give him one tonight. But to her complete and utter shock, when she opened her mouth her name fell out.

"Harper."

"Harper," he repeated slowly, his eyes traveling over her face like he was not only memorizing her name but everything about her.

The scrutiny almost made her squirm. *Almost.* But Harper Laurence was made of much sterner stuff than that. Or at least she sure as hell hoped so.

"I'm Liam." He put his beer on the bar and held out his hand.

Before she could think better of it, she was putting her palm in his. His long fingers wrapped around her hand, his skin warm on hers and somehow traveling up and over her, like she was settling into a steaming bath or wrapping herself in a blanket straight out of the dryer.

Apparently she wasn't as numb as she thought.

Oh, this was going to be bad…or really, *really* good. She was just going to have to see now wasn't she?

* * *

The second the front door of the cabin closed Harper found herself pushed up against the wall. She only had a moment to take in the rich wooden floors and walls that stretched out from the entryway to the living room.

But as she was now looking up into warm green-gold eyes and pinned against said wall by the solid weight of a perfectly muscled, attractive-as-sin man, she found that she really couldn't care less about the décor. Or anything else for that matter.

All she cared about in that moment was Liam. He was all she'd cared about since he'd grabbed that beer from the bar.

They hadn't stopped with that first drink, either. She'd gotten her shots of tequila, and Liam had been right there next to her, licking the salt and sucking the lime. But neither of them had gotten crazy; they'd paced themselves up to a nice little buzz.

And then somewhere around midnight he'd leaned in close to her ear and whispered, "Do you want to get out of here?"

"You know a place we can get a burger? I'm starving." Dinner had seemed like ages ago and she usually always got the munchies when she drank anyway.

He'd smiled as he grabbed her hand and led her out of the bar. They walked two blocks to a twenty-four-hour diner where they'd both not only gotten a burger and fries, but the best chocolate malt milk shakes she'd ever had in her life. They then sat there for three hours and talked.

When he asked questions that bled too far into the personal side—career, where she was from, why she was in Nashville—she'd just shake her head and he'd move on to something else.

She told him about her French bulldog Luna, named so because of the crescent moon shape on the dog's chest. The spot was the only white on her otherwise entirely black body. He told her about his love for music. They discussed a whole lot of nothing really…yet, it didn't feel like nothing.

Which was probably how she'd ended up going back to his house with him. She'd never gone back to some guy's house that she'd just met. But when three o'clock rolled around—and they were both stone-cold sober—she hadn't been ready for the night to end.

Hadn't been ready to say good-bye.

And that was why she was currently pinned up against the wall with his chest—and other glorious body parts—pressing into hers.

"God you smell incredible. What is that?" he asked as he put his hands on either side of her head and leaned in, skimming his nose across her neck as he inhaled.

"Honey."

"Honey?" he asked, pulling back and raising his eyebrows.

"Honey-scented lotion."

"It's been driving me crazy all night." He moved in closer, breathing her in again before he straightened and his eyes met hers. "I'm going to kiss you now. So if you have any problems with that, you should speak now or forever hold your peace."

The wording of his statement was not lost on her, but she chose to ignore it. Tonight was all about the present. All about being in the moment with this man who clearly desired her. That was what she was choosing to focus on.

So did she have any problems with him kissing her? Why no, no she did not.

She ran her hands up the front of his shirt before she placed her palms flat on his chest. The handle of her clutch was looped around her wrist and it swayed to the side of them.

"No objections." She shook her head. "I've been wondering what you were waiting for."

He tilted his head to the side and gave her a wicked grin that had her imagining him doing other things with that mouth of his besides kissing.

He leaned in close, his mouth little more than a breath away before he veered off course and brought his lips to her ear. "I was waiting to get you alone, Harper. I knew the second I tasted you I'd want everything and I wouldn't be able to stop until I got it all."

Her breath hitched at his words and her hands fisted in the fabric of his shirt, holding him tight.

He grazed her earlobe with his teeth before he trailed kisses down her jaw, his scruff rasping against her skin before he covered her mouth with his. His tongue dipped in past her lips, and the second it touched hers she understood exactly what he'd said.

She wanted *everything*, too.

His hands were no longer on the wall; one was palming her breast, the other her ass. Considering Harper's more than ample curves, he was getting two very nice handfuls. And if she had any doubts as to how much he wanted her, they were long gone as he shifted his body and his erection pressed into her thigh.

He pulled his mouth back from hers, breathing hard as he looked at her. "Damn. You taste like honey, too. So much better than I imagined." He nipped at her bottom lip before he soothed it with a kiss. "Still no objections?"

"I'm objectionless."

"Thank. God." And just like that both of his hands were on her ass and he was picking her up in one swift move, her legs wrapping around his waist.

Now Harper wasn't a tiny thing, not by any means. She was a healthy size ten with D breasts, and shapely hips with a butt to match. So it would be an understatement to say that she was impressed by the fact that he picked her up and carried her through the cabin like she was nothing. She would've said so, too, but her mouth was occupied with his tongue again.

She was vaguely aware of the fact that the light from the living room was fading as they moved down the unlit hallway. Her shoulder and back brushed against a half-open door and it gave way, moving back and allowing them entry as he pushed both of their bodies through it. She dropped her hand, letting her clutch fall to the floor where it made an audible thunk on the wood.

A moment later she was flat on her back, Liam firmly wedged between her thighs, her legs locked around his waist, and her ankles cupping his ass. His cock pressed into the apex of her thighs and she couldn't help but move, rubbing herself against him and making him groan.

He pulled back from her mouth and looked down at her. A minimal amount of light from the living room was making its way into the bedroom, and his face was mostly in shadow, which was a damn shame. His slightly long and gloriously thick brown hair was hanging in his eyes. She reached up—she couldn't stop herself—and brushed his hair back, running her fingers across his forehead before she traced his hairline.

She could just make out his grin as he reached up and grabbed her hand. He pulled it from his head and brought it to his mouth, pressing his lips to her wrist. He found her other hand on his shoulder and did the same thing, kissing that wrist, too, before he moved both of her hands up and above her head, pinning them to the bed.

"Drop your legs," he whispered as he moved his hands down the length of her arms.

She obeyed without even thinking, and he grinned again before he buried his face in her neck, opening his mouth wide on her throat. He shifted down her body, his hands now making their way along her sides while his lips moved across to the center of her chest.

"Did you know that your breasts are magnificent?" he asked before he bit the top of her shirt and pulled it down, exposing more of her chest.

She didn't get a chance to respond before he dipped his tongue between the very top of her cleavage. The only sound she made was a long low moan that filled the room.

Liam's hands were now under the hem of her shirt, his magic fingers on her bare stomach tracing circles as he moved up. He lifted his mouth from her breasts as he pushed her shirt up and over her head, her still outstretched arms making it all the easier.

He threw it to the side before he looked down at her, and she could just make out his head shaking from side to side. "Well, this just won't do. I can't see you."

He moved, sitting up and shifting to the side. Three clicks echoed in the room before a soft glow filled the space.

"That's better," he said as he settled back into his kneeling position between her legs.

He reached up and popped the top button on her jeans before he pulled the zipper down. And then he was shifting off the bed to stand, pulling her boots off and dropping them to the floor with two loud thuds. He grabbed the toes of her socks and they disappeared from her feet with simultaneous tugs. Then he was reaching up again, hooking his fingers in the top of her jeans and dragging them down her hips and legs. She shimmied, helping him in the process, and just like that she was down to her bra and panties.

Now Harper had long, *long* ago accepted the fact that she would never be a size two nor would the ever-coveted thigh gap be part of her anatomy. And that was perfectly okay with her. It had been a hard-won fight to get comfortable in her own skin.

But she had.

Adolescence hadn't been kind. Harper's family moved to Mirabelle right before the sixth grade. Starting over in a small town where most of the kids had known each other since birth—or at least kindergarten—hadn't been the easiest. Then there was the added fact that she'd been a chubby eleven-year-old who hit puberty a little bit earlier than everyone else. The girls had been downright cruel. The boys had been relentlessly horrible, too. Well, right up until she'd grown into her curves and her boobs hadn't been so *weird*.

But a man's approval hadn't been something that Harper had ever sought out. She was who she was, and her body wasn't going to change based off of what someone else wanted. That being said, she was in no way immune to the look that Liam was currently giving her. Because no man had *ever* looked at her with so much desire.

His eyes raked her body, a look of reverence on his face that made her forget everything besides him and her, in that room, at that moment.

He reached out and traced a path up her knee, to her thigh, and across the front of her panties. They were navy blue cotton with an inch of cream lace around all of the edges. Her breath caught as he paused for just a moment at the very top, thinking that he might pull them down and touch her, but instead he moved up to her stomach.

"I was wrong," he whispered, shaking his head. "It's *all* of you that's magnificent." His fingers went around her belly button before he walked them up between her ribs and to the center of her chest. He leaned over her as he ran his hand along the swells of her breasts, starting at the side of her left and going across to the right.

He touched the tattoo inked just below her right shoulder, a lotus blossom with a floating heart hovering above the opened petals. He leaned down farther, pressing his lips to the tattoo, an open-mouthed kiss with his tongue on her skin.

Harper moved her arms from their stretched-out position above her head. She wanted her hands on him, unable to wait a second longer. Her fingers speared his hair and she tugged his head up, needing something else as well.

He didn't resist for a second, and when his mouth touched hers there was a renewed frenzy in the way their tongues tangled and their breaths mingled between hungry kisses. His hands were everywhere, palming her breasts and finding her erect nipples through the material of her bra. Then on her thighs and sliding up to her butt for something to hold on to as he moved against her.

Their bodies were perfectly aligned, his jeans unable to hide the more than impressive bulge behind his fly. He was pressing into her and she was going to lose her mind in about three point five seconds.

She let go of his hair and started tugging on his shirt. She needed her hands on more of him. Needed to feel his skin on hers. The second he realized what she was after he assisted in the de-clothing mission, levering himself up on one hand while he reached behind his back with the other and grabbed a fistful of shirt. He pulled it off in one swift move and threw it to the side.

Now Harper was not one to under-appreciate the male form in all of its glory, and Liam had *a lot* of glory. His muscled arms were flexed as he hovered over her, making the tattoos scattered across his arms stand out even more.

He had a bar of music wrapped around his left biceps, and underneath it was a bird about to take off in flight. Its feet were perched on a letter "M" that was inked in solid black above the bend in his arm.

She reached up, tracing the words *Then Sings My Soul* that ran down the inside of his right biceps. And then she was touching both of his pecs, her hands gliding down. He had a light dusting of hair that ran all the way past the waistband of his jeans.

She moved down his happy trail, her fingers outlining his abs, but he stopped her hands before she made it to her destination. "Not so fast." He smiled as he shook his head. "You got to see my chest, now I get to see yours."

"Oh, so tit for tat?"

"Yup."

If he kept grinning at her like that he could have whatever the hell he wanted. "Well, then what are you waiting for?"

She arched her back and he slid both of his hands underneath her, making quick work of the hooks. The second they were undone he pulled her bra from her body.

"Perfect," he whispered as he lowered his head. His mouth landed on one of her breasts, a hand on the other. The double onslaught was almost more than she could handle: his tongue on one nipple, his thumb and forefinger on the other.

And just like that her hands were in his hair again, her nails raking his scalp. His mouth disappeared from one breast and landed on the other. His now free hand making a move south, traveling down her side before it made its way between their bodies. And then he was touching her through the thin material of her panties, his thumb finding her clit and making her body arch off the bed.

He pushed her panties to the side, his fingers running across her center before he slid two inside of her. She gasped, her head falling back onto the mattress. And she wasn't the only one making noises, either. Liam groaned and as his mouth was still working at her nipple it rumbled through her breast. What with that and the added sensation of his fingers now moving inside of her, Harper couldn't stop her body from bucking or her hands tightening in his hair.

But as good as all of that was, it was *nothing* compared to what he did a moment later. His mouth moved from her breast, his teeth grazing her ribs and his tongue trailing across her skin as he moved down.

Down.

Down.

Down.

And then he was off the bed, his fingers disappearing from inside of her as he knelt on the floor. He touched her knees, gently pushing her legs apart so that he could settle his shoulders between her thighs. His hands moved to her hips, pulling her body right up to the edge of the bed. The second she was in a position to his liking, he pushed her panties to the side and had his mouth on her.

Her body didn't simply arch off the bed when he ran his tongue along her core. She was pretty sure she levitated in the air for a good couple of seconds. She let go of his hair and grabbed on to the quilt next to her, holding on for dear life.

As to the words that came out of her mouth? Well, those were mostly incoherent. She could barely get enough air into her lungs as it was, but when he put his hands underneath her bottom and lifted her up for better access she somehow managed.

"Ohmygodpleasedontstoppleasedontstoppleasedontstop."

And he didn't stop. The first orgasm was barely finished before he had her going off again. And he stayed with her until the end, bringing her down, with slow licks of his tongue before he pulled back and kissed the inside of her right thigh.

"Yup, magnificent," he whispered as he looked up at her. He slid his hands up across her legs and to her hips where he wound his fingers in the sides of her panties and pulled them down. The second they were free he stood, kicking off his boots as he reached for his belt.

Harper sat up on her elbows and watched as he pushed his jeans, boxers, and socks off in one swift move. He stood before her entirely naked, and she wanted to use the word *magnificent* on him as well.

She took a few seconds to look him over, to take in the fact that he had toned muscular thighs and the most impressive erection she'd ever seen in her life. He walked over to the nightstand, pulling open the top drawer where he grabbed a condom. He opened it and rolled it down the length of his cock.

She wanted him on her, moving over her. Wanted him inside of her. *Now.* The urgency and need was all-consuming. She shifted back on the bed, scooting across the mattress so that her legs were no longer hanging over the edge.

"You waiting for another invitation?" she asked as she settled into the pillows.

"Maybe." His mouth quirked to the side.

God he's sexy. "Written or verbal?"

"Verbal will do just fine."

She bent her knees, her feet going flat on the bed before she pulled her thighs apart. He took a deep breath, his eyes dilating as he focused on the apex of her thighs. "Come. Here."

The bed dipped just slightly as he put first one knee down on the mattress, then the other, kneeling between her legs. His hands skimmed her sides before he placed them flat on the bed. He leaned down, opening his mouth over one of her breasts before trailing kisses up her chest, over her neck, and finally covering her mouth with his as he settled between her thighs.

One of his palms moved under her butt, lifting her as he thrust inside of her in one powerful move. Her mouth fell away from his and she found herself looking up into his green-gold gaze.

He was all that she saw. All that she felt. All that she wanted.

She reached up and ran her fingers across his strong jaw, her thumb moving against his stubble, a stubble that had rasped across most of her body. She was going to have whisker burn *everywhere.*

Worth it. So *totally* worth it.

He kissed her again as he began to move, pulling his hips back before he thrust back into her. The hair on his chest brushed her now overly sensitized nipples. She slid her hands to his back, her palms gliding over his skin as they traveled down to his ass. She hadn't gotten a rearview yet, so a hands-on exploration was necessary.

And it was glorious.

He groaned into her mouth as her nails dug into his skin, urging him on harder. He complied with gusto and she moved with him, meeting him thrust for thrust. She had no idea how long they moved like that before she pulled away from his mouth, gasping for air.

Liam buried his face in her neck, sucking at her skin before nipping at it with his teeth. The sting sent pleasure all the way down to her toes, hitting every spot in between. Or maybe that was just him hitting every spot in between.

Didn't matter. It was working. Everything he was doing was working.

"I don't think I'm going to last much longer," he whispered, his breath washing out over her skin.

"I'm almost there," she panted. Almost being the operative word, she was right on the edge. Just a few more thrusts and she…

She would…

Be…

Right…

"Oh, ohh, ohhh." She tightened around him, her body pulsing as the orgasm ripped through her.

"Thank God," Liam groaned into her neck as he found his own release.

They stayed that way for just a few moments, their sweaty bodies tangled together. Harper closed her eyes and reveled in the weight of Liam pushing her down into the mattress. She moved her hands up and down his back, memorizing him with her fingertips and cataloging everything. His hand at her hip, his lips on her throat, his breath on her skin.

He pulled his head up and looked down at her, giving her that smile of his again as his hair fell across his forehead. "I'm so glad I bought you that drink."

A laugh burst forth from her lips as she reached up and brushed his hair back. "So am I."

"I'll be right back." He leaned down and kissed the tip of her nose. "Don't go anywhere." He pulled from her body and got out of bed. She watched him walk to a door on the other side of the room, finally getting a proper look at his *very* fine ass.

Yeah, she wasn't going anywhere…for now.

Chapter Two

An Unsuccessful Walk of Shame . . .
Breakfast Included

Consciousness hit Harper about two seconds before she opened her eyes, and in that one brief moment all she knew was contentment. But then her eyes did open and reality set in. Well, it set in after she blinked a few times, the sunlight streaming through the floor-to-ceiling windows temporarily blinding her.

As her eyes adjusted she took in the open-beam ceiling—that went on for days—above her, before she turned her head to the side to find a naked man next to her.

Liam was fast asleep, his face buried in the pillow and his dark brown hair rumpled all around his head. One of his arms was wrapped around her stomach, his hand on her hip.

Everything about last night came back to her in an instant.

His hand at the small of her back as he'd leaned in close to her at the bar. His lips at her ear, the sound of his rich southern drawl filling her up with a warmth that had absolutely nothing to do with the alcohol.

She couldn't even blame her actions on drinking because she'd been fully and totally in control of herself when she'd decided to go home with him…well, unless she could count being drunk on lust. And as she remembered the countless out-of-body experiences he'd given her throughout the night, she wasn't quick to discount it, either.

The thing was, she'd spent about seven conscious hours with the man, but it didn't feel like she'd just met him. No, it felt like something much more.

But none of that changed the fact that Harper did not do one-night stands. She didn't even dabble in them, didn't even stick her toe in the water. So to say this was out of character would be an understatement. Yet there she was, waking up next to a guy she'd only just met on the morning that *should've* been her wedding.

Oh. Good. God.

The wedding that would never be to the man who had left her. Brad had been far from her thoughts. She'd been entirely focused on Liam, and why wouldn't she be? He made her laugh, made her come harder than she'd ever come in her entire life…and made her forget everything besides him and her.

She couldn't do this again. Wasn't ready for another man in her life—not that Liam wanted to be a part of her life. Hell, he'd probably be trying to get rid of her the second he opened his eyes. Harper chose not to focus on the fact that the thought of him wanting her gone was worse than anything else.

Nope. She wasn't going to do it. Instead she was going to get out of there. Stat.

Priority number one: getting dressed.

She sat up ever so slowly, gently pulling Liam's hand from her body before she got out of bed. Her clothes were scattered all around the room and she had to stop herself from groaning out loud at the sight before her. She started gathering the garments as fast as she could, cataloging as she went.

Panties: hanging from a knob on the dresser. *Check.*

Shirt: at the foot of the bed. *Check.*

Pants: on top of a chair in the corner. *Check.*

Boots: the right was in the middle of the floor. *Check.* And the left…was…just peeking out from under the side of the bed. *Check.*

Purse: sitting in the entryway of the bedroom and miraculously still zipped up…unlike her pants. *Check.*

Bra…bra…nope, no bra.

Where the hell was it?

Liam shifted in the bed, his arms flexing as he buried his face farther into the pillow. Her bra was just going to have to be a casualty. There was no time to waste.

She headed out of the room in search of a bathroom, being careful to move as quietly as possible across the hardwood floors. Every time a board squeaked her heart flew up into her throat. She made it to the end of the hallway before she found a bathroom and ducked inside, closing the door behind her with an unavoidable—and very audible—snap. But it was nothing to the flush of the toilet a minute later, though there was no avoiding that, either.

She dressed quickly, her ample chest looking downright indecent in her shirt sans bra. But there was nothing for it.

There was also nothing to do about the state of her hair, which was Bed Head 5000 no doubt do to Liam's hands. At least she could do something about the eyeliner and mascara that made her resemble a grunge band groupie.

She turned the faucet on, noises be damned at this point, and stuck her hands underneath the cool water before she took a few mouthfuls. She splashed her face, scrubbing at the space under her eyes. The hand towel next to the sink was clean and she ran the fluffy fabric across her skin, wiping up the drops. There was a stock of tiny bottles of mouthwash in the mirrored cabinet above the sink and she helped herself…might as well at this point.

When she shut the door and caught her reflection in the mirror she had to close her eyes to block out the image of who she found staring back at her. She had no idea who she was in that moment. She was not easily scared…yet there she was…running.

But really, after everything that had happened over the last few months it wasn't all that shocking.

Harper wasn't quick to fall in love. At the age of twenty-six she could count on one finger how many men had gotten that far. Brad had done much more than broken her heart; it wasn't just a crack down the center. It was shattered into a million teeny, tiny pieces. And no, she wasn't being over-dramatic.

He'd decimated her.

He'd shown up in Mirabelle about a year and a half ago, a general contractor who'd been hired by the county to fix the bridges and roads. He'd met Harper and swept her off her feet. She wasn't easily swept. Never had been.

Maybe it was because of her father. Paul Laurence had set the bar very high when it came to a good man, and all of the guys she'd dated over the years had definitely fallen short.

At least until Brad…or so she thought.

So yeah, she was running. She had no other choice and her escape time was counting down fast. She gathered her purse—all the while still avoiding her gaze in the mirror—before she stepped out into the hallway.

She was so intensely focused on getting out of there that she didn't take in the rest of her surroundings, like how the massive stone fireplace in the living room was a thing of glory, or that the cabin was settled on a lake that could be seen sparkling through the windows that made up the entirety of the back wall, nor did it register that the kitchen smelled like freshly brewed coffee.

All Harper saw was the solid wood of the front door, which was why she jumped out of her skin when the voice spoke out behind her.

"Forget this?"

Her purse flew into the air, hitting the floor with a thud. She clutched her chest and spun around. Liam was leaning back against the counter, her bra dangling from his forefinger, swaying just slightly in the air.

Okay, yes it was true that she'd gotten to see his body up close and personal the night before, but there was something to be said about seeing it in the daylight. Actually there was a lot to be said about it. She just couldn't do that much talking as her brain had temporarily short-circuited.

He was wearing nothing more than a pair of black boxer briefs and a smile, his washboard abs giving her the strangest urge to do laundry. She looked like death warmed over and he looked…well, glorious.

"Your bra wasn't the only thing that you forgot, either. I don't get a good-bye, Harper?"

"I figured it would be better," she said as she reached up and attempted to smooth her hair. She had no doubts that she did *not* succeed.

He leaned back against the counter and folded his arms across his chest, her bra now hanging at his side. "Better for whom?" His mouth quirked to the side, making him look infinitely sexier.

The jerk.

"Look, we don't have to do this whole awkward morning-after thing," she said, making a gesture between the two of them.

"Perfect." He nodded his head as he reached up and scratched his beard, the sound of his nails on his scruff reaching her ears from across the room. He used the hand that was still holding her bra and it swayed with the motion, taunting her like a freaking red flag…even though it was navy blue.

"Then I'll just get going." She took her eyes off of him, so not an easy thing to do, and went to grab her purse on the floor.

"Why?"

"What?" Her head came up and she straightened.

"Why are you leaving?"

"I thought we just established this."

"No, we established not having the *awkward morning-after thing*. We never established you leaving," he said, shaking his head.

"Do you plan on making this as uncomfortable as possible?"

"I was thinking about it. But if you head out that door I think you'll make yourself plenty uncomfortable all on your own."

"Meaning?"

"How were you planning on getting back to the bar?"

Well, that had her coming up short. "I hadn't really thought that out." She hadn't really thought anything out as was evident by her current predicament.

"It's three miles to the main road, and another five to the Second Hand Guitar. And as you don't know where you are I would imagine it would be difficult to call a cab. Also I don't think you'd get far walking in those shoes of yours before your feet started to kill you."

"Well, isn't this the perfect setting for a horror movie."

A laugh escaped his mouth and he shook his head. "I was actually going for the perfect setting for a romantic comedy. Boy meets girl, boy takes girl home and gives her multiple orgasms, boy makes girl breakfast the following morning."

Okay, she was going to ignore the romantic comedy comment. "Look, Liam, last night wasn't something that I've ever done before. I'm not the kind of girl who goes home with men I just met."

He tilted his head to the side and his grin somehow widened. "See, we have something in common. I don't go home with men I just met, either."

The corner of her lip twitched despite herself.

"Is this something you do for all of the girls you have one-night stands with?" The question was out of her mouth before she thought better of it, and she inwardly cringed at her words. She was *that* girl. The one-night-stand girl.

His head straightened and he studied her for a second, the humor in his eyes gone. "First of all, I've never made breakfast for any girl that I've brought home. And second, I wouldn't classify you as a one-night stand."

His words had her coming up short again. She couldn't get her brain to connect with her mouth to say anything.

"Let me cook for you, Harper. Then I'll take you wherever you want to go."

It was on the tip of her tongue to say no, to ask that he just drive her back now. She wasn't sure what it was, the fact that he hadn't called her a one-night stand or the intensity in his gaze, because the word "okay" slipped past her lips. And judging by the look on his face, she wasn't the only one shocked by it.

"Good." He pushed himself off the counter and crossed the space to her, reaching out to hand her the bra when he was close enough. When she grabbed it he didn't let go. His green-gold eyes focused on hers as his free hand slipped around her waist and he moved in closer. "I'm going to kiss you now."

He hesitated for just a moment, giving her a second to object...but just like the night before she found herself objectionless. She couldn't think straight around this man, not when he was speaking, or looking at her, or breathing in her general direction. And now he had his hand on her, his mouth just inches from hers.

She gave a small nod before he lowered his head. His lips gently brushed hers and his fingers tightened at her hip, bringing her flush against his body. She couldn't stop herself from sighing in pleasure, and the second her mouth was open he took full advantage, dipping his tongue inside. She wasn't the only one who'd taken a moment to freshen their breath, either, and he tasted so incredibly good.

And just like that her palms were flat on his chest, like they had a mind of their own. Yup, her ability to think straight was obliterated when he was around...but maybe thinking straight was entirely overrated.

* * *

Liam James was a heavy sleeper, had been since he was a child. This was why the alarm on his phone was loud and obnoxious and would usually go off for a full five minutes before it would even register in his sleep-hazed brain. But luckily for him he hadn't been dead to the world that morning. Otherwise he would've missed the attempted exit of his violet-eyed, black-haired goddess.

Thank the Lord for small favors, because never seeing Harper again would've been one *massive* mistake.

He'd noticed her the second she'd walked into the Second Hand Guitar, which was saying something as the bar had been packed. But then again it was *always* packed. The place was up there with the Bluebird Café on musicians getting discovered in Nashville, not to mention some already well-known names liked to stop in and do a little impromptu show. So the crowd of people was always thick with musical and nonmusical patrons alike.

Liam had his own soft spot for the bar. Whenever he was in town he practically lived there, writing more of his songs on one of those bar stools than anywhere else. Then there was the fact that he'd been discovered there himself.

Three years ago he'd been singing up on the stage when Hunter Andrews of the country duo Isaac Hunter had pulled out his own guitar and gotten up onstage with Liam. Five songs and two pitchers of beer later, Hunter had invited Liam to open a show the following evening. He'd ended up touring with the duo for the better part of a year, playing in cities across the country.

When they'd asked him to open on their most recent tour he'd said yes without hesitation.

Now, he had two albums under his belt and a decent following. But he wasn't big enough to headline his own tour yet, or to be recognized by everyone he ever met. People knew his songs and connected his name to them because of the radio. His name was way more recognizable than his face.

He'd conveniently kept his last name to himself. But that was Harper's rule, right? *Nothing personal.*

Bunch of bullshit if you asked him. Everything about their night had been personal.

Never in his life had he seen a woman that made everyone else disappear, and he did mean *everyone*. As far as he was concerned they'd been the only two people in that bar the night before…well, them and the bartender who got them drinks. But that had been more like a floating hand that appeared when they wanted another one.

All he'd been focused on getting from the second he'd seen her was her undivided attention. Once he'd gotten it, he hadn't let it go. He hadn't been wrong about her, either. There was something to be said about a woman who listed *The Godfather* and *Wedding Crashers* in her top five movies, and whose favorite fictional character was Indiana Jones.

"It's the hat that does it for you, isn't it?" he'd asked her after their fourth shot.

"Nope, totally the whip," she'd said without missing a beat.

Then there was her laugh, loud and full bodied and so damn genuine. He'd gone back and forth all night on where to focus his attention. There was a case to be made about her mouth. She had full, pouty lips that she'd painted a soft pink, and whenever she'd smile it would light up her entire face.

But then there were her eyes. Eyes so blue they were violet. He'd never seen anything like them before. Never seen anyone like *her* before. He'd been entranced by her. Yes, *entranced*. And that had all been before he'd even kissed her, let alone taken her to bed, because really the second he'd gotten inside her he'd been done for.

It had really bothered him when she kept referring to herself as a "one-night stand," because if he had anything to say about it they would be spending more than just one night together. He was determined to break down whatever wall she'd built that morning.

His first plan of attack was breakfast.

He knew the way to a woman's heart was *not* through her stomach. But it gave him an opportunity to spend more time with her, and really it wasn't a bad idea because he wasn't a shabby cook if he did say so himself, and he did.

He moved around the kitchen sipping on his coffee between cooking the bacon, cutting and frying up some green tomatoes, and mixing his hollandaise sauce. He was making his modified version of Eggs Blackstone—the added ingredient being asparagus and a few key spices to the sauce—a personal specialty of his own that he'd perfected over the years.

He hadn't been lying when he said he'd never made this for a woman he'd brought home, and that was because he never brought women home with him. Though he didn't have much of a *home* to speak of lately.

The cabin belonged to his brother, pro-hockey star Logan

James. After two years on the road, Liam discovered that his apartment was empty more than not, so he hadn't renewed his lease. For the last year or so he'd just stayed at the cabin when he was in Nashville. When he had breaks that were long enough, he'd head down to Florida—both Logan and their sister Adele had houses down there—or go visit his parents wherever they were.

His family was from Nashville, but when his mom and dad retired they sold their house and bought an RV. They'd been traveling all over the U.S. and parts of Canada for the last few years and loving every second of it. Liam wasn't the only nomad in the family these days.

The bacon popped in the frying pan and he took another sip of coffee as he flipped it.

"I don't think I've ever met a man who can poach an egg," Harper said from behind him.

He turned and stepped away from the stove as he leaned back against the counter. She was sitting at the breakfast bar, her hair now brushed and pulled up into a messy bun thing on the top of her head. She'd taken a few minutes to straighten her bedhead out and put on her bra, while he'd pulled on a pair of jeans and a T-shirt. He was just glad she hadn't tried to make another run for it.

Now she was nursing her own cup of coffee as she watched him cook.

"I have many skills as you learned last night."

"Well, aren't you cocky this morning?"

"Honey, I'm cocky every morning." He waggled his eyebrows and she shook her head at him, fighting a smile.

"You're shameless."

"That I am. Do you want some more coffee?" He nodded to her mug.

"Please."

He pushed off of the counter and went over to the coffeemaker, grabbing the pot and filling his cup as he crossed the kitchen to the bar. He reached across and tipped the pot, brown liquid filling her mug. He'd watched her fix her first cup so he knew how much room she would need for creamer, which was about double the amount that he put in his.

He left his mug on the counter as he crossed back across the kitchen to put the pot back on the coffeemaker. Then he stopped by the fridge to grab the creamer, closing the door with his hip before he walked over to her.

"So," he started to say as he poured the creamer into her coffee, "how much longer are you going to be in the city?" He'd been hard pressed to get certain facts out of her the night before. She'd pretty much stuck to her word on not telling him things that were too personal. But he had managed to get a few things out. Like that she wasn't from Nashville.

She was in town visiting her aunt and he wanted to know how much time he was going to have before she left. How much time he had to win her over. How much time he had to break down all of her walls. He was by no means done spending time with this woman.

She looked up at him as she stirred her coffee, a great debate going on behind her eyes like she was deciding on whether to answer or not. "I leave on Monday," she finally answered.

It was Saturday, so he had two days. He could work with two days.

He didn't have any other choice.

"What are you doing tonight?"

Her hand stilled, the spoon no longer going around her cup in circles. "I don't know."

"Have dinner with me."

"Aren't you getting a little ahead of yourself there, Sparky? We haven't even had breakfast yet and you already want to make plans for dinner?"

"Sparky?"

"You heard me," she said as she brought her mug of coffee to her mouth and took a sip.

"Yeah I did, and I find it interesting that you're calling me Sparky when you were the one trying to run out of here this morning like your pants were on fire."

"Yeah, that is interesting, isn't it?"

"Why were you running?"

Something flickered in her eyes...something that if he didn't know any better he would guess was a flash of pain. But it was gone just as soon as it had appeared and she covered up her moment of weakness with a coy smile.

"That's crossing over into the too personal territory." She shook her head.

"Honey, I had my mouth between your thighs last night. I think we're *way* past too personal."

"Is that a fact?" she asked, raising her left eyebrow.

He hadn't really met that many women who could do the one eyebrow lift thing, and every time she did it he found her infinitely sexier.

Something he didn't even know was possible.

Apparently it was.

"Yeah, it is." He put both of his palms on the counter and leaned forward, getting dangerously close to her mouth. Dangerously because the closer he got to her the more he wanted to forget about what he was cooking and just have her for breakfast.

She leaned forward, too, those lips of hers mere inches away. "I'm still not telling you," she whispered.

God, he could do this with her all day and not get bored.

"Do *you* enjoy being this difficult?" he asked as he reached up and found a stray strand of hair that was too short to be pulled back into her bun. He curled it around his finger and tugged until her mouth was on his.

"Definitely," she said against his lips. He kissed her for the second time that morning—not nearly enough by his standards—tasting the coffee on her tongue.

He pulled back just enough to look into her eyes, letting the curl of her hair unravel from his finger. He moved his hand to her jaw, running his thumb across her cheek. "Have dinner with me tonight."

"Why don't we see how breakfast goes first?"

"You lacking confidence in my cooking abilities?"

"Not as of yet, but if you keep standing over here your bacon might burn."

"Don't you worry about my bacon. It's perfectly fine," he said as he went in for another kiss. He might as well make the most of the moment and her readily accessible mouth. Which really wasn't a shabby moment to be in at all.

* * *

Okay, so breakfast turned out to be something that bordered on legendary. Liam could cook *cook*. If he was able to whip that dish up without all that much preparation, Harper could only imagine what he would be capable of when it came to dinner.

Not that she'd agreed to have dinner with him as of yet. She was still deciding, had been all through their meal, and was still trying to figure it out as he drove her back to the Second Hand Guitar.

But she was filled with conflicting emotions.

Her brain kept screaming "run away."

Her heart was staying silent, except for the fact that it started to pound harder when it came to anything that involved Liam.

And then there were her lady bits, as unreliable and unhelpful as ever. They were all for more time spent with Liam.

It was hard for her to resort back to her original plan of escape when he kept kissing her. The things he was capable of with his mouth just added to his fine string of talents. It was no wonder she couldn't think straight. What she needed was a little space.

Yes, space.

Good thing they were now sitting in the close-confined cab of Liam's truck. A beautiful blue and white 1971 Chevy.

"So where did you find a C-ten in impeccable condition?" she asked as she ran her hand over the tan vinyl seats.

He looked at her, his eyebrows raised high above his aviator sunglasses.

"What? I'm just as capable of appreciating a good car as the next person."

"Apparently. You're just full of surprises, aren't you?" He grinned at her before he turned back to the road.

"I thought you figured that out by now."

"Oh, I think it would take me a lot longer than this to figure you out, honey."

God. The way he said honey was sinful. How could a word be sinful? It was his voice, all deep and rich. Not too twangy, not too southern, but just right.

Oh great, apparently she was Goldilocks when it came to the timbre of a man's voice. Or maybe it was just this man's voice. It did funny things to her senses.

"You keep calling me that," she said before she could stop herself.

"What?"

"Honey."

"It's appropriate, isn't it? As you smell like it…and taste like it *everywhere*."

Oh, look at that, she was thinking about last night's activities again and imagining a repeat performance. "So, what about this truck?" she asked, unable to hide the small quaver in her voice.

"The truck belonged to my grandfather Freddy," Liam answered, apparently taking pity on her and letting her change the subject. "He's the reason it's in the shape it's in, the reason it still runs like a dream. He taught me how to drive in this bad boy. He passed away when I was seventeen and left it to me."

"Well, you've done a good job with it."

"Thanks." He turned to her again and flashed her another smile before his eyes were back on the road as he made a right and pulled into the parking lot of the bar. "Which one is yours?" There were a handful of cars still parked in scattered spots.

"That one." She pointed to the bright red FJ Cruiser.

"Well, aren't you fancy?"

"Only on the weekends." Actually the Cruiser had been a *massive* splurge for her. Her Explorer had crapped out a few years ago and she'd needed another SUV with decent space in the back.

Harper was a licensed massage therapist and split her time between LaBella—a high-end resort on Mirabelle beach—and Rejuvenate—a spa in the downtown area. She also did a few side jobs where she had to transport her own massage table. Then there were her homemade lotions and massage oils that she delivered to her local buyers.

So it had been all about the utility. Though she wasn't going to lie, she sure did love the fact that it didn't break down every other month and leave her stranded all over the county. Plus, she loved driving it. Which was why she'd decided to make this trek to Nashville a nine-hour road trip as opposed to flying.

Liam parked in front of it, putting his truck in gear before he turned fully to her, resting one of his arms on the back of the bench seat.

"So what's it going to be, Harper? Do I get to see you again?" he asked as he pushed his sunglasses to the top of his head.

Well, wasn't that the question of the morning? Harper had gotten another apologetic text from her aunt that morning. Celeste's patient—both momma and baby—from the night before were having complications from the surgery. She was going to be on call for the next twenty-four hours.

So Harper could spend the evening that would've been her wedding drinking alone and wallowing...or with Liam who made her forget things.

Decisions, decisions.

"What time?"

The relief in his eyes was immediate, and his mouth split into the biggest grin she'd seen on his face since she'd met him.

"Seven o'clock. You going to remember how to get there?"

"Uhh, probably not." She shook her head. "I'm much more of a learn-by-doing type."

"Is that so?" he asked, his eyebrows rose up his forehead again, this time more than a little suggestively.

"I didn't mean that in a dirty way."

"*Sure* you didn't." He reached over and opened the glove box, pulling out a pen and a pad of paper. He straightened, moving his hand from behind her as he started to go through the pages that were covered in a wiry cursive.

When he got to a blank page he wrote the address and his phone number in the same handwriting she'd seen on the other pages of the notepad.

"Call me if you get lost." He reached for her hand, placing the paper in her palm. And then he was leaning in, covering her mouth with his.

Yeah, she could forget for just a little bit longer.

Chapter Three

A Million Simple Things
That Aren't So Simple at All

The gravel in the driveway crunched at five till seven. Liam stepped away from the kitchen island where he was cleaning up the remnants of his dinner making.

Rosemary and lemon gnocchi, from scratch.

Pan-seared pork chops.

And white chocolate raspberry bread pudding.

Yup, if his career in music failed he could just try his hand in the culinary world. His mother had taught him well when he was growing up, and it was something he'd always enjoyed doing. Since his time in a full functioning kitchen was limited these days, he tended to indulge whenever he could cook. And since Harper was coming over tonight he was pulling out all the stops.

Every last one of them.

He caught a glimpse of her red Cruiser through the windows before he opened the front door. She was making her way up the porch wearing a dark purple dress that hit her about mid-thigh.

A bronze belt was buckled just under her chest, somehow making her breasts look bigger.

He didn't even think that was possible.

Her matching bronze strappy heels clicked against the wood with every step that she took, but she faltered for just a second when she saw him.

"Hey." Her hand tightened on the railing and she paused at the top of the stairs.

"You look stunning." His eyes did another perusal of her body as he leaned against the open doorjamb.

"Thank you," she said as she reached up with her free hand and brushed her long black hair back and behind her ear. "You don't look half-bad yourself."

As he was wearing a pair of faded blue jeans, and a black V-neck with a green and white flannel shirt, he didn't think the comparison was all that close.

She really was the most beautiful woman he'd ever seen, but it was so much more than just looks with her. He wanted to know *all* of her, more than what he'd gotten last night. More than what he'd gotten that morning.

He didn't quite understand it…didn't even really know what to do with it…but he wanted *everything*. He also wasn't sure what to do with the amount of relief that was coursing through him at seeing her again.

There was a part of him that really thought she wasn't going to come, and now that he was looking at her he found that he needed to have her under his hands.

They both moved at the same time, Harper mounting the last step as Liam pushed off the door frame. He crossed to her in three long strides, and then he was leaning down, his hands going to her hips as he pressed a kiss to her cheek.

She was probably five-foot-seven or eight to his six-foot-one, but her four-inch heels narrowed the gap between them. She turned her head and looked at him for just a second before her hands landed on his chest and she stretched up the last remaining inch to put her lips on his. And just like that his arms were wrapping around her and he was pulling her fully into his body.

His mouth opened to hers and he finally had the taste of her on his tongue again. It had been seven hours since he'd seen her. *Seven hours.* And he'd missed her.

How was that even possible? Who was this woman and what had she done with his sanity?

Oh, who cared?

"I'm glad you're here," he whispered against her mouth.

"Me too."

He pulled back and looked into her face. Her cheeks were slightly flushed and her eyes more than slightly dazed. He had no doubt his face was sporting a very similar look.

Yeah, he had no clue what was going on with this woman. But he sure as hell wanted to figure it out.

* * *

"Good Lord you can cook," Harper said as she ran the last piece of gnocchi through the rosemary, lemon butter sauce before she popped it into her mouth.

Even watching her eat was sexy as hell.

"You cook?" he asked.

She shook her head and swallowed. "Not like this." She waved her hand at the almost empty plate in front of her. She still had a bite of her pork chop left. "My mother is the culinary expert of the family. She spends hours in the kitchen."

"Your father?" Well, if she'd opened a door into the personal he was definitely going to walk right on through it.

"Not so much. But I will say that he does contribute nicely to the cause with fresh fish."

"Your father is a fisherman?"

"Among other things." She smiled, forking the last bit of food and sticking it in her mouth. She chewed and swallowed before she shook her head at Liam, leaning back in her chair. "I didn't think it was possible for you to top breakfast, but you, my friend, have managed to exceed yourself." She tossed her napkin onto the table next to her now empty plate.

Liam had no doubt about the fact that she'd enjoyed her dinner. The woman wasn't shy about her reactions, and she'd made more than a few moans around her fork as she'd eaten. And they hadn't even gotten to dessert yet.

"That so?" he asked as he grabbed his glass of wine and took a sip.

"That is so." The corner of her mouth turned up into a half smile. "You know, you've already gotten me into bed. You didn't need to work so hard to impress me to do it again."

"My trying to impress you has nothing to do with wanting to get into your pants."

"Well, that's good. Because I'm not wearing any tonight."

Liam laughed. "I picked up on that. You're wearing that dress like you're doing it a favor."

"Is that another one of your pickup lines?"

"It might be. Did it work?"

"I don't know yet." She reached for her wineglass that was on the verge of needing a refill.

"You'll keep me posted though?"

"Of course," she said right before she polished off the last of the red liquid.

"You want another drink?"

"Sure."

"Let me clean up and I'll put something together. You want some more wine or something else?"

"Well, what are the options? Do you bartend as well as you cook?"

"Not really. My skills go about as far as opening a bottle of beer or wine," he said as he indicated the now empty bottle in front of them. "Adding whiskey to ice, vodka to any juice of your choosing, or a gin and tonic."

"Gin and tonic."

"Coming right up." He pushed his chair back and stood, reaching for his plate. Harper made the same motion, grabbing her plate before he could. "What do you think you're doing?"

"Helping."

"I don't think so." He pulled the plate from her hand and motioned toward the living room with his chin. "Go make yourself comfortable. It'll only take me a second to get the rest of this put away."

"If you insist."

"I do."

She turned on those sexy-as-all-hell heels of hers and headed toward the couch. Liam took just a second to watch her walk away, appreciating everything about the rearview.

Harper looked over her shoulder, catching him in the act. "You get your fill or do you want me to do that again?" she asked, raising her eyebrow.

"Honey, I don't think I'll ever get my fill." That was a fact, and the sooner he got rid of these dishes the sooner he'd get more. He somehow managed to pull his gaze from her and went into the kitchen, quickly loading everything in the dishwasher.

He made fast work with the gin and tonics and was joining Harper in the living room in less than five minutes.

"How's this?" he asked, handing her a short tumbler as he took a seat next to her on the couch.

She took a sip and nodded. "Mmm, perfect. I haven't had a gin and tonic in a while. They're my dad's specialty and you make a pretty mean one."

"I'll take that as a compliment."

"You should."

She took another sip of her drink as she nodded to the guitar that was resting against the chair next to the sofa. "So you play, too, Mr. Music Lover?"

He'd apparently forgotten to put it away before she'd come over. A good portion of his afternoon had been spent working on a song that he couldn't get out of his head.

The interesting part? Not only was it a ballad, it was a love song. Two things that he'd never written successfully before. Sure he had lust down pat. He'd written more than a few on that subject. But this song, well, it wasn't about that.

It was completely and entirely different. Which wasn't a bad thing at all.

The reason for his current stint in Nashville was finishing up his newest record. His label wanted one more song.

"Something they haven't seen from you before," his manager Gary Kirkland had told him about a thousand times.

And there it was, his sudden spark of inspiration wrapped up in a beautiful woman. But what could he say? The woman in question was very inspiring.

At least he'd had the sense of mind to close his notebook that was sitting on the coffee table. One look at the first verse would leave no doubt as to whom his newest song was about. If he ended up recording it she'd know it was about her. She'd *have* to.

"I dabble." Apparently she wasn't the only one still keeping things a secret. For whatever reason, he found that he wasn't quite ready for her to know what he did for a living.

"You dabble?" she repeated. "And dabbling involves writing your own songs?"

His eyebrows rose in question.

"I saw that notebook in the truck." She pointed to the coffee table. "And it's filled with something that looks remarkably like songs."

"Can't get anything by you, can I?" He shook his head.

"Would you play something for me?"

"Sure." He nodded as he leaned forward, setting his glass on the table before reaching for his guitar. He was coming to the very real conclusion that he'd do just about anything she asked.

He'd had half a dozen songs make it to the airwaves, and they were regularly played to where people who were fans of country knew of at least one. He wondered if Harper knew them. If she'd ever had her radio up loud, the windows down as she sang along.

Yeah he'd always hoped his songs were something to strike a chord with people, but there was something absolutely remarkable about the idea of *his* words coming across *her* lips. He wanted so desperately for his songs to mean something to *her*.

For the first time in a long time, he was nervous as he settled his guitar on his lap and placed his fingers over the correct strings. He took a deep breath before he strummed the first chord, humming to himself before he started with the chorus.

"A day, a week, a month, a year. It would never be enough. I want forever, honey. Forever with you."

His head came up and he focused on her face. Her mouth had fallen open slightly and her eyes had gone wide.

"A million simple things that aren't so simple at all. Your hand in mine. The taste of your tongue. Your head on my chest. You stealing my heart."

A heart that was currently pounding out of his chest. This was ridiculous.

"A day, a week, a month, a year. It would never be enough. I want forever, honey. Forever with you."

He sang the chorus one last time, discovering a new chord that he hadn't known seconds before and knowing that he'd hit the nail on the head.

Harper's eyes hadn't left his, and when he finished she just sat there for a second in stunned silence before she spoke. "You wrote that?" The question was little more than a whisper on her breath.

"Yeah. It isn't finished yet though," he said as he set the guitar off to the side.

"That was…" She shook her head. "I don't even know. Amazing doesn't seem adequate."

The look in her eyes and the awe in her voice were humbling…and Liam wasn't humbled all that often. Not that he was a particularly arrogant man, but he did take pride in his passion.

"Thank you."

Her breath came out in a huff as she shook her head again. "Apparently I'm not the only one full of surprises."

"Apparently not." He grabbed his gin and tonic from the coffee table before he leaned back on the sofa, moving closer to Harper in the process.

"That didn't sound like dabbling. Why do I get the impression you've done that before?"

"Because I have. So now that I've shared that, it's your turn." He reached forward and fingered a piece of her hair, rubbing the silky strand between his thumb and forefinger. "Can I ask you a question or are you still sticking with this nothing personal thing?"

"Depends on the question."

"Why are you in Nashville?"

She shook her head as she took another sip of her drink. "Nope. Not that question."

"You enjoy doing this whole mysterious hot girl thing?"

"I wasn't aware that was a thing."

"Oh really? I'm not all that sure I believe you."

Her head tilted to the side as her cheek brushed against his fingers. "You should believe I haven't lied to you."

"Okay, so if you won't tell me that, tell me something else. Something no one else knows."

"I'm intimidated by what your voice does to me."

And now he was the one who was left speechless for just a moment. "What do you mean?"

"I don't really know." She reached up and lightly traced his lips with her index and middle finger, first the top, then the bottom.

Holy. Hell. He felt that simple touch everywhere, which was beyond complicated. But really, when was he going to learn? *Nothing* with her was simple.

"You speak and somehow make things easier." She continued as she ran her fingers around his lips one more time.

"Things?"

"Yes. *Things.*" She nodded as she leaned into him, her mouth landing on his.

He brought his hand to the back of her head, his fingers spearing into her hair as he held her to him, devouring her mouth. Every taste of her was like heaven. The words to that song were so damn true. He'd never get enough of her. Not ever.

Yeah, he was a goner. Done for.

Harper was the first to pull back, and both of them were breathing hard. She tilted her glass to her mouth, finishing her drink. She stood up and nodded to the glass in his hand. "You should finish that, too. You're going to need both hands in a second."

"Yes, ma'am." Liam followed her lead and drained the rest of his gin and tonic. She held out her hand for the glass, and when he handed it to her she turned and set both down on the coffee table.

And then she was facing him again, hiking up the bottom of her dress. He saw a flash of emerald green lace before she was crawling up onto his lap, straddling him. She braced her hands on his shoulders as she settled her lush ass on his thighs. And then she was shifting closer, pressing against his cock that was quickly making its way to full mast.

Her hands went to his chest where she slid them out, pushing his unbuttoned flannel shirt from his arms. He leaned forward, helping her remove the shirt from his body. The second his hands were free they went to her hips, sliding over the bunched-up fabric as he made his way down to her bare skin. He rested his head on the back of the sofa and looked up at her.

Her head was slightly turned and his eyes landed on the cluster of freckles just under her left ear. He had the sudden urge to lick them. Get them under his tongue. They probably tasted like honey, too, just like the rest of her.

He'd get to that later; at the moment he wanted to take in the rest of the woman currently balanced on his lap. The deep purple fabric of her dress made her violet eyes pop, her thick black lashes framing her almond eyes. Some of her hair had fallen forward over her right shoulder, a black curtain of silk.

"Do you have any idea how beautiful you are?" he asked as he pushed his hands under the fabric of her dress, his fingers finding the lace he'd seen just seconds before.

Her hands moved from his shoulders down to his chest, tracing his muscles through the fabric. "We both already know what's going to happen here? So there's no need for the flattery, Liam."

"I'm not feeding you more lines." He shook his head, one of

his hands moving up to her hip while the other traveled to the sweet spot between her thighs.

"You're no longer just trying to pick up some girl at the bar?" Her mouth quirked to the side before it dropped open on a gasp, her eyes dilating as he pressed his thumb to her clit through the thin material.

"You aren't *some* girl." He was beginning to think she was *the* girl, and that thought wasn't as scary as it normally should've been. Or maybe he was just too thoroughly distracted to focus on it.

Yeah, probably the second one. But really what else was he supposed to be focused on when she was currently bucking against him. Her hands went back to his shoulders, where she fisted the fabric of his T-shirt and held on tight.

"Is…is that so?"

"That is so." He pulled the lace of her panties to the side, running his fingers across her folds before he slipped two inside of her.

"Oh God." Her hips picked up speed as she sought more pressure.

He wanted to take her this way, but with his cock buried deep inside of her as opposed to his fingers. He wanted her naked, riding him hard as her tits bounced freely in his face.

But he really wasn't of a mind to stop her from seeking her pleasure. No, he wanted to feel her body tighten around his fingers. Wanted to hear her moans. Wanted to watch her and appreciate everything about the moment when she completely and totally lost herself.

Because the fact of the matter was that once he was inside her, it was hard to focus on everything. Last night she'd blown his mind. He had no doubt it was going to be any different tonight.

Her hands tightened on his shoulders, her nails digging into his skin despite the fabric of his shirt. Every time she moved she rubbed against him, making him harder with each brush of her body.

The sweetest torture he'd ever experienced in his life.

But with each breathy moan and gasp that emanated from her mouth, his willpower to wait for her to finish took another hit. He fought every instinct to free his erection from his jeans and get inside her, but as the condoms were in the bedroom that was a no-go.

A change in location was imminent. He could wait for her to finish. He could do that. He could breathe past the clawing desperation for her. He just needed to focus, needed to get her there sooner.

"Come on, honey. Come for me," he said as he worked her clit.

"I am. I am. Liam, don't stop." Her head fell back between her shoulders, her words going toward the ceiling.

"Not going to stop. But I need you to look at me." He wanted to see it happen, wanted to watch her unravel. He hadn't been able to last time, he'd had his face buried in her neck and had been focusing on not coming before she did. Though he wasn't going to lie, that was still a bit of a concern at the moment.

Harper's head fell forward and her eyes landed on his, dazed and maybe just a little bit lost. But seconds later she was found. Her body trembling as his name came across her lips and she let go. She fell into him, burying her face in his throat as she caught her breath.

He pulled his hand from her body, putting it on her hip. His other hand moved up, his palm going to the back of her head, burying his fingers in her hair. "You okay?"

She groaned, the vibration tickling his skin. "I don't know." She pulled away slowly and looked at him, shaking her head. "I...you do something to me that I don't quite understand."

"Good or bad?" He trailed his fingers down through her hair, tracing her spine. Her entire body shivered.

"Good. *Really* good." She pressed her lips to his, her hands now in his hair. Her nails raked his scalp as she rocked against him, trailing a path of kisses down his jaw and to his throat.

This time he was the one groaning. "I don't know how much more of this I can take."

"All right," she said as she sat back on his thighs, reaching for the hem of his shirt. He leaned forward, helping her pull it from his body. He threw it to the side while her hands landed on his now bare chest. "Sit back."

He did so immediately and she was sliding off his lap, pushing his legs apart as she settled herself on the floor, her knees resting on the thick cushioned rug beneath his feet. She grabbed the skirt of her dress and pulled it up and over her head, throwing it somewhere in the direction of his shirt.

She sat before him wearing a black bra with emerald green lace that matched her panties perfectly. "It's your turn."

And just like that the woman who was every single one of his fantasies come to life was currently kneeling in front of him wearing lace and the sexiest pair of shoes he'd ever seen in his life.

He had no doubt that whatever she was going to do to him was going to be glorious, but he'd be lying if he said he wasn't hoping for a blow job. Because really, her mouth wrapped around his dick might just be the best thing. Ever.

A dream. He surely had to be dreaming.

He never wanted to wake up.

"My turn?" he somehow managed to get out of his throat that had suddenly gone very, very dry. He was now regretting his decision of finishing off his drink.

As if she'd read his mind she reached behind her for a glass, fishing out an ice cube that hadn't yet melted. "Yup," she said before she popped the ice into her mouth and stretched up. He leaned forward just enough to get to her lips. He tasted her tongue a second before the cube was in his mouth. And then she pulled back, fishing another one out of the glass and putting it in her mouth.

Harper pushed at his shoulder with two fingers, and he leaned back onto the couch. She put her mouth on his chest, tracing the ice across his skin as she made her way down. The cold against the heat of her tongue was incredible, especially across his abs.

When the cube was good and fully melted, she sat up and reached for his belt, unbuckling it. Then her fingers were at the button popping it open, and like magic the zipper was making its way down. She grabbed the top of his jeans, her fingers hooking into the elastic of his boxer briefs, and he lifted his hips. She pulled them down just far enough for his erection to spring free.

Her hand wrapped around him, stroking from base to tip. And then her mouth was on him, her tongue wrapping around the tip of his cock before she opened up and sucked him deep. He would forever be grateful about the fact that he was already sitting down. If he'd been standing he would've been flat on his ass.

"Oh good *God*." He groaned the last word long and loud, his head falling back on the sofa and his eyes rolling to the back of his head. One of his hands gripped the pillow next to him; the other was in her hair, palming the back of her head. There was no need to guide her, she was keeping up a remarkable pace all on her own, moving up and down the length of his shaft in perfect warm, wet strokes.

Speaking of strokes, he was going to have one shortly…or surely black out because all of the blood was gone from his brain. All of it.

He opened his eyes, the need to see her working him over a necessity. "I'm…I'm…I'm going to come." Oh great, he was panting.

She drew her mouth slowly over him, her tongue doing that amazing little trick around the head again before she let him go. "Isn't that the general idea?" she asked before her lips were wrapped around him again and she proceeded to take him all the way down to the hilt. A few more expertly placed strokes of her tongue and he was letting go, pumping into her mouth and making a string of inarticulate sounds.

His head fell onto the back of the sofa and he stared up at the ceiling, trying to catch his breath.

"That was…unreal."

A soft chuckle escaped Harper's mouth as her hands went to his knees. He brought his head down just as she was levering herself up from the floor. She stood before him, his sexy goddess in green lace.

Just as soon as he figured out how to stand again he was going to have to peel her out of the few things that still remained on her body.

Maybe with his teeth.

Yeah, that sounded like a good plan. One he was distracted from a moment later when she crawled onto his lap again.

"Glad you enjoyed it."

His hands were on her thighs, moving up and over the curves of her body. Tracing her hips, the dip of her waist, the rise of her chest. "No." He shook his head. "I *enjoy* a beer after a long, hot day. I *enjoy* watching a good movie. I *enjoy* getting to work on my truck. That was…that was something else entirely."

She was something else entirely.

* * *

Harper sat perched up on the breakfast bar wearing an oversized T-shirt and her panties. Liam was standing between her thighs wearing gray boxer briefs and nothing else. A spoon hovered in front of her lips, another bite of bread pudding waiting to be devoured. She opened her mouth and closed her eyes as the richness touched her tongue.

She savored it for just a second, humming around the spoon before opening her eyes. Liam's gaze was focused on her mouth, his eyes dilated.

"Watching you eat this might be the most erotic thing I've ever experienced in my life."

She swallowed, deliberately licking her lips. "Really? Out of everything, this is at the top of your list?"

"With you, my list runs horizontal, so everything is at the

top." He scooped up another bite of the pudding and brought the spoon to his mouth.

Hmmm, of that she had no doubt. They'd added a few more things to that list of his when they'd managed to make it to his bedroom. He'd laid her out and taken his time, running his mouth over her body for a good long while. When he'd gotten her truly mindless he'd just started the process all over again.

It was a fact that Harper wasn't one to sleep with men she'd just met—the man in front of her an obvious exception to the rule. And contrary to her current actions, it took a lot for her to let a man into her bed. All that being said, she was no stranger to good sex.

Brad had never left her wanting for anything, and he'd most definitely been the best she'd ever had…

Until Liam.

She didn't really understand it, either. When it came to men in general—even before being dumped by her fiancé—she didn't get in over her head. She tested the waters of a new relationship. Dipped her toes in and waited before *slowly* submerging herself. She never just jumped right on in…

Until Liam.

It had been a lost cause to even attempt to keep up her defenses when she was around him. He was breaking them down left and right; case in point she'd come back that night. She'd almost chickened out. Almost hadn't come over. But she kept telling herself she had nothing to lose with spending another evening with him.

For the first time in three months she could see a light at the end of the very dark tunnel she'd been traveling down. And the thought of what she was leaving behind wasn't nearly as debilitating as it had been.

She was barely aware of her mouth opening, didn't know what possessed her to start speaking, but the words were out before she even knew it. "I was supposed to get married this weekend."

Liam froze, the spoon in midair as it made its descent toward the bowl of pudding. "You...you were?"

She nodded, pulling her bottom lip between her teeth and chewing on it. *You can't go back now. You've already opened your mouth. Good job.*

"What happened?" He dropped the spoon in the dish before he reached up to her mouth, pulling her lip from her teeth with his thumb. His other hand moved from her thigh, to her hip, and around to her lower back. Turned out her body craved the firm, steady weight of his palm.

"He left. Called it off three months ago."

He nodded, cradling her jaw in his hand, his thumb brushing across her cheek. "So you came here to..."

"Get away from it all. I live in a very small town. Pretty much everyone knows. The looks of pity everywhere I went were getting to be a little much, and I just didn't want to deal with it. Not this weekend."

"I get that. So you came here to spend it with your aunt?"

"Yeah."

"And then ended up spending it with me." His eyes didn't leave hers as his hand moved from her jaw, running down her neck and tugging her shirt down to reveal the very top of her breasts. He traced the swells with his fingertips before he palmed the full weight of one, his thumb rasping over her nipple through the material.

"Yeah," she repeated, now more than slightly breathless.

He leaned forward, pressing his lips to the side of her neck. "Your ex is a moron."

She laughed, a different kind of warm settling in her belly and mixing with the heat that was the constant result of his hands on her body. "Really? You've known me for all of about twenty-six hours."

He pulled his mouth from her throat and looked at her, shaking his head. "I could've told you that after twenty-six seconds. I'm sorry you had to go through that, I really am, but all I can think is, thank God he was an idiot. Because if you'd married him, you wouldn't be right here." He leaned forward, pressing his mouth to hers. "Right now." Another quick touch of his mouth that was just a little more than a taste of his lips. "With me."

Well, damn.

"How is it that I just had you and I already want you again?" he whispered, sounding more than a little baffled.

"I don't know. But you should go with it."

"Yes, ma'am." This time when his mouth touched hers he didn't pull away, his tongue finding hers as he tilted his head and deepened the kiss.

His hands were at her hips, pulling her from the counter as her legs wrapped around his waist. He was carrying her through the house again, his mouth not leaving hers as he navigated around the furniture and made his way to the bedroom.

The second she was on her back the weight of his body disappeared. The drawer of his nightstand was pulled open and then slammed shut. She sat up, pulling the shirt over her head while he lost his boxers and put on the condom. He knelt on the bed, hooking his fingers in the lace at her sides and dragging her panties down her legs.

And then he was pushing her back onto the mattress, climbing up her body and trailing kisses across her skin.

"Slow," he said as he settled between her thighs. "I want to take my time. *Need* to take my time."

"Yes," she whispered breathlessly; it was the only thing she could manage to say. Slow sounded glorious. Slow sounded perfect.

He placed one of his arms by her head, leveraging himself up as his knees moved out, pushing her legs farther apart. And then he was sliding inside of her and her back was arching up off the bed.

She wrapped her legs around his thighs, placing her feet flat on the mattress and giving herself just a little bit of leverage herself, moving with him.

His free hand went to her head, palming the side of her face as he leaned down and kissed her. His tongue thrust into her mouth, matching the delicious pace that their bodies were rocking together.

It was a slow build. Torturous and perfect, starting at her toes and climbing up her body with every push and pull of his hips. Her mouth fell away from his, her eyes closing as she gave way to the pleasure.

"Harper." He whispered her name and her eyes opened again. All she could see was the green gold of his gaze, the adoration clear. Adoration for her. "Just wait."

She wasn't sure if she could; it was all coming to the surface. Her heart was pounding out of her chest. She couldn't get enough air into her lungs. Couldn't hold off the release that was building at the very core of her.

It was all too much. Too much to take. Too much to understand. And the way he was looking at her? Watching her? Seeking her pleasure with every move he made? How could she wait?

"I can't," she gasped. "I can't hold on."

"You can." His hips slowed as he kissed her gently. "Stay with me," he said against her lips. "Stay with me, Harper. We'll get there together. Slow, remember?"

"Slow." She nodded, grabbing on to his biceps, her nails undoubtedly scoring his skin.

He did it three more times, building her right up to the edge of an orgasm before pulling back and slowing down. She wasn't sure she could handle another one. Wasn't sure if she'd survive it.

"Please," she begged. "Please, Liam."

This time his hips didn't ease up. No, they moved faster, harder, slow apparently a thing of the past. And the result was mind bending.

Her orgasm slammed into her, taking over her entire body. Her hips bucked wildly, her hands clawed at Liam's back, her lungs were going to explode. But even with all of that, her eyes didn't leave his.

The pleasure in his face was incredible. Pleasure he found in her. Pleasure they found in each other.

He didn't stop moving until they were both good and truly spent. His arms were shaking as he gave her one last kiss on the mouth. And then his lips were moving to the spot just under her left ear, his tongue rasping against her skin and making her entire body shiver as another spasm contracted her core, squeezing around the length of him that was still firmly inside of her.

"You're incredible," he groaned. "Every part of you." And then he rolled off her, pulling from her body as he fell to his back.

Neither of them moved for a minute…or five, staring at the ceiling.

"What the hell was that?" he asked through a hoarse voice.

"I…I have no idea." And that was the first lie she told him. She knew exactly what it was.

Her heart was still beating out of her chest. A thrumming so loud she could feel it in her ears. And she couldn't catch her breath to save her life.

She'd gone and done it. She'd fallen in love with him. Fallen in love with a man who she didn't even know.

How the hell had that happened?

How was it even possible?

And what in the world was she going to do?

Chapter Four

Lost

Liam knew before he even opened his eyes the following morning.

The sheets next to him were cold and empty.

The house eerily quiet.

No note.

No good-bye.

No anything.

Harper was gone.

Chapter Five

Not Alone

June 13th...five weeks later

Harper stared down at the line of pregnancy tests on the bathroom counter.

All five of them had the same answer.

Just like the five she'd taken the day before.

And the five she'd taken the day before that.

Fifteen tests and they all said the same thing: she was pregnant.

A soft whine at Harper's feet had her looking down at Luna. The little French bulldog was sitting back on her hind legs and staring up with wide black eyes. She stood, taking a couple of steps forward and laying down right across Harper's feet as she whined again.

Luna always did this when she sensed that Harper was upset...which was pretty much all the time these days.

Harper bent down, picking Luna up and cradling the small dog in her arms before she turned and slid the rest of the way down the cabinets. She sat on the bathroom floor, petting the dog's back and waiting for the world to right itself.

But that wasn't going to happen.

"I'm pregnant," she whispered, thinking that if she said it aloud she'd believe it.

Nope. Not the case.

It had been five weeks since Nashville. Five weeks since she'd walked into that bar and gone home with a man she'd just met. Five weeks since she'd spent two nights having the most mind-blowing sex of her life. Five weeks since she'd run away. Five weeks since she'd left a sleeping Liam in his bed. Five weeks since she'd turned into a coward.

She thought about him daily…multiple times a day in fact, and every time she did it hurt like hell.

She didn't get it. She hadn't even spent forty-eight hours with him and she missed him more than she'd ever missed Brad.

How? How was that even possible?

She'd gone over it all thousands of times. Replaying it in her head and trying to figure out if she could've done things differently.

But what other choice did she have? Two days with him and he'd had more power to destroy her than anyone else ever had before.

That last night with him, she'd lain there for hours memorizing the moment. Memorizing *him*. His arms wrapped around her body, his steady deep breaths on her skin, his lips on her shoulder.

When she'd pulled away from him it had been physically painful.

But she knew the pain was nothing to what it would be if he was the one to walk away from her. So in the long run what she'd done was best…

Or at least that was what she kept telling herself. What she *had* to keep telling herself. But really it was a big lie. A *massive* lie.

She'd driven to her aunt's, letting the numbness overtake her because as soon as she started to really feel things, she was going to lose it. Celeste had been home, asleep on the sofa with a marathon of her favorite cooking show lighting up the otherwise dark living room.

The second the door had closed behind Harper she'd started sobbing. To Celeste's credit it had only taken her about thirty seconds to go from asleep to fully aware of the situation. It was well into the morning before Harper had stopped sobbing. By the time she'd gotten a hold of herself she'd been desperate to get out of Nashville, needing to put as much distance between her and Liam as possible. If she didn't, she probably would've found herself on his doorstep again.

And that could *not* happen.

Celeste was the only one who knew what had happened with Liam. All of her friends and family were under the impression that her current state of mind still had to do with Brad.

They were all *incredibly* wrong.

She'd been forcing herself to function over the last few weeks, thinking it was going to get better. Turned out she was just biding her time, denial her greatest friend.

She'd ignored the fact that her period had been late…one week running into two and then turning into three. And then the morning sickness had set in two weeks ago.

Morning her ass.

She was nauseous all the freaking time. She'd kept telling herself that she was coming down with something.

See, denial.

But the proof was sitting on the counter behind her. This was the third morning in a row that she'd looked at those positives. There was no more hiding. Reality had just caught up to her.

The corner of her eyes prickled, that familiar constricting sensation taking over her throat.

You are not going to cry.

You are not going to cry.

You. Are. Not. Going. To. Cry.

These were your decisions. You *went home with him.* You *slept with him…half a dozen times.* You *got pregnant.*

She closed her eyes, taking deep steady breaths through her nose, trying to calm down her now rolling stomach. Or stop the steady stream of tears tracking down her face.

Neither of them went away. So she just sat there and continued to pet Luna.

These were your *decisions.* You *cannot go back and change things. This is how it is. How it is going to be.*

Deal with it.

And deal with it she would…just as soon as she got off the floor.

* * *

The *ohhh*s and *awe*s that emanated from the circle of women around Harper were beginning to get to her. But really what else did she expect? She was at a joint baby shower for two of her friends.

About thirty women were stuffed into the front room of Café

Lula, munching on finger foods and drinking punch. The little eatery, with its variety of bright colors scattered about here and there, was closed on Sundays, so the party had free rein.

Harper closed her eyes and took a deep, fortifying breath when another round of *awe*s resonated around the circle. It turned out to not be the best idea as her mother—who was currently sitting next to her—bit into an egg salad sandwich.

Eggs were currently enemy number one on Harper's *not-so-friendly* food list. The smell. The taste. The general thought of them. But as her mother was currently on her *not-so-friendly* in general list, she wasn't too shocked.

Delilah Laurence didn't always think before she spoke...or before she acted. And yes, Harper completely and entirely understood that mothers could be critical of their children—daughters especially—but Delilah took it to a whole other level.

She hadn't held back any of the jabs of late. But she *never* held back. Ever.

Harper hadn't even been at the shower five minutes when Delilah had cornered her and started in. As she hadn't really been eating the last couple of weeks, and her appetite had been pretty limited even before the morning sickness had kicked in, she'd lost a few pounds. The dress she'd picked out for that afternoon was a size smaller than she'd been wearing, and one that she hadn't fit into for a couple of years.

"I might not agree with this breakup of yours," her mother had said, giving Harper the ever-critical Delilah once-over. "But it does have its benefits. You look skinnier."

Wellllll, that was all about to change now, wasn't it?

No sooner had the jab from earlier crossed Harper's mind,

when her mother leaned over and whispered, "It's a good thing you have so many friends with children, now you won't feel like you're missing out."

Yup. Delilah was in for a surprise. Harper wondered if she could just wait until after the baby was born, and have the baby tell her mother the news.

Guess what? You're a grandmother!

Yeah, probably not.

Well, at least part of Delilah's statement was true. Hannah Shepherd and Paige King were both very much pregnant. Hannah was due in mid-October, Paige toward the end of September. Though the odds that Paige lasted that long were a little slim because she was carrying twin girls, her baby bump was quite a bit bigger than Hannah's.

The stack of baby supplies on either side of the women was growing considerably. As Hannah was having a little boy, hers was dominantly green and blue. Paige's was filled with pinks and yellows.

Paige and her husband Brendan already had a little boy, Trevor, who'd just turned two last month. He was currently helping his mother rip the paper off of her gifts and giving Hannah assistance with her presents as well.

Paige and Hannah had quickly become two of Harper's closest friends when they moved to Mirabelle, but the positions of best friends were and would always be reserved by Grace King—now Grace Anderson—and Melanie O'Bryan—now Melanie Hart. Grace and Mel had known each other pretty much since birth. When they'd met Harper on the first day of sixth grade almost fifteen years ago, she'd been quickly added to the fold.

Neither of them knew what was currently going on with Harper. Not talking to them about it over the last few weeks had been nothing short of painful. But Harper couldn't talk about it. She wasn't ready yet. Because if she said the words to someone else, everything would be really real.

Oh look, there was that denial again.

But her denial wasn't the only reason she wasn't talking. No, the other part was the jealously that she just couldn't get over, and the subsequent guilt that accompanied said jealousy.

Grace and her husband Jax had welcomed their daughter Rosie Mae into the world last September, and Mel and Bennett were now embarking on starting a family of their own. They were in the trying phase and enjoying every aspect of it.

Harper was happy for them, really she was.

It was just hard.

How could it not be? She was single...*alone*...and now very much pregnant. While all of her closest friends were married to men who loved them. Men who adored them. Men who would move mountains for them.

None of them was doing it alone.

At that exact moment someone who immediately had Harper amending her previous statement filled the empty seat to her right.

Almost all of her friends were married to men who loved them and weren't raising children all by themselves. Beth Boone was the exception. And her situation was *way* more complicated than Harper's would ever be.

Beth had been a couple of years ahead of Harper, Grace, and Mel when they were in high school and they'd all been friends.

When Beth had graduated, she went up to Tallahassee for college. She and Mel had been roommates for a couple of years when their time in school overlapped, and they were incredibly close.

For more than a decade, Beth's older sister and brother-in-law—Colleen and Kevin Ross—had been next-door neighbors to Mel's parents. Mel's little brother, Hamilton, was best friends with the Rosses' oldest daughter, Nora. The two kids had grown up together, running back and forth across the front yard.

Two months ago, Kevin and Colleen had died in a car accident. They'd both been killed on impact. Beth moved back to Mirabelle and was now the sole guardian and new parent to her sister's three kids: Nora, sixteen; Grant, seven; and Penny, three.

How was that for some perspective?

Penny was currently curled up in Beth's lap, her little head resting on Beth's shoulder while she sucked her thumb and observed the room through her wide, mossy green eyes. The pair could easily be mistaken as mother and daughter as they both had the exact same shade of blond hair, though Beth's eyes were a light blue.

"Would you judge me if I packed up some of that food over there and took it home in to-go containers?" Beth whispered conspiratorially. "Cucumber sandwiches and raw vegetables are an acceptable dinner for three children, right?"

The circumstances sucked for Beth returning to Mirabelle, but Harper truly had missed her friend.

"I mean I wouldn't." Harper shook her head. "But there's no guarantees to some of the other guests."

"What are you talking about?" Beth gasped in mock shock. "No one here has a single judgmental bone in their bodies."

Penny pulled her thumb out of her mouth and stretched up to Beth's ear. Harper could just make out the word *potty* in Penny's little voice.

"I'll be right back. Don't let anyone take my seat."

Harper nodded, and as she watched them walk away she couldn't help but be in awe of her friend. Beth had been thrown into the deep end and she was handling things remarkably well. In the scheme of things, Harper was treading water in the shallow end.

Barely keeping her head up from drowning.

And as if on cue, like she sensed the moment to strike, Delilah leaned over and said, "It's a shame things didn't work out with Brad; you would've made beautiful babies. Though hopefully they would've had his metabolism."

Harper was getting to the point where she didn't visibly cringe when Brad's name was said. They were now starting in on month five of him being gone, and it was no secret to anyone that Delilah partially blamed Harper for the demise of the relationship. It was also no secret that Delilah was still holding out hope that he'd come back.

She'd told her mother more times than she could count to let that pipe dream go, but it hadn't happened yet.

Harper closed her eyes and took another deep breath, reminding herself that she loved her mother. Really she did. But sometimes the woman tried every ounce of her patience. Today was no different. But she could get through this. She *had* to get through this. And really this was just the calm before the storm when it came to what was going to happen. Because when the truth came out, all hell was going to break loose.

So Harper went back to protocol number one in regards to Delilah Laurence: she locked her jaw tight and stared straight ahead, counting down to her escape.

Thirty-two minutes, twenty-nine seconds…

Twenty-eight seconds…

Twenty-seven seconds…

She looked across the circle of chairs to find Mel's amber eyes on her, eyes that very rarely missed anything. *You okay?* She mouthed.

Harper nodded. Twenty-five seconds…

Twenty-four seconds…

You sure?

Harper nodded again, forcing a smile that just made Mel's eyes narrow. She turned away from the speculative gaze of her friend just in time to catch Hannah stick a massive pink bow on the top of Trevor's head.

Twenty-three seconds…

Twenty-two seconds…

Trevor ran over to his aunt Grace who was bouncing Rosie Mae on her knee. Rosie was nine months old and giggling up a storm as she watched everything going on around her. Her strawberry blond hair, a gift from her redheaded father Jax, was held back with a green headband.

Twenty-one seconds…

Twenty seconds…

Trevor took the bow off his head and put it on his cousin's before he leaned in and kissed her on the cheek, causing another collective *aww* from around the circle.

Nineteen seconds…

Yeah, she could get through this. She *would* get through this.

The countdown continued in her head for the next half hour, and she kept up with her steady breathing all the way through the rest of the shower. She stayed strong when she said good-bye to her mother, not flinching under the final Delilah once-over.

Must. Not. Show. Weakness.

Because any sign would be spotted and latched on to.

But Harper's downfall was when she was helping clean up. She went to throw something in the trash and a plate of half-eaten food was sitting on top. The second she lifted the lid, the scent of fried chicken mixed with that pungent smell of eggs hit her like a punch to the face...or to the stomach. Really it was all things poultry that were enemy number one on the *not-so-friendly* list.

She got to the bathroom just in time, dropping to her knees and ridding herself of the tiny cup of fruit and few crackers she'd managed to eat earlier. Her stomach cramped painfully, apparently hell bent on proving to her just what was going to happen if she continued to try to put anything in it.

Her skin broke out into a sweat, her eyes watered, and her head pounded. It took her a minute to catch her breath, but the disorienting ringing in her ears was going full force. Her head spun as she stood up, forcing her to grab on to the wall for balance. She stood there for a couple of seconds, holding on to the wall as she attempted to pull herself together.

It took a lot longer than she'd imagined.

When she got her breathing under control she cleaned herself up as much as she could in the tiny stall, wiping her eyes and blowing her nose. What she really wanted was to rinse her mouth with water.

Well, if she was being honest, what she'd really like was to drink some water, but she wasn't all that sure if her stomach would be kind enough for even that at the moment.

She opened the door and took one step before she registered that she wasn't alone. She stopped dead in her tracks as she spotted Mel and Grace who were both leaning against the counter, their arms folded across their chests and their eyes focused on her.

"So are you going to start talking?" Mel spoke first.

"Or are we going to have to force it out of you?" Grace finished.

Now Harper wasn't much for losing her shit. Really, she was more the suffer-in-silence type. But as she looked at her two best friends everything hit her. The sob that broke out of her mouth a second later was one she couldn't hold back any longer. The two women converged on her, wrapping her up in their arms as she lost it.

"We're here, Harp," Mel whispered as she rubbed her hand up and down Harper's back.

"Always will be," Grace said.

When Harper managed to somewhat rein herself back in, she pulled away from their embrace.

Grace reached behind her and grabbed a tissue from the box on the counter. "Please tell us what's going on."

"Yeah. Is it Brad?" Mel asked.

Harper took the tissue, shaking her head. "No. It's something else…*someone* else."

"Someone?"

"When…*what*?" Grace's eyebrows bunched in confusion.

Harper didn't have a chance to answer either of her friends' questions when the bathroom door opened.

Abby Fields walked in, a streak of green icing on her cheek and bits of cake in her auburn hair. Abby was Paige's best friend—had been since both women were five years old—and was now an honorary member of the close-knit girls in Mirabelle. She was actually a recent transplant to Florida herself, though she lived about three and a half hours east in Jacksonville.

The woman was busy, there was no doubt. She was about two months into her new job running the PR department for St. Ignatius, one of the top hospitals in the south *and* her new official relationship with a now Stanley Cup winner Logan James. The Stampede had just won two days ago, but Abby had taken a break from the celebrations to come to the shower.

Abby took in the scene in front of her, her steps faltering as she walked into the bathroom. "Trevor discovered the cake table," she explained.

"Ahh," all three women said as they took a step back from the sinks to make room.

Grace excused herself to one of the stalls, while Harper washed her hands and Mel fiddled with her short blond curls in the full-length mirror on the back of the bathroom door.

Abby made quick work at the sink, cleaning herself up and unsnapping her purse to pull out her compact. She touched up her makeup before she turned to Harper, a bottle of eyedrops in her hand. "Allergies sure have been a bitch this year."

"Thanks." Harper managed a watery smile as she grabbed the bottle.

"No problem. And keep it." Abby nodded to the bottle before

she reached out, touching Harper's hand lightly, and then headed out of the bathroom.

Harper tilted her head back and put a few drops into each eye, grabbing another tissue and dabbing at the new stream of moisture on her face.

"Okay," Grace said as she came out of the bathroom stall and started washing her hands in the sink. "Start talking."

"Can we not do this here? Please?" Harper shook her head, doing everything in her power to hold back the fresh wave of tears that threatened.

She knew she needed to tell them. That she actually wanted to tell them. To talk to her best friends and tell them everything that was going on. She just didn't want it to be in a bathroom where anyone that was still there cleaning up could walk in on the conversation. She was under no delusions that she'd be able to keep it together when she told Mel and Grace everything.

None.

"Your reprieve is only going to last as long as it takes for everyone to leave." The severe look on Mel's face brokered no argument.

"Yup, as soon as everyone clears out we are having ourselves a little conversation. Got it?"

"Got it." Harper nodded, taking a deep breath to fortify herself.

The truth was definitely about to will out...and very, very soon.

* * *

Grace had kept her word. There was no dilly-dallying in story-telling. As soon as the last person was out the door, she flipped the lock and pulled Harper and Mel into the back of the café. She was able to do this as she was part owner of said café. Her grand-mother, Lula Mae King, had opened it years ago, and Grace was now in charge of all the baked goods.

As it was well past Rosie Mae's naptime, she'd gone home with her great-grandmother, so the women were able to talk freely. They all settled into the table and chairs set up in the back corner of the café kitchen, and Harper told them every last detail…except for one very important one.

She left out the fact that she was without a doubt in love with Liam. For now, she was going to keep that to herself.

"So I'm pregnant," Harper finished, looking both of them in the eye in turn. She took a deep breath, letting it out in a wave of relief.

They knew. She'd told someone. *Two* someones. She wasn't alone in this.

After a few beats of silence, where both of her friends digested the news, Mel was the first to talk. "Okay, I'm going to ask the obvious question here. How did this happen? You guys did…you know…use protection, didn't you? And aren't you on birth control?"

"I stopped taking it after Brad, which is why everything has been a bit irregular lately. And we did use condoms…they just didn't work."

"No kidding," Grace said slowly, still in shock. "Does he know?"

Harper shook her head. "Not yet."

"*Yet*. So you *are* going to tell him?" Mel asked.

"Yes. I am." She nodded, and she was going to have to tell him much sooner than later.

She'd long since programmed his number into her phone. She'd also spent more than one night staring at the piece of paper that he'd written said number on—and his address for that matter—all those weeks ago.

She was pathetic. Just another thing to add to the list.

One: *Coward*
Two: *Delusional*
Three: *Pregnant*
Four: *Pathetic*

She could keep going, but she wasn't really interested in feeling more depressed about the situation. She'd reached her max.

"And after?" Mel asked.

"I have absolutely no idea what's going to happen after I tell him...if he'll want to be involved, or if I'll be raising this child alone. Because I *will* be raising this child. That much I do know. Without a doubt."

"Well, that's good, but you're wrong about one thing," Grace said as she reached across the table and grabbed Harper's hand.

"Yeah," Mel agreed as she grabbed Harper's other hand. "You will *not* be raising this child alone."

And there was another thing to be added to the list.

Number five: *Foolish*

Because not telling her friends earlier had been *beyond* foolish.

* * *

The waiting area of the women's health wing of the Atticus County Hospital was almost empty when Harper and Mel took a seat, but that's what Harper had been hoping for when she'd made the eight a.m. appointment.

She'd asked Beth—who was an OB/GYN nurse and had gotten a job at the hospital when she'd moved back—to get her in as early as possible, and her friend had complied.

"You're going to need to get me another cup of coffee when we leave here," Mel said around another yawn.

"Seriously, don't your classes start at seven in the morning?"

Mel was a high school math teacher so she kept an early schedule nine months out of the year, something that Harper found to be a miracle as her friend wasn't much of a morning person…actually she wasn't a morning person in the slightest little bit. The woman required multiple cups of coffee in the morning to actually function like a human.

"Yes." Mel nodded. "But in the summer I keep summer hours, which means sleeping in."

"Your husband let you get away with that?" Harper asked as she started to fill out the forms in front of her.

Name: Harper Maria Laurence

"Are you kidding? Bennett sleeps in, too. He takes full advantage of longer mornings in bed."

Age: Twenty-six

"I'll just bet he does." She did her best to keep her voice neutral when she checked the single box.

Not alone. Not alone. Not alone. She told herself. The fact that

Mel was there was proof positive of this fact. And Harper knew beyond a doubt that Mel had absolutely no qualms about being in the doctor's office that early in the morning. Mel was making a valiant attempt at distracting Harper, and though it wasn't working all that much, she appreciated the effort nonetheless.

Mel continued talking as Harper started to fill out her address.

She lived on the third floor of a walk-up. Two bedrooms, one her "laboratory"/storage for the lotions and oils she made. There was barely enough room in there as it was, so it would definitely be too small for a baby's nursery. Who was she kidding? The entire apartment would be too small for a baby's nursery.

What was she going to do? The rent for the place was pretty much the max that she could afford as it was, and now she was going to have so many more added expenses when the baby came along.

Oh God.

"Hey." Mel's hand was on Harper's knee squeezing lightly. "Where did you just go?"

She turned to look at her friend, knowing that her wide eyes were filled with a fear she couldn't control. "I'm either going to have to be homeless with a baby or move back in with my parents."

"Okay, I don't think those are your only options. So let's stop spiraling. And how about I finish filling this out," Mel said as she pulled the clipboard and pen out of Harper's hands. "One step at a time, babe, and I don't think we are anywhere near where you just went."

"Promise?"

"Promise. Here." She reached over and grabbed the newest

copy of *People*. "Read up on what's going on with Miley Cyrus and Kim Kardashian, it will make you feel better about your life. One because you've yet to prance around wearing a slutty teddy bear onesie while doing this." She stuck out her tongue and held up two peace signs. "Nor have you been impregnated by Kanye West." She paused, tilting her head to the side as she narrowed her eyes on Harper. "I mean, Kanye isn't the father, is he? You didn't just say Liam as a code name, did you?"

"She's got jokes, ladies and gentlemen." Harper rolled her eyes, but she did have a smile creeping up her face as she focused on the magazine in her lap.

It was another five minutes before Harper heard her name called. She looked up to find Beth holding the door open. Her blond hair pulled back in a ponytail and wearing light blue scrubs that were almost the exact same shade as her eyes. Eyes that widened fractionally when she saw that Mel was sitting next to Harper.

Beth had probably just thought Harper needed to see the doctor for a routine checkup or something. She probably hadn't guessed that her friend was pregnant. But she didn't ask any questions or comment at all when Mel came with them. She just nodded before she turned and led them down the hallway.

"Weight first." Beth stopped in front of the scale. Harper handed her purse to Mel before she got on.

Hey, every little bit counted.

But when she saw the number that Beth jotted down, she cringed. She'd lost twenty pounds in the last few months, and though she didn't think that all of it was post getting pregnant, she knew that some of it was and concern for the baby filled her, causing her chest to tighten and that ever-present anxiety to perk up.

Well, her blood pressure number was going to be awesome now, wasn't it?

Chapter Six

How to Be a Grown-Ass Adult
Step One: Wait Until the Following
Week

An hour later it was official. *Officially* official. Harper was pregnant and due at the end of January.

This *was* happening.

She was now sitting at a booth in Café Lula with Grace on one side of her and Mel sitting across from them. They were all munching on some ginger cookies that Grace had whipped up.

They'd apparently worked wonders on Grace's nauseous stomach when she'd been pregnant. She had high hopes that those—along with the cup of herbal tea that was going down sip by sip—would do the same for Harper.

So far it was working…and she was only slightly jealous of the caffeine glaze in both Grace's and Mel's eyes as they enjoyed their morning coffee.

The doctor had said it could take a month or two before things evened out and her appetite got back to normal. Until then she was going to try to see if the anti-nausea meds she'd been prescribed combined with some natural remedies would do the trick.

She really didn't have any other options.

"Okay. So what's the plan of attack?" Grace asked. "When are you telling him?"

"Yeah." Mel nodded as she put her mug down on the table. "Are you calling him, or going there? Or what?"

"I don't know yet." Harper chewed on her bottom lip. "This isn't exactly information I want to tell him over the phone. But seeing him again is going to be complicated."

"Sweetie, I think from here on out we're going to have to deal with *everything* being complicated," Grace said before she took another sip of her coffee.

"I know," Harper groaned, dropping her head and gently banging it against the table.

"Okay, I have a thought that might prevent you from doing that," Mel said as she patted the back of Harper's head. "I don't think giving yourself a concussion is the answer."

Harper lifted her head and looked across the table at her friend. "What's your plan?"

"Give yourself the week. It hasn't even been thirty minutes since we left the doctor and this was all *really* official. And I think you should get out of town this weekend."

"What?" Harper asked.

"Give yourself a second to breathe," Grace agreed.

"And do what?"

"Come to Jacksonville for the Stampede party. Dale's mom can't go so there's an extra ticket and hotel room." Mel grabbed a cookie and dipped it in her coffee. "You should get away for a few days."

"Because we all know how well getting away worked for me

the last time I did it." Harper made a motion to her stomach over the table.

"This time it will be different. You'll have a responsible chaperone, and I will be sure not to leave you on your own," Mel said. "Come on. You should take advantage of a little distraction."

As the team was celebrating winning the Stanley Cup, the Stampede party promised to be a big event. And would probably be filled with distractions galore. Abby Fields's boyfriend, Logan James, was one of the bigger players on the team, and he'd developed a number of relationships with some of the members of Mirabelle. The two most important being Mel's little brother Hamilton O'Bryan, and his best friend Dale Rigels.

It had been a few months before Dale's seventeenth birthday when the doctors had found the brain tumor. The surgery to remove it had been done immediately and he'd gone through chemo afterward. Now he was three months into remission. Logan had come to visit Dale during his recovery, and they'd kept up with each other ever since.

As Mel's husband Bennett had become a bit of a mentor, and big brother to both boys, he and Mel were going with them to play chaperone. So what was one more person to watch over? Even if she was a grown-ass adult?

Harper grabbed another cookie and bit into it; she might as well take the time while she had it...because everything was about to change very soon.

Who was she kidding? It already was changing.

Had changed.

* * *

On a normal day Harper worked until after five, sometimes six. But that day was not a normal day. Not only had it been incredibly slow, but she finished up before three, which was the biggest godsend.

If someone were to ask her what had happened that day, it would've been hard for her to remember. She'd pretty much just gone through the motions of everything. But how could she focus when she couldn't shut her brain off from the all-consuming anxiety and worry...or continuously thinking of *how* she was going to tell Liam.

Before she knew it, she was pulling up in front of her parents' house and putting her Cruiser in Park. She leaned back in the seat, taking just a moment to collect herself before she went inside.

The rule of show *no weakness* around her mother was more important than ever. There would be no pregnancy revelations to anyone else until she told Liam. At least she knew that much.

She took another couple of steady breaths as her eyes focused on the two three-story Victorian houses in front of her.

Harper's family had moved to Mirabelle fifteen years ago. It was right before she was about to start middle school and she hadn't been exactly thrilled about leaving her life in Atlanta. But now she couldn't imagine growing up anywhere else.

The two houses were pretty much smack dab in the middle of downtown and they stood about thirty yards apart. Besides the different paint colors—one sage green, the other dark blue—they were identical in every way.

Well, there was another difference. The green one was a residential home and where Harper lived from the age of eleven to eighteen. The blue was the St. Francis Veterinary Clinic...though a case could be made that Harper had spent almost as much time there as the house.

Her father had inherited the clinic from his uncle, and as it was the only vet in the area, it stayed pretty busy. She'd always been there helping out especially when they'd started the pet adoption/foster portion.

Mirabelle was part of Atticus County, and the only animal shelter in the area was a kill shelter. So for a couple of years, the clinic had been the temporary home to as many cats and dogs that could be taken in and saved from being euthanized. Harper would spend many hours playing with them and giving them as much attention as possible.

These days, there were a number of foster homes that would take in the animals until they were adopted. It was a much better option than them living in cages for weeks on end.

Or being put down.

The St. Francis Foster Pet Adoption program was one of the reasons that Harper needed to stop by her parents' house. Her mother was putting together baskets for a fund-raiser, and she'd asked for some of Harper's lotions and oils.

Which was something Harper found *beyond* interesting.

There were a number of things that Delilah Laurence didn't approve of, and her daughter's career choice was near the top. Though this didn't stop her from hitting Harper up for the homemade "lotions and potions" that everyone else *loved,* not to mention a donated gift certificate for massage "services rendered" had been requested more times than could be counted.

None of that changed the facts: a massage therapist was *not* a way to make a living.

The words had never actually been spoken, but Harper was pretty sure that was one of the reasons her mother had liked Brad so much. He was successful. So when her career as a massage therapist failed her "husband" would be able to take care of her.

Not only had that not worked out, but now Harper was pregnant without any husband at all.

Oh, look at that, her anxiety was spiking again.

Well, might as well give herself a small reprieve and go over to see her father before she had to face the firing squad that was her mother. The constant contention that she had with her mother was non-existent in the relationship she had with her father. She was a daddy's girl through and through.

When she walked inside the clinic she was greeted with the customary squawk of Gabby, the white and yellow cockatoo perched at the currently empty receptionist desk. The bird had been surrendered to the practice ten years ago when the owner died, and was now the unofficial mascot of the practice.

"Hello." Gabby flapped her wings as she adjusted on the stand.

Harper walked over to her, always the first order of business when she visited, and scratched the bird's chest. "Hey, pretty girl," she purred. Gabby's feathers ruffled in delight at the attention. "Where is everybody?"

"Getting our middle of the day caffeine fix." A deep voice—along with boots walking across the hardwood floor—echoed down the hall behind the desk.

Harper looked over just as Finn Shepherd walked into the reception area.

Until about a year ago, her father had not only owned the sole practice in Mirabelle, but he'd been the only vet. When Finn had graduated from veterinary school and moved back, he'd been hired onto the practice. The additional doctor had been more than needed. The workload having increased significantly over the years, and as her father was getting older it was a bit of a worry for Harper.

As it turned out, her father was adjusting just fine to sharing the practice. But as Finn was pretty much the son Paul never had, it wasn't all that surprising. Harper had grown up with Finn. Not only were they in the same year in school, but he'd been in and out of the practice learning everything he could since he was sixteen.

Before Brad had been in the picture, Harper's mother had always wanted her to end up with Finn. Though there was no denying that the man was attractive beyond words—what with his sapphire blue eyes, thick black wavy hair, and black-framed glasses that only added another layer of sexy—she'd always looked at him like a brother. And he'd always looked at her like a sister.

Besides, these days the only man she was thinking about had green-gold eyes and a deep, rich voice that set every part of her on fire. A man that she knew almost nothing about…except that she was in love with him. Oh, and she was carrying his child.

God, when had her life gotten so complicated?

Well, there was no time to focus on that because five seconds after Finn came into the room, another set of shoes echoed down the hallway. These were definitely heels as opposed to work boots.

"Ohhh, do my ears deceive me or is that one of my favorite

girls?" The kind face and gray-haired head of Janet Peterson popped through the doorway, her own steaming cup of coffee in hand.

Harper was only slightly bitter that she couldn't join in with her own cup. She was exhausted and really wishing she could get a little pick-me-up, too. Even with her limited coffee intake over the last couple of weeks, she was still a caffeine junkie. Admitting it was half the battle.

But as Janet's coffee was usually strong enough for a spoon to stand up straight, Harper wasn't going to tempt fate or mess with the delicate balance of her stomach. Besides, she shouldn't be drinking the stuff now anyway.

Janet was pretty much the backbone of the clinic, and it ran on more than just her coffee-making skills. She'd been working the receptionist desk for the last thirty years, and was still going strong in her sixties.

Before Harper could even respond to the question Janet asked, the woman had set down the coffee mug and pulled her into one of those soul-affirming hugs. Really, Harper should stop by every day just for one of these.

When Janet pulled back, Paul walked into the room, his mouth splitting into that customary grin when he laid eyes—the exact same shade as Harper's—on his daughter.

No matter what was going on, at least some things hadn't changed.

"Hey, sweet pea." He pulled Harper into his arms, giving her a kiss on the temple like he always did, before he let go and took a step back.

"Hey, Daddy."

"You get off early?" he asked, checking his watch.

"Yeah, my last appointment canceled. And it was a bit of a slow day."

"It's been slow here, too," Janet said as she reached for her coffee and took a sip. But the words were barely out of her mouth when the door behind them opened.

Gabby squawked again—no need for a bell over the door when they had this bird—as Tripp Black walked into the building. Tripp was Mirabelle's resident fire chief, a job he'd had for the last two and half years ever since he'd moved to the area. He was another insanely attractive man with thick brown hair, and warm chocolate brown eyes. But again, Harper had only ever been friends with the man.

As he was wearing his navy blue uniform pants and a gray polo with the Mirabelle Fire logo, she was guessing he was on duty. He made his way into the room and she noticed he was cradling a rather large ball of white and brown fur in his massive arms.

The ball of fluff shifted, or should she say balls. There were two puppies in Tripp's arms, and while one lifted its head from the crook of his elbow, the other burrowed deeper into his chest whining.

"Didn't know where else to take them. Someone abandoned these little guys at the station. No one even saw them drop the cardboard box at the door, but we did hear the barking."

This was a better alternative than what most people did, which was abandon their unwanted animals on the side of the road. Something Harper would never understand for as long as she lived.

That was what happened to Luna. She'd been no more than

two months old when someone found her wandering through a neighborhood. She had no collar, was starving, and covered in fleabites. Her father had never seen the dog before the day she'd been brought in, so he'd had no idea who the owner was.

Weeks went by with no one looking for or claiming the puppy. As Harper had been the one fostering her—and had gotten attached faster than it took to blink—the adoption had been obvious.

As Luna was a purebred French bulldog, Paul always suspected that it was a local breeder who'd just let her go without a care. She was most definitely the runt of the litter and had a slight limp as her left back leg was just a tad bit shorter than the rest.

Apparently imperfection was a reason that meant someone or something wasn't worthy to live. All a pile of garbage if you asked her. This was one of the reasons why Harper firmly believed there was a special place in hell reserved for people who were that cruel and heartless.

"Let me see." Finn moved closer, holding his hands out.

"I'd take the girl." Tripp nodded to the one who was sniffing the air around her. "The boy seems to have clinging issues with me."

Finn grabbed the puppy that was mostly white, just a few brown spots on her head and back, and pulled her into his chest. He touched one of her front legs, moving his hand down. "Well, I don't think they are going to stay little for very long. This one's paws are pretty big compared to her body."

"Definitely a mix," Paul said, moving forward and taking a look.

"They're going to be massive. Probably why someone abandoned them." Janet moved forward, scratching the chest of the puppy that was in Finn's hands. She preened, wanting more affection.

"Can you start lining up a foster family while we get them checked out?" Paul asked Janet.

"On it." She nodded as she headed for her desk and pulled out an address book.

"And if we can't find a foster family I can take them home," Finn said.

"I don't know if this one is going to let you take him from Tripp's arms." Harper reached over and ran her hand down the puppy's back. Even though she could only see about half of him, he looked to be evenly light brown and white all over his body. "You might just need to adopt him permanently." She looked up at Tripp and grinned.

"I don't think my town house would hold up to this guy. My yard is a postage stamp."

"Hey, haven't you been talking about getting a house? Problem solved." Finn raised his eyebrows, his blue eyes lighting up like it was the most brilliant plan in the world.

Tripp's mouth turned down into a frown as he shook his head. "How about you just get them checked out first before you assign me a new roommate?"

"You just stopping in to say hello, or did you need anything?" Paul asked Harper.

"Needed to drop some stuff off for Mom and see if you guys wouldn't mind watching Luna this weekend," she said as she gently scratched her nails down the puppy's back. For the first time he slowly lifted his head from where it was buried in Tripp's elbow.

"Where are you going?"

"Jacksonville. There's an extra ticket for the Stampede party," she answered, barely paying attention to anything besides the dog's face. He looked like a little teddy bear and he closed his eyes in pleasure when she started scratching under his chin.

It took her a second to realize that all three men had stopped talking. She looked up to find three sets of eyes looking at her in shock.

"What?" she asked, not stopping the attention she was giving to the puppy.

"You're going to a party with the most recent Stanley Cup winners?" Finn's voice didn't spare an ounce of envy. "Do you even watch hockey?"

"Sometimes." She shrugged. Meaning when it was on one of the TVs at the Sleepy Sheep she'd occasionally look up at it and see a game. The only sport she really followed was baseball, and that was because Grace was a hard-core Boston Red Sox fan and her friend's fandom had carried over.

"Sometimes?" Tripp asked aghast. "I think we're friends with the wrong people," he said to Finn. "We need to get in with Dale and Hamilton."

"You think we can bribe them with a dog?" Finn eyed the girl puppy in his arms that reached up and pawed at his face. He scratched her under the chin and she leaned into his chest, nuzzling his neck.

"I don't know. I think we're going to have to think bigger. You got any horses you're willing to trade?" Tripp asked.

Not only was Finn a vet, but he worked out at his aunt and uncle's farm helping with the horses they trained and boarded.

"Not at the moment." Finn shook his head. "But I'll get back to you."

"I want to hear more about this trip of yours," Paul said, focusing on Harper. "And your mother and I watching Luna shouldn't be a problem. But you should double check with your mom anyway."

"I'll go do that now and let you guys get them checked out." She gave the puppy in Tripp's arms one last good scratch before she kissed her father on the cheek, said good-bye to everyone, and headed outside.

She grabbed the box of lemon oils and lavender lotions from the back of her Cruiser before making her way to the house. When she walked inside, she was enveloped in the seventy-two-degree blast of air that was the standard in the Laurence household.

"Mom," she called out as the door closed behind her.

"In the kitchen," Delilah answered.

Darby, her parents' border collie/mutt mix, came sprinting into the hallway barking excitedly.

"Shhh, nothing to get worked up over," Harper told the dog. "It's just me."

The familiar scent of the Angelo family's homemade marinara sauce, or gravy as her mother called it, filled Harper's nose as she made her way to the kitchen. Her mother's side of the family was Italian, and a good amount of extended family still lived in Italy. Her mother and aunt had been born and raised in the States, and certain traditions had carried over. Like cooking…and Catholic guilt.

"I brought the stuff for the baskets," Harper said when she

walked into the room to find her mother at the stove, spooning the gravy into rows of mason jars. No doubt these were going to be added to the baskets as well.

"Oh good." Her mother turned around, eyebrows raised and mouth pursed as she did the Delilah-once-over. "You look exhausted."

Code for *you look like crap.*

Well, wasn't that a lovely greeting?

"It's just been a long couple of days." Harper put the box on the counter before she knelt down and petted Darby. The dog started sniffing her hand like she was attempting to inhale it. No doubt trying to figure out what other dog—besides Luna—Harper had come in contact with.

"Hmmm. I'm beginning to think it's been a long couple of months with you."

Truer words couldn't have been spoken. "It has been. Which is why I was actually planning on going out of town this weekend with Mel and Bennett and the boys. Would you mind watching Luna for me?"

"Didn't you just go out of town a couple of weeks ago? You know constantly running from your problems isn't going to make them go away."

Well, Harper was wrong. *Those* were truer words.

"Mom, can you watch her for me or not?"

"You know I have no problems watching Luna. She's probably the only grandchild I'm going to get anyway."

Well, two out of three accurate observations wasn't too bad for Delilah. Her mother sure was in for a surprise.

Chapter Seven

You're Gone and I Can't Move On

The sun was sitting low in the sky, a smear of bright yellow surrounded by a pinkish orange. The orange turned to a magenta, then transitioned into a purple and finally ended in a deep blue. There was an area where the purple met the blue that was the exact same shade of violet as Harper's eyes.

Damn. Liam was so beyond screwed.

It had been almost six weeks since she'd walked out—since he'd woken up without her—and he still couldn't stop thinking about her.

It was ridiculous.

There was no way for him to find her, either; she hadn't given him anything in the way of that information.

Nothing personal.

Well, he'd thought that rule had been bullshit from the very start. Everything about the time they'd spent together had been personal, both in and out of bed. Every word spoken. Every time she'd laughed in his ear. Every single touch. Every single *everything*.

Yet, she'd left anyway.

She'd just used him to forget. *Used* being the key word. And part of him felt like the biggest hypocrite in the world for being so pissed about it, because he'd done it before. He'd spent the night with someone with no intention of it being anything more than sex. But that hadn't been the case with Harper, and that's why this whole situation just didn't feel right.

Why *he* didn't feel right.

He'd said it before, she'd been more than a one-night stand, or as it turned out a two-night stand. Because there'd definitely been *more* between them than the sex. He *knew* it. Knew it beyond a shadow of a doubt. But there was absolutely nothing he could do about it now.

She was gone.

Maybe if he told himself that enough he'd start to believe it. Start to move on. Because he wasn't any closer to *moving on* now than he was six weeks ago.

And there'd been plenty of opportunity. There was always plenty of opportunity. But he wasn't interested in any of the women he'd been around. Wasn't interested in going to bed with someone else to fill the void.

It wouldn't be fair to the other person…because all he'd be thinking about was Harper. And in the end, he'd just make the void bigger. He couldn't pretend. Couldn't act like that weekend was just a passing thing. Couldn't act like Harper was just another girl.

Because she wasn't.

Which was probably why Liam was more than a little upset with his manager's newest PR plan. Liam was pretty sure his frustration was permeating through his pores at this point. Gary Kirkland was a man all about opportunity, and obnoxiously persistent when he needed to be. He firmly believed that a "relationship"—real or not—with a very popular starlet was the best thing for Liam's career at the moment.

Kiera "Kiki" Jean Carlow was one of the lead actresses on *Mason-Dixon*. The show was about two families from small towns on opposite sides of the line, one in West Virginia and the other in Pennsylvania. It had a Romeo/Juliet thing going on with a feud dating as far back as the Civil War.

Kiki played the villain, the girl trying to steal the hero away from the heroine, and everyone loved to hate her.

Even though the show was supposed to take place on the actual Mason-Dixon Line, they filmed in a city right outside of Nashville. So Kiki was never too far away. The girl was a good actress. He'd give her that without argument. But her sweet-as-pie persona when the cameras were off was the real act. She was much more like the villain she played on the show. Conniving and manipulative.

Everything was a game to her, and she liked to play as many people as she could.

He'd witnessed it in full force, too. He wouldn't exactly call the time he'd spent with her dates so much as forced proximity. It hadn't taken him very long to realize he didn't want his name—or anything else for that matter—anywhere near hers. He'd known that months ago…and he most definitely knew it now after Harper.

Not that it mattered, because again, she was gone.

Liam stretched his legs out, his boots sliding across the

wooden floorboards of his brother's back porch as he slowly rocked in his chair. The humidity in the air was in that transitioning stage of unbearable to mostly tolerable, and the breeze coming off the Intracoastal Waterway that ran behind the house wasn't too shabby, either.

Or maybe the supposed cooling in the air had more to do with the fact that he was on his third beer of the evening. The bottle was sweating in his hand, trying its damnedest to stay cold. But no matter, it would be finished in another couple of minutes.

Liam had been in Jacksonville, Florida, for the last two weeks, going to the final games of the Stanley Cup playoffs where he got to witness the Stampede's—and his brother's—victory firsthand. Now he was sticking around for the big celebration that was the following evening.

Might as well, it wasn't like he had any place else to be before the next leg of the Isaac Hunter tour started the following week. So he was getting in some time with his siblings and parents who'd also come into town for the festivities.

They'd all had dinner that night, a meal prepared by his mother Edie, sister Adele, and Logan's new—and very serious—girlfriend Abby. The three women were now sitting at the dining room table chatting as Liam, Logan, and their father Dustin sat outside.

Logan and their father were carrying on a conversation while for the most part Liam sat there in silence. Brooding, as he was prone to do of late. But he supposed that was to be expected when he was comparing a woman's eyes to the sunset.

Fucking sap.

He needed to shake this off. Needed to pull his head out of his ass and move on. Sure his time on this side of things was few and far between as he was normally the one doing the leaving. But he'd gotten over stuff like this before, and he'd damn well do it again.

Right?

It was a little before eleven when his parents headed upstairs to go to sleep, and it was just Logan and Liam sitting out on the porch, fresh bottles of beer in both of their hands.

Maybe more beer wasn't the answer at the moment…he tended to do stupid things when he was drinking, like hit on gorgeous girls at bars. An image of Harper filled his brain and he was tipping his bottle back immediately. Maybe if he drank enough he could kill the memory cells of her.

Or probably not as she was permanently branded into his brain.

"So, you going to tell me what's eating at you, or would you prefer to suffer in silence?" Logan asked after about five minutes of nothing but the cicadas talking to each other.

Liam stopped rocking and turned to look at his brother. Most of Logan's face was in shadow as the only light was coming from the dining room behind them—where Adele and Abby were still talking as they finished a bottle of wine. But shadow or not, Liam had no doubt as to the expression of concern on his brother's face.

Logan was three years older than Liam, and as they'd shared a bedroom for fifteen years growing up, it was safe to say that they knew each other pretty well. And distance or time apart hadn't changed that.

Not only were they brothers, but they were best friends.

And if anyone looked at them side by side, there was no doubt that the men were related. They'd both inherited their father's strong jaw, though Logan's and Liam's were just slightly dusted with scruff whereas their father sported a clean shave. Then there was their green-gold eyes that were the perfect mix of their mother's golden brown and their father's sage green. The really big difference was their hair, Logan's shorter and the lighter brown of their father's, while Liam's was an inch-ish longer and the dark brown of their mother's.

"It's up to you and I'm not going to bust your balls either way. But if you think this," Logan waved a hand in the air at Liam, "whatever it is that you've got going on has escaped anyone's notice in our family…well, you my friend are pretty fucking delusional." He finished before he brought his beer to his mouth and tipped back the bottle.

Liam took a deep breath and let it out on a sigh, turning back to the water as he took a drink of his own beer. He wasn't sure how long they sat there in silence, probably long enough for Logan to give up on Liam answering.

The thing was, if there was anyone to talk to about this, it was Logan. He and Abby were a pretty recent thing, and it was nice to finally see Logan happy after all these years, because he'd been through some dark times. Eight years ago, Logan's daughter Madison had died of leukemia. It had happened right after her fifth birthday.

That was the darkest moment of Liam's life, too, and he missed his niece every day.

Madison's mother hadn't really been around before, during, or after. She'd walked out on her daughter, and Logan had been pretty careful with his relationships since. Well, that was the case until Abby.

Liam had never seen his brother in love before.

"I met someone," Liam finally said into the darkness.

"No shit."

"Did you know immediately when you met Abby?"

"Know what? That she was it for me?" Logan asked.

"Yeah."

Logan was quiet for a second before he cleared his throat and spoke. "When I first met her I knew two things: that she was a pain in the ass, and that she was a *hot* pain in the ass."

"Well, never let it be said that you aren't romantic."

Logan laughed. "But to be completely honest with you, it's sometimes hard to see something you aren't looking for."

"So when did you see it?"

"That first night we spent together. But it still took me a while to figure it out after that. I'm guessing that wasn't the case for you?"

"No." Liam reached up and scratched his jaw, the sound of his nails on his beard rasping in his ears. "I figured it out immediately."

"*Damn*, seriously? You fell in love? No wonder you're a mess."

A humorless laugh escaped Liam's lips. "Understatement."

"Who is she?"

"Someone who doesn't feel the same way." He took another mouthful of his beer before he started from the beginning of the story. About halfway through Logan went inside to grab more beer. He came back with a full six-pack of bottles that they started in on as Liam finished the whole long, sorted tale.

"So then I woke up the next morning and she was gone." He was leaning forward, his elbows resting on his knees as he looked out into the dark backyard.

"And there's no way for you to find her?"

"Nope, the only thing I know is that her name is Harper and she isn't from Nashville…oh, and she has an aunt who works at a hospital there."

"She made it pretty much impossible for you to find her. And she doesn't know who you are?"

"No. She never said her last name, so I never told her mine."

"So there's no way for her to find you, either?"

"No, there is. She has my phone number. Knows the address to the cabin. She could find me if she wanted to. She just *doesn't* want to. Which is why I should let this go but…" he dipped his head and stared down into the empty bottle in his hands.

"But you can't." Logan finished for him.

Liam lifted his head and looked over at his brother. "Which is something I can't wrap my mind around because it's been over a month. That's always been plenty of time for me to bounce back…even with relationships that lasted years. Yet this woman, who I was around for thirty plus hours—some of that sleeping—I can't bounce. So tell me what that's about, because I'd really like to know," he said, unable to keep his voice even.

"Shit, that makes two of us."

"You want to hear the most pathetic part?" And this where the anger he'd been feeling for the last six weeks started to boil over.

"Always."

"Get me another beer and I'll tell you. I'll tell you what a complete and total jackass I've become." What number beer was he on now? Nine or ten? He had no idea except for the fact that his buzz was making the transition to drunk.

Logan opened another bottle, passing it to Liam before he grabbed one for himself. "Okay, hit me with it."

"I wrote a song about her for the new album."

"Really?"

"Yup. The label wanted something *more* from me. Something that was different than anything I'd given them before. I showed them the song and they loved it. It's the first one they want to release."

"You've been playing it at shows?"

"Yup."

"And how's that going for you?"

"Reliving it over and over and over again? It's fucking fantastic." He took another mouthful of beer, trying to wash down the bitterness.

Didn't help.

Singing that song made him feel like the world's biggest schmuck. "Who knows? Maybe it will get to the point where it's cathartic or something."

"Or something," Logan said with as little conviction as Liam felt. "You think she'll know it's about her when she hears it?"

"I don't know." He shrugged. "I think it's blatantly obvious that it's about her, but then again I thought it was blatantly obvious that there was something between the two of us. I was wrong on one account, wouldn't be too shocking if I was on the other."

"Okay, so let's just say she hears it, and does figure it out, and for whatever reason finds you. What would you do if you saw her again?"

Liam had actually thought about this a lot. What would he do if he saw Harper again? What would he say?

"No idea." He shook his head as he leaned back in the chair, looking up at the ceiling and the spinning fan above them. "Maybe walk away like she did."

"You really think so?" Logan asked. "I mean you're pissed, this is evident, but you're also in love with her. Love makes a man do stupid things."

"You talking from experience?"

"Absolutely."

"Well, I think I've already proven the stupid part in regards to her."

"Yeah, and maybe you aren't the only one. Could it be possible she felt the same way and ran scared? You did say she'd just recently gotten out of a serious relationship."

"Possibly." Liam closed his eyes, the spinning of the fan not making his head feel any clearer. "Doesn't matter now. The only thing to do is move on." He waved his hand blindly in the air. But his words came out hollow, no conviction. Because at the end of the day—infuriated with her or not—it didn't *feel* done. He wanted to tell himself that was the alcohol thinking for him.

It wasn't.

"I don't believe that." And apparently neither did his brother. "If you really thought it was done, you wouldn't be this angry about it."

"Maybe. Maybe not."

"Oh no, of this I know. There are few women in the world that can inspire that much passion in a man. And I've never seen you like this before."

Liam pulled his head from the back of the chair and opened his eyes. "Because nothing like this has ever happened to me before." And as he stared out into the darkness he had a pretty good idea it never would again.

So really, anyway he looked at it he was fucked.

Royally.

* * *

Liam adjusted his tie for about the fortieth time that night as he scanned the packed ballroom of the Brogan-Meyers Hotel. What he was looking for? He had no idea.

The hundred or so tables filling more than half the room were covered with black tablecloths and gray roses. Fitting as black and gray were the Stampede's colors. A deep male voice crooned through the speakers that surrounded the space, giving the people on the dance floor an excuse to pull their partners close. Waiters with trays of alcohol and the tiniest food he'd ever seen circled around the room.

"Stop doing that." Adele swatted at Liam's hand. "I don't think I've ever seen a man fidget as much as you."

Well what did she expect? He was not a suit kind of guy, and the long gray noose around his neck was beginning to get to him. But his sister had been insistent on the tie, saying he'd stick out like a sore thumb without one. His only consolation was that she'd let him wear his cowboy boots.

And yes, he did mean *let him*.

But really, arguing with her was pointless. One, she always won. And two, when it came to fashion, she was always right.

The girl had the unmistakable talent to capture any time period with a skilled perfection, and she tended to bounce around eras when it came to her own style as well. Tonight she had on a black and gold lace dress that he suspected was from somewhere around the fifties, though he wasn't sure if she bought it or made it. Either was a possibility.

At the age of twenty-five, Adele was the head costume designer on one of the most popular shows on television. *Ponce* was the Florida version of *Downton Abbey,* taking place at the Ponce de Leon Hotel in St. Augustine during the early nineteen hundreds. It was full of more drama than anything he'd ever watched before, and yes, he did watch it.

What? It was his sister's show. Plus, he wanted to know if Beauregard was going to end up with Abigail or Rosamund. His money was on Rosamund.

"Champagne?" A waitress stopped in front of them offering a tray of glasses.

"Please." Adele smiled as she reached up to grab one. Liam's eyes focused on the tattoo on her right wrist of a threaded needle and a stitched heart. Much to their mother's dismay, he wasn't the only James with an ink addiction.

"I'm good, but thank you." Liam held up his glass of bourbon before he took a sip. The waitress moved on to the people next to them and he found himself scanning the room again.

"What are you looking for? An escape route?"

He turned back to his sister and shook his head. "No. Just looking around."

"Mmm, hmm." Her eyes narrowed and he suddenly found himself under the type of scrutiny that would make lesser men cower. Adele had taken more after their mother's Spanish side of the family than their father's Irish side. Her sharp golden brown eyes missed next to nothing, and baby of the family or not, she had the ability to make him squirm. "What's going on with you anyway?"

"What makes you think something is going on with me?"

"Because I'm not stupid. And you and Logan sat out on the porch last night getting drunk."

"We do that all the time. Besides you and Abby sat inside getting drunk. What's going on with you?"

"Nice subject change." She frowned at him before she reached up and pushed a dark brown curl behind her ear. Her hair was naturally straight, but she'd done something ridiculously complicated with it tonight. Some kind of fancy, curled and pinned just right, up-do thing that no doubt matched the era of her dress. And she pulled it off elegantly even with the tiny diamond sticking out of her nose and the streaks of bright red in her hair.

"I like to think so."

"You're a pain in the ass you know that?" Her frown deepened. "And I'm not going to be distracted, so what's going on with you?"

"How do you know that it wasn't Logan needing a drunken conversation? Something could be *up* with him."

"How do I *know* nothing is up with our brother? Because he looks like that the majority of the time now," she said as she pointed across the room, and Liam's gaze followed automatically.

Logan was standing behind Abby, one of his hands on her hip as he bent his head low to whisper in her ear. He was about a foot taller than her, but she made a little bit of an effort to close the gap with her heels. She was stunning in her red dress, and there was no doubt she'd worn it in an effort to tempt Logan as he had a thing about seeing her in the color. He had nicknamed her Red after all, though that had more to do with her hair than anything else.

Abby turned to face Logan, both of his hands now gripping her waist as she ran her palms up the lapel of his tux. Whatever she said to him had him grinning down at her like a fool.

"Logan is so beyond happy that it's ridiculous," Adele continued, and Liam turned back to face her. "Not only because he's in love, but because his team just won the Stanley Cup. Yet you," she poked him in the shoulder, "spend a few hours outside on the porch with him getting drunk and he comes inside looking somber. So yes, I know it's you. Who is she?"

"How the *hell*?" He looked at her, shaking his head.

"I really wish you and Logan would give me more credit and stop trying to hide things from me."

Yeah, maybe that was his own fault. Underestimating Adele was never smart.

"Her name is Harper. I met her a few weeks ago in Nashville."

"Groupie?" she asked, narrowing her eyes in that intimidation stare he was so used to.

Again, Adele might be the baby of the family but she was just as protective of Logan and Liam as they were of her. She in no way approved of the hangers on, using her brothers because they were somewhat famous. Though, Logan had a lot more stardom than Liam did, and the rink bunnies were more prolific than the music groupies.

"No, not a groupie." Liam shook his head.

Adele opened her mouth to ask something else but was interrupted as they were joined by Logan, Abby, and two teenage boys.

Apparently the rest of this conversation was going to have to wait.

"I wanted to introduce you guys to Dale Rigels," Logan said, patting the back of the shorter, and slightly thinner of the two. "And Hamilton O'Bryan." He then patted the back of the taller boy with thick black-framed glasses and a goofy grin.

The names immediately registered in Liam's brain, and he forced himself to switch gears from the conversation he'd just been having with his sister to focusing on the two boys.

Last February, Logan had gone to visit a kid in remission. It was something Abby had set up when she'd still worked for the Stampede PR department. Abby's best friend lived in the same small Florida town as the two boys, and they were all family friends.

Logan was never one to jump in the spotlight. He liked his private life private and wasn't about being exploited, or exploiting anyone else for that matter. He firmly believed that just because he was semi-famous didn't give anyone the right to know about his personal business. It was one of the reasons he and Abby had butted heads so hard in the beginning. He'd been pretty unwilling to work with her.

But when she came to Logan and asked him to visit Dale, he'd said yes without hesitation. If there was one thing that he couldn't say no to, it was a kid in need. And he hadn't stopped with that one visit, either. He'd developed a relationship with Dale and Dale's best friend Hamilton. Keeping up with Dale's treatments, knowing that the kid was in remission, inviting him to Stampede events, and even paying for the kid's medical bills.

That was just the type of guy Logan was, biggest heart on the planet.

"It's great to finally meet you," Liam said, shaking both boys' hands in turn. Adele did the same, smiling warmly at both of them, clearly knowing exactly who they were as well.

"You know who we are?" Hamilton asked in awe.

"Yeah, Logan talks about you both all the time."

"But you're…you're Liam James."

"Hamilton here is a bit of a fan," Logan explained.

"Are you kidding? What you can do with an electric guitar is ridiculous. That part in the chorus of 'My Kinda Summer' is genius."

"Genius?" Adele raised her eyebrows. "I believe that's a first."

"Thanks." Liam shook his head at his sister. "You play?" he asked, returning his focus to Hamilton.

"Guitar? A little. I'm not that great."

"Don't let him fool you," Dale said. "He plays about ten different instruments."

"Really? Which one is your strongest?"

"The piano."

"Nice." Liam nodded. "Well, next time we're in the same area be sure to have your guitar. We can play together."

"You're serious?"

"Absolutely."

At that moment another guy joined the group. He had about an inch in height on Liam, and his arms were massive and looked to be testing the jacket of his navy blue suit. The short dark blond hair on the top of his head matched the length of the beard on his face.

Abby stepped in, making quick introductions. "This is Bennett Hart, Hamilton's brother-in-law. And, Bennett, these are Logan's siblings, Adele and Liam James."

"Nice to meet you." Bennett shook Adele's hand first before he turned to Liam. "Liam James, the singer? I didn't realize the family connection."

"That's because I only claim him every once in a while," Logan said before he took a sip of the same bourbon that Liam was drinking. They both were whiskey drinkers.

"You know I don't know what I ever did to the two of you." Liam shook his head.

"You want a list?" This coming from their mother, who was hand in hand with their father as they joined the group. "Because I can give you one in alphabetical order."

"Oh great. This is going to be fun. I think I'm going to need another drink before the roast begins."

"Hmmm." Adele narrowed her eyes. "With the stuff we've got on you, you might need two."

"Don't worry." Logan clapped Liam on the back. "We won't embarrass you in front of everyone. By the way, Mom, Dad, let me introduce you to Dale, Hamilton, and Bennett."

Dustin and Edie chatted with the three men, both of them knowing the story behind Dale just as much as Liam and Adele.

"So is it just the three of you that were able to make it to tonight's event?"

"No," Bennett answered. "My wife and our friend are here. But they seem to have disappeared."

"We didn't disappear," a blond with curly hair bouncing around her shoulders said as she joined the group, leading a woman who followed behind her. "I was just getting a drink for Harper and me."

He knew it was her before her name even hit his ears.

Harper's gaze was caught by something on the other side of the room as she joined the group, her head turned away on that slender neck of hers. A neck that was exposed.

He spotted the cluster of freckles that were under her left ear. Freckles he'd kissed more than once. Freckles he'd know anywhere.

Harper was here.

He'd found her.

Chapter Eight

Found ... Again

It was one of those slow motion moments, like when Liam had first seen Harper at the bar, where everyone and everything disappeared besides them. As her head turned to face them, his heart started beating out of his chest and he stopped breathing.

And then those violet eyes were on him, going wide as she choked on her drink. She coughed, covering her mouth.

"Are you okay?" the blond with curls asked, turning around.

The sound of someone else's voice so close brought Liam back to the room filled with people and the reality of the situation.

It had been six weeks since he'd seen her. Six weeks of thinking he'd never see her again. Six weeks of being out of his mind, and here she was. Standing in front of him.

"I'm fine," Harper said when she caught her breath. "Just swallowed wrong."

"This is my wife Mel," Bennett said, introducing the new guests to the circle. "And our friend Harper Laurence."

Harper Laurence.

"And these are Logan's parents, Dustin and Edie James," Bennett continued with introductions. "His sister, Adele, and his brother, Liam."

The shock in Harper's eyes was giving way to something else that he wasn't quite sure of. Where he was pretty sure he hadn't breathed since he saw her, he thought she was about to hyperventilate.

"Liam James," she whispered.

Ahh, so she'd *just* figured it out.

"You want an autograph?" Well, he'd apparently found his breath and his voice. But he couldn't help himself.

"Liam!" his mother gasped. "Don't be impertinent."

"Don't worry, Mom, Harper and I know each other." He tilted his head to the side as he looked at her, the smile on his face not one of amusement. "We met a few weeks ago."

This time it was Mel choking on her drink, coughing hard as she tried to catch her breath. He knew the look in her eyes had nothing to do with him being a singer. Apparently Harper had mentioned him, and that weekend, to her friend.

Liam didn't have to look at his brother or his sister to know that the two of them were playing a tennis match, looking between him and the woman in the blue dress. He couldn't bring himself to look away from her again, afraid that if he did she'd disappear.

"You look *magnificent* as ever, Harper." His eyes dipped, taking in the rest of her. Her mouth was painted a deep red, and her black hair was up, all piled on top of her head. She was wearing a form-fitting midnight blue dress and those damn bronze strappy heels she'd had on the second night…the last night…the night she'd knelt down on the floor between his legs wearing nothing but those heels and lace.

A blush started to creep up her chest, maybe because the word *magnificent* had her thinking about his mouth on her breasts. Or her completely naked underneath him. He knew that's what it made him think of.

"Holy shit," Logan whispered low enough for only Liam to hear, but even at that volume he could clearly hear the surprise in his brother's voice.

Well, he could just join the fucking club.

"Small world, isn't it?" he asked.

"You two know each other?" Abby looked between the two of them, and then her eyes went wide. Apparently she knew a little something about the situation, too. Liam wondered for a brief second if Logan had mentioned something or if she'd heard about it from Harper herself.

Then he realized he didn't care. He didn't care who knew what. All he cared about was the fact that she was here.

What he didn't know was how he felt about it. Yeah he was angry, there was no doubt about that, but a sense of relief was running through him, too. And then there was the need to touch her. He wanted so much to grab her and pull her close. Take her mouth again because it felt like forever since he'd gotten to taste her.

"When did you guys meet?" Bennett asked, looking a little bewildered. He obviously didn't know what was going on, and the only other people in his boat were the two boys, and Liam's parents.

"In Nashville," Harper answered.

"I had no idea you knew Abby or Logan," Liam said.

"We met through Abby's best friend Paige. She lives in our hometown and is married to one of our very close friends." Mel was speaking now, probably trying to take some of the attention off her friend. It didn't work. The majority of the eyes in that circle were on Harper. "We've known Abby for years."

"Well, isn't that fascinating?" Edie asked, and there was something in her tone that made it clear she was picking up on the tension as well. She might not know what had happened, but she did know her son, and Liam was hiding nothing. He couldn't.

"Yup, fascinating." He downed the last of his bourbon.

"Where are you guys from?" Dustin asked.

"Mirabelle, Florida," Bennett answered. "It's a tiny town on the beach about three and a half hours west of here."

"And the world just keeps getting smaller," Adele said.

"No kidding." Harper tipped back the last of her drink.

She'd barely finished it when a waiter came up, taking the empty glasses from the group. Not a second later there was another waiter, offering up some filled glasses.

"No, thank you." Harper shook her head. "Actually, I need to get some air. Liam, do you have a second?"

His instincts were at war with each other. Part of him really wanted to be the arrogant bastard he knew was in there and not give her anything she wanted. She hadn't given him the courtesy, so why should he give it to her?

But that part of him was small in comparison to what the rest of him was screaming for…to get her alone and get some answers.

"Sure." He nodded his head, finding that he wouldn't have been able to say no, pissed or not.

Harper gave a friendly smile to the group, one that he knew took everything in her to achieve. She reached out as she turned, grabbing Mel's forearm and squeezing tight before she let go, her hand shaking.

* * *

So, *that* just happened.

The last three minutes weren't really processing fast enough. Harper was in shock, so unbelievably unprepared for seeing Liam. And not only that, but meeting his entire family.

It's lovely to meet you, Mr. and Mrs. James. And oh, by the way, I'm carrying your grandchild.

Her step faltered at the words that echoed in her head, and she stumbled a little bit. A hand was suddenly at her side, another at the small of her back. And just like that she had the sure and steady weight of Liam's palms on her body, his fingers gently pressing into her and holding her firm.

"You okay?" His mouth was at her ear and she turned instinctively to look at him.

He was so close. Those green-gold eyes of his focused on hers, eyes that hadn't hid anything from her before. But now…now she couldn't decipher them to save her life. There was a hardness to them she didn't recognize.

Hardness she had no doubt put there.

"Harper?"

Just the sound of her name on his lips had her back in that

cabin, no one but him and her. Nothing but the feel of his hands on her skin, his mouth at her ear as he moved inside her.

Making love to him had been so real. So raw and bare, everything stripped away besides the two of them.

But that was gone now.

"I'm fine," she forced herself to say before she turned away from him.

She had no idea how she was going to get through this. She wasn't ready, was supposed to have the rest of the weekend to figure things out, and then even after that there still should've been more time until she was doing *this*. Until she was face-to-face with him and telling him...telling him that she was going to have his child.

There was supposed to be more time.

But she'd known the second she'd seen him there wasn't going to be any more waiting. She couldn't do it. Couldn't possibly be around him for any length of time and not have him know the truth. And she wouldn't be able to walk away without telling him, either.

He deserved to know and she wasn't going to be a coward. Not this time around. She was going to bite the bullet, ready or not.

His hand didn't move from the small of her back as he came up next to her and guided her through the crowded room. His hands on her body were killing her, splitting her heart in two. But she didn't want him to stop, because it was probably going to be the last time he ever touched her like this.

The familiar ache she'd known for the last few weeks settled over her, and her chest tightened for about the eighty-sixth time since she'd seen him. The second they were outside and away from the crowd, his hand disappeared from her body.

Oh, look at that, her chest tightened for the eighty-seventh time.

The ballroom of the Brogan-Meyers Hotel was located on the roof of the building, which just so happened to be the thirtieth floor. There were a few people out on the terrace that ran around the floor, and Harper kept walking until no one was near them.

She went to the railing before she stopped and turned to look at him. Somehow she managed to speak first. "I had no idea you were going to be here."

"Funnily enough, I guessed that." His eyes moved over her face, like he was seeing her for the first time. Like he didn't know her. And at the end of it all, they didn't know each other...not really.

Case in point, he was *Liam James.*

The country musician. The country musician whose albums she had. The country musician who wrote the songs "It Ain't Me, It's You"; "Buckle Up"; and "Mother Trucker." Songs that she'd sang along to quite loudly more times than she could possibly count.

She *knew* his music, so how was it possible that she hadn't made the connection? She'd even had her own private show.

Maybe it was because when he was around her she couldn't think straight to save her life. Maybe that was the reason.

"I owe you an explanation." She started to run her hands up and down her bare arms.

The sun had only gone down about an hour ago, the temperature dropping to the mid-seventies. It was still warm, even with the breeze coming from the water, but it didn't matter, she suddenly found herself very cold.

"You mean for leaving and not saying good-bye?"

"Yes." She nodded slowly. "For that."

"By all means." He gestured to the space between them. "The floor is yours."

Her mouth went dry and she regretted downing the last of her ginger ale. "I've thought about this more times than I can count. Gone over what to say to you. But now that you're here, and I'm looking at you, none of it seems right. I don't know where to start…I didn't expect it to be this hard."

"Did you think it was going to be easy?"

"No…" She shook her head. "No, I didn't think it was going to be anywhere near easy. Nothing about you has been easy. Not from the moment I met you. I couldn't in my wildest dreams have imagined you. Couldn't have predicted that weekend. What it was like to be with you. It was unreal. Everything that happened…I don't even know how to describe it."

"But it was real, Harper." He took a step toward her, closing the gap between them. "And you walked away."

"I was scared."

"That's a bullshit excuse. Everyone gets scared." She couldn't help but flinch at the harshness of his words. "You don't think it freaked me out?" he asked, taking another step toward her, their shoes almost touching.

He was only about an inch or two taller than her with her heels on, but she still had to tilt her head back to look up into his face. His expression was fierce, his eyes so intense that she was desperate to look away, but she couldn't. Not for the life of her.

"You don't think it was scary for me, too? That's never happened to me before. Meeting someone, and having this...I don't even know what it was, but it was something powerful. Something real." He reached out, his hands landing on hers and stopping her palms from constantly moving up and down her arms.

Her next breath was sharp, the contact of his skin on hers overwhelming her beyond anything else. How was it possible to miss something so much? Something she'd only known for such a short amount of time?

"You think a single second of it was easy for me?"

"No." The word fell from her mouth on a whisper.

"And then you were gone." His hands disappeared from her body and he took a step back from her. "Dammit," he all but shouted as he turned away from her, his hands going to his hair as he walked a few steps to the side. He leaned against the half wall that ran around the balcony, resting his forearms on the top and looking out to the city below them.

She came up next to him, placing her palms flat on the concrete wall. She watched the twinkling lights of the cars and buildings below them for a few moments before she spoke. "It wasn't easy you know. Leaving you."

He turned at her words, his hair falling across his forehead and into his eyes. She wanted to reach over and push it back.

Not appropriate.

She pressed her hands down onto the concrete, the grit digging into her skin. "It was one of the hardest things I've ever done."

"Yet you did it anyway. Why?"

"I thought it was safer."

"Safer?"

"Liam, I'd just gotten out of the most serious relationship that I'd been in. *Ever*. Brad, my ex, he broke me. I'm not over-exaggerating, either. He really did, and that was after being with him for a year and a half. I knew you for less than forty-eight hours, and somehow you had more of that power than he did." Her throat tightened, the corner of her eyes prickling as tears started to brim. "I've never done anything like that before." She tried not to wince as her voice cracked on the last word.

God no, you are not doing this. Pull yourself together and do not cry.

He straightened, turning toward her and focusing on her face. "I know. You don't go home with men you just met." He repeated her words from that morning after. The first time she'd tried to leave.

"But it isn't just that, Liam. I don't sleep with guys on a first date, or the fifth date, or the twelfth date. It takes a lot of time for me to get to that point. But with you, there was no time. It just…happened. And it's never been like that before…the sex I mean, because that wasn't just sex. That was something else entirely. Especially that last time…it…it terrified me. So I ran." She blinked, and the prickling in her eyes turned to a burn, the tears falling. "I'm sorry, Liam. I really am," she said as she reached up and wiped at her cheeks, running her fingers under her eyes. "I don't think I've regretted a decision more in my life."

"Yet you didn't do anything to fix it."

"Would you believe me if I told you I was going to? I think I've stared at your number on my phone, my finger hovering over the Dial button, almost every night since I left."

"So you do still have my number." His breath came out on an aggravated sigh as he shook his head. "Do you have any idea how incredibly frustrating the last few weeks have been? After meeting you, I've second-guessed everything. I can understand you being scared. And I might be able to understand you running. But what I can't understand is that after all this time you still have done nothing, even though you've regretted your decision. So no, I don't know if I believe you, Harper. I don't know if I believe you were really going to do anything."

"I deserve that."

The full ramifications of the whole situation didn't hit home until that moment. Okay sure, she wasn't expecting him to get over everything that had happened and just forgive her for walking out. She wasn't that delusional.

In the end though, not only was this man the father of her child, but she was most definitely in love with him. And now he might not want anything to do with her.

What had she done?

He turned away from her again, bracing his hands on the wall as he dropped his head between his shoulders and looked down at the city. "I don't know what to do with any of this. Where to go from here."

"I don't, either. But…but there's something else you should know…something that you *need* to know," she amended.

He straightened, pulling his head up and looking at her. "And what's that?"

"Liam, I…" The words caught in her throat.

Say it, Harper.

Say. It.

Tell him now.

NOW!

"I'm pregnant."

For a moment nothing was registering on his face. It was blank, frozen, like the rest of him. He'd even stopped breathing.

Harper just stood there, not sure of what to do or say, waiting for him to speak first.

"W-what was that?" he finally asked.

"I'm pregnant," she repeated. "With your child."

"But we used condoms. Lots of them."

"Apparently they didn't work."

"And you aren't on birth control?" His tone was accusatory, like she'd planned it.

"Seriously? You're blaming me for this?"

"I'm not blaming you. It's just…normally there are backup plans in place."

"Well, there weren't."

"And you're sure it's mine?"

She flinched at the question. "Wow, we really don't know each other, do we?"

"It's a fair question."

"You're wrong about that. Nothing about this entire thing is fair." Try as she might she couldn't keep the bitterness out of her voice.

"Really, you're going to get upset with me for asking what I think is probably a fairly common question, after the bomb that you just dropped?"

"The bomb that I just dropped?"

"Yes. What did you expect, Harper? For me to be overjoyed at the fact that I might've gotten you knocked up?" His voice rose, carrying across the wind, and quite possibly to the people on the other side of the balcony.

She took a step back from him, her stomach so tied up in knots at this point that she was pretty sure the ginger ale wasn't going to stay down for much longer. "There is no *might've*, Liam, and I'm not going to stand here while you imply that I'm a whore."

"I didn't say that."

"I told you before, you're the only person I've been with since my ex, whether you choose to believe that or not. This baby is yours. If you want to be a part of his or her life, that's up to you." She took another step back, taking up again with chafing her palms against her arms. Fresh tears welled in her eyes, but they were more from anger than anything else. "You figure that out and let me know. Abby can get ahold of me."

She turned, heading back for the ballroom, but had barely taken three steps when he called out after her.

"So you're just going to run again?"

She looked back at him over her shoulder, focusing on the hard stubborn line of his mouth that was so foreign to her. "I don't see you trying to stop me." She turned from him and walked away.

Chapter Nine

No Going Back. No Starting Over.

Liam stared down into his glass of bourbon, his third since sitting at the bar in the lobby of the Brogan-Meyers Hotel. The glass just couldn't seem to stay filled and the ice cubes looked lonely.

He obviously hadn't gone very far after leaving the balcony. Alcohol or not, driving sure as shit hadn't been an option. His head was spinning, still reeling from everything that had happened that night.

He'd found Harper…or had she found him? Oh, who the hell cared? He'd already been confused beyond reason before she'd gone and told him she was pregnant.

With his child.

And every time he closed his eyes he saw her crying. He hated seeing women cry. *Hated it*. But this was something different. Something that tore at every inch of him. And he'd done nothing to comfort her. Nothing because he couldn't get over his own anger. Nothing because he was apparently the biggest dick on the face of the planet.

"So this is where you disappeared to. See, I told you we should've checked the bar first," a female voice said behind his back.

"Yes, yes. You were right. Again. Happy?" a deep male voice answered.

Liam didn't stop staring into his empty glass. He didn't need to look over to see that his brother and sister were standing next to him.

"I'm always right," Adele said. "And just as soon as the two of you start accepting it, things might go a lot smoother." She leaned into Liam's shoulder, grabbing the glass in front of him. "How many of these have you had?"

"Since sitting down?" He looked up and glanced over at them. "Three."

"Shit," Logan whispered. "Are you chugging them? It's only been forty minutes since you followed Harper out onto the balcony."

Really? It had only been forty minutes? It felt like it had been an eternity since he'd watched her walk away.

Somehow that was almost as painful as when he'd woken up without her.

Almost. At least this time he knew where to find her.

"Can we get three more of these?" Adele asked when the bartender came to their end of the bar. "We'll be over there." She pointed to the empty circular booth in the corner before she wrapped her hand around Liam's arm and forcibly pulled him from the bar stool he was sitting on.

As he didn't want his sister dragging him across the room like a little boy, he didn't resist. They all settled into the booth, Adele in the middle with Logan on the left and Liam on the right. They were positioned in such a way that he could see both of them.

"Start talking," Adele demanded pretty much the second their butts were in the seats. "And feel free to just jump right on in with what happened tonight, because Logan already filled me in on the Nashville stuff."

Well, that was good, because diving back into that would make his head an even bigger mess. Who was he kidding? It was a disaster as it was. So really what was a little more chaos at this point?

He looked down, his palms flat on the table. The old saying, *I know it like the back of my hand*, repeated in his brain. But as he studied his own hands, hands that were scared and calloused over the years, hands that were his livelihood, hands that he *thought* he knew, he realized he knew absolutely nothing.

He started talking, his words coming out like he was telling a story that wasn't his. But it was his story. This was the new reality.

A waiter came over about halfway through, sliding the drinks onto the table. Liam grabbed his but didn't take a sip. He wrapped his fingers around the cool glass, focusing on that as he got to the climax of his conversation with Harper.

"So she's pregnant," he said before he finally allowed himself to take a sip.

Neither Logan nor Adele said anything for a good couple of seconds. Liam put the glass down on the table as his eyes came up, focusing on his brother and sister.

"And it's yours?" Logan asked, his brow furrowed and his mouth flattening out to a grim line.

"Yeah." He nodded. Because despite his words to Harper earlier, he did believe her. And he wasn't sure if that just made him an even bigger fool.

"Wow." Adele breathed the word on a sigh, grabbing her own glass and downing a good amount of it. "This just keeps getting more and more complicated."

"You can say that again."

"And you believe that she was going to tell you? Even if she hadn't run into you tonight?" The look on his brother's face was getting more and more severe by the second, and it didn't take a genius to figure out why.

Logan had cherished being a father, no doubt more than anything else in his life. He'd loved his daughter from the very start and had always wanted her. Madison had never been a burden. Never been anything he'd ever regretted. And even though Madison's days had been short, she'd been treasured for every second of them.

Liam looked down to the tumbler in his hand, tilting it to the side, the ice clinking against the glass. "I think she would've told me…" But what did he really know?

"Okay…so we've established the fact that this woman, who you're in love with—"

"*Thought.* Thought I was in love with." Liam corrected his brother.

"Right," Adele scoffed at that, and both men turned to look at her. "Come on, you saw what happened when she walked up. You were about to come unglued. No one in that circle can deny your reaction." She looked at Liam, her eyes brokering no argument. As per usual she'd missed nothing. "Or her reaction to you for that matter. And you better believe that Mom was entirely aware something was up, because the second the two of you stepped away, she oh-so-very-not-so-casually started asking questions about Harper to everyone in that circle who knew her."

"Fantastic," Liam grumbled, though it wasn't all that shocking. That was Edie James for ya. "You guys probably know more about her than I do at this point."

"I don't think so." Logan leaned back in the booth, stretching his legs out in front of him. "They stayed pretty tight lipped. I have no doubt Mel knows exactly what is going on, and she didn't reveal more than she had to about her friend."

"What did Abby say?" Adele asked as she ran her finger around the rim of her glass. "She's known Harper for years. We want some insight, we should talk to Abby."

But for whatever reason, that prospect wasn't all that appealing to Liam.

"No." He shook his head. "I don't want to learn about Harper from anyone besides Harper." Because the thing was, he still wanted to learn *everything* about her. Wanted to know all he could about her. That hadn't changed, and he didn't think it ever would.

He put the tumbler down on the table, closing his eyes and pinching the bridge of his nose. His fingers were cold from touching the glass, and they felt good on his overheated skin.

"I just keep wondering what would've happened if she hadn't left. Happened with her, you know?" He dropped his hand, his eyes opening as he looked across the table at his siblings. "But then again it changes nothing with the baby. That would've happened regardless, and I'm not walking away from my kid."

My kid.

Something warm settled in his chest at those words. Something that had nothing to do with the alcohol. He was going to be a father.

"Well, obviously," Adele said immediately.

"I didn't doubt that for a second." Logan shifted in his seat, leaning forward and resting his elbows on the table. "But how are you going to proceed with Harper?"

Wasn't that the question of the hour?

"I have no idea."

"Well, you aren't in this alone, Liam." Logan lifted his glass, clinking it to Liam's before he polished off the last of the liquid in it.

"And we're going to be here no matter what to help you through it all." Adele reached across the table and put her hand over Liam's. "Because we're family."

Family...yeah, a family that was only going to get bigger.

* * *

The air conditioner on the opposite side of the hotel room kicked on, blasting cold air into the space. Harper snuggled down deeper into the mattress, pulling the comforter tightly around her shoulders.

She had absolutely no desire to get up. The moments of sleep throughout the night had been few and far between. All together she'd say she probably got about four hours, and she was going to pay for it dearly today.

After the balcony incident the night before, Harper hadn't even attempted to rejoin the party. She'd made a beeline for the elevator and headed straight down to her hotel room. It had been the longest five minutes, fighting with the tears that had been simmering at the surface. Though a few escaped, trailing down her cheeks, she'd wiped them away the instant they'd fallen.

But the second her hotel room door snapped shut behind her there'd been no holding back. As was expected, she got sick first. Of course she would, heaven forbid she go ten hours without throwing up. The medicine she'd been taking had been working, but it wasn't a match for her stress level in that moment.

And then she'd taken a shower, the heat in no way getting rid of the chill she just couldn't seem to shake, even though it was June in Florida. Though she was pretty sure the shaking had more to do with her sobbing than anything involving temperature.

When she'd managed to gain an ounce of composure, she got out of the shower to find Mel sitting on the bed, already changed into her pajamas. Though Harper wasn't sharing with anyone, Mel had a key card for the room to come and go as she pleased. Just one look from those concern-filled amber eyes, and Harper had lost it. *Again.*

That was how they'd spent most of the night, Mel not leaving to go be with her husband no matter how much Harper insisted. And to be honest, the prospect of spending the night by herself was not a pleasant one, especially as sleep had been an elusive bitch.

All she could think about was Liam. That pained look in his eyes. His frustration. His anger. His words.

What did you expect, Harper? For me to be overjoyed at the fact that I might've gotten you knocked up?

Overjoyed wasn't the word she would've used, but neither was *knocked up.* It had just sounded so harsh coming from his mouth. Like this baby was unwanted.

Her hand automatically went to her belly, her palm pushing up her shirt and landing on her skin. The baby was obviously too small to be felt in any capacity—unless she counted her morning sickness, which she might be inclined to—but he or she was still in there. Growing.

Harper wanted this baby, and she would love this child no matter what. That was a love she didn't doubt in the slightest.

Unlike another love.

Liam filled her vision, but it wasn't the man in the blue suit with the hard eyes from the night before. No, it was the man from the bar all those weeks ago. The man with the quick smile and the gentle hands. But she couldn't deny the fact that when he'd touched her last night, those hands of his had still been gentle. Still made fire burn inside her. Still made her ache in the sweetest, most painful way.

That oh-so-familiar tightening started up at the back of her throat, but she refused to give into it again. She wasn't going to cry today.

Was. Not. Going. To.

She pulled the comforter from her body and slowly sat up, her head tender from the night before and her stomach uneasy. For whatever reason, the nausea was usually tolerable in the morning and got worse throughout the day. Apparently Harper liked to be an anomaly.

But the twinges this morning seemed to be even less than they normally were. It was just a slight rolling of the stomach and she was able to push it back with a few steady breaths. Maybe the medicine was working. Or maybe it was *finally* getting the massive weight off her chest that was the anxiety of talking to Liam.

Yeah, maybe it was that.

Harper got out of bed and walked over to her suitcase, searching for a change of clothes. The only light coming in the room was a tiny sliver from a crack in the heavy drapes. She was careful as she looked around among the chaos, trying not to make any noise to wake Mel. She finally found an outfit and headed to the bathroom.

She shut the door behind her before she flipped the light on, glancing at her reflection in the mirror as she set her clothes on the counter. It wasn't as bad as it could've been. Sleeping on wet hair was never the best option, but she'd be able to pull it back no problem.

As for her eyes? Well, thank goodness she had sunglasses, 'cause those bad boys weren't going down anytime soon. She turned away from the mirror, no use worrying about her appearance at the moment. She had absolutely no one to impress. She was long gone from that.

She made quick work, using the bathroom before changing into jean shorts and a sherbet orange shirt that was made of a thin cotton material. It hung loose past her waist and probably wasn't the most flattering, but it was comfortable and as she was going to be spending a few hours in the car it would do just fine.

She pulled her hair up into a ponytail before she washed her face and brushed her teeth. Her pajamas were lying on the floor and she snatched them up before walking out of the bathroom.

Natural sunlight was streaming into the room now, the curtains pulled back from the window showing downtown Jacksonville in all of its morning glory.

Mel was sitting in the middle of the bed, her curls a wild halo around her head as she looked down at the phone typing out a text. She hit Send before she looked up, rubbing at her eyes sleepily. "How you feeling?"

"About the same." Harper crossed the room to her suitcase, shoving her pajamas in among the other clothing wreckage. "What about you? You're the one who had to deal with a crying mess all night." She looked up, attempting a smile and hoping it would detract from the two beyond-puffy eyes she was sporting.

"Pshh, that's nothing." Mel waved her hand in the air. "Once I get some coffee, I'll be just fine."

"Coffee, oh, how I miss thee."

"That sounded a little Shakespearean."

"Stick around and I just might start spouting sonnets. It will be about how much I want a full fat, full sugar, fully caffeinated, piping-hot gift from the java gods with whipped cream on top…and a caramel drizzle," Harper said wistfully.

"Yeah, I think you're a few months away from one of those." Mel said the last word around a yawn as her phone chimed. "I told Bennett to grab you a cranberry juice. He's at the café now."

"You've trained him well."

"I have." Mel nodded as she got out of bed. "I'm going to head across the hall and get dressed. Checkout is in an hour; that enough time?"

"I'll be down there." Harper pulled the zipper closed on her bag; she was already done with half her packing as it was.

She was also beyond ready to get home. She would've driven

back the night before if she'd had her own car…or if she'd been in any state to drive. But as neither had been the case she'd just wallowed in her own misery in the hotel room.

God, she was pathetic.

"Hey." Mel stopped in front of Harper and grabbed her arm. "It's going to work itself out. It might be hard, but it won't be insurmountable, no matter what happens. And like Grace and I established earlier, you won't be alone through it."

Harper took a deep breath and let it out on a sigh. "I know. I just wish…I just wish I hadn't messed up so epically with Liam."

"You can't change anything that's happened, babe. All you can do is learn from it and move on from here. At least he knows now."

"Yeah, at least he knows now," Harper repeated.

She just wanted to know what he was going to do with the information.

* * *

The June sun was high in the sky and shining brilliantly when Harper walked out of the doors of the Brogan-Meyers Hotel. The Florida humidity wrapped around her like an oppressive blanket. Not only was she immediately pleased with her wardrobe selection, but she was happy she had pulled her hair up. There was nothing quite as uncomfortable as her hair sticking to the back of her neck.

The outside entrance of the hotel sat under a massive awning. Golden brown pavers covered the area, creating a circle that could easily fit four cars all the way around. In the center sat an enormous fountain with four mermaids playing in the water.

Even under the shade of the expansive awning, the sun was too bright for Harper's sensitive eyes. She pushed her glasses down from the top of her head and settled them on her nose. Bennett had already grabbed her bags from the room and was currently at the back of the SUV parked at the curb. He was loading the bags while Mel went inside to finish checking them out. Harper would've waited inside with her friend, but she needed some fresh air before they loaded up in the car. Plus, the line of people had made her antsy.

As Harper rounded the car, she spotted Dale and Hamilton who were setting up their things in the third row of seats. Harper would have the middle to herself again. Maybe she'd stretch out along the bench seat and take a nap for the three-and-a-half-hour ride. Though, odds were her brain wouldn't be able to stay quiet long enough to let her doze off.

"You got everything?" Bennett asked her as she walked up to him.

"Yup." She nodded.

"I got you another juice; it's in the cooler with some bottles of water. *Organic* apple this time." He looked over at her and waggled his eyebrows.

"Ohhh, fancy."

"You know it. That's how we roll." He stacked another bag into the trunk just as Dale stepped around to the back of the SUV.

"Did you seriously just say, *that's how we roll*?"

"Yeah, you got a problem with it?" Bennett asked.

"No problem." Dale shook his head. "Just didn't realize how hip and cool you are." The sarcasm was dripping from his words.

"You know, it's a long walk back home, buddy."

"Like you'd leave him," Hamilton said, joining the group. "Mel wouldn't let you."

"Fair point."

Both boys grinned before they grabbed bags from the rolling cart and started loading them into the back, allowing Bennett to take a step to the side.

His gray-blue eyes were uncovered and he looked Harper over with concern. "You feeling any better?"

"I think I'm about as good as I'm going to get for a while."

He nodded, wrapping his arms around her and pulling her against his solid body. He pressed a kiss to her temple before he pulled back, his hands on her shoulders. "I don't know exactly what's going on, but I'm not oblivious enough to not see that *something* is going on. I got your back, Harper. No matter what it is."

"Make that two of us," Hamilton said as he continued to load the car.

"What am I? Chopped liver?" Dale asked. He stopped and looked over at her. "Make that *three* of us." He pointed to his chest. "I got your back, too."

One of the few genuine smiles she'd felt in days turned up her lips, but a second later it was sliding off her face.

Hamilton's gaze was fixed on a spot over Harper's shoulder and he waved, calling out. "Hey! Liam!"

Harper spun around immediately, her heart now lodged in her throat as her eyes focused on the man crossing over to them, cowboy boots and all.

And *dammit*, she couldn't stop herself from admiring the *all*.

His jeans looked like they were made for him, and the V-neck of his green T-shirt was pulled low by the aviator sunglasses that hung from the collar, exposing the very top of his chest.

Even with his eyes uncovered, she couldn't read anything in them. Between that and the set line of his mouth, she didn't find anything promising in his expression.

"Were you staying here, too?" Hamilton asked as Liam joined the group.

"No, I've been staying with Logan. But I was wanting to catch a word with Harper before you guys hit the road. Is that okay?" His gaze focused on her, and for just a second she saw hope flicker through his eyes. But it was gone just as quickly and she was pretty sure she might've imagined it…or it was a trick of the sun.

"Yes." She turned to Bennett, whose eyes were focused intently on her. "Ten minutes?"

"Take as long as you want. We'll be here."

She made a move to step away but Bennett grabbed her hand, making her stop and look back at him.

"Right here, Harper," he said only loud enough for her to hear. "If you need us."

"Thanks." She squeezed his hand before she stepped away, following Liam. When they walked out into the sun he pulled his glasses from his shirt and slid them onto his face. He led them to a patch of green on the side of the hotel, heading for the black metal bench in the corner that was shaded under a massive tree.

They sat on opposite ends, as much distance between them as possible. The space felt forced…wrong.

All wrong.

Liam took a deep breath, letting it out as he rubbed his hands across his jeans. "I'm sorry about last night. I was a dick, and no matter anything that's happened, you didn't deserve that."

"I…" Her brain went momentarily blank. "I, um…"

Nope. Nothing.

"I believe you," he continued. "I believe the baby is mine…or ours really." He stopped rubbing his hands across his jeans and reached up, running his fingers through his hair. "Wow, that sentence didn't exactly seem real coming out of my mouth."

"I know what you mean," she said, finding her voice. "I was in denial until a week ago."

"What was a week ago?"

"I finally took the pregnancy test, or tests really. And there were plenty of signs that I ignored…or tried to ignore."

"How many tests did you take?" he asked, dropping his hands. Some of his hair fell across his forehead, and just like the night before she wanted to reach up and brush it back.

"Fifteen," she said as she settled her hands on the bench next to her, tapping her fingers against the warm black metal. She needed something to do with her hands besides touching him.

"Seriously?"

"Five a day, three days in a row. And I think I was still in denial until my doctor's appointment the other day. So really, coming to grips with this after about twelve hours is pretty impressive on your part."

"So…this was only just confirmed?"

"Yeah." She nodded slowly.

"And who else knows?"

"Mel and my other friend Grace."

"So you haven't told your parents?"

"No. The plan was to tell you first." Yeah, she'd planned a number of things that hadn't exactly happened. Hadn't been close to happening.

"You should know my parents know."

"They do?" *Oh. Dear. God.* They probably thought she was the worst person in the world. Well, maybe not the *absolute* worst…but pretty far up there.

"They travel all over the continent these days, so there's no telling when I'll see them again. It isn't exactly information I want to inform them about over the phone. So I told them this morning, and my brother and sister found out last night."

So his entire family knew. And none of hers did. She was going to have to change that very soon.

"How did they take it?"

"They're all supportive. My parents are kind of used to unconventional at this point. This isn't the first time something like this has happened."

For a second her mind reeled, thinking that he had other kids from other women out there…apparently she was no better than he was last night. But then something clicked in her brain, making her heart twinge in pain. "Are you talking about Logan and his daughter?"

Madison had been the little girl's name, and the image of the "M" tattoo on Liam's arm flashed through her mind, the bird taking flight above it. He'd gotten the tattoo for his niece who passed away.

"Yeah." He nodded.

Harper knew about Logan and his daughter, not only because

it had been big news a couple of months ago, but because of Abby's involvement in the whole debacle. It had almost ended Abby's relationship with Logan, but in the end they'd found their way back to each other.

Maybe there was a possibility something like that could happen again…

"After Madison, they have a very different perspective on things." The pain in his voice was palpable, not all that shocking as Liam and his family had dealt with an extreme loss. Death of a loved one was never easy…but the death of a child?

Unimaginable.

Yup, if his family thought that she was going to keep this child from Liam, they would without a doubt *hate* her.

"Liam, I swear I was going to tell you. If…if you believe anything, please believe that." The desperation to fix this was clawing at her insides.

"I do. I believe that."

Okay…well, that was something at least.

"So what about your doctor's appointment? Was everything okay with the baby? With you?"

"They're doing a complete blood workup, but those results won't come back for a week or two. But everything they were able to check at the appointment was good. Well, for the most part. The nausea has been hard to deal with, so they gave me some medicine to help with that."

"So you've had bad morning sickness?"

She couldn't stop the scoff that escaped her throat, couldn't help herself. "That title is full of false advertising. The mornings are actually the easiest. Afternoons are when it really hits the hardest. If it gets worse than what I'm currently dealing with I need to go back in. But as it is, my next appointment will be in a month."

"Did they give you a due date?"

"January thirtieth."

"And did you hear the heartbeat?" He shifted closer to her.

"No, not yet. It was too soon. That should happen at the next appointment."

"I want to be there," he said immediately. "I don't want to miss it."

"Okay."

"I don't want to miss *any* of it, Harper. I don't want to screw this up."

Her hands tapped out a faster rhythm against the bench. "I think I already took care of that. I messed up. Made this harder…and I'm sorry."

"So, what do we do? What do you want?"

"I'd like to get to know you."

The flash of frustration in his eyes was apparent, and he let out a bitter huff through his nose. "I wanted that six weeks ago."

"I…I know. I wish there was a way to start over." Her throat had to work hard to get those last words out, tightening around them.

"We can't start over. Too much has happened." His mouth made that hard stubborn line again. The finality in it clear as day.

So that was it. They couldn't *start over.*

She turned away from him, looking over at a couple walking their dog on the opposite side of the little park. She closed her eyes hard in an attempt to block out the image of the people in front of her, but instead different images filtered through her brain.

Liam walking up to her at the bar. Liam pressing her against the wall as he kissed her for the first time. Liam singing to her, his voice resonating in her bones. Liam looking down into her eyes as he moved inside of her. As he consumed every part of her.

But that was over. Apparently there was no finding their way back.

So that was where they stood…the only way he was going to be a part of her life was through their child. That was just how it was going to be. Splitting holidays, one Christmas with, the next without. Meeting halfway so that Liam could have him or her for the summer.

People did it all the time. Shared their child.

This was how it was going to be. And she was just going to have to accept it.

Chapter Ten

Catching Up

The next ten minutes were in no way easy for Liam. He was fighting with every ounce of his strength to keep his hands to himself, because all he wanted was to reach over and touch Harper.

It took everything in him not to pull her into his chest. Took everything in him not to wrap his arms around her, press his nose into that spot just underneath her ear, and inhale. Even now, the scent of honey filled his nose with every breath, testing his will.

As her eyes were his biggest source of insight, and her sunglasses currently covered them, he couldn't be completely sure of her emotions. But she was fidgeting, something that until last night he wasn't used to seeing her do. And for whatever reason she seemed just as confused and lost as he did.

He had no clue what to do about any of it. It was hard for him to get over how mad he still was at her.

She'd left.

Yes she'd explained it, said she was scared. And he got that, really he did, because he'd been terrified. But that didn't change the facts.

She'd left.

The sting of waking up alone was still there, itching underneath his skin. And it had absolutely nothing to do with his pride. Hell, that had gone out the window about a second after he'd met her. After he'd seen her really. And it wasn't like he'd regained it, either. Case in point his ridiculous love anthem that would be officially released to the airwaves in a few weeks' time.

He tried not to cringe at the thought of it. Yup, the second that was out there, the only name for what he was would be a fool.

And then there was the fact that she'd waited so long to tell him about the pregnancy.

Okay…so she'd just confirmed it a week ago…and then the doctor's appointment to *really* confirm it had only been a few days ago. Denial was a word she'd used in describing the time gap between suspecting and knowing.

And denial was a word that he was becoming fully acquainted with as well.

Because he really thought he could do it, really thought he could get through it all without making a bigger ass out of himself. And he almost did, too. Made it through the part where he programmed her number into his phone—and he was going to ignore the relief of finally having it. Made it through the appointment confirmation of her next doctor's visit that he would be going to—and which was conveniently during a break of the Isaac Hunter tour. Made it through walking the short distance back to the hotel where her friends were waiting by the car.

But he couldn't have things stay that way. Couldn't let her leave like this. Because at the end of it all, *he* couldn't walk away. He still wanted her.

They were ten feet from the car when he gave in. He pulled his sunglasses from his face, hanging them on his shirt, before he grabbed her hand. He was unable to ignore the relief that coursed through him at finally touching her. She came up short as she turned to look at him.

"You want to get to know me?" His hold on her hand tightened, and he closed the distance taking a step forward.

"Yes. I do," she answered without hesitation.

"Okay, new rule: no barriers." He reached up, pushing her sunglasses into her hair and revealing her eyes. She winced at the sudden brightness, but she didn't look away from him.

What he saw first was surprise mingled in her eyes, violet eyes that he'd been unable to get out of his head for the last few weeks. But underneath the shock they were tired and sad…sadder than anything he'd seen on her face before.

Considering everything, that was saying a lot. He hated seeing that look there. *Hated* it.

"Like I said earlier, we can't start over. It's not possible with everything that's happened. Certain things can't be undone." He let go of her hand, grabbing on to her hip and sliding his palm around to her back. His other hand moved to her face, cradling her jaw.

"Like me leaving."

"There are a number of things, and that's one of them." He nodded slowly. "I wish I could forget that part. I really wish I could, but it happened, and it sucked something serious."

"Believe me it sucked for me, too. I'm sorry, Liam. I don't think I'll ever be able to tell you that enough."

"I know that. I do. And, though we can't erase it, we can move past it. And even though we can't start over, we can catch up." His thumb brushed her cheek.

"And how do we do that?" Hope flickered in her eyes, a hope that was running through him as well.

"One day at a time." He lowered his head and pressed his lips to hers gently, just a slow simple brush before he pulled her bottom lip into his mouth. His hand moved back, palming the base of her skull as he tilted his head and deepened the kiss.

She opened for him immediately, like she needed to taste him just as much as he needed to taste her. And then her hands were at his sides, tightening in the fabric of his shirt.

He didn't care that they were surrounded by people, most of them strangers and a group of four that he had no doubt were watching their every move. Nope, he didn't care in the slightest. All he was focused on was the fact that the woman in his arms was not only holding on to him, but kissing him like her life depended on it.

When he pulled back from her a minute—or two—later, they were both good and truly breathless. He leaned down, resting his forehead against hers.

"Despite everything that's happened," he whispered, "I still want you, Harper. That hasn't changed." *Will probably never change*. He moved just enough to where he could press his lips to her forehead.

She pulled back and looked up at him. "So how does this 'no barriers' work?"

"Honesty. We share *everything* personal."

"So the exact opposite of six weeks ago."

"Exactly. We talk. Every day. *And* at a minimum we learn three new things about each other daily."

"Like what?" she asked, her mouth quirking to the side and giving him the first smile he'd seen on her face since finding her again.

"Like, I'm twenty-nine, have an older brother and younger sister, and I'm a musician."

"I already know all of those things about you."

"But I don't know any of those things about you," he said as he continued to move his thumb across her jaw.

"Okay, I'm twenty-six, an only child, and a massage therapist."

"That's interesting, both of our careers are dependent on our hands."

Speaking of hands, hers were now climbing up his chest, something he had no problem with in the slightest.

"You have to go again," she said as her fingertips brushed his collarbone.

"I hate Brussels sprouts, I have a *slight* fear of heights, and I hope our child has your eyes."

Her hands stopped moving, her fingers now laying against the base of his neck. "Liam." She breathed his name and he did the only thing he knew. He kissed her again, savoring everything about the taste of her on his tongue.

He didn't want to say good-bye to her. Wasn't ready for it. He'd just found her. It was too soon.

"We're going to figure this out," he said against her mouth.

"I know. No barriers." She repeated the new plan.

"Exactly."

When the SUV pulled away from the curb five minutes later—taking Harper with it—the only thing that helped the ache in his chest was the fact that he was going to get to see her in less than two weeks.

Let the countdown begin, and let it get to the end as fast as possible.

* * *

Liam's deep, rich voice filled the tiny space of Harper's bedroom while she unpacked and did laundry. As she had neighbors on all sides of her—some a little bit older who had never hesitated to complain—she had to listen to music at somewhat subdued levels. Though she was pushing the boundaries a tad bit tonight, her volume just a little louder than usual. The current song coming through her speakers was "Wild and Reckless."

"Tearing down the road in the middle of the night. My only guide the glow of the moonlight…" she sang along.

It was Liam's first big song and she knew every single word of it. Again, the fact that she hadn't made the connection that he was Liam James was freaking ridiculous. How had she never Googled what he looked like before?

She still couldn't believe how they'd found each other again, either. Because really, what were the odds? Slim, that was for sure. But hey, considering the fact that she'd gotten pregnant even with the use of all those condoms, maybe the odds were a little skewed.

She dropped the basket of laundry onto the bed and immediately put her hand over her belly.

But her getting pregnant was not an unlucky occurrence. It might not be the most optimal timing in the world, but this was her child...Liam's child...*their* child.

He was going to be involved, and the relief at that fact was freeing. And then there was the added bonus that she hadn't screwed everything up beyond repair.

I still want you, Harper. That hasn't changed.

Those words kept repeating in her head, and that—combined with the low rich timbre of his voice crooning through her apartment—resonated through her body. The power that his voice had over her was scary as all hell, and the fear she'd felt all those weeks ago was still present, niggling at the back of her mind.

There was no denying the fact that she was in love with him. It hadn't been some overwhelming rush of hormones six weeks ago. It hadn't been just great sex...*really* great sex. It had been him. Liam James.

But there was no more running. She couldn't. The future held a good amount of unknown that wasn't comforting in the slightest, but wasn't that life? There were no guarantees with anything...

She wished they'd had more time. Wished they hadn't had to leave, and she had no doubt that Mel, Bennett, and the boys would've given her more time. But Liam hadn't had the time. He'd needed to catch a flight to California, and he'd looked genuinely unhappy about leaving her. He'd wanted more time, too.

That hadn't been a figment of her imagination, had it?

I hope our child has your eyes.

More words that kept repeating on a loop.

There was a lot of uncertainty coursing through her, but something she felt in her bones was that Liam James was a man of his word. So she was going to go with that, uncertainty and all.

At least the overwhelming anxiety that had been plaguing her for the last few weeks had lessened significantly. She guessed it was because of the truth finally being out there and all. Well, the truth being out there to Liam…she still had to tell her parents, a prospect that wasn't in the slightest bit appealing.

But she didn't need to worry about that tonight…that was on the docket for tomorrow.

She'd actually planned on telling them everything when she'd gone to pick Luna up that afternoon, but her father had been out at a farm checking on a sick colt. She couldn't tell one without the other there…and really the thought of telling her mother alone was terrifying.

So yeah, she didn't need to worry about that until tomorrow.

Her cell phone rang on the nightstand next to her, vibrating against the wood. Liam's name flashed on the screen and she grabbed for the phone immediately, hitting the Accept button before even thinking about it.

"Hi." Her heart was beating erratically out of her chest.

"Hey, I…" He trailed off for a second, the phone going silent. "Are you listening to my music?"

"Crap!" She dropped the phone into the pile of clothes before she practically pole-vaulted over her bed to get to the speakers set up on her dresser. Luna jumped up from her dog bed in the corner and started barking as Harper fumbled with her iPad. It took her a couple of tries before she was able to mash the Off button successfully.

Well…that had just happened.

"Luna, shhh." She picked up the still barking dog and held her to her chest.

Luna let out a few more chuffs before Harper set her on the bed. The dog stopped barking as she spun in a circle, making herself comfortable on a throw blanket by the pillows.

It took Harper a second to successfully retrieve her phone from the still warm pile of clothing, and she heard Liam's chuckle coming through the speaker before she even had it to her ear.

She cleared her throat before talking. "Sorry, I, uh…dropped the phone."

"Yeah, I noticed that." The smile in his voice was evident. "Luna not a fan of my music?"

"Wh-what?"

"She was barking."

"Because I woke her up when I made a mad dash across the room."

"Ahhhh, I see." He chuckled again, the rich warmth of it settling low in her belly. "So, what are you doing?"

"Unpacking and washing laundry."

"Well, aren't you a party animal?" The teasing in his voice wasn't helping with the erratic state of her heart.

"Yup. What are you doing?"

"Settling into the hotel."

"Your flight was okay?" she asked as she propped the phone between her ear and her shoulder and started twisting a washcloth in her hands. Why was she so nervous? It wasn't like this was their first conversation, yet she was barely able to think of what to say. Next thing she'd be asking him about the weather.

"Yeah, but I came to a conclusion."

"A conclusion?"

"This whole catching-up thing is going to need to be balanced."

"Balanced?" Or she'd just turn into a parrot and repeat the end of all of his sentences.

"Yup, I want an entire conversation where I get to ask you anything. You know way more about me than I know about you. And I'm at a disadvantage as a lot of information about me can be found on the Internet."

This was very true. Case in point, the entire ride back she'd been regaled with interesting tidbits about Liam.

As it turned out, Hamilton was a *huge* fan, so he knew quite a few facts without the assistance of the World Wide Web. And fan or not, the vetting process on whether Liam was good enough for Harper began, and Dale had been more than happy to help out. The two must've looked up every ounce of information that could be located about the guy, and repeated it for everyone else to learn.

The only person in the car who knew about the pregnancy was Mel, but as they'd all been witness to Liam making out with her in front of the hotel, they obviously knew *something* was up in some capacity. Couldn't exactly miss it, now, could they?

For the most part, Liam wasn't much for being in the spotlight when he wasn't on the stage; must've been a family trait as Logan was pretty similar on that front. Liam had dated a few semi-famous women—an actress or two, other musicians, a model—and those facts had all come with somewhat painful pangs. But as none of those relationships seemed to have been all that serious, she was able to breathe a little easier.

There was a part of her that had felt guilty about learning this information…like it was an invasion of privacy. But in the end, it was information that she was pretty sure he would've told her himself and really none of it was anything that was all that personal. It was observations from outsiders. She'd found out more about him within the first hour of meeting him than what the boys had pulled up on their phones.

"You Google me yet?" Liam asked, a shuffling on his side of the phone like he was moving papers around.

She pulled her bottom lip into her mouth…chewing on it as she tried to figure out how to answer.

"Honey, remember the new rule: no barriers."

She dropped her lip from her teeth, smiling at the fact that he was calling her *honey* again. "*I* didn't."

"Ahhh, so it was one of your companions. My money is on Dale and Hamilton."

"You'd be correct." She dropped the towel she was still twisting and sat on the edge of the bed, holding the phone to her ear with her hand.

"Well, in that case I get *two* conversations of asking you questions. And you don't get any follow-ups until then."

"Oh, is that so?" Her eyes focused on the mirror across from her and she was taken off guard by just how massive that grin on her face had gotten.

She'd never seen anything like that before.

"Yup, and I've made a list."

"Really now?" She grabbed a pillow and placed it on the space behind her on the bed, lying back and settling in.

"Spent the entire flight working on it, too. Could take hours to work through."

"Well, then you should get started."

"Question number one." Papers rustled again and he cleared his throat. "When is your birthday?"

"July thirty-first."

"Question two: Where were you born?"

"So you're starting from the *very* beginning?"

"The more interruptions you make, the longer this is going to take. I have *a lot* of questions, honey."

Honey. Yeah, her grin was somehow still growing. She was going to have to get a grip, because not only was it hard to talk around it, but it was going to crack her face in two any second now.

"Atlanta, Georgia, and it was four seventeen in the afternoon," she answered.

"You being sassy will not make this process go any faster, either."

She had absolutely no problems whatsoever with a long conversation with Liam. How *shocking*.

* * *

Harper ended up staying on the phone with Liam until well after midnight. When they'd hung up—both more than a little reluctantly—she'd passed out with a massive smile on her face. A smile that had been there the entire time she'd gotten ready that morning...and hadn't budged in the least bit on her drive to Café Lula.

The first order of business that morning was breakfast with Mel and Grace, where she was grilled for about an hour. Even though Mel had known a lot of what had happened over the weekend, she hadn't been privy to all of the facts of Harper's conversation with Liam. Mel had been kind enough to refrain from interrogating Harper in the car—something she couldn't have done without revealing the pregnancy. But neither Mel nor Grace refrained from asking Harper every question under the sun over coffee.

Well, coffee for the girls and green tea for Harper. It was her first caffeine in weeks and she was going to happily enjoy every sip of it between answering—in great detail of course—all the questions thrown at her.

The beginning of the conversation consisted of Grace's opened-mouth shock interspersed with more *are you kidding me*'s than Harper could count while the party portion of the weekend was recounted. And by the end of the conversation, both Mel and Grace were grinning just as much as Harper was.

"Well, this sure has taken a lovely turn," Mel said happily.

"No kidding," Grace agreed.

"So you guys are going to get to know each other?" Mel drummed her fingers across the table. "Just talk for a little while?"

"Yeah. Maybe this way we can actually get some talking in without, well—"

"Screwing each other's brains out?" Grace finished.

"Exactly." She nodded, taking another bite of her cranberry orange muffin that was settling surprisingly well with her tea.

Keeping food down for the win.

Harper's phone was face-up on the table and it buzzed against the wood, alerting her of a text from Liam. She grabbed the phone immediately, sliding her thumb across the screen as she read the words.

Surprises on my morning run.

When she opened the text conversation—empty until now—a picture popped up of about forty peacocks blocking the path. A second later the three floating dots indicating he was typing were moving on the screen.

How are you feeling this morning?

Exhausted, but well worth it. She even tagged on a smiley face emoji for good measure. *Looking forward to many more late-night conversations.*

Who says we need to wait for the late night? I'm going to need my three facts about you before noon.

Yes, sir, she typed quickly before she looked up to find both of her friends staring at her.

"What? It's Liam."

"Really?" The mock surprise in Grace's voice was beyond exaggerated. "We had no idea."

"Which just goes to show how oblivious we are, as that smile you're rocking is giving the sun a run for its money on brightness this morning. Good thing I have my sunglasses." Mel tapped the pair sitting on the top of her head, and they fell down onto her nose.

"Was it this blinding when she was around him?" Grace asked Mel. "Because I might need to invest in sunscreen stock when I get to meet the man. And when is that going to be?" she asked, turning to Harper.

"In two weeks. He's coming to my next doctor's appointment."

"Is he now?" Mel pushed her glasses back into her hair before she rubbed her hands together. "And staying for *how* long?"

"We haven't discussed that."

"And *where* will he be staying?" Grace this time.

"We haven't discussed that, either."

"Well, maybe you should discuss it. When are you guys talking on the phone again? And I don't mean texting," Mel said before she finished off her muffin.

"Tonight."

Harper already had the countdown going down in her head. It was the only thing distracting her from the inevitable conversation she was going to have with her parents in just a few hours.

* * *

It was a little after seven when Harper pulled into her parents' driveway that evening. She spent a solid five minutes sitting in the car, staring up at the house while she prepared herself for what was going to go down.

And while she was at it, she listened to the rest of Liam's song that was currently playing through her car's speakers. Because obviously she'd been listening to his music at any and all opportunities all day.

"You only get one chance at this life. So live it up, live it up right…"

Yup. That was the plan. Living it up right.

She couldn't help but think of the last time she'd had to prepare herself for a very similar conversation not five months ago. She'd sat her parents down at the dining room table and just ripped the Band-Aid off.

Brad is gone. The wedding is off.

Paul had said good riddance. *"Any man who doesn't realize what he has with you, isn't good enough for you."*

Delilah had cried…Harper predicted a repeat showing of that performance tonight.

As it was after seven she was hoping they'd already eaten dinner. She wanted this for two reasons. One, her parents would no doubt ask her to join them, and food just wasn't going to be an option for Harper tonight—less so because of nausea and more due to the fact that her stomach was tied up in knots. Reason two, she had no doubt both of her parents weren't going to be pleased with the news…and might in fact lose their own appetites.

No need to ruin everyone's dinner.

The last chords of the song echoed around her. She reached up and shut off the ignition, taking one last deep breath before she got out of the car and headed for the house.

"It's now or never," she whispered as she walked in the front door.

Actually it was *now* or *now*.

She found both of her parents in the living room at the back of the house, the evening news chirping away in the background while Paul read the newspaper on the sofa and Delilah played solitaire on her iPad, reclining in her chair while she mumbled about corruption in the government.

"Knock, knock," she said as she rasped her knuckles on the door frame.

It was then that Darby was alerted to another person in the house, rousing from her deep sleep as she bolted off her bed in the corner and ran to Harper.

"Hey, sweet pea." Paul folded his newspaper and stood up, giving Harper a quick kiss on the temple.

"Were we expecting you?" Delilah asked, closing her iPad and setting it down on the coffee table in front of her. She pushed the pop-up footrest of her recliner down, sitting up and putting her feet on the floor.

"No." Harper shook her head. "I was hoping you guys had a second, though. I need to talk to you about something."

"Something serious?" her father asked, his brow furrowing in concern as he sat back down.

"Yes." She nodded before taking a seat on the empty space next to her father on the sofa.

She'd barely settled down when Delilah blurted out, "Tell me you didn't lose your job."

"No." Harper shook her head, trying to swallow the sudden lump in her throat and wishing she had a glass of water. "I'm still gainfully employed."

"Well, that's a relief."

The humorless laugh that escaped Harper's mouth was unavoidable. "Yeah, I don't know that you'll be saying that in a second, Mom."

"Harper?" Paul shifted forward, placing his forearms on his knees.

Better out than in.

Say it.

Say. It.

"I'm pregnant and—"

"Tell me it's Brad's," Delilah said, cutting Harper off before she could get any further.

"Oh my God." Another humorless laugh escaped Harper's mouth as she closed her eyes and rubbed at her forehead.

Well, it hadn't taken any time at all for Delilah to go there. Awesome, just what she needed to make this conversation better.

She opened her eyes again and shook her head at her mother. "As Brad left five months ago and I'm about eight weeks along, that isn't something that's a possibility."

Harper's eyes focused on her father who moved his arms from his knees and shifted back in his seat. He took a deep breath, his face now showing nothing as to what he was thinking or feeling.

Harper knew that look, when her father went from being expressive to revealing nothing. She'd seen it so many times. Usually it was when people came in with their hurt or sick pets, and before he even got a good look, he had a pretty good idea of what was going to happen. He was very rarely wrong, but until he thoroughly examined the animal, he hid that initial diagnosis from the owners. Which was what he was doing right now.

"When?" he asked.

"When I went to Nashville…during the weekend that was supposed to be the wedding."

"Nashville?" Delilah repeated. "When you were supposed to be supervised by your aunt Celeste?"

Otherwise known as Delilah's sister.

"Mom, I'm twenty-six. No one supervises me."

"Well obviously." She gestured to Harper aggressively. "Look what's happened."

"Delilah," Paul said sternly, effectively shushing his wife. "Who is this guy and how did you meet him?"

"His name is Liam James and I met him at the Second Hand Guitar."

"At a bar! You met him at a *bar*?" Delilah shouted. So really Paul had effectively silenced his wife for all of about ten seconds. That was something at least.

"Liam James…Liam James," Paul repeated, ignoring his wife. "Why do I know that name?"

"He's a musician."

"A *musician*? Oh. My. God. Like he plays on the side of the street for dimes?"

"No, Mom. He doesn't play on the side of the road for money. He's actually very successful."

"Successful?! I can't believe this!" She stood abruptly, the force causing her chair to move back, the feet screeching across the hardwood floors. "Can. Not. Believe. This. Why do you keep doing this to me? First you call off the wedding. Then you get knocked up by some stranger." And with that she stormed out of the room.

Neither Harper nor her father said anything as Delilah's footsteps echoed up the stairs. And it was only after the bedroom door slammed shut that Paul finally did speak.

"Liam James is the guy who sings 'Against the Odds'?"

"Yes." The word came out on a whisper.

"And he knows that you're pregnant and that he's the father?"

"Yes."

"And he's going to be involved?" he asked, still revealing nothing.

"Yes."

"Okay." Paul nodded slowly, clearly still trying to process.

"I'm sorry, Dad. This isn't how things were supposed to happen." She didn't look away from her father's gaze. She couldn't. She was still waiting for it to reveal something.

Anything.

"How do you know?" he asked, tapping his forefinger against his chin.

"What?"

"How do you know it wasn't supposed to happen exactly like this?" And there it was, the twitch to his lower lip. "Sometimes you have to believe that things happen for a reason. And that's how I'm going to look at this, because I can't think of my first grandchild from my only daughter any other way."

Hope. All she felt was hope at her father's words. "You're not disappointed in me?"

The twitch in his lower lip turned to a smile. "Not even in the slightest. No one is perfect, sweet pea." He reached for her face, touching her chin and pushing it up, his wordless way of telling her to hold her head high. "If we were, life would be pretty boring."

A soft laugh escaped her mouth. "Yeah, you can say that again."

"Your mom…she'll come around."

"You sure about that?" Harper raised one of her eyebrows, not so sure of her father's statement.

"You know how well she deals with shocking news."

"You mean she doesn't."

"Exactly. But she'll get there, and you know how I know?"

"How?"

"Because she loves you. And she's going to love your child, too. She's just got to adjust. And she will."

"Promise?"

"I promise," Paul said as he pulled his daughter in for a hug. Holding her close for a good minute before he grabbed her shoulders and pulled her back so he could look at her face. "So tell me about him. Tell me about the father of my first grandchild."

Her dad's mouth flickered up at the corners when he said the last word, his eyes twinkling more than a little bit.

For the first time since Harper walked in the front door, she took a full breath without that painful constriction over her chest. Yet another reason she'd been beyond stupid to keep the truth to herself. Once it was out there, she'd felt so much better. Could breathe again and not feel like she was suffocating in the slightest.

The truth will out. And for her, when it was out it was so much better.

Chapter Eleven

The Elephant in the Room

When Liam first started opening for Isaac Hunter, he was lucky if the seats in the auditoriums were half-filled. The people around the stage were usually only those who were staking out their spots for the main show, while the other forty percent of the space remained empty. But within the last year, the seats had started to fill up before he hit the mike, and the people around the stage were the majority of the crowd that were going to show up for the night.

People were no longer *forced* to listen to him. Now they were there because they *wanted* to hear his set.

That being said, the size of the crowd had never had any effect on his performance. He put on a good show no matter the circumstances. He had to. It was his job. But never had that part of his job been as difficult as it had been during those weeks right after Harper had left him in Nashville.

He'd opened for fifteen concerts during that time, and for every single one of those performances it had taken everything in him not to phone it in. This was not the case anymore.

It had been eleven days since he'd seen Harper in Jacksonville, twelve since he'd found her, and in that time he'd opened for eight concerts. For Liam, each performance had been better than the last. If anything, the show he was currently rocking out on the stage might just be the best so far. And when he got to "Forever"—the song he'd written about Harper—he killed it.

Maybe it was because when he sang the song it was no longer physically painful. He'd been able to get the words past his throat without feeling like the biggest tool on the face of the planet. Maybe it was because he was talking to her on a daily basis. Maybe it was because he was going to see her in less than twenty-four hours.

Maybe it was everything that had to do with her.

So okay, things weren't perfect yet. Far from it. She actually still didn't know about the song he'd written about her. Well, he was pretty sure she didn't know more about it than when he sang it to her in May. And as it wasn't going to be released on the radio for another couple of weeks, he figured he still had a little time.

He just didn't want to freak her out again. They were in a good spot, or as good as it was going to get when all they had going was electronic communication. So he was taking advantage of the time, because it was going to take time to figure out what was going to happen with them. No matter what, she would be a part of his life forever. She was the mother of his child.

He was going to be a father…a freaking father. That was a reality he knew and though it was more than a little scary, it was an exciting scary. The kind he wanted to run toward and not away from.

"I don't know what's gotten into you lately." Isaac grinned at Liam as he walked backstage, the crowd chanting his name at ear-splitting levels. That was something new. "But you better keep it up. That, my friend, was *incredible.*"

"Thanks." Liam tipped back a cold bottle of water, so thirsty it was kind of ridiculous that he hadn't noticed it until now.

"Go take a breather. We'll see you onstage for "Practice Makes Perfect," and you better bring your A-game for the guitar solo," Isaac called after him.

"Always do." Liam grinned as he headed for one of the rooms at the end of the hallway.

The second the door closed behind him, he reached for the back of his T-shirt and pulled it over his head. It had been hot out on the stage and he needed a clean one that wasn't sticking to his skin.

But before he could grab another shirt he was reaching for his phone. As was the norm of late, when he hit the Home button the screen lit up showing texts from Harper. He found himself grinning like an idiot—something else that was becoming the norm—as he entered the code and pulled up their text conversation.

My three facts of the day:

1. When I was in the seventh grade I played the part of Esmeralda in The Hunchback of Notre Dame for our school play.

2. I know the lyrics to every N'SYNC song by heart (I know. Don't judge me.)

3. I've seen Jurassic Park more times than I can count. And when I see it on TV I have to watch it.

Her last text was followed by a picture of a TV, the Tyrannosaurus rex from the movie running across the flat screen. She was zoomed out far enough that he could see her legs propped up on an ottoman. There was a yellow blanket spread across her lap and Luna was nestled between the folds, her little black head just peeking out and looking up at the camera.

Liam studied the rest of the picture, taking in what was around the TV. It was sitting on a black entertainment console with candles, picture frames, and books filling the shelves. There was a floral painting hanging on the light green wall above it.

Tomorrow he was going to see the room in person. He was going to see her. That fact added to the current euphoria pumping through his body.

The baby wasn't the only exciting thing he wanted to run to—sprint to more accurately. He wanted Harper even more than he had in May. Even more than when he'd spotted her across that bar and been drawn to her like a freaking moth to the flame.

Even though she'd left him without a word, even though she'd waited through all those weeks and still not called him, even though he'd been a mess, it hadn't changed the fact that he wanted her.

Seeing her again in Jacksonville? Having her in his arms again? Yeah, that had confirmed it all. He was without a doubt in love with her. Really and truly head-over-ass in love for the first time in his life. *That* was what had gotten into him.

Oh, look at that, the ridiculous grin on his face was only getting bigger.

"Well, that's a smile if I've ever seen one."

And just that fast, his smile was gone. Every single time Liam heard that voice, his entire body tensed. Actually it was more like a cringe. He took a second to brace himself before he looked up to find Kiki Jean Carlow.

He understood why the woman was in Los Angeles; she owned a home here and spent the summer months in the city. What he didn't understand was why she was in his room.

She was leaning against the door frame that led to the bathroom, one of her arms stretched above her blond head. The move pulled up the bottom of the low-cut shirt she was wearing. She somehow managed to expose all of her tanned-toned stomach—complete with twinkling diamond belly button ring—as well as her chest.

The move did absolutely nothing for him. *She* did absolutely nothing for him.

"What are you doing in here, Kiki?"

"I thought we could take advantage of your downtime. Don't you have an hour before you need to be onstage again?"

"Yeah, that won't be happening. You need to go." He turned away from her, walking to the small closet in the corner and grabbing a clean shirt. But before he could pull it over his head, hands were running across his bare chest, skimming down his abs to the top of his jeans.

He moved fast, snatching her hands away from his body and turning around. "What are you doing?" He let go of her and stepped away.

"You should really stop denying the attraction between us, Liam, and just give into it already." She looked up at him, pouting her lips and batting her eyes. "Besides the fact that we'd have a lot of fun, it would be *fantastic* publicity. And as we're going to be working together, you should really start playing nice."

"Excuse me?"

"I'm going to be in your new video. Or didn't you know?"

Liam's mind reeled. The next video he was making was for "Forever." Over his dead body would Kiki be in the video for the song that was about Harper.

"I don't think so."

"You don't believe me? Just call and ask your manager. He was the one who talked to my agent."

"I don't care what he has to say. You aren't going to be in it. And you need to get out of my room." He moved farther away from her and headed for the door. He opened it and pointed to the hallway where more than a few backstage people passed by. "Now."

"Okay, Liam." She smiled as she walked to the door. "But it's just a matter of time before we get together." She reached up, running her fingers across his still bare chest as she passed by him.

It took everything in him not to slam the door behind her. The second it was shut and locked he had his phone out, pulling up his manager's number to get this sorted out.

Because there was no way in hell.

* * *

Harper had seen her mother a number of times since telling her the baby news. The first handful of encounters hadn't been exactly pleasant. They always involved someone dissolving into tears—Delilah—or someone shouting—Delilah again.

But after everything that had happened in Jacksonville, Harper had resolved that she was very much done crying about this.

She had her father's full support, she had her friends by her side—all of whom now knew the full scope of what was going on, and she had Liam. Sure she and the father of her child were still in the process of figuring things out, and for now, that was enough.

And though her mother wasn't in any way, shape, or form as accepting of the situation as her father, she was still more than happy to make as many demands of the situation as possible.

The one that Harper was currently giving in to? Liam was flying into Tallahassee in two hours. And their first stop after he landed? Her parents' house for dinner.

Yeah, Harper was picking her battles, and Delilah's insistence that she meet the father of her future grandchild didn't seem like a smart one to fight.

And besides, at the end of the day, she really wanted to fix things. There was no point fighting about it anymore. What was done was done. There was no changing this pregnancy. Only moving forward.

Their relationship had never been the easiest, and differences or not—because there were *a lot* of differences—this was her mother.

And as it had been made very clear to Harper, there was no starting over, only catching up. So Delilah was just going to need to catch up, and Harper would wait until she did. Again, this was her mother after all.

Before Harper went to pick Liam up at the airport, she stopped by her parents' house to drop off Luna and the fresh-baked apple pie she'd picked up from Café Lula.

"Paul?" Delilah called out. "You're home early."

Harper walked down the hallway, leaving Luna and Darby in the entryway while they did their customary sniff-over. "Dad's still at the office," she said as she walked into the kitchen.

Delilah looked up from the kitchen island where she was peeling potatoes, her mouth going from relaxed to pursed and her nostrils flaring. Her eyes immediately dropped back down to the task at hand where she was now peeling so vigorously it was any wonder there would be any potatoes left at all.

"Hello," she said as the *tppt-tppt-tppt-tppt-tppt-tppt* filled the kitchen.

"Luna is running around with Darby and I brought the pie." Harper held the box in the air.

Tppt-tppt-tppt-tppt-tppt-tppt.

"You can just set it there." Delilah nodded to the counter before she dropped the potato into a pot next to her and grabbed another one before she started up again.

Tppt-tppt-tppt-tppt-tppt-tppt.

Harper set it down in the spot indicated before she took a deep breath and walked over to the space right in front of her mother, leaning against the counter that separated them. "Can we get this out of the way before I go pick Liam up?"

"What out of the way?"

Tppt-tppt-tppt-tppt-tppt-tppt.

"The bright pink elephant in the room. Though it might be a blue elephant, I'm not sure of the color yet."

The potato and the peeler both fell onto the cutting board and Delilah looked up in fury, wiping her hands on her apron. "Is this funny to you, Harper? Some sort of joke? You're having a child with a man who you barely know, a man your father and I have never met."

"Yes, but the part where you and Dad have never met him will be rectified in…" Harper made a dramatic show of looking at her watch. "Oh, about three hours."

"Is this still you trying to be funny? Because I'm not seeing the humor here."

Harper wondered if her mother saw the humor anywhere. "I know, Mom. But I don't know what else you want me to do. You're going to meet him tonight. We are coming straight here. Not even stopping at my apartment beforehand."

"So he's staying with you?" Her lips pursed even tighter, something that Harper didn't even think was possible.

"Yes. He will be staying with me while he's in town."

"I'm not happy about that."

"I know, Mom, but my time with him is already limited and I'm not going to waste any of it driving back and forth from wherever he would be staying."

"Is he going to be sleeping on the couch?"

"Probably not." God, was she really having this conversation with her mother? Besides the fact that it was more than somewhat painful/awkward, she really had no idea what was going to happen with Liam in the sexy times department.

Though if she were entirely honest with herself, she was hoping they wouldn't be doing all that much sleeping in her bed. Her wanting him definitely had not changed…and good Lord the last few weeks on the phone felt like the longest foreplay of her life.

"See. You have no regard for your actions." Delilah shook her head as she picked up the potato and peeler again.

Tppt-tppt-tppt-tppt-tppt-tppt.

"It isn't like the full consequences of my actions haven't already been realized." Harper waved her hand down in front of her belly as her mother looked up, dropping the now peeled potato into the pot.

"Oh, so you've already sinned so you might as well sin some more?" She grabbed another potato.

"I didn't say that." Harper rolled her eyes and was thankful that her mother's gaze was directed down again. "Do you think Brad and I weren't having sex, too?"

For the second time another clatter of potato and peeler hit the cutting board. "Are you deliberately trying to upset me?" Delilah asked. "I know that anything and everything with Brad is good and truly out the window at this point. There is no need to rub it in my face."

"You think that's what I'm trying to do? Because it's not. You've put Brad on this pedestal that you refuse to take him down from even though he left me. He. Left. Me. You do know this, right? He called off the wedding. Not me. He didn't love me, Mom. So why can't you let it go? Let him go?" Harper's voice had progressively gotten louder as she'd gone on. By the end of it, she was surprised by the max volume she'd reached.

And so was Delilah, whose eyes had gone wide with anger and righteous indignation. But a second later that look was gone as her mother's entire face fell. Delilah averted her eyes for a second while she took a deep breath, trying to collect herself.

And the next words that came out of Delilah's mouth were the very last that Harper ever expected to hear.

"Because when he left I lost part of you," she whispered.

"What?"

Delilah's eyes came up and she focused on her daughter. "Brad was the first relationship you shared with us. The first man you introduced to your father and me. The first time you let us in to that aspect of your life. And I saw quite clearly how happy you were with him, and how much it devastated you when everything fell apart." Her voice cracked on the last word.

"Mom?"

"I just wanted it to go back to how it was. Where you shared that part of yourself with us. Because when he was around, that perpetual wall between us was lower. I could look over it. It wasn't that I couldn't let go of Brad, it was that I couldn't let go of you. When he left you shut me out completely. That wall was higher and thicker than ever. So him coming back was the only solution I could think of."

Harper was pretty sure she was going to need someone to come along and pick her jaw up from off the floor. "I had no idea," she said when she managed to find her voice. "Why didn't you tell me this before?"

"I didn't know how to." Delilah started to blink rapidly and turned away again.

Well, this had been...unexpected. Harper had never known her mother felt that way.

She reached across the counter and grabbed her mother's

hand, whose gaze came up again immediately. Delilah's eyes were brimming with tears. Harper was long used to tears of anger coming from her mother, but not tears of this caliber.

It was slightly unnerving, and causing her own eyes to mist up.

"Mom, you and I need to work on our communication skills with each other."

"Yes. We do." She nodded as she reached up with her free hand and ran her fingers under each eye.

"You should know that I shut everyone out after Brad left. It wasn't just you." Harper let go of her mom's hand and rounded the island.

Delilah didn't hesitate, pulling her daughter in for a hug. They stood there for a good couple of minutes, both of them sniffling.

"I want you to be a part of my life, without walls," Harper whispered before she pulled back and looked into her mother's face. "But you've got to let Brad go. And you've got to give Liam a chance. I know that the circumstances aren't the best, but he's a good guy…a great guy in fact. One who didn't walk away from me, even when I walked away from him."

"He's still going to have to earn my approval," Delilah said resolutely.

"I think he's up for the challenge."

Or at least she sure as hell hoped so.

* * *

The show the night before ended just before eleven o'clock, and afterward Liam went out for a drink with Isaac and Hunter. He needed something to rebound from the foul mood Kiki had put him in…and from the news he'd gotten from his manager.

It wasn't "Forever" that Kiki had been cast in, but she was going to be in a video with him.

Liam had collaborated with Isaac and Hunter for a couple of songs on their last album, and the next one getting released was "Beyond the Limits." Their label had this genius idea to connect the song to the beyond the law aspect of *Mason-Dixon*, which meant that a number of the female cast members were going to be in it. Liam, Isaac, and Hunter would be playing the love interests.

Liam's partner? Kiki.

He'd lost it.

But there was nothing to do to change it. Their record label and the show had already struck up a deal. The contracts had been signed, sealed, and delivered. And Liam wasn't exactly in a position in his career to be making demands of the caliber it would take to change it.

The tie-in with the show was an obvious one, and it was going to give Liam a hell of a lot of exposure. As his album was coming out in a matter of months, exposure like this wasn't something he could really argue with.

So he was just going to have to suck it up and deal. He didn't have to be happy about it, though. And really he needed to push all of the nonsense to the back of his brain for now. It wasn't what he should be focused on when his plane landed at the airport in Tallahassee.

No, what he needed to be focused on was the fact that he was going to see Harper. And that he was meeting her parents for the first time. For the moment that was all that was important. A really good first impression was a must, and him being in a bad mood wasn't going to help that in the slightest.

Add to that the fact that he had a serious case of nerves that he was going to see her—What? He couldn't help it. The woman messed with his emotions—and he was more than a little sluggish.

He was now surviving off of five hours of sleep and two massive cups of coffee. One beer with Isaac and Hunter easily turned into two and he hadn't made it back to his hotel until just before one in the morning. But late night or not, he didn't have to fight with his alarm when it had gone off at six o'clock. He heard it the second it started and was out of bed and in the shower within minutes.

But the moment he saw Harper all of that sluggishness disappeared. Instantly.

He spotted her the second he rounded the corner to the exit. She was standing on the other side of security wearing a knee-length green dress that clung to her breasts but hung loose at her waist. Slight waves were in the black curtain of hair that hung around both of her shoulders.

She was pacing, back and forth between the wall and the set of chairs in the middle of the space. He was about twenty feet away when she turned to make her way back to the wall and looked up. Her gaze landed on him, those violet eyes of hers widened and she froze. Well, for the most part, she pulled her bottom lip into her mouth as she took a deep breath, her shoulders rising and falling.

When he was about three feet away her lip fell from her teeth.

"Hi," she whispered just a little bit nervous herself it seemed.

"Hey." He closed the gap, setting his guitar case on the ground before he reached for her. His arms wrapped around her body, pulling her in close.

Harper came willingly, her arms sliding around his waist as she pressed her face into his neck. They both relaxed in unison, all of the tension and stress melting away with one simple hug. But really there was nothing simple about it. Nothing simple about anything that involved him and her.

Liam didn't realize it until that moment—until the moment he was able to press his nose to her hair and inhale that sweet honey scent that drove him out of his mind—but it was like he'd been holding his breath since the last time he'd seen her. And the relief of having her in his arms again was almost knee weakening.

"You're here," she whispered against his neck, her breath hitting his skin on each syllable.

"I'm here." His mouth was now at her temple and he couldn't stop himself from pressing his lips to the spot.

Harper turned her head, and before either of them could say or do anything else, their mouths found the other's. His hand moved up, his fingers spearing in her hair as he tilted his head and deepened the kiss.

After a minute—or two—Liam forced himself to pull back. He cradled her jaw in his hand, running his thumb back and forth across her cheek as he looked down into her eyes.

"I could stand in this airport and kiss you until the end of time." A soft laugh escaped her mouth, and he couldn't stop himself from leaning forward and capturing it with his lips in another lingering kiss. "But we probably shouldn't be late."

"No, we shouldn't. You have people to meet."

"Very important people. I've been preparing myself all day on winning your mother over with all of my charm."

"Is that so?" One of her eyebrows rose high as she gave him a sideways smirk.

"Yup."

"We had a bit of a heart-to-heart before I came to pick you up." Her palms skimmed up his chest, her hands on his body driving him out of his mind.

How in the world was he going to make it through the next few hours?

Going to her parents' house tonight was not his first choice. He'd be the biggest liar on the face of the planet if he said he didn't desperately want to get Harper alone. He had absolutely no doubt that if it was just the two of them in any room they would both be naked within minutes...probably seconds.

Yeah, that was going to have to wait.

"Really? I'm guessing it was good." He forced himself to focus on the conversation and not the fact that she was about to give him a hard-on in the middle of the airport.

"Yup, very good. But she's still going to put you through your paces tonight."

"I'm more than ready."

"Good." She fisted her hands in his shirt as she stretched up, her lips hovering just above his. "I'm really happy you're here," she said before she opened her mouth over his.

What was he supposed to do besides kiss her back? So what if they were a couple of minutes late.

Chapter Twelve

Sleeping Arrangements

So what prompted the heart-to-heart?" Liam asked when they were both loaded in Harper's Cruiser and heading south to Mirabelle.

He'd been more than a little curious about the conversation she'd had with her mother. Especially as the tension between the two of them had been a constant worry and stress for her over the last couple of weeks.

Harper's thumb stopped tapping out a rhythm against the steering wheel. She cleared her throat, shifting in her seat. "Uh…our sleeping arrangements."

Well, wasn't that a fascinating topic? Liam turned his whole body as he looked at her. She didn't move, just continued to look straight ahead out the windshield, a slight flush starting to creep up her neck.

He wasn't sure if she was embarrassed or…something else.

"Oh really now?" He couldn't stop the grin that turned up his mouth.

"Yeah, she asked if you'd be sleeping on the couch during your visit."

"To which you responded?"

She hesitated for just a second, the corner of her mouth turning up mischievously. "Probably not."

Yeah, she wasn't embarrassed. She was thinking about them in bed together, too. Good, because that was pretty much all he was thinking about. How could he not when every single time he breathed in her honey scent his dick twitched in response?

Down boy.

"And she didn't like that?" he asked.

"Not particularly, no." She shook her head, her black hair falling over her shoulder.

"Your mother does know we've had sex, right?"

"I do in fact think she is aware of this." She took her eyes off the road for a second as she glanced over at him, her eyes covered by her massive sunglasses, before she turned back to the road.

"You know, if it would be better to appease your mother, I can just sleep on the sofa."

The car rolled to a stop at a red light and Harper turned again to look at Liam. "You can't be serious." There was no longer a hint of a smile on her lips.

"In the spirit of catching up and all." The sentence was barely out of his mouth before the smile took over. It was too much for him to keep a straight face as Harper's eyebrows had bunched together in disapproval.

Yeah, he objected to that statement just as much as she apparently did.

"He's got jokes, ladies and gentlemen." She turned back to the road as the light turned green and her foot eased down on the gas pedal. "Don't quit your day job."

Yeah, he was flat out grinning now at her obvious adverse reaction.

God, how he wanted her. Let him count the ways. Yup, she made him wax poetic like nothing or no one else had before.

He found himself reaching over before he even realized it—a reflex of need if he'd ever had one—and running his fingers down her arm. Feeling the warmth of her skin on his palm.

She shivered as she glanced over at him. "Yes?"

"How long are we going to be at your parents'?" he asked, letting her know full well exactly what he wanted.

"A couple of hours."

"And then I get you all to myself?" He grabbed her hand, lacing her fingers with his and bringing it to his mouth.

"And then you get me all to yourself."

The car ride from the airport to Mirabelle took about an hour, but Liam wouldn't be able to tell anyone about the drive besides the few landmarks that Harper specifically pointed out to him. He vaguely remembered a pickup truck graveyard, where about thirty different rusted metal vehicles sat decaying. And the few lighthouses that were stationed on the river that ran parallel to the road.

But that was pretty much it because he wasn't paying attention to anything that was going on outside of the car. Nope, he only had eyes for the woman next to him.

How shocking.

Besides he needed to take advantage of the precious time he

had with her before they got to her parents' house, and to prepare himself for the evening.

Now Liam would be lying if he said he didn't have a small case of nerves as he made his way up the steps of the Laurence household. Yeah, he'd had to charm past girlfriends' parents on several different occasions…but obviously not with these extenuating circumstances.

And they were some seriously *extenuating* circumstances.

There was no plausible deniability in the "I'm having sex with your daughter" department. The proof was in the pudding. Fact: Harper was pregnant. Fact: Liam was the one who'd gotten her pregnant.

And he was going to need to prove that he was much more than the sperm donor.

Much, *much* more.

They walked into the house hand-in-hand and were immediately greeted by two dogs. The larger of the two was on the heels of the tinier one. Liam recognized Luna from all the pictures that Harper had sent him over the last couple of weeks. The dog wriggled her tiny little black body as she circled him, sniffing his shoes.

Luna let out a few friendly barks in greeting, the other dog joining in both the barking and the sniffing.

"This is Luna, and Darby, my parents' dog."

Liam set the black bag hanging from his shoulder on the chair next to the door, letting go of Harper's hand before he crouched down to pet both dogs.

"Hey girls." He ran his hands down both of their backs a couple of times before lightly scratching their chests. They closed their eyes, both of their back legs thumping against the wooden floor in a steady tap.

"Well, that took you absolutely no time at all to win them over."

"And I didn't have to buy either of them a drink first or anything." He winked up at Harper.

"More jokes? What did I tell you about those?"

Liam straightened, grabbing one of her hands and linking their fingers together as his other hand slid around to her back. He brought his face in close to hers, their mouths mere centimeters away. "Oh, you like it. Admit it."

"Maybe a little."

He pressed his lips to hers, because really why wouldn't he? He would forever take advantage of any and all opportunities that involved them kissing, or touching, or well, anything for that matter.

But just as it was getting really good—her tongue being in his mouth—someone cleared their throat.

Harper pulled away, spinning around. Liam looked up to find her father in the hallway. He had light brown hair, Harper's eyes, and an unreadable expression covering his face. His eyes dipped to where Harper's hand was held in Liam's for just a second before they came back up, focusing on Liam's face and still revealing absolutely nothing.

So much for good first impressions.

Harper's hand tightened in his before she let go, taking a step toward her father. "Hi, Daddy."

"Hey, sweet pea." Mr. Laurence wrapped his arms around her, kissing her on the temple before pulling back. "This him?" He looked at Liam.

"This is him." Harper nodded.

Liam stepped forward, sticking his now free hand in front of him as he moved. "It's nice to meet you, Mr. Laurence."

Mr. Laurence's hand tightened as he shook Liam's firmly. "So you're my daughter's new boyfriend."

"Yes, sir."

"Hmm." Mr. Laurence's eyes looked Liam over again, for a good couple of seconds that almost—*almost*—made Liam squirm. "Well, all right then. You can call me Paul. No need for this sir or mister nonsense. You want a gin and tonic?" he asked, letting go of Liam's hand as the corner of his mouth twitched, the only indication that he might possibly be okay with how things were.

Or maybe was somewhere in the realm of being okay. He was apparently accepting enough to make him a drink.

The sudden shift had Liam coming up short, but he recovered almost instantly. "Absolutely," he said, and nodded.

Liam grabbed the bag on the chair, slipping the strap on his shoulder. And then he was reaching for Harper's hand—a hand that she was holding out for him as she gave him a sideways smirk—and they walked to the kitchen, following behind Paul.

"Well, that's one hurdle down," he whispered to her.

"Don't get ahead of yourself, sparky. The next one is going to be about as easy as clearing the Empire State Building," she said right before they walked into the kitchen.

Delilah Laurence was at the oven, pulling a pan out and setting it on top of the stove. All Liam could see was the back of her, the same thick black curtain of hair as Harper's hitting her right between the shoulder blades. She was just a tad bit shorter and more slender than her daughter, but as she turned and he saw her face, the relationship was obvious.

Same full lips and almond-shaped eyes, though hers were a light blue as opposed to the violet that Harper and her father shared.

"Ahh, you're here." Mrs. Laurence pulled the oven mitts from her hands as she crossed the room, setting them on the kitchen island before she untied her apron and put it on the counter as well.

"Mom, this is Liam."

"Mrs. Laurence." He nodded. "It's nice to meet you."

Harper's mother folded her arms across her chest as she looked him over. The scrutiny in her eyes *well* surpassed what he'd been through just moments before with Paul. "So you're the father of my first grandchild?"

Well, she was just going to jump right on in now, wasn't she?

"Yes, ma'am," he answered, still implementing his *don't look away* strategy. It was like staring down the barrel of a loaded gun.

"Harper says I need to give you a chance, so I'm going to."

"I won't disappoint you, Mrs. Laurence."

"Good." That one word was dripping in skepticism. The *we'll just see about that* heard loud and clear by everyone in the room.

All right. He could deal with this. He wasn't going to cower. He refused. Getting her approval was an obstacle he needed to figure out, and he would. There wasn't any other option, because in the end he *was* going to be with Harper.

"I brought you and Mr. Laurence something for having me

over tonight," Liam said, holding up the bag in his hand. He might as well start with presents.

"Paul," Mr. Laurence corrected while Mrs. Laurence said nothing.

She had no problems with *ma'am* or *missus*. He apparently would not be calling her Delilah anytime soon.

"Harper told me you were the family chef and an excellent one at that," Liam said as he pulled out the square box from the bag. It was about one foot by one foot, four inches tall, and made of solid wood.

Mrs. Laurence's eyes widened in surprise; she apparently hadn't expected him to come bearing gifts.

One point to him.

She set the box on the counter, pushing back the metal hook that kept the box latched, and lifted the top. Inside sat three separate trays stacked on top of each other, each sectioning off sixteen different tins of spices. So forty-eight in total.

"They're specialty spices from this shop in Nashville. They blend all of them and grow most of them. They have hundreds so I tried to get you a good assortment."

Mrs. Laurence lifted one of the tins, popping the top and inhaling deep. She repeated the process a few times, exploring the different aromas. Liam totally got it. He'd spent *hours* in the little shop trying to figure out which ones to buy the first time he'd shopped there. And the second. And the third. Okay, every time.

He'd called the owners a week ago to put the box together, and they'd shipped it to him in California.

Mrs. Laurence put all of the tins back in the box before she ran her hands across the smooth top of the cherry-stained wood. Her fingers traced the embossed company logo branded into the wood before she looked up at Liam, a warmth in her eyes that definitely had not been there just moments before. "Thank you. This was very thoughtful."

Okay, maybe *five* points to him.

"You're welcome. They're my favorite spices to cook with, so I thought you might enjoy them."

She nodded, running her hand across the top again, almost reverently.

"And this is for you," Liam said as he pulled out another box and handed it over to Paul.

"Well I'll be. Two gifts." Another twitch to Paul's mouth that almost, *almost,* looked like a smile.

He pulled off the top of the box to reveal the parts of a hand-made fly fishing rod that was—in Liam's humble opinion—one of the best. "It's a Flanagan. Harper said that you were a fisherman on your off time."

"You fish, too?" Paul asked.

"Yes, and that's the same one that my brother, father, and I use."

"This is…impressive." Paul looked back down at the rod in his hand, examining it further. "You bring yours?" He brought his gaze back up to Liam's.

"Don't leave home without it."

"You and I are going to go fishing sometime. We can catch something for Delilah to use her fancy new spices on. That sound good to you?"

"Sounds perfect."

And just like that Paul's mouth split into a grin.

One parent down. One to go.

* * *

Harper was in a daze throughout all of dinner. How could she not be? She'd been shocked pretty much the second she and Liam had walked into her parents' house.

Not only had the man brought gifts. But he'd gotten the most personal gifts of...well...*ever*.

The thing that *really* got to her? He'd known what to get from something she'd said *months* ago. When Liam had made her dinner in Nashville, she'd mentioned that her mother loved to cook and that her father fished.

And he'd *remembered*.

He'd *freaking* remembered.

Liam had won Paul over, something she'd noticed pretty quickly. She also knew it had more to do with how Liam was with her than from that fishing rod. Though the rod hadn't hurt in Liam's endeavors.

As for her mother, well, that was going to take a little bit more time. But he was making pretty good progress with her, considering it was only the first night.

They left just before eight thirty, laden with multiple Tupperware containers filled with roast beef, mashed potatoes, grilled zucchini, and apple pie. Luna lay in Liam's lap during the five-minute ride to her house, him scratching her belly as she lay on her back entirely blissed out at his attention.

Harper pulled up in front of her apartment building and put

her Cruiser into Park. Liam's gaze focused on the building in front of them where about thirty little apartments were stacked three high and ten across on ten-foot-high pylons. The sun was setting over the beach that stretched out behind it.

"So this is home," she said as a sudden wave of nerves overtook her. She knew what was going to happen when they went inside and she was both excited and maybe just a little bit scared. "It's kind of small, but I wanted to live on the water and the options in my budget are somewhat limited."

"I'm sure it's perfect. Lead the way."

Harper grabbed the food while Liam got his bags. Luna was on a retractable leash, and she walked over as far as it would stretch to a patch of grass next to the parking lot. She did her business before walking over to the stairs and waiting for Liam and Harper.

Liam followed behind Harper and Luna as they made their way up the three flights of stairs. The entire time all she was thinking about was the fact that he could probably see right up the skirt of her dress.

Good thing she was wearing sexy panties, because…well…obviously. He was probably going to be seeing them in a matter of minutes.

Oh, would you look at that her palms were sweating, so much so that she dropped her keys when they got to the door. After a good ten seconds of fumbling with them she managed to get them in the lock.

When they walked inside, Harper let Luna off the leash—who immediately headed for the back bedroom to most likely put herself to bed—before heading for the kitchen. "Make yourself comfortable."

Bags hit the ground and Harper was fully aware of Liam's boots as they walked around the hardwood floors of her apartment, taking everything in.

The walls were a light green, soft enough to not overpower other things in the room while bringing in the tones from random accents like the painting above her TV and the floral pillows on her overstuffed gray couch.

Two bookshelves took up the corner in the right filled with books, random knickknacks, and picture frames. The shag rug on the floor was salmon—another color pulled from the painting and the pillows—and teal curtains hung from the window on the other side of the TV.

The only thing separating the living room from the kitchen was a bar. Two backless stools sat in front of it, and on the far right side a variety of mismatched and beyond varied wineglasses—that she hadn't used in months—hung from little brackets attached to the cabinets above.

More light filled the rooms as Harper flipped a switch in the kitchen, heading for the refrigerator in the corner. Her kitchen was small with bright lemon yellow walls that she painted herself because she loved the way they popped with the black and white tiles that covered the counters.

It had taken her months to figure out the right feel to the kitchen. The perfect find? An antique cherry wood table, with four matching chairs, that sat in front of the white French doors. More teal curtains were in here, pulled to each side and tied back with a yellow sash that matched the walls in the kitchen. On the other side of the doors was a back deck that overlooked the water.

That was where she spent most of her evenings, her feet

propped up on the railing as she watched the sunset. Small space or not, she'd made it her own…made it her home. And now Liam was in it.

He was here.

Harper pulled away from the refrigerator, closing it behind her as she headed for the living room. Liam was standing in the middle of the room and filling it in only the way that he could.

"I like it." He nodded, still looking around. "It feels like you."

"Yeah?" she asked as she leaned against the door frame, fiddling with the ring on her finger. Spinning it 'round and 'round.

"Yeah."

"Well, that's good. Because that's your bed." She let go of the ring as she pointed to the sofa. "In the spirit of appeasing my mother and all with separate sleeping arrangements."

To be honest, Harper was beyond shocked that her mother hadn't brought that subject up again before they'd left for the night. Didn't matter that she'd embargoed certain topics from her mother earlier before picking Liam up from the airport. Another off-limit topic was marriage or discussion of the future. If Harper and Liam hadn't discussed it yet, it wasn't going to be brought up over dinner.

Nor would it be discussed now for that matter. Liam's eyes narrowed and the banked heat that had been simmering since she'd picked him up from the airport blazed over in an instant.

"You know," he said as he stalked toward her, shrinking the space between them, "getting your mother's approval means a lot to me. But I'm going to tell you right now, being in the same town as you and not being in your bed would be beyond difficult for me. But being under the same roof? Impossible."

He was right in front of her, the smell of his cologne over-whelming her in an instant.

It was a scent that she'd been dreaming of since the last time she'd seen him. A scent that had filled her head the entire time they'd spent in the car. A scent that had her heart beating fast and her head swimming in the best kind of way.

One of his hands went to her waist and was now sliding around to the small of her back as he pulled her from the wall and right up against him. Her hands went to his hips, an attempt to steady herself, but her hands on his body was a surefire way to get her entirely unsteady. Add to that the fact that he was pressed up against her.

And there went touch. It belonged to him as well.

"That so?" she somehow managed to ask as she looked up at him.

"Honey." His voice dropped low when he said *honey*. That one word filling her ears and moving to her chest before it spread through her entire body. "The only person who is going to stop me from finally waking up next to you tomorrow morning is you."

Bye, bye hearing. It was his.

"Me?"

"Yeah. You. Do you want separate sleeping arrangements?" His voice somehow dropped even lower with the last question and the words vibrated through her.

"No." She shook her head.

"And what do you want?" He moved so that their faces were only inches apart. His green-gold eyes were all that she saw, tak-ing over her sight as well.

Such an easy answer. "You."

"Good." And just like that his mouth was on hers and she was opening up for him immediately, needing his taste on her tongue.

He'd taken over all of her senses. She was gone. He owned her. But she'd already known that. Had known that when she'd first met him.

"I need *you*, Liam," she whispered against his mouth.

"You got me. Now where's your bedroom?"

Chapter Thirteen

Promise?

Liam followed behind Harper, his hand firmly in hers, as she led him to her bedroom. There were more French doors in here as well, and a quick glance showed they led out to the same back deck as the ones in the dining room. The setting sun filled the space with a warm light.

Pinks, reds, and oranges streamed through the glass panes and reflected on the walls. Besides the queen bed, that was the only thing Liam took in as his gaze was now fixed solely on the woman in front of him.

Good Lord she was stunning.

His hands were on her body again, moving up and down her sides as he pressed his lips to hers. And then he got to that spot under her ear, opening his mouth over that patch of freckles that he loved to taste so damn much.

"I don't understand it." Harper gasped, her hands fisting in his shirt.

"Understand what?" He moved his lips down and across her jaw, kissing every spot he could get to.

"I feel like I've been missing this for years. Missing *you* for years."

He pulled back, his hands going to the back of her head, his fingers spearing through her hair. "I'm going to let you in on a little secret. I missed you even before I met you."

She gasped at his words, her hands tightening at his sides. "You never cease to amaze me, Liam James."

"And I'm never going to stop."

"Promise?"

"I swear." He moved one of his hands down through her hair, pulling his fingers through the strands as he traced her spine. "I got you a little something, too, you know."

"You what?"

"A gift. I couldn't help myself. I saw it and I knew I needed to see it on you." He reached for his front pocket, fishing out the necklace that he'd dropped in there only moments before.

He pulled his hand up, the delicate silver chain dangling from his finger. The pendant at the end swayed back and forth, the amethyst stone and the ring of tiny diamonds that surrounded it catching in the sunlight that streamed through the open windows.

Another gasp escaped Harper's mouth as her eyes moved from the necklace to him. "It's beautiful."

"Of course it is; it matches your eyes. Now turn around."

She did so, gathering her hair to the side as he unclasped the chain and looped it around her throat. When it was in place he leaned forward, kissing the back of her neck. She dropped her hair as she spun to face him again.

"Thank you." She reached up, fingering the pendant. "But I didn't get you anything."

"You're wrong there, honey. You're giving me the greatest gift of all." He reached out, his palm going flat on her belly. "This baby."

"Liam." She stretched up, pressing her mouth to his.

"I don't want anything else," he whispered against her lips. "Well, besides seeing you wearing nothing besides that necklace, that is."

"I think that can be very easily arranged."

"Good." But he knew for a fact that as soon as he started to strip Harper out of her clothes he was going to be good and fully distracted, so he started to undress first.

He reached behind him, grabbing a fistful of shirt and pulling it over his head as he kicked off his boots. But before he could reach for his belt, Harper's hands were there, sliding the buckle out and pulling down the zipper of his jeans.

He needed his mouth on her, and the second his lips brushed over her neck she let out a soft sigh, her body melting into his. And just like that he got a little waylaid from his mission, and it didn't help that Harper was now pressing herself firmly into his erection.

Focus, man. Pull it together.

He reached up, palming one of her breasts and she cried out as her body stiffened.

His head came up immediately and he cradled her face in his hands.

"Sorry, they're just really sore."

"Harper, don't apologize."

"I just…I know how much you like them." Uncertainty flickered through her eyes and it almost did him in. "I don't want you to be disappointed if it's a little different this time around."

"Disappointed?" That word should never, *ever,* be equated to sex with her. "Not possible."

"Liam, that's not true. I'm pregnant and my body is changing and—"

"Do you trust me?" He cut her off as he leaned forward and nipped at her bottom lip, their eyes not breaking contact.

"Yes," she whispered.

"Good. And you should know," he said as he dropped his hands to the skirt of her dress, slowly working the fabric up, "I was amazed by your body the first time I saw it." The skirt was at her hips and he tugged, pulling it past her ribs, and her breasts, and over her head. "And if anything I'm even more enamored with it now. And you know why?"

He dropped the dress to the floor as his eyes raked over her body, taking in everything. Her breasts were currently decorated with a cream and black lace bra, and matching panties covered her hips.

"Why?" she whispered, her hands falling to her sides.

He reached behind her back, unhooking her bra and pulling it from her arms before he fell to his knees. "*Because* it's changing." His hands slid across her hips as he pulled her close and pressed his mouth to her belly.

Her fingers were in his hair, her nails lightly raking against his scalp.

"You. Are. Perfect." He kissed a circle around her belly button between each word. And he had to stop himself from saying the rest of the sentence that was on the tip of his tongue.

And. You. Are. Mine.

She was concerned that things would be different this time around? That there was a chance he'd be disappointed? Well, that was the most ridiculous thing he had ever heard in his life.

For one, he still held firmly to the fact that she was the most beautiful woman he'd ever seen. Two, absolutely nothing was going to change that. Three, she was carrying his child. *Their* child. If that wasn't the sexiest thing in the world, he had no idea what was.

And four…well, he was in love with her. In love with *everything* about her, from her body to her mind and *all* that there was in between.

Speaking of between…

He hooked his fingers in either side of the fabric of her hips before he pulled down, sliding her panties down her legs. And then his mouth was at the very core of her, doing everything in his power to make her lose her mind.

It didn't take very long before her unsteady breaths started to fill the room, and when his tongue found her clit she was gasping his name.

"Liam, I…I can't…can't do this standing up."

"Lie down."

The second she was flat on her back on the bed he had both of her legs over his shoulders and he picked up right where he'd left off.

He had her coming across his tongue twice before he moved his mouth up, trailing his lips across her stomach and her ribs before he was on his feet. He pushed his jeans and boxers down, pulling his socks off as he freed his legs.

Harper was lying at the center of the bed, and he kneeled down, the mattress dipping as he pulled her legs apart.

"What do you want to do about protection?" He had to ask before they went any further, before he lowered himself on top of her and completely lost his mind.

Her eyes dipped to his cock for just a second before she looked back up at him, the sexiest grin tilting her mouth. "Well, I know your swimmers are overachievers, but I don't think you're going to get me pregnant again."

"Not what I was talking about." He shook his head as he touched her knees, his palms sliding up the inside of her thighs.

Maybe touching her wasn't going to help him in staying focused. Who was he kidding? She was naked—except for that necklace—and spread out in front of him. He was lucky he was stringing sentences together at this point. And really the thought of being inside of her with nothing between them was enough to obliterate his brain.

He'd *never* had sex sans condom.

"I'm clean." He forced himself to look at her eyes as opposed to her gloriously naked body. "I haven't been with anyone else since well before you and I was tested before that."

"I'm clean, too. They did a full blood work up at my first doctor's appointment."

"Good," he said as he leaned over her. He pressed his lips to her belly again, lingering there for a minute before he moved up her body. He spread more kisses across her ribs, stopping when he got to her breasts.

His gaze met hers as he lowered his mouth to one of her nipples and ever so slightly ran his tongue across it. This time she didn't stiffen or flinch in pain. Quite the opposite in fact, her eyes closed as her head fell back onto the pillow and she moaned his name.

He repeated the move on her other nipple making her body writhe. He spent a minute or two showing her breasts the admiration they deserved, gently palming both as he ran his fingers and mouth across the softest, sweetest skin known to man.

"So beautiful," he whispered as he brushed his lips over the swells. "Every. Single. Inch. Of. You." And then he was moving up past her neck, and *finally* ending at her lips.

He settled between her thighs as they both staked claims to each other's mouths. Harper's hands were on his back, moving lower and lower until she grabbed his ass and thrust her hips up. She apparently wanted him inside of her just as desperately as he wanted to be there.

He pulled his mouth away from hers, looking down and finding her gaze.

"I need you, Liam." That was the second time she'd said those words tonight and they'd killed him both times.

Killed. Him.

Everything about her killed him, and what she did next was no exception. She reached down, stroking his cock before she guided him inside of her. He slid in the rest of the way, ever so slowly until she was wrapped around him to the hilt.

Good God, he wasn't going to survive this. What he *was* going to do was lose his damn mind. Nothing had ever felt this good. Nothing. Ever. In the history of anything.

He pulled out before he flexed his hips and slid back inside of her. A soft moan escaped her mouth as her body arched off the bed. The movement offered her breasts up and who was he to deny himself?

He lowered his mouth and gently swept his tongue across first one nipple and then the other. Her hands were in his hair, holding his head to her breasts. He slowly rocked his hips moving in and out of her at a torturous pace.

"Liam," she gasped as she lightly tugged on his hair.

He pulled his mouth away from her chest and looked up at her. She dropped one of her hands, running her fingers down the side of his face and across his jaw, her nails rasping his beard.

"Harder." Her eyes darkened as she said the word.

Harder? Okay, so she *was* trying to kill him. It was taking everything in him to not lose every ounce of his control.

"I don't want to hurt you." He turned his head and kissed her fingertips.

"You won't." She pulled her legs up, her thighs cradling his body as she planted her feet on the mattress and thrust her hips up against him.

"Harper," he groaned, dropping his head and trying to hold on.

But there was nothing for it. She grabbed his hand, putting it on her hip and making him squeeze tight as she continued to forcefully move against him.

When he looked up at her again he caught her gaze, and the need in her eyes was too much for him, but the next words out of her mouth were what really sent him over the edge.

"I trust you."

He covered her mouth with his, breathing in her gasp and the moans of pleasure that followed. His hand on her hip tightened and he held on to her as he moved.

As *they* moved.

Together.

Neither of them held back, both of them taking every ounce of pleasure that they could find in each other. He was doing everything in his power to hold on to his release and wait for hers, but he wasn't going to be able to hold out much longer.

It was all *too* good. *Too* perfect. Moving inside of her. Breathing her in. *Finally* being with her again. Finding what he'd been desperately missing. Finding her.

When he pulled back and looked down at her—at her black hair spread out across the pillow, at those violet eyes that were lost in pleasure, at the flush that was covering her skin, at her mouth that was gasping for air in between moaning his name in pleasure—his control snapped.

And not a moment too soon, either. Her hands were on his ass again and she was moving wildly underneath him. He levered himself up on his other arm and thrust into her powerfully.

Over. And over. And over again.

Harper's back was arching off the bed as she cried out his name. Her body pulsed around him and he let go, spilling inside her. Neither of them stopped moving until they were both good and truly spent. And as his hips slowed he leaned down, pressing his mouth to hers.

"You were right," he whispered between kisses.

"About?"

"It *was* different." He pulled back just enough so that he could look into her eyes.

"And it's more." She smiled up at him.

"So much more," he agreed.

* * *

Harper's pregnancy wasn't a secret to any of her friends. After she'd told her parents she'd gone and revealed the news to everyone else. In a few weeks' time it would've been difficult to hide as she would be showing. Not to mention there were certain things she wasn't doing…like drinking coffee or alcohol. Dropping those two habits was more than noticeable.

It wasn't like Harper had a problem with alcohol or anything. She could be in social settings and not have a drink, but she would normally indulge in more than a few glasses of wine a week.

Also, there was the fact that one of her closest friends owned a bar. As she would usually go into the Sleepy Sheep for a beer and hang out at least one night a week, it didn't go unnoticed by anyone in their circle when she stopped.

And finally, as her friends were breeding like a bunch of Catholic rabbits, the signs were all there and more than obvious.

Another thing that Harper hadn't kept from everyone was who the father was. So when they found out that Liam was going to be in town, it was *demanded* that they get to meet him. As Harper's parents' got first dibs, her friends got second.

They weren't the only ones making demands on a meet-and-greet, either.

Liam's siblings—Adele and Logan—had made the trip over the night before along with Abby and another one of the Stampede players, Jace Kilpatrick. As it turned out, Jace was not only good friends with Logan but Liam as well.

Jace was the only person Harper hadn't met—even briefly—during her trip to Jacksonville weeks ago. The four of them were all staying at the Seaside Escape Inn, a massive house right on the water that doubled as Hannah and Shep's house. It was also where everyone was meeting up for a Fourth of July cookout that afternoon.

The inn was actually the reason Hannah had migrated to the south…or really the catalyst. Being madly in love with Shep was the ultimate motivator for her moving to the area. When her grandmother Gigi had passed away and the will had been read, Hannah had been surprised to find out that not only had her grandmother bought the inn that the two had spent a summer in thirteen years previous, but that she'd left it to Hannah.

The renovations on the three-story building were still ongoing, but there were enough rooms finished for Abby, Logan, Adele, and Jace to stay there no problem. Which was good as they were all spending a few days in Mirabelle while Liam was in town, too.

When she and Liam pulled up to the driveway of the inn, he let out a long low whistle. "Well, this is impressive."

"Wait till you see the inside. It's gorgeous."

"I have no doubt." He shook his head before he looked over at her. "Don't move," he said before he turned away and opened the passenger door of the Cruiser and jumped out. He rounded the front and walked to her side, opening her door as she moved in her seat to face him.

"Such a gentleman."

"Hmm, I don't know about that." His mouth quirked to the side as he put his hands on her thighs and moved them up under the skirt of her light blue dress until he got to the edges of her panties. "I had ulterior motives." He leaned forward and pressed his lips to hers.

"I can see that," she said as she looped her arms around his neck.

"I'm letting you know right now, it's going to be a problem for me to not have my hands on you whenever we're in the same room." He kissed a line down her jaw and to her neck, pressing his lips to the amethyst pendant that hung just above her breasts. "Same goes with my mouth."

"I've noticed that as well. You making up for lost time?"

"Not possible." He shook his head, his hands moving out from under her dress and to her hips, before he wrapped them around her waist and helped her out of the car. He leaned into her body as he smoothed his palms down the skirt.

"And why's that?" she asked as she looked up at him.

"Because I'd have to make up for the twenty-nine years of my life before I met you."

How in the world was she supposed to respond to that? Didn't matter. He didn't give her a chance to speak anyway. He kissed her again, his mouth parting hers as his tongue dipped past her lips.

"Come on, it's time for me to impress all of your friends."

She was more than a little dazed as he grabbed her hand and

guided her away from the car, closing the door behind her. But dazed or not, as he led her up the stairs, she had no doubt he was going to succeed with the impressing-her-friends part.

No doubt at all.

Now as to her impressing his family and friend? That was still up in the air. She'd be lying if she said she wasn't more than a little nervous, her first—and very short—impression with Logan and Adele had been less than stellar. She was the girl who walked out on their brother after all.

But they hadn't even made it into the house before they ran into Logan and Abby, who were making their way down the stairs from the second floor. Logan was walking behind her, pulling at the skirt of her yellow sundress.

"Would you stop that?" She spun around and swatted at his hands when they got to the landing.

"Come on, Red, I didn't get a good look at your bathing suit. I just want one more peek at the bottoms," he said as he reached for her again, but she dodged his hands.

"Oh, I think you got to look plenty when you stripped me out of them earlier. You're the reason we're late."

"It isn't my fault you came parading out of the bathroom in nothing but a tiny red polka dot bikini. Really it's your fault we're late."

Liam cleared his throat, making both Abby and Logan look over. "You two need a second?"

The flush that crept up Abby's chest was immediate, and while she looked horrified all Logan could do was grin. "See we aren't late at all. Liam and Harper just got here."

Harper hadn't met Logan before that encounter in the ballroom at the hotel. And yes she'd seen him in pictures and on TV, but his resemblance to his brother wasn't as obvious as it was when they were standing right next to each other. Sure they didn't look like identical twins, but it was more than apparent that they were brothers, complete with the same green-gold eyes.

"Yeah, and you don't see him trying to lift up *her* skirt," Abby said.

"I wouldn't be too sure about that." Liam shook his head.

"You're just as bad as your brother." Abby frowned at Liam as she walked over. But when her gaze shifted to Harper a smile broke out across her lips before the two women embraced. "You look to be in considerably better spirits than the last time I saw you."

"I wonder why that is," Logan said as he closed the gap as well. "It's nice to see you again, Harper. And in less surprising circumstances." Before Harper could say anything Logan had pulled her into a hug, too.

Some of her tension and worry melted away in an instant. "Same." She nodded.

"You ready to be entirely overwhelmed?" Logan asked as he gave his brother a quick hug, both of them doing the man-pat-on-back thing before they let go. "There are more people in that house than we're even related to, and they are all beyond fascinated to meet you, my friend."

"So we shouldn't keep them waiting any longer I think." Liam reached for Harper's hand again. "Lead the way, honey."

"You know they're going to like me better than you," Logan said from behind them.

"We'll just see about that." Liam turned and looked at his brother over his shoulder.

Abby sighed, looking at Harper. "Children I tell you. One man-child against another. Good luck."

Harper bit down on her lower lip trying not to laugh. The back-and-forth between the brothers making her feel at ease...though, really, the person she was most nervous about meeting was their sister.

When they walked into the house it was to find the usual bedlam that was a get-together with her friends these days...only more so as their numbers were continually growing.

On the other side of the massive dining room table, Harper spotted a good number of people through the French doors, talking as they hung out on the wraparound porch. The grill was already going and Shep was the one manning it. Bennett, Tripp, and Finn were with him, all with a beer in hand. Mel was standing next to Beth who was kneeling down slathering her seven-year-old nephew Grant with sunscreen.

But Harper didn't head that way; instead she led Liam to the Tuscan-villa-themed kitchen that any master chef would covet.

Shep was the one making use of the space more than anyone else, because Hannah's talents in the kitchen were pretty much limited to sandwich making. And not all that shockingly Harper spotted her friend seated at the island in the middle of the kitchen. She was chopping fruit while she chatted with Adele who was busy slicing cheese and stacking it on a plate.

Brendan and Paige were at the stove, both stirring something in their respective pots. His free hand was on her lower back, moving in slow steady circles. From behind, it barely looked like

Paige was pregnant…Harper had no doubt this would *not* be the case for her.

Liam let out another low whistle. "What I could do in here," he said as he looked around the room.

Adele spotted them first, putting her knife down as she slid off the stool. "Well, look who it is. The man of the hour." She crossed the room, her eyes dipping down to Liam's hand that was still holding Harper's.

Though a second later he had to let go of said hand so he could hug his sister. "Man of the hour?" he asked as he wrapped her up in a hug.

"Yup." Adele nodded as she pulled back. "They've been *anxiously* awaiting your arrival. But I'm much more interested in who you arrived with." And with that, Adele's sharp golden brown eyes were focused on Harper.

The shrewd once-over was one that Harper was more than used to, how could she not be when she'd received it so many times from her mother? But Adele's was less one of being critical, and more one of assessment. She was fact-gathering. This was something Harper understood entirely as she was doing the exact same thing to Adele.

Their meeting in Jacksonville had been less than optimal…and to be quite honest, Harper had really only been focused on Liam at that more than stressful moment in time. But now she got to take in the full picture of Liam and Logan's sister.

Adele was stunning, no doubt about it. Good family genes were a given when it came to the Jameses. She'd inherited the same height as her brothers, coming in at five-nine or five-ten. Her statuesque figure only added to her imposing air.

"I've been waiting to hug the woman who's turned my brother inside out. It's something not easily done," she said, now grinning hugely.

"It's nice to properly meet you." Harper couldn't help but reflect the grin on Adele's face. And when the two women embraced, the last of her nervousness melted away.

Just. Like. That.

Chapter Fourteen

Anytime, Anywhere, Anything

Harper was more than impressed at how Liam was keeping track of everyone at the house. She had no doubt it wasn't an easy thing in the slightest as there were almost fifty people in attendance.

Not only were her friends there, but a plethora of her friends' parents (hers included), grandparents, cousins, aunts, and uncles milled around. Yet somehow he was keeping up with most of them as well.

But his effort in the moment wasn't all that was getting to her. No, it was that everything she'd told him he'd remembered.

Everything.

He'd apparently been more than paying attention during all of those lengthy conversations they'd had every day over the last two weeks. Which shouldn't have been all that surprising after what had happened at her parents' the night before, but it did surprise her. He was able to figure out more than most of her friends before introductions.

Not only did he immediately know the name of Trevor when he spotted the two-year-old who belonged to Brendan and Paige, but he also knew the name of the three-year-old girl that the boy was walking around hand-in-hand with.

"Penny." He nodded his head at the tiny toddler. "Baby sister of Grant," he said before he looked to the little boy who was currently getting another slathering in suntan lotion by his aunt Beth. "And Nora who's been out there for most of the afternoon." He indicated the Gulf of Mexico with his beer bottle over the railing of the porch they were standing on. "Learning how to surf from Jace, hockey player for the Jacksonville Stampede and licensed surf instructor."

"Hey that one doesn't count in your wealth of knowledge." She shook her head. "Jace is your friend."

"Why not?" His brow furrowed. "He's here, and I know who he is."

"Do your sister and brother count, too?" she asked, pursing her lips together and narrowing her eyes.

"If I can identify them, they count."

"If you say so." She rolled her eyes but couldn't stop the grin from taking over her face.

"Anyway, back to what I was saying. Nora was out there learning to surf with Dale, Hamilton, Preston, and Baxter. Preston is your friend going as far back as high school. While Baxter has only been in the inner circle for the last few years since he and Preston started a relationship. Baxter and Preston are now married, a new development that happened in…" he trailed off for a second before he snapped his fingers, the month suddenly coming to him. "January." He finished before he took a swig of beer that just so happened to be one of Shep's creations.

Another fact that was known by the man next to her: not only did Nathanial Shepherd own a bar, but he brewed his own beer that he sold in said bar. Liam was to be given his own personal tour later in the week.

And it didn't stop there.

She didn't need to remind him that Jax and Grace were the parents of the adorable Rosie Mae. Though the infant was currently in her father's arms, the matching red hair between father and daughter being enough of an indicator of the connection.

"Grace isn't hard to identify, either, as the tiny blond snuggled up against Jax's side keeps grabbing his ass." Liam raised his eyebrows as his own hand traveled south of the border and squeezed Harper's ass.

"Really?"

"What? I told you that I made no promises of keeping my hands off you."

"That you didn't."

He *really* hadn't, a fact that in no way escaped a single one of her friends. And the second Liam stepped away to go "jam out" with Hamilton who'd brought his guitar with him, Harper heard all about it.

"Good Lord. That man is *all* about you," Paige whispered out of the side of her mouth as she sidled up next to Harper. Or really *waddled* up next to Harper, her ever-growing belly preceding the way. "How you doing?"

"I'm doing okay." Harper nodded, leaning against the railing and looking out to the emerald green waters that stretched out in front of her. "I'm still trying to figure it all out and Liam doesn't even flinch. He just...*goes with it.* Like this is how it's supposed to be."

"That's how he's always been," someone said as they came up on Harper's other side.

She turned to find Adele, also holding a bottle of Shep's beer in her hand, and now wearing a pair of retro sunglasses, complete with sapphire blue rhinestones on the top corners.

Abby was right behind her, joining the small group.

"Twenty-five years of having Logan and Liam as brothers." Adele shook her head. "And they both fall harder than I've ever seen them fall within months of each other. That's crazy, right? Now, one could ask themself, *what are the odds?* But it isn't about the odds."

All eyes were on Adele, but it was Paige who asked, "And what's it about?"

"Fate. It was just a matter of time before the two of you crossed paths."

"And how do you figure that?" Harper couldn't stop herself from asking.

Adele tipped the neck of the bottle of beer in her hand toward Abby. "Because, Abby here is a permanent fixture in Logan's life. So whether it was two months ago in Nashville, or two weeks ago in Jacksonville, or a year from now when I have no doubt Abby and Logan will be walking down the aisle—"

"Oh really now?" Abby interrupted her apparent future sister-in-law.

"Yes, and I'd be more than happy to make that bet with you

right now. There really isn't any other option besides the two of you getting married."

Abby opened her mouth, but nothing came out before she snapped it back shut, speechless.

"Anyway," Adele continued, "the two of you would've no doubt found each other, and Liam would've been just as *unflinching* then as he is now. It isn't just because you're pregnant that he's not walking away."

Now Harper was the one who was speechless. But before she could find her tongue to say anything, Paige's mother Denise was at the door, summoning Paige and Abby to help her with something in the kitchen.

And then there were two.

"It's beautiful here." Adele nodded to the water as she took a step forward and leaned on the railing.

"Don't you live on the water, too?"

"Yeah. I just love it down here near the beaches. I mean, I miss Nashville sometimes, but there really is something about waking up to the water crashing against the shore right outside your window."

"I agree to that."

They stared out at the water for a minute, the sun momentarily covered by a white fluffy cloud.

Harper was about to say something. What? She didn't know because the next words that came out of Adele's mouth had her brain going blank.

"Don't hurt him." Even though the *again* was left off the end of that sentence, both of them were aware of it lingering in the air around them. "My brothers are the best kind of men out there."

Adele turned, and Harper mirrored the movement, looking at the woman next to her. "And if you ever tell them I said that, I will deny it to my last breath."

"Understood. Thanks for not hating me. For giving *me* a chance."

"We all make mistakes." Adele shrugged. "I believe in second chances…not so much third chances, though."

"I agree with that."

It was then that Logan was at the French doors calling their names. "You guys should get in here. Something epic is going down."

They both turned and headed for the house, and before they stepped inside she heard what was so epic.

Liam was singing "I'm Gonna Be" by the Proclaimers.

He was sitting at the very back of the living room, Hamilton on his left and Dale on his right. Dale didn't have a guitar in his hands, but he was making use of them by tapping out the rhythm of the song against the legs of the chair he was sitting on. But even though his lips were moving, he wasn't very loud.

"Of course this is what he's singing," Adele said as she took the spot next to Harper. There wasn't that much space left as most of the people from the party were filling the room. "The eighties is his favorite decade when it comes to music."

"I actually knew that one," Harper said as she glanced over. "David Bowie is at the top of the list."

"Yup, and I'll bet you money he pulls out a Bruce Springsteen song before the end of the night."

"Well, Shep will appreciate that. He's a huge Springsteen fan."

"I'm going to need you to get a little bit louder there, Dale."

Liam broke away from the song for just a moment, but Hamilton carried on by himself, not breaking stride. And when Dale and Liam rejoined a second later, Dale was definitely singing louder than before.

When they got to the chorus Liam's eyes came up, focusing on Harper with an intensity in his gaze that instantly had her stomach fluttering.

"See, it's that right there," Adele whispered in Harper's ear. "That look he just gave you. I'd swear on anything that my brother will never walk away from you."

Harper really wanted that to be true. Wanted it to be true more than anything.

* * *

Someone had brought whiskey to the day's festivities and it was cracked into about an hour before the fireworks show started. The fact that it was Tennessee whiskey only sweetened the whole experience.

Not all that shocking, Logan and Jace were right next to Liam with their own glasses, and they'd been joined out on the wrap-around balcony by Brendan, Jax, Bennett, Shep, Finn, Tripp, Baxter, and Preston.

He remembered all of that without writing anything down, *and* would be able to repeat it back immediately no problems at all. He was just that good.

And he was feeling good. Like really *freaking* good. Not just because of the liquor—that was actually the smallest portion of the pie—but because of *everything*.

The first perfect moment of the day? Waking up next to Harper that morning.

Consciousness had hit him about two seconds before he'd opened his eyes, and in that moment all he'd known was contentment. When his eyes did open a second later that contentment transformed into something else. Sheer joy didn't seem like an adequate enough descriptor.

Elation? Euphoria? Jubilation?

No, they weren't strong enough for the reality of it.

She'd been snuggled up against his side, her head on his shoulder and her hair spread out across his arm like a blanket. One of her arms had been lying across his chest, with her palm resting right over his heart. She'd still been asleep, her warm steady breath washing out across his skin every time she exhaled.

It was the most perfect and peaceful moment that ever existed.

For anyone else it might not have been that big of a deal, but it was the first time he got to wake up with her in his arms. Something he'd wanted desperately from the very beginning. And as he'd looked down at her, finally getting it, he found himself praying that it wasn't the last time he woke up exactly like that.

He wanted every morning with her. And though he knew that wasn't a possibility—especially with his chosen career—he wanted as many of them as it was possible to get.

He wanted all of the nights that preceded them, too. Wanted to spend as much time as it was possible wrapped up in sheets, wrapped up in her. Wanted to talk about everything with her laugh lingering in the air. Wanted to make love to her for hours on end. He wanted to fall asleep next to her before they would wake up and start all over.

And he wanted everything in between.

All of it.

The second perfect moment of the day? Making love to her that morning.

Another thing he could do every morning for the rest of his life.

The third perfect moment? All of the other moments.

He was getting to meet her friends, talk to them, learn more about her, see her life up close and personal. Yeah, he was feeling good because of the whole day. And not only was the day not over yet, but when it did end he was going to get tomorrow with her, too.

And the day after that.

And the day after that.

And the day after that. The thing was, he wanted *all* the days.

Every. Last. One. Of. Them.

Her laugh—a sound he would know anywhere—carried across the porch and the instinct to look over at her was automatic.

Harper was holding Penny in her arms, the little girl's hands on the sides of Harper's face. Penny was moving in and out, coming in and kissing Harper's nose before she pulled back and they both giggled like crazy.

It was a preview of what was to come. Harper holding their child and their laughs filling his chest, making it expand like a balloon.

He was going to marry that woman. He knew it with every fiber of his being. She was his. Had been since the moment he'd seen her.

"Now there's a look that most of the men in this circle are very familiar with," someone next to Liam said, causing him to pull his gaze—more than a little reluctantly—from Harper.

He looked around to find all eyes on him.

"And what look is that?" Jace asked.

"What look is that, Shep?" Brendan tipped his glass at his friend.

"That would be the *I'm going to do anything to keep her* look," Shep answered, looking a tad bit smug.

"Show of hands," Bennett said. "Who's been there?"

There was an immediate lifting of hands around the circle…everyone except Jace, Finn, and Tripp.

"Though you might need to amend said statement from *her* to *him* for those two." Jax nodded at Preston and Baxter.

"True story." Baxter grinned as he held up his tumbler to Preston, who immediately clinked his glass in cheers.

Preston took a drink of his whiskey before he turned to Liam and asked, "So tell us, Liam, why are you good for *our* Harper?"

"Yeah." Brendan nodded. "You're going to need to get the approval of everyone here."

"How did you pass this test with Abby?" Liam nodded at his brother.

"I'm not sharing my secrets with you." Logan shook his head.

"Probably bribed them all with hockey tickets," Jace said.

"Actually, the only person here who's benefited from that is Bennett." Finn pointed at the man across the circle from him.

"And why is that?" This from Tripp who was now shaking his head with a mock frown turning down his mouth.

"You've been holding out on them?" Liam put his drink down

on the railing and rubbed his hands together, grinning. "Any of you guys country music fans? Tour's coming this way in a couple of months."

"See, I knew I liked him," Finn said.

"What makes you think you're guaranteed a ticket?" Baxter asked.

"Yeah? If anyone's going to get tickets, it's going to be Grace and me." This from Jax.

"And how the hell did you figure that one?" Tripp raised his eyebrows skeptically.

"Because, my wife is best friends with Harper," Jax answered.

"Then I'm just as likely to get tickets as you are," Bennett argued. "My wife is best friends with her, too."

"Hey, hey, hey." Preston shook his head. "It's already been established you get to go to hockey games, so you, my friend, are out of the running for concerts."

"And besides, Finn and I would beat all of you out anyways," Shep said.

"Oh really? And how in the world did you figure that one?" Brendan frowned.

"Harper and Hannah are like this." He held up his hand with his fingers crossed. "I grew up with Harper. Finn grew up with Harper. Hell, Finn is practically Dr. Laurence's other son. And the icing on the cake? Harper is godmother to baby Nate."

"Bullshit." Jax shook his head. "You just pulled that one out of your ass."

"Hey babe?" Shep called out to Hannah who was a few feet away, her feet propped up as she leaned back in a lounge chair. She was chatting with Paige who was right next to her in exactly the same position. "Who are baby Nate's godparents?"

She glanced over just long enough to answer, "Finn and Harper."

Shep didn't say anything, he just grinned hugely as he took a drink of whiskey.

"Sorry boys, I still win over all of you," Brendan said, looking around the circle. "Not only is Liam here my sister's best friend's boyfriend. But he's also my wife's best friend's boyfriend's brother. That makes us practically family." Brendan clapped Liam on the back.

Liam laughed. "How about this? I'll get all of you tickets."

"Well, that was easier than expected," Tripp said.

It was at that moment that Harper came over, her arms now empty…well, they were for a second before she wrapped them around Liam's waist. She placed a kiss on his mouth before she pulled back to look at him. "Hey."

"Hey." One of his hands went to her waist while the other reached up, and he pushed a strand of her hair back and behind her ear.

She turned from him and looked to the group of men. "If you all will excuse me, I'm going to pull him away before the show starts."

"No problem." Finn nodded.

"Yeah, I should go find my wife." Bennett looked around and spotted Mel on the opposite end of the porch. He headed off in that direction as Shep, Brendan, and Jax also broke off.

"Lead the way," Liam said before he stole his own kiss from her lips.

One of her hands slipped down, grabbing his that was at her

waist and twining their fingers together. She took a step away before she pulled him down to the opposite side of the porch, him following behind her.

"You leading me into dark corners?" he asked.

"Mmm, hmm," she hummed. "Easier to do things in the dark."

"What sort of things?"

"You'll find out now won't you?" She didn't stop when they got to the empty end of the deck, instead rounding the corner and leading him up a flight of stairs to the second floor…and then another flight of stairs to the third floor.

Shep had explained to Liam earlier that the inside renovations had yet to be completed on the top story of the building, so no one was occupying these rooms. Not only that, but the automatic floodlights hadn't been set up, either. Besides the moon, stars, and glow of the lights from the first floor, they were almost in total darkness.

The moment they got to the far side of the porch Harper turned and looked up at him. Her face was half in shadow, but he could still see the reflection of the moonlight in her eyes.

"You have a good time today?" Her free hand ran up his abdomen until her palm was flat over the center of his chest, her thumb moving back and forth.

Could she feel his heart beating as hard as he could? Did she know she owned it?

"I did." He moved closer to her, making her take a few steps back until he caged her in against the railing. "But you've left a few things out in our conversations over the weeks. Like the fact that those people down there are *much* more than your friends. They're your family."

"They are," she said without hesitation. "Absolutely, they are."

"I liked seeing that. How much they care about you. That they would do anything for you." He leaned in, kissing her mouth before he trailed his lips down. "It didn't take that long for me to get there with you, you know." He skimmed his nose across her jaw until he got to her ear, his lips brushing across her skin during the journey and making her shiver despite the warm summer air. "Actually, no time at all."

"To get where?" she asked, more than a little breathless.

He pulled back, looking into her eyes as he spoke the next words. "Where I would do anything for you. Anytime. Anywhere."

"Anytime? Anywhere?" She raised her eyebrow.

"Yes."

Her palm moved up to the collar of his shirt, her hand fisting in the fabric and pulling him close. "Kiss me," she whispered against his lips.

His mouth covered hers in an instant, both of his hands now framing her waist and holding her to him. She sighed as her body molded to his, her hands going up to his head and her fingers spearing in his hair.

"You taste like whiskey." Her mouth moved against his, her warm breath coming out in huffs.

"You taste like honey...you always taste like honey." He caught her bottom lip between his teeth, biting down lightly before he pulled it—along with one of her low throaty moans—into his mouth.

A series of pops sounded in the distance, and lights from the opening fireworks shone bright behind Liam's closed eyes. He pulled back from Harper's mouth, opening his eyes just as a red firework exploded with a loud boom. It illuminated her face, her eyes focused on his and showing that she was more than a little desperate for him.

Anytime. Anywhere. Anything.

He gripped her hips, spinning her so that she now faced out to the water. He was just able to make out the sound of protest from her lips before another round of booms filled the sky.

"Spread your legs and watch the show," he growled in her ear as he pressed his front to her back, his hands skimming down her thighs until he got to the hem of her dress. He pushed his palms up and under the fabric, now sliding across her bare skin.

"So soft." He pulled her earlobe into his mouth, giving it a small nip with his teeth at the same moment that he ran his fingers across the front of her panties. "And warm."

Four separate streaks of white shot out diagonally from the right, and then a second later streaks of blue came from the left, crisscrossing in the middle.

He pushed the cotton fabric of her panties to the side, slipping one and then two fingers inside of her. He discovered that she was much more than warm. Yeah, she was hot and wet.

And she was all his for the taking. Which he would be doing. Right now in fact.

Chapter Fifteen

No Going Back

Liam, what if someone looks up?" Harper gasped, her head falling back on his shoulder as he moved his fingers in and out of her in slow, delicious pushes and pulls.

The thought of someone seeing them was terrifying…and maybe just a little bit thrilling.

Dear God, these pregnancy hormones were getting a little out of control. Or maybe it had nothing to do with being pregnant and everything to do with the man who was currently working her over.

"Keep your eyes open." His voice was ragged in her ear. "And if anyone sees us they'll just think we're watching the fireworks. They can't see where my hands are."

Okay…okay this was a good point. The wooden posts of the railing that ran around the porch were close enough together that it would be almost impossible for anyone to see. Plus, there was the added fact that the skirt of her dress was also providing some good camouflage.

So really she just needed to look like she wasn't getting pleasured out of her mind...which would be about as easy as driving a semitruck through the eye of a needle.

And about two seconds later he made it five thousand times harder. His other hand was now joining the party and he was pressing his fingers to her clit. There was no way in hell she could stop herself from writhing against him, her ass pressing into his erection and the back of her naked thighs rasping against the denim of his jeans.

The sky in front of her exploded with colors. Green, blue, red, and white bursts filling the view before the sparks rained down in a sizzle. He moved his lips to her throat, opening his mouth and running his tongue across her skin.

"Liam." His name on her lips was a plea as she reached for the railing, grabbing hold of it and giving herself better leverage to move.

"I'm going to need you to not move so much."

"I—I can't help it."

"You're going to make me come if you don't stop."

She turned and looked over her shoulder at him just as the sky lit up with a dozen blue rockets. "I don't see why that's a problem."

"Because I'd rather be inside you."

"Then why aren't you?"

To say that Liam moved fast would be an understatement. He pulled his hands from inside her, grabbing her waist and spinning her around again. Within a few seconds he had her backed up into the very corner of the porch. There were about five feet of shutters on either side, creating a ninety-degree barrier around them and completely blocking them from view of anyone down below.

But barrier or not, if someone came up to this level now, there would be no hiding what was going on in that corner. A fact that had escaped neither of them.

"You know there is the possibility that we could get caught?" he asked as he hooked his fingers into the sides of her panties and shimmied them down her thighs.

"I do," she said as she nodded.

He kneeled down in front of her, lifting first her right foot and then the left, and freeing her legs. "So if you want to stop," he straightened as he put her panties in the pocket of his jeans, "speak now or forever hold your peace."

She couldn't help but smile at those words because they were the same he'd said their first night together...when she'd been reckless and wild just like this.

Apparently that was their MO.

"I'm objectionless." But as her hands were now at the front of his pants, pulling at his belt buckle, her words might be a tad bit redundant.

She had the button out and the zipper down, before she gripped the sides of his jeans and slid them down his hips. Her hand wrapped around his cock the second it was free, stroking him from base to tip.

"Nope, inside you." He pulled her hand away. "You're going to need to hold on for this."

Before she knew it, his hands were at her thighs, pulling her body up, her back sliding up against the wood. Her arms looped around his neck on reflex, her legs wrapping around his waist.

He pushed inside of her in one powerful move as the sky lit up. The brilliant white light illuminated his face and the intensity in his gaze was staggering. He moved in and out of her in sure, steady thrusts and her mouth fell open in a gasp…or a moan…or both. She couldn't be exactly sure as the air around them was filled with the *boom, boom, boom*s of the fireworks…that and she really didn't care because it felt so good.

His mouth captured hers, his tongue pushing past her lips and claiming her fully.

What the hell was she talking about? He'd claimed her fully months ago. She belonged to him completely.

Entirely.

He brought her right to the brink of an orgasm before his hips slowed, keeping the release at bay. Which she was beyond grateful for because she wasn't ready for this to be done. She needed more time. More time with the air erupting around them while he moved inside her.

She hadn't told him she was right on the brink. She hadn't been able to say anything even close to coherent. He'd just known. And why wouldn't he? The man knew her body better than anyone ever had before.

But it was more than her body. So much more. He knew her heart…knew her soul.

He pulled his mouth back from hers, his erratic breath hitting her lips in bursts as he rested his forehead against hers. "You feel so good. I'll never get enough of you."

"Promise?" The word escaped her lips before she could think better of it, and not a second too soon as another round of rockets exploded, this time making everything glow green.

He pulled back and fully looked her in the eyes, his skin now reflecting the red and blue fireworks that had just gone off. And then his mouth was at her ear, the low, steady timbre of his voice blocking out everything else around them.

"I swear."

And just like that the need for him was clawing at every part of her. She moved her hands to his head, making him turn to kiss her, while she used every bit of leverage she could gain from the wall to move up and down the length of his cock.

Liam moved, too. Harder and just rough enough to cause the perfect friction between their bodies. She was the one who found her release first, going off and pulsing around him. But before she could recover for even a second he had her detonating again. This time somehow even more powerful than the last.

He pulled his mouth from hers, burying his face in her throat as a groan erupted from his throat and vibrated across her skin. His hands tightened on her thighs, his fingers digging into her flesh in the sweetest sort of pain as he came inside of her.

The second they were finished, he turned around and she dropped her feet from where they were crossed around his back. He leaned against the shutters, sliding down until his ass was on the floor. She was straddling him, her body still wrapped around him in every way.

They sat there for a moment, looking at each other in stunned silence…well, silence besides the constant bangs from the fireworks that filled the air around them. But Harper barely heard the rockets exploding in the air over the sound of her heart pounding in her ears. Her hands went to his shoulders, bracing herself as she leaned forward and pressed her lips to his.

She wasn't sure how long they stayed like that, but when they pulled apart the air around them was quiet, the fireworks show apparently over.

"We should get back down there." He reached up, tracing her hairline. "Before someone notices we're missing and comes looking for us."

"I suppose you're right." She stole one last kiss—her tongue still tasting the whiskey that lingered in his mouth—before she moved off his lap and stood. She immediately felt the absence of him inside her, and by the sound of regret that escaped his lips she guessed he missed being inside her just as much.

He stood up, too, pulling his jeans back up and buckling his belt. He pulled her panties from the pocket of his jeans and handed them to her, but there was no point in putting them back on until she could sneak into the bathroom and get herself cleaned up.

When she made a move to start heading for the stairs he grabbed her hand and pulled her back until she was fully up against his body, both of this hands at the small of her back and holding her to him.

"I meant more than just sex, Harper."

"What?"

"Me never getting enough of you. It's *everything* that has to do with you."

"Good thing you swore on it." She grinned up at him. "Now that it's out there, there's no going back."

"Honey, sooner or later." He moved one of his hands to her chin and gently pressed up, tipping her head back. And then he was leaning down, his lips hovering just above hers. "You're going to figure out there was no going back for me the moment I met you."

He kissed her one last time before he reached for one of her hands. And as he led her back down the stairs to join everybody else, she knew it was neither sooner *nor* later…

She'd already figured it out, because there was no going back for her, either.

* * *

Sunday morning dawned much like Saturday, Liam waking up with a sleeping Harper in his arms. They went to Mass with her parents at the one and only Catholic church in town, and when Mrs. Laurence found out that Liam had been born and raised Catholic he got another couple of points without even trying.

After church they went to brunch at LaBella. Liam had been more than interested to see where Harper worked, and the high-end hotel and spa was a pretty fancy setup.

Besides the storm that blew in, Sunday night was a quiet affair. Just the two of them—and of course Luna, who jumped every time thunder rolled across the sky—curled up on the sofa with the newest episode of *Ponce* playing on the TV. Apparently Harper was a pretty big fan of the show, and she was also #TeamRosamund.

Liam took Harper to work on Monday, that way he could use her cruiser to get around town. Not only did she trust him with her vehicle, but she gave him a key to her apartment to come and go as he pleased. Both of these facts had him grinning like an idiot.

But she had that affect on him.

It was late that morning when Liam headed over to the inn to hang out with Adele, Logan, Abby, and Jace...and he brought Luna with him, too. What? The storm still hadn't passed and the little dog was legitimately terrified. How was he supposed to leave her when she'd been shaking like a leaf and staring up at him with eyes that begged the question: *you aren't going to leave me, are you?*

For the most part they just hung out in the more than spacious suite on the second floor. And everywhere he went, Luna was right by his side. Not only that, but the second he sat down she was immediately hopping up on his lap, circling once, and then curling into a ball.

"Wow," Adele said in mock shock. "Winning over her canine? It's a good sign when her dog loves you, too."

His hand that was scratching the top of Luna's head paused as he looked over at his sister. She was sitting at the opposite end of the sofa. Her hair was all pinned up in her customary curls, a purple bandanna tied to the side acting as a headband. That was all he saw of her as she was wrapped up in a throw blanket. The dark gloomy weather and blasting air conditioner were making for perfect snuggling conditions.

"Too?" he asked.

"Don't be dumb. That girl's in love with you just as much as you're in love with her."

"That so?"

"Oh, so you guys *haven't* had that conversation yet." She didn't even attempt to keep the surprise out of her voice.

Nope, they weren't discussing that at the moment. It was true he and Harper *hadn't* had that conversation…yet. He wasn't all that ready to rock the boat. Things were going well…*really* well in their journey to catch up.

"Speaking of winning over a woman's canine." Liam didn't hesitate in flipping Adele's line of questioning on her. "Where is your dog?" But his question wasn't a necessary one as they both knew exactly where Katharine Hepburn—Adele's dalmatian—was currently hanging out.

Even from the living room of the suite, the telltale noise of the dog's nails hitting the tile in the kitchen could be heard. Adele's eyes darted over and landed on Jace who was currently making a sandwich for his on-the-hour snack. The guy ate like a Hobbit, had about ten meals a day.

"Katie is just hoping he gives her something." Adele shook her head.

Okay, so it was true that the dog would never turn down a treat, and yes she did follow Jace every single time he went into the kitchen. But this weekend wasn't the first time Liam had noticed that Katie was at Jace's side almost as much as she was at Adele's.

And the man treated the dog like she was his, too.

"Fess up, Del."

"Fess up about what?" she asked with an air of obliviousness that in no way fooled him.

"You're not the only one in this family who's observant. I see the way you look at J—"

Her foot shot out, kicking Liam hard in the thigh. "Shut up," she hissed at him.

"No, you better start talking before he finishes making his

fifteen-layer club." Liam nodded to the kitchen with his chin.

Adele sighed, taking a moment before speaking. "Nothing has happened."

"And do you want it to?"

"There's nothing to happen, Liam. We're just friends. Besides"—she shrugged like it didn't really matter—"he's got plenty of other women to occupy his brain and his bed to not think about me that way."

The plenty of women statement was true. Jace filtered through them faster than a person could blink. A playboy at heart with a charming smile, shaggy dark-blond hair, and aquamarine eyes. He was the king of a one-night stand, which was one of the reasons Liam wanted his baby sister to stay away from him.

And okay, so Liam might be a bit of a hypocrite as he'd gotten Harper into bed on that first night, but as was evident, *that hadn't been a one-night stand.*

But Liam didn't get a chance to ask any more questions as Jace came into the room, Katie at his side.

"Look, I taught her a new trick." He set his plate on the coffee table, grabbing a carrot before he stepped back and faced Katie.

"Sit," he commanded the dog, and she fell onto her haunches instantly, her tail wagging erratically across the floor like a windshield wiper.

"Still," he told her, holding the carrot up high, and Katie's tail stopped moving.

"Stay." He reached forward and set the carrot on top of Katie's snout. "Stay," he repeated as he stepped back. Katie's eyes were entirely focused on the carrot, her body not moving as she waited for permission.

"Get it," Jace told her.

Katie threw her head back, the carrot popping up into the air for just a second before it landed in her mouth.

"Good girl." Jace rubbed her head affectionately. "Smart girl." He handed her another carrot before taking a seat in the chair, grabbing his plate and digging into his sandwich.

Liam's gaze went back to his sister for just a second, a longing in her eyes that said quite clearly she wanted to be the girl on Jace's mind. Her eyes met Liam's and that longing was gone in an instant. A wall slamming down to hide how she felt. A wall that was not the norm for his sister.

She might be intense, might be intimidating, might be scary as hell sometimes, but the girl loved with her whole heart. She was kind and witty and had more brains than Logan and Liam put together.

Any guy would be lucky to have her...but would Jace be good enough?

Maybe...maybe not.

But as Liam learned full well, there was no controlling who you fell in love with. And his sister *was* in love with Jace. *Damn.*

Adele's eyes widened in horror, seeing the knowledge in Liam's face, and she gave a slight shake of her head in denial. A denial he didn't believe in the slightest.

At that moment the front door opened, and Abby and Logan walked in with their hands filled with grocery bags. Adele shot off the sofa. "You guys need help?" she asked almost sprinting across the room.

Yeah, Adele could run all she wanted. It was going to catch up to her sooner or later.

* * *

By some miracle there was a lull in the downpour that had been going on all day, and it lined up perfectly with Harper getting off work at six o'clock. Liam picked her up when she finished and about ten minutes after they got to the inn, the sky opened up again and let loose with full force.

Though the evening promised to be a much less involved endeavor than the Fourth of July, it still wasn't all that small.

Abby was in town so it was a given that Paige, Brendan, and Trevor were there. Grace and Mel weren't going to miss any opportunity to get to know Liam, so they'd come with their husbands in tow. The giggling Rosie Mae wasn't going to be left out of the evening's festivities, nor were Dale and Hamilton. And last, but certainly not least, Shep and Hannah were there as their kitchen and dining room were the ones being occupied. It was the optimal cooking space as all three of the Jameses were in charge of making the Spanish-themed cuisine.

Apparently cooking was a talent that all three of them enjoyed. The table was now just a resting place for all of the empty dishes, and everyone was sitting around talking and laughing. Liam had his hand on the back of Harper's neck, his fingers tracing the very top of her spine.

His hands on her felt so good that she couldn't bring herself to pull away, which was a problem as she'd had to go to the bathroom for a little while now. The full bladder thing was no joke during pregnancy.

"I'll be right back," she whispered to Liam. He nodded, gently squeezing the very base of her neck before he let go. She pushed her chair back and headed down the hallway.

On her way back she spotted Luna and Henry—Hannah and Shep's gray cat—playing in the living room. Henry was more like a rambunctious little dog himself, and the two of them were wrestling in between playing tug-of-war with an old sock.

Adele's dog Katie wasn't having any of those shenanigans. When they bumped into her comfortable lounging position on the rug, she gave them a somewhat disdainful look—well, as disdainful as a dog was capable of—before she got up and headed to the dining room with the adults.

Dale and Hamilton were in the kitchen with Mel and Bennett, stacking dishes on the counter. Harper veered off and headed in that direction instead, stationing herself at the sink and turning the faucet on. As the water heated up, she grabbed the massive glass bowl that had held the paella, wiping away the tiny remnants in the trash before putting it under the steady stream of steaming water.

When she reached up for the soap on the windowsill, her eyes caught on the porch on the other side of the glass window in front of her. Her mind automatically flashed back to last Saturday with her and Liam two floors up, her legs wrapped around his waist while he moved inside her…

Hands landed on her hips making her jump, and Liam's mouth was at her ear. "This doesn't look like you coming right back."

"I'm just trying to help."

He reached up and he hit the handle on the faucet, making the stream of water stop. And then his hands were at her hips again, turning her around.

"You aren't cleaning up, Harper. Not going to happen."

"Liam, I'm more than capable—"

"I know you are," he cut her off. "But you aren't going to. Know what you can do though?"

"What's that?" She looked up at him as his palms moved up along her sides.

"Tell me what you were thinking about that has you all flushed?"

"I'm not flushed. It's the hot water."

"The hot water making your eyes dilate, too?" He shook his head, calling her bluff. "You know I'm sure we can sneak out there if you want. Have an encore performance." He indicated the porch with his chin, his eyes not leaving hers.

"The rain is blowing in sideways. We'd get soaked."

Something downright wicked flashed in his eyes and he leaned down to her ear. "I think you're going to have that problem regardless."

"You're terrible," she said, laughing as he pulled back, his mouth split in a massive mischievous grin.

"I am." He waggled his eyebrows. "Now, no washing dishes for you." He pressed his lips to hers in a quick kiss before he stepped back and gently pulled her away from the sink. "I got this."

"And what am I supposed to do?"

"Keep me company," he said as he turned the water on again and finished washing the bowl that Harper had started. "Tell me about your day."

"I can't guarantee that it will be all that interesting."

"It was *your* day, of course it will be interesting."

She leaned back against the counter, the grin on her face not to be helped, as she started talking.

* * *

Liam spent Tuesday at the inn as well, Dale and Hamilton joining them. As both boys had requested more music sessions, Liam
was happy to comply. It hadn't taken him very long to figure out
why his brother had gotten so close to the two teenagers. They
were great kids and Liam found himself enjoying their company
more than he could've ever anticipated.

On Wednesday, they all went out to the horse farm that Shep
and Finn's aunt and uncle owned. It had been years since Liam
had gone horseback riding, and when he was finished up he was
feeling it on every inch of his body. Luckily, Harper took pity
on him and she spent the evening showing him just how good
her massage skills were...and after that she showed him just how
good her riding skills were.

Thursday was way less exhaustive. Liam, Logan, and Jace in-
dulged in a tour of the Sleepy Sheep's new brewing facility and an
afternoon tasting of Shep's beer. The evening was again spent in
Harper's apartment, with Liam making her dinner. Pretty much
any opportunity he had to get her alone, he took advantage of it.
Yes, he wanted his friends and family to spend time with her, and
he wanted to get to know all of her friends and family, too. But as
he was about to be leaving her for two weeks, he was getting just
a tad bit stingy.

And besides that, the Jacksonville crowd still had another few
days left in Mirabelle, and he knew for a fact that Adele and
Harper were hanging out when he was gone. So he didn't feel all
that guilty. Actually, he didn't feel guilty at all.

By Friday he was settling very nicely into their routine. Had it really only been a week since he'd been in Mirabelle? It felt like it had been much longer, like they'd been part of each other's everyday lives for years now...and would be for the long haul if he had anything to say about it.

It was something that he just *knew,* and something that was confirmed more than ever when they went to her doctor's appointment that afternoon. Beth had worked them in for the last slot at the end of the day, and as they sat in that waiting room he found that he was just a little bit anxious.

And why wouldn't he be? They were going to hear their child's heartbeat. He would put money on the fact that he'd never been so excited in his life. And though the anticipation was overwhelming, it was nothing to how he felt when it actually happened.

He was sitting on a stool right next to her, his hand in hers when the steady rhythmic beat filled the room. Never in his life had he heard a more perfect sound.

He could barely breathe, could barely move, couldn't get over the fact that he and Harper had created something. They'd made a life. *Together.* Just the two of them. It was the greatest thing he'd ever do.

Ever.

So yeah, he was in more than a daze for the rest of the evening. All through dinner with her parents...and dessert...and then during their drive home, him behind the wheel of Harper's Cruiser as he was more than familiar with how to get around town at this point. He'd been driving most of the week after all, dropping Harper off at work in the morning and picking her up in the evening.

Their little daily routine.

It was more than he could've ever imagined. She was more than he could've ever imagined.

* * *

Saturday morning was the first since Liam had been in Mirabelle that Harper woke up alone. It wasn't the best feeling in the world…actually it really sucked. But as he was leaving in, oh, six hours to go on tour for two weeks, she was going to have to get used to it.

And when it all came down to it, this was how it was going to be with a life with him. He was a musician and his career was only getting bigger. How they were going to figure this out was a question that she was trying not to worry about. It was too soon. It had barely been over a week since he'd been there, three since they'd found each other again…and about two months since they'd met.

Two months? Really? How had it only been that long?

Okay, she wasn't going to spiral this early in the morning. She needed to find Liam, and as she heard a pan hitting the stove in the kitchen, she had a pretty good idea of where he was.

A quick trip to the bathroom was a must. Again, full bladders weren't to be messed with. After brushing her teeth and washing her face, she grabbed her robe on the back of the door before heading out into her apartment.

Liam was at the stove, the only article of clothing on his body his gray boxer briefs…and one of Harper's aprons. She had two, one black with bright pink frills on it. The other blue and green stripes. He'd picked the black frilly one.

Of course he had. It took everything in her not to laugh as she leaned against the door frame and watched him while he talked to Luna.

Yes. *Talked* to Luna. The dog was sitting at his feet, looking up at him with imploring eyes and no doubt waiting for him to drop a piece of bacon…or cheese. That dog would do backflips for a piece of cheese.

"Listen," he said, waving the tongs at the dog. "I know that you have fun with Henry, understandable. He's a fun little guy. But that's the point, Luna. He's a *male*. And men are dogs, which I'm sure is confusing to you as he's a cat. But you get my point."

This time Harper couldn't stop the laugh that bubbled out of her chest. Liam spun around, and Harper was able to get the full picture of him in that ridiculous apron. And the small laugh morphed into a full-on belly laugh.

"What?" he asked, setting the tongs on the stove before he walked over to her.

"You look ridiculous."

"Hey, black is slimming and way more flattering than stripes." His hands landed on her hips before they moved to the belt at her waist.

"Whatever you say."

"This one has better coverage. And you were supposed to sleep in. I was going to bring you breakfast in bed."

"What is it with you and eating in bed?"

"At least this time it was going to be food." His eyes left hers as he slipped the belt loose, the two sides separating and his hands sliding down to her bare thighs. She was only wearing a tank top and a pair of panties. "I take it back." He shook his head as he reached up and ran his fingers across her nipples, the thin fabric doing nothing to lessen the sensation. "I want you for breakfast."

"I think your bacon might burn."

"How many times do I have to tell you to stop worrying about my bacon?" He started kissing her a second before he reached down in a quick move, grabbing her thighs and picking her up.

She gasped against his lips as he carried her across the room, and then he was setting her down on the counter. His mouth lingered on hers for a moment or two before he pulled back and went to the stove, flipping the bacon.

Then he went to the fridge, pulling out a carton of cranberry juice and pouring her a glass. It was the first thing she drank every morning, and it had taken him no time at all to remember that fact.

It had taken him no time at all to remember a lot of facts. Like that she liked her bananas the most when they just started to get spotted. Or that even though her nausea wasn't nearly as severe, all things poultry still weren't agreeing with her. Or that she preferred prime numbers when it came to just about anything…like grocery store lines or the volume on the TV. Yeah it was, weird but he just went with it.

He went with everything.

Her throat constricted as she stared down at the juice glass in her hand. Her head came up and she looked back over to Liam who was at the stove, flipping the knob and turning off the burner. The tightening feeling in her throat was now accompanied by the burning at the corner of her eyes.

"You want some of my Potato Sensation?" Liam asked as he

grabbed plates from the cupboard next to him. "I made toast, too."

She couldn't stop the sniffle that happened next, either. It seemed to fill the kitchen, bouncing off the tile. She bowed her head, running her thumb up and down the glass.

"Hey, hey now." Liam was back to her in an instant, pulling the juice from her hand. He touched her chin, pushing her head up. "Honey, what's going on?"

"I don't want you to leave." And just like that she burst into tears.

It was something she wished she could blame entirely on the pregnancy hormones, and though those no doubt had something to do with it, they weren't the only factor.

He pulled her into his chest, his hands moving up and down her back. "I know. I don't want to, either. I'll be back in no time at all."

"And then you leave again."

He took a deep breath, letting it out slowly before he leaned forward, resting his forehead against hers. "We're going to figure this out, honey. We are."

"Promise?"

"I swear."

The certainty in his voice was a small relief…she just wished she felt as certain.

Chapter Sixteen

I Want Forever, Honey, Forever with You

Liam was more than capable of being a patient guy…in certain circumstances. He could handle long lines with ease, didn't really lose his temper while driving, never really watched the clock waiting for time to tick down.

That was until Harper had come along. Turned out when he wasn't with her, all he was thinking about was how long it was going to take to get to her again. This constant unsettled feeling had been going on since May, and though it was different than it had been when he couldn't find her, it was no less intense.

Twelve days. Twelve days since he'd seen her and he was losing his damn mind.

And the morning he was currently having was bringing everything to a boil. The Canadian and Great Lakes leg of the Isaac Hunter tour was over, but there was something else on his schedule that he needed to do before he could get back to Harper.

Shoot the video for "Beyond the Limits."

The song was supposed to be a tie-in with the outlaw aspect

of *Mason-Dixon,* but the location for the video was in Louisiana as they were doing a bayou Bonnie and Clyde thing. The forty-eight-hour shoot was now apparently going to take seventy-two.

Something that he was in no way pleased about as he was out in the middle of the swamp, the summer sun beating down on him with an intensity that just shouldn't be legal for ten o'clock in the morning. Not to mention the air was already so thick it was like he was breathing in soup.

And the real reason he was about to lose it? All of this was keeping him from Harper.

If he could go back in time to last year when Isaac and Hunter had asked him to help out in writing the song, he would've said no if it meant he could be anywhere besides the *middle of the fucking swamp* in that moment.

So yeah, his patience was almost non-existent.

Maybe it was the fact that his shirt was sticking to him, the sweat trickling down his back. Or that the smothering heat was suffocating him. Or it could be that Miguel, the director of the video, had shot the scene with Kiki running her hand up Liam's thigh while they sat on the back of a boat on the bayou three times already.

It could also quite possibly be because the guy wanted another take.

This scene was a compromise to what they'd originally wanted, which was Kiki straddling Liam's lap as she leaned down for a kiss.

He'd flat out refused, having a pretty heated conversation with Gary that they were going to have to figure something else out. And even with the edits to the video, Liam was in no way happy.

While all he wanted to do was go take a shower and wash off the feel of her hands on his body, Kiki was enjoying every moment of it.

"Like this?" she asked, moving closer and pressing her chest against Liam's arm. She turned her head, her voice dropping low as she looked over at Miguel, whose eyes were focused on Kiki's legs that had been covered in baby oil.

Why that was necessary when they were both already sweating in the heat, he had no idea.

"Yeah. Just like that, sweetheart." Miguel winked. "And roll."

Kiki turned back to Liam, her eyes looking up at him as she batted her lashes. "You want this, baby. You want *me*," she murmured. "You need to admit it to yourself."

Liam pulled away from her, the need to distance himself too much to not listen to.

"Cut." The exasperation in Miguel's voice apparent. "We need to do that again."

"I need a break." Liam stood, not even turning back as he jumped off the boat to the shore and headed to the trailer that had been set up for him.

The second he stepped inside he was enveloped with the cool air from the air conditioner. He went to the mini-fridge in the corner and grabbed a bottle of water, downing it in seconds.

He wiped his mouth with the back of his hand when he pulled the bottle away. His eyes caught on his phone that was sitting on the table and he reached for it automatically, pressing the Home button. Harper had texted him earlier that morning and he unlocked the screen, pulling up their full conversation.

Painting my toes pink this morning while I can still bend this way.

#5   31-10-2019 03:36PM
tem(s) checked out to 06495000823597.

TLE: Hero
RCODE: 50000000128503
E DATE: 21-11-19

TLE: Instant attraction
RCODE: 50000000239201
E DATE: 21-11-19

TLE: Unsung
RCODE: 36495014577575
E DATE: 21-11-19

Attached was a picture of her sitting on the bathroom sink, wearing short-striped pajama bottoms and one of his Jacksonville Stampede T-shirts that he'd left at her apartment. She was looking up at the camera, her hair thrown up in a messy bun as she blew him a kiss.

God he missed her. And the need to be with her was overwhelming. "Forever" was going to be released next week, but the promo for it had already started. He'd done more than a few interviews about it in the last couple of days.

And he wanted to tell Harper about it face to face. Which was why the delay in getting to her was killing him.

He needed to finish this video now. Get it over and done with and be on his way. He put his phone back on the table, grabbing another bottle of water before he headed outside. As he rounded the half a dozen trailers that had been grouped together he came up short when he overheard his name.

"Liam is fine, Miguel. I just want to make sure that I look good for this," Kiki said sweetly. "This video is a big deal for me and I need you to get all of my best angles."

"Sweetheart, I got all of your best angles. Believe me. You look good in everything that I've shot."

Liam moved just enough to peek around the side and catch a glimpse of the pair. Kiki was running her hand up Miguel's chest as she looked up into his eyes. "Just a few more takes." She stretched up and kissed Miguel's jaw. "I promise I will make it worth your while."

"The label is already starting to ask questions with the delay, Kiki. I don't think I can push this out longer."

"You could try though, couldn't you?"

White-hot anger flowed through him. "Are you kidding me?" Liam asked as he rounded the corner.

The pair jumped apart as they moved to look at Liam.

"You're the reason I'm still stuck here?" He looked at Kiki, so over this woman in every capacity known to man. "You're un-fucking-believable, you know that? I'm done here."

He didn't spare another word, another breath in their direction, before he turned around and walked away.

* * *

Eight nights and eight mornings—that was all it took for Harper to get completely and totally dependent on Liam being next to her when she went to bed…and him being there in the mornings.

It was strange really as she'd spent about fifty times as many nights and mornings with Brad. Yet when he left, the empty space next to her in bed wasn't *nearly* as significant. Sure, she'd missed her ex when he'd left, but not like this.

Nothing like this. This was more like a gaping chasm.

She talked to Liam every day—multiple times a day actually—which was all that was getting her through it.

He'd been delayed another day at the video shoot…the video shoot where Kiki Jean Carlow was apparently going to be crawling all over him.

Liam had been completely and totally up front with her about what was going to be happening. He'd also told Harper that he wasn't interested in the actress at all…which only helped a little bit.

Not that she didn't trust him, because she did, but it didn't stop the jealously that coursed through her in the slightest. She wasn't even remotely prepared for any of it. Wasn't aware it was possible to miss someone so much.

God she was going crazy. She knew it, too. Not only was she exhausted all of the time, but she would cry at the drop of a hat, and over ridiculous things, too. A commercial for tires made her cry the other day. Yeah, that's right. *Tires*. And then when she couldn't fit into her jeans two days ago she'd had somewhat of an emotional breakdown. *Over jeans*.

Though to be fair to herself, that was the first day that she noticed a drastic difference in her body. She was starting to show and she was going to need to go maternity clothes shopping very soon.

Her hips were getting wider, her boobs perilously close to spilling out of her bras, and then there was the tiny bump above her belly. She'd never really had the flattest stomach known to man, and she definitely didn't now.

Not that she had a problem with said baby bump in the slightest…it was just that Liam wasn't there to see it. And it made her emotional.

The only thing going for her was that the nausea was non-existent and she could eat regularly without problems…but that was pretty much about it.

He'd told her the night before that he was going to be delayed another day, which had put her into a pretty spectacular funk. And because the universe was apparently against her this week, when she got to the spa for work on Wednesday morning—the longest day of the week in her opinion—it was to find Bethelda Grimshaw in her room at Rejuvenate, waiting for a massage.

Bethelda-*freaking*-Grimshaw.

Yup, one of the regular clients at the spa was none other than the gossip hag of Mirabelle. As no one *ever* wanted the woman as a regular client, she was rotated among all of the therapists.

Apparently it was Harper's week for the short end of the stick.

"Ahh." Bethelda smiled, eyeing Harper over her cat-eyed glasses. "I get you this week. You look considerably better than the last time I saw you. No longer wasting away in despair over your failed relationship? Getting back up to your fighting weight I see."

Oh great, a fat reference.

"I am doing better, Mrs. Grimshaw." Harper did her level best to paste a smile onto her face and not gag at the fact that she'd just addressed the woman as *missus*. "Thank you."

"I also noticed you're back in the ring with another man. You do move fast don't you? Don't really waste time between rounds."

Now a slut reference. Perfect.

"How about we get started?" Harper asked, wanting to get this over with as soon as possible.

"Yes." Bethelda's eyes did another sweep over Harper's entire body.

She had a very strong instinct to cover her belly with her hand, to shield her baby from this woman. But she resisted. A move like that would be ample fodder for this woman to write about. As it was, Harper had no doubt that her Voluptuous V. nickname would be gracing another Bethelda Grimshaw blog post very soon.

She couldn't freaking wait.

* * *

Starting her day with Bethelda Grimshaw was a pretty accurate precursor for how the rest of Harper's day was going to shape up.

She had back-to-back clients and barely any time to breathe. Which might've been a good thing as one of her clients had apparently bathed in patchouli before she'd come in. The scent was so pungent that Harper's small reprieve in no more nausea was non-existent.

After lunch, Harper went to LaBella where she was treated to a couple on vacation yelling at her for her inability to "squeeze" them into her already packed book for the day. And then she was forced to listen to a tourist who spent the entire hour on the phone talking to someone about "the injustice of *Daddy* not buying her the convertible Porsche for the days that she just didn't feel like driving her Beamer or Audi."

There was a "no phones" policy in the spa, but it had long ago been established that if the clients didn't follow it, there was no way to enforce it.

Speaking of phones, she'd forgotten her phone charger. Since she'd also forgotten to charge it the night before, it died somewhere around two o'clock. The short charge on her drive from the spa to the resort had only bought her about a half hour.

Texting Liam throughout the day had become part of the norm, so not having that when she was already in a foul mood was just adding fuel to the fire at this point.

She was at the spa until well after seven, just in time to get caught in the downpour from the thick black clouds that had been threatening all day. They were an excellent indicator of exactly how she felt, too.

The second she stepped out from the overhang of the spa the wind whipped up, making her umbrella flip and getting her soaked in an instant. She shoved the useless bit of scrap metal and cloth into the trash can at the end of the walkway before sprinting to her car.

When she shut the door behind her it was like she'd just climbed out of a pool. She shoved her keys in the ignition, turning over the engine before she opened the vents and turned on the heat.

Summer or not she was shivering, the cold making her teeth chatter and every inch of her skin breaking out in goose bumps. There was a cardigan in her backseat and she snatched it up, attempting to wipe some of the water from her skin. Her ponytail was dripping and when she squeezed the material of the sweater over her hair it instantly soaked the fabric.

Harper threw the now sopping cardigan into the seat next to her, before she found her phone in her purse and plugged it into her car charger. The spinning wheel popped up, indicating it was getting some juice, but it would be a good couple of minutes before it loaded up. The song on the radio ended and rolled into another as she put her Cruiser in Reverse and backed out of the parking lot.

She wanted more than anything to take a steaming hot shower when she got home, but the lightning that cracked across the sky a second later shoved that idea out of her head. She was going to have to settle with food warming her up.

She was going to make the most decadent grilled cheese sandwich possible with the ingredients in her fridge before she heated up the tomato soup her mother had sent home with her the night before. Then she was going to curl up on the couch with Luna in her lap, a cup of hot chocolate in her hand, and talk to Liam in whatever form was available.

It would be her choice to FaceTime with him as she'd like to see his face more than anyone's in the world, but she'd make do with just his voice if she had to.

And as if the universe was *finally* on her side, his voice filled her car making her warm in an instant.

"I firmly believe that it's the things you have to fight for that are worth the most. The struggle makes it *more* in the end."

It took her a second to realize *how* hearing his voice was a possibility—her brain was just that frazzled—but he was talking to her through the radio. Well, not to *her* exactly, but to the DJ who was interviewing him.

It was the country station she always listened to on her satellite radio. Nellie Westin did the morning show and she interviewed musicians all the time, getting them to do a live performance at the end. They'd usually replay segments of the interviews throughout the day and week.

Harper had no idea Liam was supposed to be on it.

"More what?" Nellie's northern accent came through the speakers. She was born and raised in Detroit, which was actually where her show was broadcast. Liam had been there two days ago.

"More *everything*. In my experiences, the greatest things in my life have not come easily."

"This is the theme of your newest album, which will be available in a few months if I'm not mistaken?"

"Yes, ma'am, *Unsteady Ground* will be out the last Tuesday in October."

Always the southern gentleman. Harper's mouth split into the first genuine smile she'd had since going into work that morning.

"Ladies and gentlemen, I just got ma'amed by someone who's about two seconds older than me. You southern boys sure are polite."

"Sometimes. Depends on the day." A low laugh escaped his lips and Harper would bet money on the fact that he had a slightly mischievous smile on that face of his.

"Well, I don't doubt that. Now don't let me get sidetracked here. Let's get back to this new album of yours. There's a song on *Unsteady Ground* that's already creating a lot of buzz. 'Forever' hasn't been officially released yet, but you've been playing it at concerts and your fans are going crazy over it."

Harper pulled into the parking lot in front of her apartment, putting the car in Park and turning the engine off. The radio was still running as she leaned back in her seat to listen to the last of the interview.

"Yeah," Liam continued. "It's a different song than anything else I've done."

Harper could just see him sitting there in the studio, those massive headphones on his ears while he reached up and ran his hand across the back of his neck.

"It's a love song isn't it?"

"It is. And a ballad, two things I've never really delved into before…or at least not successfully. But this song was one of those *stars align* moments."

"And how exactly was that?" Nellie asked.

"I found the right muse…the *perfect* muse actually."

And this was the part where Harper stopped breathing.

"Would I be correct in guessing that this song is based off something that actually happened? Off an actual woman? Because I'm not going to lie, Liam, there are quite a few fans out there, besides myself, who are more than curious."

"'Forever' *is* based off true events," he confirmed.

Harper still hadn't taken a single breath.

"And I wrote the song within twelve hours of meeting her. It was the fastest I've ever gotten anything out on the paper. And it's the clearest melody I've ever heard in my head."

"Are you willing to confirm the fact that you did fall in love at first sight. That the song is true?"

Wait? What did she just ask? Harper's hands were wrapped around the steering wheel in a death grip. Her fingers going white against the black.

"I uhhh…you're really going to put me in the hot spot today aren't you?"

"It's kind of what I like to do. Also, you're totally blushing right now."

"I have no doubt about that. I'm not going to answer that one, though. Not because I don't know the answer, but because I haven't exactly had that conversation with the woman in question. The first time I say it, I want to say it to her."

Okay…okay…what was going on? What was *even* happening? He…he was in love with her?

"Oh my *gawd*. I wish you guys could see him right now. He's positively smitten. Though I think the cat's out of the bag on that last question. So it's a safe guess that she's still in your life."

"She is," Liam answered. "We spent the Fourth together. I got to meet her friends and family and she met mine."

"So it's serious?"

Another low laugh filled Harper's car, giving her goose bumps for entirely different reasons than earlier. "Yeah, it's safe to say that it's pretty serious."

He could say that again.

"Can we get her name?"

"Not today. But I'm certain who she is won't be a secret for that much longer."

"And why's that?"

"Because if I have anything to say about it, she isn't going anywhere."

"A man who knows what he wants…or in this case *who* he wants. Got to love that. Well, you guys might not get to know the name of the girl behind the song, but you will get to hear the song. Our Twitter and Facebook followers are chomping at the bit. So while Liam gets his guitar ready, I'm going to repeat the facts that all of you need to know. He's still going to be on tour for the next couple of months opening for Isaac Hunter, so get your tickets while you can. 'Forever' will be released for purchase next week, and the entirety of *Unsteady Ground* will be out the last week of October. I've had the privilege of listening to it all the way through; it's your best yet, Liam."

"Thank you," Liam said, the humbleness beyond obvious to her.

"I only speak the truth, and without further ado, this is 'Forever.'"

Liam's fingers ran across the strings, the first chords of the song flowing through the speakers.

Harper knew the song instantly. Knew it before a single word left his mouth. It was the same song she'd heard all those months ago…in a cabin…in Tennessee.

"Love at first sight was something I'd never seen."

She closed her eyes, sinking back into the seat, her heart pounding erratically out of her chest.

"But you walked in and became every single one of my dreams. Violet eyes and the lips of a goddess. I knew I'd want more than just one kiss."

Violet eyes.

"A day, a week, a month, a year. It would never be enough. I want forever, honey. Forever with you."

Yes, she'd heard that part of the song already…but it was different now. So much different. It was how he sang *honey,* like it was her name. It was as if he could taste it on his tongue…taste *her* on his tongue.

"A million simple things that aren't so simple at all. Your hand in mine. The taste of your tongue. Your head on my chest. You stealing my heart."

It was then that she realized she was crying. The tears streaming down her face. Well, at least it was a better reason than a tire commercial. God, it was *every* reason. All the reasons.

He'd written a song about her. It was unreal.

The chorus repeated twice, *"A day, a week, a month, a year…"*

But it was the very end of the song that really did her in. The end of the song that had her sobbing.

"You were something I never knew I always wanted. Something I never knew I always needed. And now that I know, I can't let go. I need forever, honey. Forever with you."

He finished up with the last chords, and his fingers strumming the strings of his guitar could've very well been moving across her skin. That was how much she felt the song. Felt his words. Felt him.

I need forever, honey.

Need. That last verse…it was…God, it was everything.

She reached forward, shutting the radio off. It was the end of his interview, and if it wasn't his voice she was listening to, she didn't want to hear it. Instead she sat there in that parking lot, the rain pinging off the roof as she replayed the song in her head. Kept those words—*his* words—running on repeat.

He'd fallen in love with her from the very start…well, that's what she believed based off what she'd heard in the last ten minutes. But she wanted to hear it from his mouth. *Needed* to hear it.

She jumped as her phone went off in the cup holder next to her. She looked over to see a picture of Liam laughing lighting up the screen. Her hand shook as she reached over and grabbed it, her thumb sliding across to answer it.

"Hey," she barely whispered past her constricted throat.

"Harper, what's wrong?"

One word. One teeny-tiny three-letter word and he knew something was up in an instant. The concern in his voice wrapped around her and she closed her eyes, trying to find the ability to talk without losing it again.

All she was able to do was sniffle.

"Honey, please talk to me. What's wrong?" he asked again.

"Nothing's wrong." She reached up, running her fingers under her eyes for what she was sure was the billionth time that night. "I just heard your interview on Daybreak with Nellie Weston…and the song. I heard 'Forever.'"

A rush of his breath blew out across the speaker, and if she didn't know any better she'd swear she could feel it across her neck. She could just picture him, standing there, his head bowed as he ran his hand through his hair.

"Where are you?" The moment the question was out of his mouth, lightning cracked the sky in half and the thunder followed within an instant, echoing around her…and in the phone next to her ear. A second later she heard Luna barking madly through the speaker, too.

"No way," she whispered.

"Get up here."

Her phone was in her purse immediately, most likely still connected to the call. She didn't know. She didn't care. She wrenched her keys from the ignition, dropping them into her purse, too, before she opened the door. She shut the door behind her and ran for the building.

The moment she got beneath the overhang she slowed, being careful on the stairs. As her head cleared the landing for her floor, she saw Liam at the door to her apartment. She walked straight into his outstretched arms and he pulled her inside, not letting go of her as he shut the door and locked it behind them.

Chapter Seventeen

Love at First Sound

There was a slight moment of chaos as the air around them was ripped open with another clap of thunder. The walls of the apartment shook as the sky behind the closed blinds lit up again. Luna hightailed it out of the room, most likely going to burrow in the dog blankets on her little bed.

She was over this whole storm thing.

Liam wrapped his arms around Harper, pulling her fully into his chest and pressing his face to her sopping-wet hair. He didn't care that her clothes were drenching his. All he cared about was the fact that she was in his arms.

"You're here," she whispered, holding on to him just as tight.

"I'm here." He nodded before he pulled back and looked down into her beautiful face, the face of the woman he loved. Wet hair clung to her cheek and he reached up, pushing it away. "So you heard the interview…and 'Forever'?"

"I did." She pulled her bottom lip between her teeth before she let it fall free. "Why didn't you tell me when you were here before?"

"Because, that song...Harper, I meant every word of it when I wrote it in May. And I still mean every word of it now. I wasn't sure if you were ready to hear it. But I knew I couldn't wait anymore." He shook his head, letting out a huff of frustration. "What is it with us and timing anyway? Ten minutes...I would've been able to tell you myself in ten *damn* minutes."

"Tell me now. You still haven't exactly said it you know."

"Haven't said what? That I'm in love with you? Have loved you from the second I saw you? I haven't said that?"

Her mouth split into the most perfect smile as she stretched up and pressed her mouth to his. And then she pulled back, reaching up and touching his jaw, her fingers rasping his beard.

"Love at first sight, huh?"

"Without a doubt." He nodded, leaning into her touch.

"For me it was at first sound. I knew it when you sang 'Forever' to me the first time."

Good Lord his heart was pounding erratically out of his chest. "What was at first sound? You still haven't exactly said it you know." He couldn't help but mimic her words from only moments before.

"I fell in love with you, Liam James. And I'm still in love with you."

He moved in close, his lips brushing hers. "Promise?"

"I swear."

And just like that his mouth was covering hers, parting her lips and his tongue delving inside. He needed her closer. He *always* needed her closer.

She shivered against him, no doubt the air conditioner getting to be too much with the fact that she was still soaking wet.

"I need to get you out of these wet clothes." He skimmed his nose across her jaw as he pulled her farther into the room and away from the steady stream of cold air coming from the vent above them.

"You just want to get me naked."

A low laugh escaped his mouth, his lips brushing her cheek. "I always want to get you naked."

He loosened his arms from their hold around her waist, his hands dropping as he moved back a little. He couldn't stop himself from taking just a second to look at her, those wet clothes plastered to her body. She was a sight to be seen, that was for sure, but it wasn't worth her being uncomfortable.

Not even a little bit. So he reached for the hem of her soaked shirt and pulled up.

"Windows," she said, looking around.

"All closed." He tugged again and she lifted her arms without hesitation.

She sucked in a sharp breath as the fabric left her skin. Her nipples were erect, clearly visible through the white cotton of her bra. He reached back, unsnapping the clasp and pulling it away from her body.

The only light in the room was coming from a side table lamp; the overcast sky outside wasn't helping with visuals at all, either. But even with the poor lighting, Liam had known the differences in Harper's body the second he'd seen her coming across the balcony. There was also the fact that he'd had her pressed up against him for the last couple of minutes, and he'd noticed them then as well.

It was hard for him to believe it had only been two weeks since he'd seen her. Maybe the changes weren't as obvious to someone else, but as he was intimately familiar with her body, they were apparent to him immediately. The slight curve of her belly was just a little bit more pronounced, her hips wider, and her breasts larger.

They'd gone up at least a size and his fingers itched to weigh them in his palm. He reached up tentatively, his thumb brushing over her nipple. Her entire body shuddered, but this time he knew it wasn't because she was cold.

"They don't hurt so much anymore," she said as she covered his hand with hers and squeezed. Her eyes closed in pleasure, her head falling back on her shoulders as he covered her other breast with his palm and squeezed both of them in unison.

"God I've missed my hands on you."

"Me too."

"And my mouth." He kissed her neck before he trailed his lips down her chest and laved his tongue across one of her nipples, needing to taste her.

Harper's moans filled the room, her hands finding their way to his hair like they always did. He shared equal admiration to her other breast—he was just considerate like that—before he worked his way down her body until he was kneeling in front of her. Now level with her belly, he leaned forward, kissing her baby bump.

God, every time he thought about the full scope of what they created he couldn't be anything besides ecstatic.

This child was a miracle.

He looked up at her, that constricted feeling in his throat making it hard to speak, but he said it anyway. "I love you, Harper. I love you so much. And I don't regret how we started, or anything that has to do with this baby." He ran his palm across her belly. "And I never will."

"I don't, either." She shook her head, tears falling from her eyes.

He pressed another kiss to her stomach, right next to her belly button. And then he reached for the snap of her jeans before he pulled down the zipper. It took him a second to shimmy the wet fabric down her legs, but he managed, pulling them along with her panties down. He pulled her flats from her feet before he freed her legs entirely.

The need to be inside of her was slightly overwhelming him...or *really* overwhelming him. He stood up, reaching behind his back and grabbing the neck of his T-shirt before he pulled it over his head. The button and zipper of his jeans were already opened, Harper's hands there before he had a chance.

The second his legs were bare—his jeans, boxers, and socks in a pile on the floor—he pulled her over to the couch, sitting down while she crawled up onto his lap. Her knees sunk into the cushions on either side of his thighs, her hands braced on his shoulders as she lifted up and lowered herself down onto his waiting cock.

"Oh God," she groaned as she lifted up and sank back down.

Liam on the other hand was left momentarily speechless because everything about the moment was perfection. It was heaven. *She* was heaven. Her warm body wrapped around him, her hands on his chest, her sighs of pleasure filling his ears, her glorious tits bouncing in his face as she moved.

Speaking of glorious tits…his hands landed on her hips, his fingers digging into her flesh as he leaned forward, opening his mouth over one.

"Liam," she gasped, her fingernails scoring his skin.

"Right here." He placed opened-mouth kisses across her chest—letting his lips linger at the amethyst pendant he gave her—as he made his way to the lotus flower tattoo under her shoulder.

She continued to move, rising up and circling her hips before she fell back down against him. The back of her thighs hit the top of his as he pushed up into her over and over again. His release was imminent, building at the base of his spine, but she needed to get there first. He wanted her pulsing around him when he found it. Wanted her going wild above him.

Lightning struck again just as Liam looked up at Harper. The flash of brilliant white filled the room, lighting up everything. Her skin and eyes glowed, making her look ethereal.

So beautiful and she was his. The love of his life. Now and forever. He'd yet to fully wrap his mind around the conversation they'd just had. He wasn't sure if he ever would. Harper loving him back was something *beyond* everything. Something other-worldly.

Yeah he *really* wasn't going to last much longer.

"Touch me." She pulled one of his hands from her hip, moving it between her thighs. His fingers found her clit, circling over the spot and finding a rhythm of pressure that had her hips moving faster. "Harder," she demanded.

Not one to deny the woman what she wanted, he increased the pressure. He'd never be able to deny her anything ever again. Because she owned him in every way.

Her head fell back onto her shoulders, screaming toward the ceiling as she cried out. The second her body started to tighten around his cock, his orgasm slammed into him like a freight train. Full steam ahead and nothing to stop it.

They fell apart in each other's arms, Harper's mouth landing on his. Her tongue moving against his as her hips slowed. She was still pulsing around him, wringing out every last drop of his release.

Her mouth disappeared from his as she collapsed against him, her head resting on his shoulder. He pulled his hand from between their bodies, grabbing her hip again as the other moved up and down her back, his fingers tracing her spine.

Her skin was damp, sweaty from their bodies moving together and from her hair that was still dripping wet. She shivered, snuggling into his chest and seeking his body heat. He spotted a blanket on the cushion next to them and snatched it up, wrapping it around her shoulders.

"Come on, let's get you warm and dry." He shifted on the couch, pulling from her body before he stood. Getting her in a hot shower would've been the best option, but as the sky was still lighting up every few minutes, that wasn't going to happen.

Her legs banded around his waist, her arms tightening around his neck as she held on to him. He headed for the bathroom, setting her down on the counter before flipping the switch on the wall.

They both blinked in the light, Harper taking just a little bit longer to adjust than him. He reached to the side, turning on the faucet in the sink so the water would heat up.

"Don't move."

"Couldn't even if I wanted to." She shook her head, giving him a sleepy smile.

He leaned in, giving her a kiss on the nose before he pulled away, disentangling himself from her legs and stepping out into the hallway. He grabbed a pink washcloth and a fluffy blue towel from the linen closet before he went back to Harper in the bathroom. The water jetting out of the sink was starting to steam and he stuck his hand underneath, gauging the temperature before submerging the washcloth. He rang it out, lifting the folds of the blanket still wrapped around Harper.

He touched her knee, pushing her legs apart so he could run the warm cloth up the inside of both of her legs, taking special care in the middle. When he was done getting her cleaned up, he tossed the cloth in the hamper before stationing himself between her still spread thighs.

He reached for the tie at the back of her head and with gentle fingers he slowly worked it down her wet hair. When it was free, he grabbed the fluffy blue towel, and soaked up as much of the water as he could. And then he was spearing his fingers in her hair, loosening the strands and massaging the pads of his fingers against her scalp.

Her eyes fell shut almost instantly and she groaned. "God, that feels good."

She melted against him, her head falling on his shoulder as he continued to work her over. She was practically purring after a few minutes. "I think I'm going to fall asleep just like this."

"Did I exhaust you with our sexual acrobatics out there?"

"That and I haven't been sleeping all that well. I can't lie on my stomach anymore and it's hard for me to get comfortable. And…I don't like you not being next to me."

His ministrations paused for just a second, more than slightly taken aback by her words. "I don't like it when you aren't next to me, either."

One of her hands palmed the back of his neck, her fingers moving against the very base of his hairline. Her head moved from where it rested on his shoulder and she pressed her lips to his jaw.

"I love you," she whispered between steady breaths, her exhales hitting his skin. And then she moved her head up, looking into his face. "Earlier…you said you had no regrets in regards to the baby."

He dropped his hands, one bracing her hip while the other ran across her stomach. "I don't."

Her eyes had followed the path of his hand, watching as his palm moved back and forth. "And what about with us?"

"What do you mean?"

"Do you have regrets when it comes to us?" she asked again, still not looking at him.

"Harper." He reached up, touching her chin and gently forcing her gaze up. "Why are you asking this?"

"I shouldn't have run from you. I shouldn't have left you in May." Her voice caught on the last word and the pain in her eyes was bleeding into his heart. "I hate that we missed time because of me." Tears ran down her cheeks when she blinked. She shook her head, closing her eyes.

"Hey," he whispered. His hand at her hip slid around to the small of her back and he moved in closer. "Look at me," he demanded firmly, and her eyes opened immediately. "Harper, you can't play this game. Everyone makes mistakes, honey. Everyone has those moments they want to take back."

"I know that…I…" She blinked again, more tears falling from her eyes. "I ran because I knew. I knew I was in love with you then and I didn't know how to deal with it. I told you before…Liam, forty-eight hours in and you had the power to destroy me. I was *terrified*."

"I screwed up, too, you know. That night on the balcony…letting you walk away." He took a deep breath and let it out on a sigh. "I let my pride get in the way. I didn't know what to do. Didn't know how to react, and I messed up. But in the end, no matter all of the mess-ups and mistakes, we were going to end up here anyway."

"How do you know that?" She wiped at her eyes and sniffled.

"Because there isn't any other option. Harper, this thing with us, it's never happened to me before, and I *know* it will never happen for me again."

"You know what your sister said?" She gave him a watery smile as she reached up and ran her fingers across his jaw.

Oh great. What *had* his sister said? "I have no idea. When it comes to Adele there is no telling what will come out of her mouth."

"She said this was fate. That it was just a matter of time before we crossed paths."

"Did she now?" He raised his eyebrows now more than interested in what his sister had spouted off.

"Yes. She explained that even if we hadn't met in that bar, our paths would've crossed because of the fact that Abby and Logan are together. So whether it was in Nashville, or at the Stampede party…or wherever, we would've found each other."

"And what else did my brilliant sister say?"

"That pregnant or not, you would've wanted to be with me."

That was a fact. "Yup, Adele is one of the smartest women I know. Don't tell her I said that, though. She already *thinks* she's smarter than Logan and me. She doesn't need to *know* it."

"So you believe in fate?" she asked.

"Not before. Not before you walked into that bar. But there were a number of things I didn't believe before I met you."

"Such as?"

"That you can love someone so much it physically hurts. That you can know within an instant that they're your future. Adele's right. I would've found you sooner or later, and I would've wanted you then, too. There's no doubt in my mind."

"I wonder if I wouldn't have run then? If it was later, you know? Because maybe I wouldn't have been terrified…and I wouldn't have hurt you."

"Maybe…" He said the word slowly. "But when it comes right down to it, it doesn't matter. We were *supposed* to meet then, Harper. We were supposed to meet in that bar. And you were supposed to come home with me that night. Because if we changed anything, we wouldn't have *this* baby." His palm still covered her belly, his thumb moving across her skin.

"No, we wouldn't."

"So I wouldn't go back…I wouldn't do anything differently. Not a second. You leaving, as much as it sucked…as much as I hated every moment of it, maybe it needed to happen. Maybe it means no running in the future."

"You'd know where to find me now if I did. There's nowhere to run to."

"You see, that's the thing." He shook his head, tipping her chin up even farther as he leaned in, looking down into her eyes. "I'm waiting for the day you realize there's nothing to run from."

Her violet eyes widened and her mouth dropped open in a shallow gasp, but besides that she made no other sound.

"I want *you*, Harper. I want all of you." His hand was at her throat, his thumb holding her chin in place so she couldn't look away.

"I want all of you, too," she whispered, more than a little breathless.

"I'm yours." His lips hovered just above hers, and he couldn't resist covering them. Kissing her and dipping his tongue inside to taste the perfection that was her mouth. Devouring her as she devoured him right back.

She pulled away, looking up at him as her palms slid down his chest to his abs. "Only mine?" she asked, flexing her hands and causing her nails to bite into his skin.

"Only yours."

"Good." One of her hands was wrapping around his cock that had most definitely found its second wind, and she was lining him up with her entrance. "Show me."

He claimed her mouth as he flexed his hips, pushing into her in one swift move. Being inside of Harper in any capacity was enough to short-circuit his brain, but being inside of her with no barriers...yeah, he still wasn't quite over how amazing it was.

Who was he kidding? He'd never get over it.

Her legs came around his waist, her feet locking at his lower back and her heels digging into his ass. He grabbed on to her hips, holding her steady so she wouldn't slide across the counter as he moved in and out of her.

It was only a matter of time before he had her good and truly breathless again, her hands clawing at his back as she rocked against him.

He pulled one of his hands from her hip and palmed the back of her head, his fingers spearing in her hair as he looked down into her eyes.

"And you're mine." He entered her in a powerful stroke.

"Yes," she gasped.

"Say it," he demanded, pulling out of her before thrusting back in.

"I-I'm yours." Her nails bit into his back harder and he'd swear she probably drew blood.

Could not give less of a shit.

"Promise?" he asked.

"I swear."

There was something about looking down into those violet eyes of hers, so bare and honest and full of love for him, that made him feel like a fucking king.

She was his.

His mouth crashed down on hers, the kiss imitating their bodies. Rough, passionate, naked hunger for each other. Only ever for each other ever again.

He knew her orgasm was coming seconds before it happened. Her back arched, thrusting those magnificent breasts of hers against his chest before her body tightened around his cock.

Her mouth fell away from his. "Oh God. Oh God. Oh Goooooooood."

And just like that he was gone. Spilling inside of her as his release overtook him.

It was remarkable that he was still standing. Really it was. But the thought of pulling away from her was unbearable. He needed her skin on his. His lips on her shoulder…and her neck. His mouth went to the freckled spot just under her ear, kissing it before going to her cheek, and then moving over to find her mouth again.

The world might be raging around them…but there inside of Harper's little apartment, all he knew was peace.

They'd *finally* found each other.

Chapter Eighteen

The Correct Way to Eat an Oreo

Liam was only going to get seven days of settling back into his daily Mirabelle routine with Harper before leaving town again. Though this time Harper would be going with him for a little trip.

Her twenty-seventh birthday was the following week, and after their talk of fate the other night, he kind of had to marvel at the fact that the release of "Forever" was the exact same day. So yeah, they were really going to celebrate and in style.

He was taking her to New York for four days. He didn't have any shows that he needed to perform at while he was there. No interviews. No recording. No meetings. Nothing.

It would be just the two of them lost in the city together.

After that, she would be returning to Mirabelle while he would be leaving for the next leg of the Isaac Hunter tour. This time to Australia…for two and a half weeks.

The fact that he was going to be half a world away from her was not something that made him even remotely happy. Add to that the fact that it would be the longest he'd go without seeing her since they'd reconnected in Jacksonville.

Yeah, he didn't want to think about it. It made him twitchy. Made his skin itch in the most uncomfortable way because there was no way to scratch it. No way to make it go away.

He was just going to have to get through it, though. *They* were going to get through it. But like he'd said so many times before: there wasn't any other choice.

So for now he was just going to focus on the four days before them. He'd gotten a room at The Plaza, a suite that cost more than anything he'd ever paid for in his life.

He was most definitely pulling out all the stops. Doing things he'd never done for a woman he'd been seeing before. But he wasn't just *seeing* Harper. He was in love with her, and he wanted the weekend to be beyond special. Something for her to always remember.

On Friday, the actual day of her birthday—and the song release—he made dinner reservations at Le Petit Fromage. The restaurant was booked out to the end of the year, but the owner and head chef was one of Hunter Andrews's childhood friends.

Liam and Harper toasted the evening with sparkling apple juice over what had to be the most decadent meal he'd ever eaten in his life.

The following night he took her to see a show on Broadway. He'd watched her more than the actual show. But as he was usually hard pressed to pay attention to anything besides her, it wasn't all that shocking.

And really who could blame him? She was wrapped in a blue sequined dress, the back dipping down in a low-V to just above her ass. It was a feat to be sure that the dress somehow managed to contain her breasts. It had to have been because of the intricate pattern of crisscross straps in the back. And since Adele had designed and made said garment—one of three dresses that were his sister's birthday gift to Harper—he wasn't surprised at all.

After the show they headed outside the theater, the crowd of people swarming around them as they waited for the limo he'd rented. Yup, a limo.

Harper's hand was in his as she leaned against his side, her head resting on his shoulder.

"You tired?" he asked, pressing his lips to her temple.

It was almost eleven at night and they'd been up early to "explore the city" as she'd put it. Something they'd done mostly on foot. Though, she hadn't been walking around in the skyscraper heels she was currently wearing.

"Yes…and hungry." She peeked up at him, biting her bottom lip. "Dinner feels like it was ages ago. What are the chances we could get a burger before we go back to the hotel?"

"I'd say they're pretty high."

"And French fries…and a milk shake, too."

"Whatever you want," he said, knowing that those words applied to pretty much everything.

When the driver showed up they asked him to take them to the best—and fastest—burger place he knew of. He didn't even hesitate, pulling off into traffic and cutting through the bright lights and tall buildings.

Harper was more than a tad bit desperate to get comfortable. Her shoes reaching the max of what she could handle for the evening. The second they walked into the hotel room she kicked off her heels. Her next stop was the bedroom, the bags of food in her hand. She'd grabbed a blanket from the sofa on her way, spreading it out over the white quilt before she climbed on top.

She was now sitting in the middle of the bed, her legs crossed in front of her as she unpacked the food from the bags and created her own little picnic. She grabbed a French fry and dipped it in the garlic aioli before popping it into her mouth.

Her eyes closed instantly and a moan filled the room. "Oh my God. These fries are heaven sent."

She opened her eyes and grabbed another one, dipping it in the sauce, before she looked up at him. "You going to join me or just stand there and watch me eat?"

A case could be made for just standing there and watching her, because it really was a fascinating sight. Her hair was still piled up on top of her head in that complicated updo thing, and the skirt of her dress pooled in her lap just below her belly, that bump still too small to look for unless someone *knew* they were looking for it.

For whatever reason, the fact that she was going to eat a burger in that fancy dress had him grinning like a moron.

The woman never ceased to amaze the hell out of him no matter the circumstances.

"What?" she asked before she took a drink of her milk shake.

"God, I'm so in love with you. You're amazing, you know that?"

"Amazing?" She raised an eyebrow. "Really? That's the qualifier you want to use when I'm about to inhale this burger?"

"Absolutely." He nodded as he loosened his tie and made his way over to the bed. He dropped the jacket of his suit on the chair before he kicked off his shoes, and then he sat down next to her on the bed.

She dipped another fry in the sauce and held it out for him. "Tell me these aren't incredible."

He leaned forward, taking the fry in his mouth along with the very tips of her fingers. "Incredible," he agreed after he swallowed. "The fries, too."

"Don't look at me like that." She narrowed her eyes as she shook her head.

"Like what?"

"You know *exactly* what. Here." She grabbed one of the wrapped burgers and handed it to him. "Eat before it gets cold."

"Yes, ma'am." He turned, sliding up the bed and settling his back against the headboard before unwrapping the burger.

How was it that with everything they'd done during this trip, this was his favorite moment?

* * *

Their last morning in New York came complete with dark gray storm clouds looming low over the city. They were a pretty good indicator for Liam's mood, too. He had to leave Harper today and he was in no way looking forward to it.

It was taking a great deal of self-control to not let his somber mood take over. He didn't want there to be any dark spots on their trip this weekend.

But sometimes things were *way* out of a person's control.

He'd just been on the phone with the airline for ten minutes confirming their flights, and when he walked back into the bedroom it was to find it in exactly the same state it had been when he walked out.

The bed was covered in Harper's clothes, her suitcase sitting in the middle and still just as empty. She was standing in the middle of the room staring down at her phone. Her shoulders were slumped forward and she was chewing on her bottom lip. She was so focused on the device in her hands that she hadn't even heard him come in.

"What's wrong?"

His voice made her jump, her phone flying into the air before she caught it again. Her head came up, her worried eyes focusing on him. "Sorry. You scared me."

"I see that. What's wrong?" he repeated as he set his phone on the nightstand and crossed the room to her.

She pulled her bottom lip into her mouth and started chewing on it again. She was waging the debate of whether or not to tell him, deciding if it was important or not. But anything that was upsetting her this much was clearly important.

"The truth, honey. Remember our agreement, no barriers good, bad, or ugly." He reached up, pulling her bottom lip from her teeth.

"Oh, it's ugly all right."

Great. He'd had to share his own bit of ugly news with her last week with the whole Kiki debacle in Louisiana. But he wasn't keeping anything like that from Harper. That was how things got out of hand.

"Have I ever told you about Bethelda Grimshaw?"

"She a villain from a kid's book?"

A small laugh escaped Harper's mouth, but it did nothing

to counteract the look in her eyes. "Half of that is correct. She's a villain all right, but she isn't fictional. No matter how much I wish that were the case. She's from Mirabelle and she writes this blog."

"What kind of blog?"

"Where she drags other people from town through the mud."

"What do you mean?"

She didn't say anything, just handed over her phone. And as Liam read, his ears started ringing.

THE GRIM TRUTH

BREAKING UP ISN'T SO HARD TO DO AND NEITHER IS MOVING ON

It's only been a handful of months since Voluptuous V.'s fiancé (Human Ken Doll) ran out of town and left her high and dry. As we all know, he had absolutely no desire to walk down the aisle and commit to the woman for the rest of his life.

Completely understandable if you ask me especially as it didn't take VV any time at all to find another man to fill her bed. And who is this mystery man you ask? Well, as to that I'm still unsure because Scruff McGruff is most definitely not from around here.

I know, I know I've been a *tad* bit outspoken when it comes to *others* invading our quaint little town. Really, what can I say? I'm a traditionalist. And I know that I'm not the only one who feels this way, either.

But I digress. That is a different rant for a different day. Back to the real topic at hand: who is this man?

I've spotted McGruff a handful of times over the last couple of weeks, but not consistently. He blows in and out of town with the wind. But maybe that's what it takes for VV to keep a man. If he isn't around her for long periods of time he can handle her/the relationship.

If we can even classify it as a relationship.

This little affair will probably be over soon enough as it is. Once McGruff is finished fooling around, he will blow out of town like the last man in VV's life.

And he won't be looking back, either, because the view is starting to look a little rough around the edges. VV is starting to pack on the pounds again and it isn't a pretty sight.

But to each their own, maybe McGruff is into that sort of thing... which just makes me question him all the more. And this is why it would be good to know who he is while he's still around.

So if any of my loyal readers have any ideas, you let me know. I'd be more than happy to spread the word as to who VV is currently spreading it for.

"Voluptuous V? What the hell is this?" He looked up at Harper, rage boiling in his veins. "Is this a joke?"

"I wish it was. She started doing it years ago. Her way of..." She trailed off and shrugged, unsure. "I don't even know what. Maybe it's her way of getting back at the world for someone who slighted her. Last week she came in for a massage and I just knew

I was going to be popping up in her headlines again."

"Again?"

"Yeah. She had fodder for weeks after Brad left. And I've been on there a number of times over the years. This isn't the first time she's called me fat or implied that I'm a whore."

This was the biggest bunch of bullshit he'd ever read in his life, and he'd been in the tabloids before, so he *knew* bullshit. "How does she get away with it?"

"She says it's all fiction. Though everyone knows exactly who she's talking about. Which is surprising as no one claims to read it, yet they always know what's going on."

"You read it regularly?"

"No, I don't." She shook her head. "One of my coworkers texted it to me. She thought I might want to know about Bethelda's call to arms to figure out who you are. I'm actually surprised she didn't know the answer to that yet. But as my friends and family won't be talking to her, it's going to take someone else recognizing you. Which, you know, is really just a matter of time at this point."

The worry in her eyes was more than he could take. "Come here." He wrapped his arms around her, pulling her into his chest as he pressed his nose to her hair. It managed to have a calming effect on his entire body.

And really, when it came down to it? All of this outside nonsense was insignificant. What was important was the woman in his arms.

"I'm sorry," she whispered as she kissed his neck.

He moved back just far enough to look down into her face. "Why in the world are you apologizing to me?"

"Liam, once she figures out who you are, it's going to go much further than just some local blog. And when she gets her hands on the fact that I'm pregnant? I don't even want to know."

"Doesn't matter." He shook his head. "I flat out refuse to let whoever the hell this woman is mess with our relationship. I refuse to let anybody mess with it. People can write whatever they want to write. At the end of the day, we both know the truth."

"We do." She nodded.

"And what's the truth?" He cradled her jaw in his hand, tracing her cheek with his thumb.

"Are you testing me?" She raised her eyebrow.

"Just making sure you remember. What's the truth, Harper?"

"That I love you and you love me."

"Exactly. Everything else isn't important. Come on." He grabbed her hand and turned, leading her to the bathroom. "We aren't letting anyone put a dark smudge on this trip. We're ending on a high note."

"A high note?"

"Yup, you screaming my name when you come in the shower."

* * *

Bethelda's little call to arms in figuring out the identity of Liam/Scruff McGruff took seventeen days to finally yield the answer she'd been looking for, and with it a few more facts. It came out the day before Liam was flying back to Mirabelle from Australia.

THE GRIM TRUTH

ROCK A BYE, BYE BABY

It's all fun and games until someone gets knocked up. Yup, that's right folks, she's not fat. She's just pregnant. VV is procreating, Lord help us all. And the knocker-upper? Well, I'm guessing it's a certain mystery man who has been hanging around our area for the last few weeks. But he isn't that much of a mystery anymore.

The man in question is actually a country musician (name rhymes with Shmiam Shames) if you feel so inclined to classify him as that. The man doesn't have all that much talent to speak of, but at least he's pretty. Though I will say his taste in women is rather questionable.

I was pretty curious to know *how* VV sunk her claws into a semi-famous singer. But it's really all because McGruff sunk something else into her. Another case of "I can't keep my pants on despite my nose...or all common sense, logic, or reason." Because *really* if he'd just taken a few moments to think he wouldn't have gotten himself into a situation like this.

Who *really* knows what drew him to VV in the beginning, but I'm sure that the only thing really keeping him around now is the fact that she just might be carrying his child. For his sake, he really should get a paternity test (along with a few other tests if you know what I'm saying. Who knows what the woman is carrying besides the bun in the oven).

I still don't really see this whole relationship lasting. It's got an ice cubes chance in hell if you want my oh-so-humble opinion. But we shall just have to wait and see now won't we?

Yup, so the pregnancy was out along with Liam's identity. And there were certain words in that stupid article that had stung more than others. But it didn't send Harper over the rails. She knew for a fact that Liam wasn't with her just because they were having a child. He'd made that quite clear.

He loved her.

Bethelda didn't have the power to take that away. No one did.

But there was a part that did infuriate Harper beyond all reason: Bethelda insulting Liam. "Not all that much talent to speak of" her ass.

"Forever" had been officially released almost three weeks ago and not only had it already cracked the top one hundred downloads on iTunes, but it was steadily climbing. Country music stations were getting frequent requests for it, and Harper heard it on the local station daily.

Those were the facts. Another fact was that Bethelda was probably suffering from gonosyphilherpes and it was beginning to affect her brain at this point.

Actually, Harper was still surprised that it had taken that long for someone to figure out who Liam was. Maybe it was because Bethelda's minions hadn't known what they were supposed to be looking for. How were they to know that he was a celebrity of any sort? Harper hadn't known who Liam was when'd she'd gone home with him that first night…or after spending the weekend with him.

No, she hadn't found out until six weeks later.

She supposed that was the power of the radio though. You knew the voice and the name, but not necessarily the face. Well, not until the name got a whole lot bigger. Kind of like Tim McGraw, or Keith Urban, or Taylor Swift. Liam's touring mates were another prime example. If Isaac Dylan or Hunter Andrews walked into a bar, a lot of the people in it were going to know exactly who they were.

But Liam was gaining on recognition, and it was only going to grow as the video for "Beyond the Limits" was scheduled to be released in less than a week. Not only was Liam going to be singing right alongside Isaac and Hunter, but there was the association with *Mason-Dixon*…

And Kiki Jean Carlow, otherwise known as Harper's least favorite person of all time…and yes, the woman had beaten out Bethelda.

Bitch was tryin' to steal her man.

Liam had told Harper everything about that entire situation, everything that had gone down on the video shoot and before then. Kiki had apparently ruined the song for him and he wasn't looking forward to the video being released in any way, shape, or form.

And after he'd told her about it, she wasn't, either. Liam with another woman made her go about fifty shades of jealous. And they weren't pretty shades, either. More like a wheel of the ugliest colors a person could think of, like rust or taupe or mold green.

But she knew what was going on, and there would be no surprises on her end. It was a fact that made her slightly guilty that she still hadn't told Liam about the newest Bethelda article.

Though to be fair, he'd been in the air during a twenty-four-hour flight…and when he'd gotten back to Mirabelle they hadn't exactly spent a lot of time talking. They'd spent hours getting reacquainted in other ways, which she hadn't had a problem with in the slightest as she was a veritable hornucopia.

And good Lord did the man deliver in everything she'd needed. He left absolutely no doubt in her mind as to how much he loved her body or that he still wanted her just as much even though it was changing.

And was it ever changing.

She'd gained back the majority of the weight she'd lost, filling out her curves to the fullest. Her breasts were now in the DD range and the bump at her belly was no longer a slight rise. She was visibly showing and her clothing was no longer camouflaging the pregnancy. It was well past the point of the expertly draped dresses and flowy tops that she'd bought with her mother a few weeks ago doing the trick.

Obviously, as Bethelda had figured it out. And she was going to tell Liam just as soon as she got home. But really how was she going to have told him when she'd been at work all day and he'd been sleeping to get over the jet lag/time difference.

A time difference that had been the bane of her existence for the last two and a half weeks.

But she didn't have to deal with that now. What she did have to deal with was the crowd of people currently at the Piggly Wiggly at five thirty on a Friday afternoon. And of course she had Liam on the phone helping her shop, because why wouldn't she?

"So what's today's craving?" his voice rumbled low in her ear. He'd only just woken up and had called her while still lounging in bed.

Really, why in the world should she give a flying flip to that stupid Bethelda article when there was a sexy, scruffy, gorgeous man waiting for her to get home?

Yup, *perspective*. That was what she was learning. See, being rational was possible even while pregnant.

"Tacos for dinner, and Oreos for dessert." She sidestepped the man in the Jimmy Buffett T-shirt who'd been blocking her path pretty much the entire time she'd been shopping. He had no regard for anyone else in the aisles shopping around him.

"With milk?" Liam asked, his voice magically pulling her away from her annoyance at Mr. Cheeseburger in Paradise. Asshole in the Piggly Wiggly was more like it.

Again, it was all about *perspective*.

"Is there any other way to eat them?" She grabbed the hard-shells and put them in the cart.

"You dunk them right away or lick the center first?" The grin in his voice was obvious.

"Liam, could you have made that sound any more inappropriate?"

"I could try."

"Oh, I'm sure you could." Harper propped the phone between her ear and her shoulder as she grabbed the cart again and started pushing, heading for the produce section.

"Do we have the ingredients to make fresh salsa?"

"Let me check." He shifted in bed and the sheets ruffled through the phone.

While he went to the kitchen, she hunted for ripe avocados, because guacamole sounded like the greatest thing ever.

"That's a negative, rubber duck. You're going to need to get onions, tomatoes, cilantro, and lemon juice. Geez, woman, did you go grocery shopping at all while I was gone? You've got nothing here unless we're going to eat peanut butter and jelly."

"And this is why I'm at the grocery store. So shut it."

"Did you just tell me to shut it?"

"Yeah I did." She headed to the tomatoes and threw a couple into a plastic bag. "What are you going to do about it?"

"As soon as you get home I'll show you. And it will be a very similar experience to how I eat my Oreos."

A shiver ran down Harper's back as a blush crept up into her cheeks. "Is that a promise?"

"You bet your sweet ass it is."

"Language, Mr. James."

"Oh, you like my mouth. And feel free to call me mister when you get home and I use it on you."

Home. Home to him. God, how she wished all days were like this.

"Deal. I'm getting off the phone now. You're distracting me from shopping."

"Translation: you're getting all hot and bothered as you look at the eggplant."

"Hanging up now." She snatched a bag of cilantro as she rounded past the herbs.

"Love you."

"Love you, too." She grinned hugely as she hung up, sticking her phone in her purse before she went to grab an onion to add to the cart.

Five minutes later she had everything she needed and was heading to the front of the store. There was a line at each of the open registers, so she went to number ten at the very end because it seemed a tad bit shorter. Her prime number tendencies weren't all that important in the moment. All she wanted was to get out of there and get to the man who was waiting for her.

Waiting to do wicked things to her with his mouth. Yes, that was a good thing to focus on. A much, *much* better thing to focus on.

The line shifted and she moved forward, loading the groceries onto the belt while the woman in front of her paid. When the last item was up on the belt she stepped back and glanced over to the stand next to her, her eyes catching on the tabloids. There were the usual articles discussing the supposed demise of another A-List couple, or if so-and-so was coming out of the closet, or how aliens had abducted what's-his-name.

But none of those were what caught Harper's eye. No, it was the tabloid with a massive picture of Kiki Jean Carlow front and center. She was batting her baby blues at the camera and grinning. Right next to it was a separate—and smaller—headshot of Liam.

Has Kiki Jean Carlow Found Love with Musician Liam James? Is She the Girl from His New Hit Song "Forever"?

Seeing his name connected to Kiki's almost had Harper losing it right there in the middle of the Piggly Wiggly. As it was, her heart was pounding out of her chest, her palms had gone sweaty, and her ears were ringing.

It was automatic, her flipping through the pages to get to the article. She stopped breathing when she found it.

More pictures were here, these with Liam and Kiki actually together. One was of them sitting in a club, the photo slightly blurry but clear enough to see him leaning closer to presumably hear her speak. Another of her leaving what looked to be a room backstage; he was shirtless and she was running her fingers down his chest. The last was from the video shoot, the two of them walking side by side, his hand on her hip as he looked down at her.

Yup, just like that, *perspective* was gone. She was going to be sick.

Chapter Nineteen

I'll Be Your Man

Liam was starting another load of laundry when Harper walked in the front door. Luna bolted from her comfortable position all snuggled on the bed and ran through the living room to get to her owner.

He shut the lid of the washer and closed the accordion doors before heading down the hallway.

"Groceries in the car?" he asked as he rounded the corner. He'd told her to call him when she was close and he'd get them out. But as her arms were laden with four reusable bags she hadn't listened.

"There wasn't that much." She shook her head, barely sparing him a glance as she headed for the kitchen.

He made a move to grab the bags but she didn't let go. "Wasn't that much? You're carrying your weight in groceries." Okay, maybe a slight over-exaggeration. But still, he'd told her he would get them.

"I've got it." She pulled away and stepped around him.

He followed automatically, an uneasiness settling over him. *What the hell was going on?* They'd just been on the phone not twenty minutes ago and everything had been fine. Now she wouldn't look at him.

"Harper, what's wrong?"

"Nothing," she said as she pulled the milk, cheese, and sour cream from the bag and walked over to the refrigerator.

Bullshit.

"You lying to me now?"

Her back snapped in tension as she straightened, shutting the door a little harder than normal as she spun around. There was a fire in her eyes, passion in her cheeks, and fury on her mouth. "Did you just call me a liar?"

"No, I asked if you were lying. Not the same thing."

Her eyes narrowed and she took a deep breath, letting it out through her nose. She walked back over to the bags, pulling out a magazine and tossing it on the counter. "That's what's going on," she said, pointing.

His eyes dropped to the magazine, scanning the front and seeing his picture next to Kiki's with a headline that immediately had his own temper flaring. He didn't need to read what was inside to know it was all a bunch of lies.

Apparently it didn't matter that he'd been one hundred percent honest with her from the get-go, she thought he was cheating.

He looked back up to her, doing everything in his power not to lose his damn mind. "Tell me you don't believe that."

"You don't even know what it says."

"I don't need to, Harper. Anything connecting me to Kiki is horseshit."

"I know that!" she shouted.

"Really? Do you? Then why the fuck did you buy it?" he shouted right back. He didn't mean to, but good God, she was killing him. "Because if you believe a word of that garbage for a single second, then you don't know me at all!"

The instant her eyes filled with tears he knew he'd missed the mark. Had gone too far and let his temper take control. This didn't have to do with trusting him. Whatever was in there had scared her and she didn't know how to deal with it.

"Harper—"

But she turned and walked away. Out of the kitchen and down the hall to the bedroom, and before the door shut, her sob echoed down the hallway.

"Dammit." He followed, refusing to let her walk away. He'd done that once before, not stopped her when she'd left him on that balcony. He wasn't doing it again.

Never again.

* * *

Harper was losing it. She was *freaking* losing it.

Another sob broke out of her chest and she tried to bury it in the pillow, her body curling in on itself as she started to shake uncontrollably.

God it hurt. Everything. Her lungs that were having difficulty pulling in air. Her head that was pounding. Her heart that was throbbing. All of it.

The bedroom door opened, Liam's bare feet moving across

the wooden floor before the bed dibbed and his arms wrapped around her. His front solidly pressed to her back.

"Honey, please don't. Please don't cry," he whispered, his lips on her neck.

It just made her cry harder.

She knew that stupid article had been garbage. The article that implied "Forever" was about Kiki. The article that implied Kiki and Liam had been seeing each other for months. It didn't matter that Harper knew the truth. Didn't matter that she trusted Liam implicitly.

Because it still hurt so badly she couldn't breathe.

She wasn't sure how long they lay there before she calmed down. Before she wasn't gasping in air. Before the crying had changed from sobbing to a wave of tears running down her cheeks every time she blinked.

His hand found hers, his palm covering the back of the fist she'd made. She was clutching on to the pillow and he tugged lightly until she let go, her hand relaxing.

"You're who I want, Harper." Their hands moved down and when he brought it to her belly he flattened her palm against the not-so-slight bump, his hand still covering hers. "You and this baby. Please tell me you know that." His nose skimmed her neck, the scruff of his beard tickling her skin. "Please tell me you know how much I love you."

She rolled to her back, looking up into Liam's face as he hovered above her. The green-gold of his gaze was all that she saw, the raw honesty in his eyes so real.

"I know." She reached up with her free hand—he still had the other pressed to her belly—and touched his jaw. "This isn't about me being pregnant and hormonal you know…well, it's not all about that."

Okay…maybe she hadn't been nearly as rational as she thought…or not at all. She'd apparently just reached the limit of what she could take before she'd lost it.

"Tell me what it's about." He leaned down, resting his forehead against hers.

"There are pictures in there, Liam. And even though I know what's going on in every single one of them, seeing that? It…it just hurts." She blinked and fresh tears fell from her eyes, tracking down her temples. Most got caught in her hair but the light tap of a couple hitting the pillow filled her ears. "This isn't going to be the last of it, either. Bethelda figured out who you are…and that I'm pregnant."

"What?" His head came up at her words, and he looked down into her eyes again. "When?"

"Two days ago. That blog isn't hard to find, babe. It's only a matter of time before someone finds out the relationship between the two of us. Especially the way "Forever" is getting bigger and how everyone wants to know *who* it's about. It's…it's only going to get worse."

"I know." He smoothed his hand across her hair.

"And then the video for 'Beyond the Limits' is going to be released, and not only is that going to take off, but…but I have a feeling those pictures are going to be *nothing* in comparison to what's in that video."

"Don't watch it."

"You think it's going to be that easy?" she asked desperately, wanting to hear him say yes.

"No. But God I wish it was."

"What would you do if you saw a picture of me with another man? Pictures that were taken while you and I were together? Pictures of his hands on me? Even if you knew the context."

Pain flashed across his face. "It would kill me. It isn't going to happen again."

"You can't promise that."

"No, I can. This hurts you. And I can't change the past but I can prevent it from happening again in the future."

"And what happens when you piss your label off?"

"Oh, that would be a headline I'd love to see: '*Liam James storms off set because he refuses to hurt the love of his life.*' Let's just see what happens after."

"Love of his life?" Harper repeated, a small smile turning up the corner of her mouth.

"Yeah, didn't you know?" He pressed his mouth to hers, in a soft and slow kiss that morphed into frenzied in seconds.

Mainly her doing.

The sudden shift in what her body needed was so strong that she couldn't for a second deny it. *Him.* She needed *him.* Would *always* need him.

He shifted to hover over her and she spread her legs, making space for him between her thighs that now cradled his hips. His hand was up and under the skirt of her dress, and he wound his fingers in the lacey band of her thong. One good tug and he ripped the material from her body.

Her hands were at the front of his athletic shorts and she pushed them down just enough to free his erection. He thrust inside her and the cry that emanated from her mouth was one that couldn't be helped.

"You okay," he gasped as his hips stilled.

"Yes. Don't stop." She grabbed the back of his head and brought his mouth back down to hers, pushing her tongue past his lips to taste him.

He started to move, pulling back before driving into her again. She didn't need to tell him harder, because he was giving her just what she needed.

Him.

Over. And over. And over again.

* * *

Liam hadn't had a place that he *really* thought of as home in years. Sure the cabin in Tennessee was where he'd spent the long stints of his off time...but that was Logan's place. Not his.

But now? Now Harper's apartment felt more like home than any place ever had before. Mirabelle had started to feel like home...way more so than Nashville. He wasn't sure when exactly that shift had happened, all he knew was that it *had* happened. And he had absolutely no doubt that it pretty much had *everything* to do with Harper.

God he loved that woman. Loved her so much he couldn't think straight. But hey, him not being able to think straight had pretty much been the case from the second he'd met her...

No, from the second he'd seen her.

For years all he'd been working for was his career. All he'd wanted was to make music. Was for people to listen to the songs that he'd created and get *something* from them. *Anything* from them.

But ever since Harper had come along his focus had shifted. What he wanted was morphing to encompass a whole hell of a lot more. Being on the road and not seeing her, not getting to experience every moment of watching her body change, of watching her grow with *their* baby...well, it was physically painful actually.

He just had to keep telling himself that they could get through this. That they *would* get through this. Australia was the biggest hurdle to deal with—as he'd been on the other side of the world—and they were past it now.

The last month of the tour was all on the East Coast, and mostly in the south. He'd be able to see her way more often than before. Even if the trip was only as long as twenty-four hours, his butt would be on a plane.

And once that was over, he was off for a few months...until it all started again.

But that was something he didn't need to worry about. The next tour was a good ways down the road, and would be happening well after the baby was born.

He and Harper had discussed a few pre- and post- baby topics. Like the fact that he was going to be there for the birthing classes, or that there would be nothing circus themed in the baby's room if it included clowns. They freaked Harper out. They'd also talked about the holidays and that if his parents wanted to do Thanksgiving in Nashville it would probably be fine, but since she'd be eight months pregnant when Christmas rolled around they should spend it in Mirabelle.

And of course they'd talked about what they were going to have. The boy versus girl debate was ongoing, and it wasn't like they had a preference either way. The only factor they were hoping for was healthy. It was the possible name selections that they were going back and forth on.

His top picks? Chloe if they had a girl. Caleb for a boy.

Her current favorites? Well, it depended on the day really. She couldn't decide between Piper and Mackenzie for a girl. And Bentley, Donovan, or Sawyer for a boy.

They'd gone through a number of them…more than he even knew. When he'd been on tour there was always a phone call first thing in the morning. Or when he was with her, a whisper low in his ear in the middle of the night. And as he was throwing suggestions out right and left as well, they texted each other possibilities throughout the day.

They hadn't exactly agreed on anything as of yet.

Though the field was cut in half on Monday at Harper's next doctor's appointment. They were having a girl.

A baby girl.

Knowing the gender was another step that brought them that much closer to the day. One more piece of information to get them prepared for the future.

He still had no idea where they were going to raise their child…Nashville or Mirabelle or anywhere else for that matter.

If they lived in Nashville they were going to need to buy a house. If they stayed in Mirabelle…they were still going to need to buy a house. Her apartment wasn't going to cut it. There was absolutely no doubt about that. Her tiny spare bedroom was barely a closet. A cupboard under the stairs probably boasted more space.

The few things they'd bought or received for the baby weren't even being stored at her apartment. They were keeping them in a spare room at her parents' house because there was no extra space to find anywhere.

They needed room and rooms to grow. All of them. Space for multiple additions to their family. Yup, *multiple* additions to *their* family.

He wanted everything with her.

And her apartment wasn't going to fit the bill when it came to building said family. The lease ended in October, a little bit more than a month away. She'd mentioned moving, talked about renting a place farther in town. The prices dropped as the distance from the beach increased.

But that wasn't exactly what he had in mind for the future. Nope, he wanted something *way* more permanent. He wanted *forever.*

He'd spent all of those nights in Australia—when he was *half a freaking world away*—thinking about it. And he knew what he needed to do first. A man-to-man conversation with Paul Laurence was priority number one.

Tuesday provided just such an opportunity. They were driving up about two hours north of Mirabelle to go fishing. Harper was ridiculously happy about the fact that he was going to be spending the day with her father. And as he genuinely liked Paul, he was looking forward to the day as well.

The plan was to leave at five o'clock in the morning when Paul picked him up at the apartment.

But Liam didn't hear the alarm and it was Harper who woke him, her hand on his chest before it slid down and wrapped around his dick.

"One for the road?" she whispered in his ear.

And just like that she successfully managed to get him up twice over.

* * *

The sun was still sitting low in the sky and hadn't cleared the forest that surrounded them when Liam and Paul got to the lake. The humidity wasn't too terrible yet and as they would be in the shade of the trees it looked to be a pretty good setup.

The entire ride up Liam had been trying to figure out how to broach the subject...just jump right on in. Or segue into it at some point during the day. Or...

"I can smell you thinking over there." Paul's voice interrupted Liam's thoughts.

They were both standing at the back of the truck putting their rods together. Liam turned to the man next to him and caught the corner of Paul's mouth doing that slight twitch that meant he was amused.

"I'm trying to figure out how to ask you a question."

"Well, you want my advice? Just come out and ask me already." Another twitch moved his lip.

"I want to marry your daughter."

"That didn't sound like a question."

"It wasn't." Liam shook his head. "It's a fact. It's also a fact that

I love her more than anyone and I want to spend the rest of my life with her. That's never going to change, either. And I know she's who I'd want no matter the circumstances. I don't want to marry her just because she's pregnant. I want to marry her because she's it for me."

"I still don't hear a question in there."

"Because none of that is in question."

"Then what is?"

Liam took a deep breath before he asked. "Do I have your blessing in asking her to marry me?"

"There it is." Paul looked over, his head tilted to the side just slightly. Though the man was wearing sunglasses, Liam could feel his penetrating gaze doing a rather extensive study. "You know, Harper's ex didn't ask for my blessing when he asked Harper to marry him. He wouldn't have gotten it, either, because he wasn't the man she was supposed to marry. Not all that shocking as he walked out on her in the end."

"Moron," Liam muttered under his breath.

The twitch in Paul's mouth curved up into a smile before he turned back to the task at hand, grabbing another piece of the rod to attach. "Lucky for you, huh?"

"Something I find myself thanking God for every day." Liam cleared his throat, reaching up and scratching the back of his neck. "So you two ever talk about the fact that you didn't think he was good enough?"

"Yeah we did, a number of conversations in fact. And at the end she always told me she was sure about him. But I always sensed that flicker of doubt. Which was why I kept asking. A year and a half and he never quite proved himself to me. And you know, beginning circumstances being what they were, I wasn't all that hopeful about you, either. But for my daughter's sake I was going to give you a chance."

"And hope that I was smarter?"

"Oh, you proved that long before I met you, Liam. You didn't walk away from her."

"I know what it's like to lose her. To think there's no chance of getting her back. I don't ever want to feel like that again."

"Definitely smarter than Brad." Paul nodded. "Still didn't mean you were worthy of her."

"If you're waiting for some revelation as to that, I think you will be waiting for a long time. Because honestly? No one will ever be worthy of Harper. I knew it before. Knew it the first time I saw her. Knew I would spend the rest of my life trying to prove myself. And, circumstances being what they are, I understand it even more. No one will be worthy of my daughter, either. Ever."

"It takes a real man to understand that." Paul put the rod on the back of his truck before he turned his entire body to face Liam. He folded his arms across his chest as he leaned against the hitch. "You know how many times I've asked Harper if she was sure about you?"

"How many?"

"Once. The night she told me she was pregnant. When I met you I didn't need to ask anymore. The first thing I saw was you looking at my daughter like she was your entire world. You want my blessing to marry her? You've got it, Liam." Paul extended his hand out.

Liam was a little taken aback by the last words that Paul had spoken, and it took him a second to get over the shock and reach out, grabbing the proffered hand and shaking it.

"Welcome to the family, son."

* * *

Harper got to her parents' house just after six o'clock, Darby and Luna greeting her when she walked in as per usual. She'd dropped Lune off before work since she and Liam were going to have a late evening with dinner and everything else.

"Hey guys," she said, getting down low and scratching both of their heads.

"Harper?" Delilah called out.

"Be there in a second."

She gave the dogs about another minute of a good rubdown before she straightened and headed for the kitchen. Delilah was at the stove, the cast iron skillet popping with oil.

"Hey, Mom." Harper came up next to her and gave her a kiss on the cheek just as Delilah dropped a dollop of dough in the oil.

"Hey, sweetie." Delilah leaned into the kiss.

It wasn't like their relationship had done a complete one-eighty in the last couple of weeks, but they were working on it. It was definitely better than it had been, and her mother had accepted the fact that she was going to be a grandmother.

So Harper had that going for her.

"They back?"

"Yeah, about thirty minutes ago. They're both getting a shower."

"Separately I hope," Harper said as she reached for an already cooked hush puppy.

Delilah turned and looked at her, not impressed with the joke.

"I know, I know. I did *not* get my sense of humor from you." She grinned before she took a bite.

"*Clearly* you did not. It's definitely from your father."

"Has to be."

"Mmm hmm." She nodded as she dropped another dollop into the oil. "Hey, your father and I pulled a few things for Baby Girl from the attic yesterday. We put it in the room with all of the other stuff."

Baby Girl. God, they were having a little girl. Every time she thought about that fact the most perfect, indescribable flutter ran through her belly. Though there were quite a few flutters lately. *Baby Girl* was moving around. Nothing drastic as of yet. No kicking hard enough for Liam to feel.

Harper knew how anxious he was for that moment to happen.

"Baby Girl?" Harper had to ask, as this was the first time her mother had addressed the baby with that moniker, and Harper would be lying if she said she didn't love it. "That's what we're referring to her as now?" Harper turned, popping the last of the hush puppy in her mouth as she leaned back against the counter to get a perfect view of her mother's face.

"Until you and that man of yours figure out a name."

"That man of mine?" Those words sounded kind of perfect coming out of her mouth, and yes all evidence pointed to the fact that he was her man, but…but sometimes minds changed.

Where the hell had that come from? Harper was more than slightly shocked by that last thought, and it caused a painful pang in her chest.

She was just being ridiculous. It was just another small moment of insecurity. She shook it off and focused on her mother again.

"Yes." Delilah's face came up and focused on her daughter. No joking in her gaze to be found. "That man of *yours*. Anyone who writes a song about you has to be your man. Right?"

Right…the song. "I sure hope so," Harper agreed. Actually those words were more like a prayer.

"It's a good song you know. And it's doing pretty well from what I've gathered."

"It is." She nodded still a little distracted, but then her mother's words resonated. "Where are you gathering this?"

"The Google," Delilah said entirely straight faced.

It took everything in Harper not to laugh. "The Google? Really?"

"Yeah, I know how to look things up. You know, not only is he talented, but he's very photogenic. Not very many people look as good in pictures as they do in real life. He's got fantastic genes."

"He does. Good thing he's the man I'm breeding with." The smile that turned up her mouth was genuine…her small moment of crazy pushed to the back of her mind.

"This is true. At least you have excellent taste in attractive men. *That* you get from me." Delilah looked over and grinned.

"I sure did. Can I go up and see what you pulled from the attic?"

"Go for it."

"Thanks." Harper leaned in and placed another kiss on her mother's cheek before she turned and headed for the backstairs at the side of the kitchen.

The "storage room" was actually Harper's old bedroom. It was the very last room at the end of the hallway, right across from the bathroom. The door was shut and the fan was going. She wondered if Liam was still naked behind that door. Drying off after he got out of the shower. For just a second she was tempted to knock and walk in there.

No. Stop it right this very second. You are in your parents' house. Your. Parents'. House. No no no.

Holy hell, five minutes ago she'd been contemplating the idea that Liam might leave her…and now she wanted to jump him. Sometimes she wondered if it was the pregnancy hormones that were making her crazy or if she was just crazy.

It's the pregnancy, she reassured herself as she veered off and headed to the left.

The door was partially cracked and when she stepped inside her old bedroom her eyes landed on exactly what her parents had pulled from the attic. Her heart flew up into her throat and that flutter ran through her belly again.

It was the antique cradle that she'd been rocked in as a baby, the very same cradle that her mother and aunt had been rocked in as well. The light brown wood was still in pristine condition even after fifty plus years.

She took a step forward, reaching out and running her fingers across the side, tracing the detailed woodwork. Lilies had been carved into the wood, wrapping around the entirety of the piece of furniture.

The corner of her eyes prickled, and when she blinked the tears fell down her cheeks.

The bathroom door behind her opened and she turned, looking over her shoulder as Liam stepped out, steam making a haze behind him. His hair was wet, a slight curl in the strands that hung low across his forehead.

"Hey," she sniffed, reaching up and wiping her fingers across her cheek.

"What's wrong?" He was across the hall and reaching for her within seconds.

"Nothing." She shook her head, more tears falling with the motion.

"Then why are you crying?" Now he was the one reaching up, his thumb wiping away the fresh tears that tracked down her face.

"This." She turned, her hand on the wood again as she traced the flowers. "My parents pulled it down from the attic. It was made in Italy, one of the few things my grandparents had shipped over when they moved to the States. Nonna Sofia loved lilies so Papa Jack had it made for her."

"Sofia," Liam said slowly, rolling the name on his tongue. He reached out for the cradle, too, his fingers right next to her and tracing the flowers on the wood. "What about Sofia Lillian?"

They looked at each other at the same time. A smile was turning up the corner of his mouth as his free hand went to her stomach, his palm flat on her belly.

"That's it." She grinned back at him, her hand covering his. "That's her name."

Liam leaned down, pressing his mouth to hers. "We just named our daughter," he whispered against her lips. And then he was kneeling down in front of Harper, both of his hands on her belly as he leaned in. "We just named you. What do *you* think about Sofia Lillian?" he asked.

It was at that moment that it happened, a small pop hit the

side of her belly. Liam looked up at Harper, his eyes going huge. "Did that just happen? Did she just kick my hand?"

Harper could only nod, the look of sheer joy on Liam's face making her momentarily speechless.

His gaze dropped down again. "You like your name, Sofia Lillian?" he asked as another kick hit his hand. "It's amazing." He shook his head before he leaned in and pressed his lips to the spot. "God, this is incredible."

And this time it was a sniff from the doorway that filled the room. Harper and Liam both looked over at the same time to see her mother standing there, tears falling from her eyes.

"I'm sorry." She took a deep breath like she was trying to compose herself. "I came up to see what you thought about the cradle. I...I didn't mean to...to interrupt. You're going to name her after my mother?"

"Is that okay?" Harper asked.

"It's more than okay." Delilah nodded, her bottom lip quivering.

Liam got to his feet again. "You want to feel your granddaughter move?"

The question was barely out of his mouth before Delilah was moving across the room. Liam grabbed her hand, placing it over the spot that Sofia had been kicking. It took a moment before another pop hit the side of Harper's abdomen.

Delilah looked up at Harper, the delight in her eyes exuberant. "Sofia Lillian. It's a beautiful name."

"Liam figured it out." Harper grinned at him.

"I'm glad you like it, Mrs. Laurence."

Her eyes moved from Harper's face to Liam's, and she shook

her head. "Delilah." She reached out and grabbed his hand, squeezing it. "You should call me Delilah from here on out."

Well, apparently Harper was covering the full range of emotions today. And as she hadn't been prepared for any of this, it took everything in her not to lose it right then and there.

Chapter Twenty

How to Burst a Bubble
In Under a Minute

As Harper was going to be heading up to Nashville with Liam for a few days, she was fitting in as many clients who wanted to schedule a massage before she left town. Her last one wasn't going to finish up until after nine on Wednesday night, so Liam went to the Sleepy Sheep to grab a beer.

Finn was working behind the bar that evening. The man might be a full-time veterinarian, but he still put in a few hours at his family's bar every once in a while. Ever since Shep started brewing beer in mass quantities, his nights at the bar had been cut down. And it was still an important feature to have a Shepherd presence at the place as much as possible. According to Harper, the Sleepy Sheep was an institution in Mirabelle.

Tripp and Bennett were at the bar, too, though the two of them were getting a drink as opposed to working it.

"You flying solo tonight?" Bennett asked as Liam took a seat next to him.

"Yup, Harper is working late. What about you? Where is your lady love?"

"Over there." Bennett pointed to a booth in the corner where Mel, Grace, and Beth were all giggling over their glasses of wine. "She's having a girl's night. Beth needed to get out, Mel is taking advantage of her last few late nights before school starts again, and Grace is enjoying an evening while Jax is on baby duty. I get to drive them all home when they've had enough. I think they are working on their second bottle now."

"Almost finished with it, too." Finn nodded as he slid a beer down in front of Liam. "Should make for an interesting night when you get home with your wife."

"It should." Bennett grinned hugely.

Liam couldn't wait for the day that he could say that: *home to his wife.*

Soon and very soon, at least he hoped. *Prayed.* He'd gotten more than just Paul's approval in regards to asking Harper to marry him. After dinner, he'd been helping Delilah dry the dishes at the sink when he'd asked her as well.

She'd reached over and grabbed his hand, much like she had earlier in the evening. "Paul already told me about what the two of you discussed." She'd grinned up at him. "You have my blessing, too, Liam."

Now he just needed to figure out how to ask Harper. He wanted it to be special…memorable.

"What was your big gesture?" he blurted out, turning to Bennett next to him.

"What?" Bennett's eyebrows pulled together over his eyes.

"With Mel. The big gesture to get her to marry you?"

"Oh." Dawning recognition overtook his face. "You're going to ask Harper."

"Yeah, and it should go without saying that this conversation is embargoed."

"Obviously." Bennett nodded.

"Dammit." Finn's hand hit the counter, making Liam jump. "Shep is probably going to win the bet. He had his money on the end of August as to when you were going to propose."

"You guys made a bet?" Liam asked.

"Yeah." Tripp nodded. "I forget how many of us were in the pool, but the winner gets over four hundred dollars at this point. Your brother and sister are in on it. Abby too."

"Seriously? When did this happen?"

"Fourth of July," Bennett answered before he took a sip of his beer. "So you wanted to know about grand gestures?"

"Yeah."

"I didn't really have one in *asking* Mel to marry me. I kind of messed up a couple things at the end there, spectacularly so, and pushed her away. When I realized she was it for me? That she was the home I'd been looking for? Well, all I knew was I had to get her back. She was the future that I wanted, so I proposed and hoped to God that she forgave me."

"I see that she did."

"Yeah, I'm one lucky son-of-a-bitch." Bennett's eyes moved over to his wife again, and the undying adoration for her was beyond clear.

"His grand gesture was before he even figured out that he was in love with her," Tripp interjected.

"How in the world does that work?"

"I helped her with a project at the school. Building bookcases for the library with her students."

"Jax was the same way with Grace. He built her a house," Tripp said. "A house that a lot of us helped out with in the making. Took months to do, too. A lot of planning. And for most of it Jax wasn't even dating her."

Bennett laughed. "He was running in the opposite direction actually. The guy was a little stubborn in the beginning. Refused to accept reality."

"A little bit like you?" Liam looked at Bennett.

"A little bit like me."

Well, that most definitely hadn't been a problem for Liam. He knew exactly what he wanted.

"What about Shep?" Liam asked.

"He was going to give it all up. Move to New York to be with Hannah. Turned out she didn't want to go back to New York as much as she wanted to stay here with him. The inn was the home she wanted."

"And Brendan?"

"Ahh, Brendan is a special case." Bennett shifted on the stool, resting his elbows on the bar. "He was pretty much all in the second he met Paige. It was more a bunch of little gestures like getting her a job and asking her to move in. She wasn't set on staying here until Brendan made her feel like she'd found home again."

"I have a question." Finn raised his eyebrows high over his thick black-framed glasses. "Where is home going to be for the two of you? You and Harper going to settle down here, or is she going to move up to Nashville?"

"Nashville isn't really home to me, and I wouldn't want to take Harper out of hers. I think staying here is the better option. So as to where we are going to settle down? Well I hope it's here."

"You hope?" Tripp was now raising his eyebrows, too.

"We haven't exactly talked about it in depth."

"Maybe you should." Bennett frowned. "Time is ticking, my friend. That baby of yours is going to be here before you know it."

"Tell me about it."

"I have a question, too." Tripp leaned forward. Bennett was sitting in between them so he was trying to get a better view. "How is it that *you* are asking about big, grand gestures? Isn't there a song currently on the radio that's about Harper?"

"Yeah. If that isn't big and grand enough, then he and I are screwed when it comes to finally settling down." Finn nodded at Tripp.

"I think a case could already be made for us being screwed in settling down," Tripp said as he finished the last of his beer. "Pretty sure it's the bachelor life for me."

"At least you won't be alone now," Finn said, and grabbed the empty glass before he got a clean one and poured Tripp another beer. "You've got Duke to keep you company."

"Duke?"

"As in *The* Duke. And that dog is a menace." He glared at Finn. "A small bear is more like it. There is no way in hell I'm getting my deposit back when I move, either. He chewed through a door. *A door.*"

Finn grinned as he passed Tripp the fresh beer. "Hey, I told you he needed space to move around. Frankie is doing just fine settling into my house. She hasn't chewed through any doors."

"Yeah, well you got the puppy that wasn't a neurotic basket case."

Finn turned to Liam in way of explanation. "Tripp found two puppies a couple of months ago. They were abandoned at the fire station. He adopted the male. I adopted the female. He's having some difficulties."

"Apparently," Liam agreed.

"At least he's doing better than he was." Tripp took a sip of his beer before he set it back down on the bar. "When I brought him home he was scared of everything. Would run and hide at the drop of a hat. It's a small wonder the thunderstorms didn't give him a heart attack."

"Yeah, well give him a yard and he will be doing even better," Finn said.

"I'm working on it. House hunting isn't going very well. I'm going again tomorrow."

"See, Tripp, you are capable of the big grand gesture. It's just for a dog as opposed to a woman."

"Here's a big grand gesture, asshole," Tripp grumbled, and flipped Finn off.

"Maybe you should go with him." Bennett turned to Liam. "You want to settle down here. So show Harper that you're all in. Show her what you want. Show her that you're ready for this."

"I am." He had been from the start.

"Okay." Bennett nodded. "Then prove it."

* * *

Liam spent the majority of the next day going from house to house with Tripp and Tammy, the real estate agent he'd hired. They looked all over town at more properties than he could even remember. Some out in the middle of nowhere that were surrounded by acres of land and cattle, with the closest neighbor miles away. Others were more centrally located, some nicer neighborhoods that were slowly growing and had more of a family feel. And there were a number of homes on the water, some scattered across the coast and others on Whiskey River.

Harper had made comments before about how much she loved living on the beach, so those were the ones that he paid especially close attention to. And when they walked into the last place he knew he'd found the one.

It stood on the typical pylons that were the foundation for the majority of the houses on the water. The house itself was two stories high, five bedrooms, three and a half baths, a newly remodeled kitchen, and a massive sunk-in living room that looked out to the water. And it wasn't the only room that had a spectacular view, because the master bedroom had floor-to-ceiling windows and French doors that led out to the wraparound porch. They'd be able to watch the sunrise from their bed if they placed it just so.

He wanted it.

The problem? Someone had already put an offer in on the house. So he did what he needed to do. He put in an offer as well...which was slightly stress inducing considering he hadn't talked to Harper about it, nor had she seen it yet.

But it was the one...and he *really* wanted it. *Had* to have it.

There were certain perks to not being a struggling artist anymore. He had more than enough money in the bank that he didn't need to worry about getting pre-approved for a loan. What he did need to worry about was if he got the house. It was an integral part of the plan.

Another part of the plan was trying to keep it a surprise. But keeping anything from Harper had proved to be a failure for him. He just needed to figure out how to work around it if she asked him for a play-by-play of his day.

She didn't get home until after ten o'clock that night, and the second she walked in the door she collapsed on the sofa and put her feet in Liam's lap.

He started to rub her arches with his thumbs, applying just the right amount of pressure to make her moan long and loud.

"*Yessss.* God. Right there. Please don't stop." Her head was thrown back against a pillow, her eyes closed as she melted into the sofa cushions.

"Honey, you keep talking like that and you are going to be getting an entirely different sort of massage." Obviously sex would be a more than fun way to distract her from conversations.

Harper cracked an eye and looked at him. "I don't know how good it will be. I think I'm about two seconds from passing out. An extended weekend sounds like the greatest thing *ever*." Her eye fell closed again as she pulled her arms up and over her head in a good stretch. The movement caused her shirt to pull up and expose her baby bump.

"That so?" He increased the pressure, moving to the ball of her foot.

Her back arched up and she moaned again. Yeah, he wasn't sure how he was going to get through this.

"Barely had a second to sit down let alone take a break. My feet hate me…but you are pacifying their sensibilities now."

"Oh, am I?" He speared his fingers between her toes, stretching them just so.

"*Yessss.*" She moaned the word again. "You are. Even talking is exhausting, so tell me about your day. How was dinner with Dale and Hamilton?"

Her follow-up saved him.

After house hunting, Tripp and Liam had gone to get burgers with the boys. As Liam wouldn't be back in Mirabelle for a couple of weeks, they'd asked if he would hang out with them before he left.

He relayed that part of the day, concentrating on massaging Harper's feet and hoping she didn't ask anything else. But he realized his worry was for nothing as she was now breathing slow and steady from her side of the sofa.

She was asleep.

* * *

Their flight out of Tallahassee left just before noon the following morning. Harper hadn't packed anything so she'd had to get up early to get all of her things in order. As it took Liam about ten minutes to get his stuff together, he went for a run.

And then came back all hot and sweaty…which made her get all hot and sweaty. That was just par for the course really. He'd always had that effect on her…from the very start.

There was a nervous anticipation coursing through her from the second she'd woken up, and when she walked into the cabin late that afternoon she knew why. They were returning to the place where it all began.

But as the second they walked in the door she had to go and get changed and freshen up from the flight, she didn't have all that much time to dwell on it.

Since Harper hadn't seen her aunt in months, nor had Liam met Celeste, she was pretty excited about the evening. Reed, Celeste's boyfriend, had made a reservation at Bourbon and Brine, one of the hottest spots in town. It was just after seven when they arrived at the restaurant, and the place was packed with people lingering around the hostess station waiting for a table to become available.

A group of people moved to the side and an excited exclamation of "Harper!" filled her ears. Celeste navigated over to her, Reed following close behind.

"Hello, my sweet niece," she said as she pulled Harper into an embrace.

"Hello, my wonderful aunt." Harper hugged her back, so ridiculously happy to see her.

"Let me see you." Celeste's hands slid to Harper's forearms as she took a step back and did a once-over. "You look wonderful. You feeling okay?" Her voice dropped low on the last question so that it would be hard for the crowd around them to hear.

"Yeah. Everyone is doing very well." Harper's hand went to her belly immediately.

"That's what I like to hear," she beamed, letting go before her eyes moved to Liam. "And you're him, huh? The man who has fallen in love with my niece?"

"Yes, ma'am. I didn't have a chance from the second I met her."

"I like you already. And it's Celeste. None of this ma'am non-sense." She winked at him before introducing him to Reed.

The hostess came up to them, menus in hand, and led them to their table. Liam walked behind Harper, his hand on the small of her back as they made their way through the room. Her eyes caught on a couple of the plates, the delicious smells filling her nose.

Good Lord she was already starving. She wanted to order everything she saw. And when she sat down and looked at the menu, she was even more confused.

"What are you going to get?" Liam asked, leaning in close to her.

"Well, the pan-seared filet with the mushroom bacon risotto sounds amazing. But then so do the pork chops in the cherry wine reduction with the asparagus soufflé."

"You just want to share? Both of those sound good to me."

"This is why you're my favorite." She grinned as she folded her menu.

The meal was perfection. *Per-fec-tion.* And by the time they were done eating and talking, Harper was so full it would be a wonder if she could walk out of there…especially after the caramel crème brûlée.

But she somehow managed.

After dinner they said good-bye to Celeste and Reed at the door. They were taking advantage of their evening out. While Harper was ready to crash, Celeste was ready to party.

"Reed is taking me dancing," she said as she shimmied. "But I'll see you tomorrow."

Liam had gotten three tickets for the concert he was performing at a club in downtown Nashville. It was a smaller venue than the arenas he'd been opening in, but he was the headliner for this one.

"Tomorrow." Harper nodded as she hugged her aunt and then Reed.

When they walked outside, the hot summer air was still a tad bit stifling, and the crowd outside was making Harper a little claustrophobic. The two guys manning the valet station were having trouble keeping up with the current rush.

Liam braved the crowd while Harper stood off to the side. A group of women—all dressed to the nines—moved to make way for him. It was like Moses parting the Red Sea.

When he walked past, the brunette in the purple stilettos leaned over and whispered into the ear of the blond in the hot pink romper.

"Nuh-uh." Romper's mouth dropped open as her head whipped back around to get another look at Liam. But while she was getting another look, Stilettos was telling the other girls in the group.

Before Harper even knew it, three of the five women had pulled out their phones and were blatantly snapping pictures of Liam. At least one of them tried to make it look like she was taking a selfie.

A possessiveness that was still very much new to Harper took over. She wanted to reach over and throw every one of those damn phones on the ground and stomp on them with her heels.

Romper caught Harper's eye, which she was doing her damnedest to not let turn into a death glare.

"That's Liam James," she whispered to Harper in explanation.

"I know." Harper nodded. "What do you think his girlfriend is going to make of the fact that you guys were just taking pictures of his ass?"

"Who cares? He's *hot*." The blond with the bob shrugged as she touched up her bright red cherry lips, pouting them as she looked into the mirror of her compact.

"Isn't he dating Kiki Jean Carlow?" The redhead in the skintight black dress looked around. "You think she's here?"

"Nah." Cherry lips shook her head. "She'd be surrounded by people fawning all over her. But more is the better for me. I'm going to get him to take me home with him."

Oh, look at how quickly that had all morphed into a boiling rage coursing through Harper's veins.

"And what makes you think you're the one he's going to want to go home with?" Stilettos fluffed her hair as she pulled the top of her dress down more than just a little bit.

"It's obvious. He prefers blonds." Cherry smacked her lips together as she closed her little compact and tossed it, along with her lipstick, into her purse.

"Harper, honey," Liam called, pulling her gaze away from the women. He was waiting just on the other side of the stand, holding out his hand for her. "They're pulling the car around now."

The group of girls all openly gaped at Harper, and as she walked by Cherry she couldn't help herself. "Actually, he doesn't prefer blonds and he's going to be taking *me* home tonight."

Liam's eyes narrowed, studying her face as her hand slid into his. "What was that about?"

"Nothing, I just told her I liked her hair." The lie might've fallen easily from her lips, but it felt wrong. All wrong.

He took a step forward, his free hand going to her face. "You sure?"

"Yes." She nodded, forcing a smile as she leaned in and kissed him.

But even the taste of his lips couldn't take away the bitterness in Harper's mouth.

Chapter Twenty-One

The Power of a Lie

The bitterness was still lingering the next day. Harper did everything in her power to not let the little incident at the end of dinner the night before upset her. But it had gotten under her skin and was now festering.

It was one thing to be out somewhere and see other women checking out your man. It was quite another to know that there were women out there who had absolutely no regard for the fact that he was in a relationship.

But this was what it was going to be like if she was with him.

No, there was no *if*.

She was going to have to get used to it. His fame was only getting bigger, so this was the life she was signing on for.

She'd been living in a bit of a fantasyland perpetuated by the bubble that was Mirabelle. That tabloid article a week ago had been a small taste of reality, and it had been just as bitter as the events of the evening before.

But it was nothing, *nothing*, to what Harper went through on Saturday night.

In the beginning she'd been excited about seeing Liam perform live onstage. It wasn't something she'd experienced and she wondered what it would be like to be a part of the crowd.

And as always, Liam's music resonated through her body, settling deep in her bones. And it wasn't just Harper who was enjoying the music. Sofia was moving, like *really* moving. She was kicking up a storm in Harper's belly.

"He's talented." Celeste shook her head in awe as Liam got to the guitar solo for "Music Shaker, Money Maker."

"He is." Harper grabbed her aunt's hand and pressed it to the spot that was being used like a soccer ball.

Celeste grinned over at Harper. "She likes Daddy's music, too, huh?"

"Apparently. She's having a rave in there."

The last chords of the guitar solo faded away and the crowd around Harper cheered, screaming Liam's name. It was one of those moments that she couldn't quite process. Watching him up on that stage. Seeing him, *hearing* him sing his heart out.

And he was hers.

But not *all* hers. Not when he was up on that stage. This was the part that she had to share. In a way, when he was performing he belonged to everyone in that room. Belonged to his fans that knew every word of his songs…and the women in the crowd who were eye-sexing him.

Just like that Harper's heart started beating hard and her stomach rolled, but this time it wasn't from Sofia's acrobatics. She closed her eyes, taking deep steady breaths.

"You okay?" Celeste asked.

"Yeah." Harper nodded, opening her eyes and looking over at her aunt. "I just need to go to the bathroom."

"I'm coming with you." She turned to Reed next to her and said something to him before they headed through the crowd.

But before they could make it there, Harper saw something that made her feel five thousand times worse.

Kiki Jean Carlow was standing at the opening of the hallway, signing autographs for the crowd of twenty or so people that surrounded her. They were mainly girls, most in frayed jean skirts, cowboy boots, and flannel shirts tied up and above their midriffs. Kiki was wearing a similar outfit.

Harper stopped dead in her tracks, unable to move on. It was like watching a train wreck...a train wreck that was her life.

"So it *is* true?" One of the girls next to Kiki gushed. "You really are dating Liam James?"

"Just flew in from California to get here. Wouldn't miss it." Kiki beamed.

"So 'Forever' must be about you, right?" someone else asked. "Since he just wrote it recently."

"You guys don't miss anything, do you?" she asked as she grabbed another picture and scrawled her signature across it.

"That's so cool."

"*Gawd*, you're lucky."

"The luckiest." Kiki's gaze came up and landed on Harper. The look of cold recognition was clear; she knew exactly who Harper was. "Did you want something signed, darlin'?"

Darlin'.

Ohhh, Kiki could sign something all right. Harper's fist… right after she threw up.

She said nothing. She couldn't open her mouth. A sick queasy pressure tightened her stomach and her feet were moving before she was even conscious of it. Her heart was now pounding out of her chest and there was a ringing in her ears. The ability to pull air into her lungs was nearly impossible as the people pushing in around her increased.

She had to get out of there. Stat.

There was no way she was going to last long enough to get through the line that snaked out of the women's restroom, so she bypassed it, pushing through the doors at the end of the hallway and outside.

She made it about twenty feet past the entrance, and away from the people gathered around getting a smoke, before she'd gotten to the limit. She reached for the wall, holding her balance as she leaned forward and threw up against the side of the building. Hands were moving across her back, pulling her hair back as she emptied her stomach.

Celeste.

When the heaving stopped, she held on to the wall and tried to keep herself upright while she started to hyperventilate.

"Come on." Celeste helped guide Harper away from the wall and to the curb. The second her butt was on the ground she dropped her head between her knees. Celeste's palm rubbed across her lower back in slow circular motions. "You need to breathe, babe."

Breathing. That would be good. Maybe if she got some air into her lungs the black spots on the edge of her vision would go away.

Maybe.

She had no idea how long they sat there, but it felt like forever for her to catch her breath. When she was finally able to pull her head up, she looked over at her aunt. "I need to get out of here."

"I think that's the best idea."

"I need to tell Liam."

"I'll take care of that when we're in the car. Let me see if I can get ahold of Reed." She pulled out her phone and dialed, her hand not stopping with the slow steady circles at the small of Harper's back. "He isn't answering." She frowned after a minute. "I'm going to need to go in there and get him. Are you going to be okay?"

"Yeah." Harper nodded. "It isn't like I have anything else to throw up."

Celeste's mouth formed a concerned line. "Okay, I'll be right back."

Harper sat by herself for a couple of minutes before sitting still became too much to do. She needed to stand. Walk around a little. Get the feeling back in her legs.

But when she stood and turned around she wished she hadn't. She suddenly didn't have legs anymore. Kiki was standing there, arms folded across her chest, making her breasts pop over the top of her low-cut shirt.

She was alone. Her little entourage hadn't followed her outside.

"So you're the girl?" Kiki asked, a slight sneer in her eyes as she looked Harper over. She clearly wasn't impressed. "I saw your picture pop up on his phone when you called him once. We were in bed at the time—"

"No, you weren't," Harper cut her off. "You think we haven't discussed this little game you're playing? Think again. You aren't going to get in my head."

The flash of delight in Kiki's eyes said *wanna bet?* "At first I wasn't sure if he'd fallen for a chubby girl. Or if he knocked you up. A little bit of both it seems."

"Go to hell."

"Oh, darlin', is that any way for an expecting mother to talk?" Her gaze dipped to Harper's belly, and the malevolent delight behind those icy blue eyes was unmistakable.

On instinct, Harper's hand went to her little bump, shielding Sofia and confirming Kiki's assumption in one fell swoop.

"Oh, this will make for a fascinating story. I couldn't have written it better myself. A love triangle. I'll be the woman scorned, and you'll be the tramp who stole my man. And even though Liam is *meant* to be with me and he *wants* to be with me, he can't be, because he got you knocked up. It's kind of perfect actually. Everyone will love me, and hate him…but oh, they will *despise* you."

"What's your problem?"

She shrugged. "I don't have one. This is just fun."

"So this is all just a game to you?"

"Pretty much. And since I can't have what I want, why should you?"

It was at that moment that Celeste was out the door, her eyes narrowed as she looked between Kiki and Harper, and she made a beeline to them. "Why don't you go somewhere else and spread your poison?"

"Maybe you should talk to your little friend over here about not *spreading* hers. Though, getting knocked up is an interesting strategy on getting a guy. Not what I would use, but different strokes for different folks. Good luck with"—she motioned at Harper's belly—"that."

And then she was walking away, heading back to the building and disappearing through the side door.

"Harper—"

"I don't want to talk about it." She turned, staring down at her shoes and trying to breathe again. The panic was simmering just under the surface and she needed to push it down. "I just want to get out of here."

"Reed is getting the car."

"Okay." Harper nodded, chewing on her bottom lip in an attempt to keep her mouth closed. She couldn't stop replaying the last few minutes, and it was just making her want to start vomiting again.

Was this *really* what it was going to be like? Was this the price to pay for being with Liam? Her name in the tabloids as his popularity grew. Combating lies. Dealing with other women wanting him.

Her lip fell from her teeth, trembling as the sob broke out of her mouth.

"Sweetie," Celeste whispered next to her.

Harper turned automatically, her aunt's arms wrapping her up in a hug and holding her close as everything came crashing down again.

* * *

It was about halfway through the show when Liam couldn't find Harper in the crowd anymore. One minute she'd been there, the next she was gone. He hadn't had a problem keeping track of where she was before, his eyes *always* landed on her. Not only that, Celeste and Reed were missing, too.

Though he told himself that they'd probably just moved a little farther from the stage, the unsettled feeling only grew through the last hour. And if he'd checked his phone during the two minutes he was backstage before the encore, he wouldn't have gone back out.

There was a missed called and voice mail from Celeste followed by a string of texts. He pulled up the texts first:

9:38 pm—*Harper didn't feel well and needed to get out of there.*

9:39 pm—*She's going to be okay. We're going to my house.*

10:15 pm—*Call me when you get out. She's in bed.*

She's *going* to be okay? Meaning she hadn't been when Celeste had sent those. And she hadn't been okay enough to call or text him herself. He immediately pulled up Celeste's phone number and hit Dial. Two rings vibrated in his ear before the line clicked.

"Hey, Liam," Celeste said, the light playful tone he'd come to associate with her the last couple of days was gone.

"How is she?"

"Better, she drank some tea to try and settle her stomach and then took a shower."

"Settle her stomach? Did she get sick?"

"She had a bit of a panic attack."

"Panic attack?" He was pretty sure he was about to have one.

"Liam," Celeste said his name calmly. "Harper is fine."

"And Sofia? She's okay? They don't need to go to the hospital or anything?"

"No, Liam. Your daughter is fine, too. If I'd thought that I needed to take them to the hospital, I would've."

"Okay." He closed his eyes, his hand gripping the chair in front of him as he bowed his head. He knew Celeste was a doctor, one of the best in her field, but he wouldn't believe Harper was fine until he saw her with his own two eyes.

"Why don't you head over here?" She managed to read his mind through the phone. "You two can stay the night. She needs to rest, so waking her up isn't the best option."

"I'm leaving now." Liam looked around the room, grabbing his bag on the floor and shoving his stuff inside it. "I'll be there in ten."

"See you then." But before the line disconnected she added, "They are both going to be fine, Liam. Breathe and don't drive like a mad man to get here."

Yeah, that was going to be easier said than done.

When he walked out of the room there were still a number of people milling around. Normally he'd pop out and do a little meet-and-greet, but there was no way in hell that would be happening tonight.

He needed to get to Harper.

But before he could make it to the back door Kiki was blocking his path.

"I don't have the time or patience for you tonight." He shook his head as he sidestepped her.

"I met your girlfriend…or is she your baby mama?"

He stopped dead in his tracks and slowly turned around. "What?"

"She seemed to be having a bit of a breakdown. Poor thing, and in her condition, too." She shook her head pityingly. "Threw up all over the side of the building."

"Kiki, I'm going to tell you this once." He took a deep breath, the fact that she'd been anywhere near Harper was making it difficult for him to not lose his shit. "Stay the fuck away from her."

"Don't worry, Liam." She tilted her head to the side as her eyes narrowed on him, a mean smile on her mouth. "I've gotten everything that I need."

He said nothing as he turned around and started heading for the back door again. He was done with this conversation. Whatever else she had to say wasn't important.

Getting to Harper was all that mattered, getting to her and finding out *exactly* what had happened.

* * *

During the entire car ride Harper had sobbed uncontrollably, her head in Celeste's lap. When they'd gotten to the house they'd sat in the car—parked in the driveway with the air conditioner running—for a good ten minutes before Harper had calmed down enough to get out. At that point, all she'd wanted to do was take off the clothes that smelled like vomit. That and to wash off the last hour of panic and sweat that had settled on her skin.

The hot shower had been helpful, and the tea had calmed her stomach…but nothing was helping her heart. The ache at the center hadn't been dulled in the slightest. And try as she might she couldn't shut her brain off long enough to fall asleep.

She'd been lying in the bed in her aunt's guest room for what felt like forever, staring at the wall and doing everything in her power to not start crying again. She was also fighting with the need to have Liam in bed with her while at the same time wanting space to breathe.

How was she going to do this? How was she going to deal with this kind of life and not lose her damn mind every single time something like this happened? It was too much…way too much for anyone to deal with in normal circumstances, but these weren't normal circumstances.

It had been less than four months since she and Liam had met each other. Two and a half since they'd found each other in Jacksonville. It was more than a little terrifying when she looked at it that way, especially as she'd only had a handful of weeks with him in between all of that.

Barely any time at all, and was it enough to really *know* each other?

Had they *caught up* in such a short amount of time? Was that possible? She wasn't sure. She did know that she was in love with him…and that he loved her. But did that mean they were ready for all that was going to follow?

Sofia would be here in five months. Five. Months. It was all happening too fast. She just wanted more time to figure it all out. Time she didn't have.

Lights lit up the window behind the closed blinds as a car pulled into the driveway.

Liam.

The engine turned off and a car door shut a moment later. She counted the seconds, breathing with them and finding a steady rhythm as the front door opened and closed…and then two minutes of whispered murmuring between Liam and Celeste.

The bedroom door opened four minutes and twenty-nine seconds from when his truck had pulled into the driveway. He moved around the room slowly, trying not to make too many sounds.

There was a shuffling as he pulled off his shirt, and then his boots hit the wooden floor with two barely audible thuds as he set them down one at a time. His belt buckle rattled only slightly before the snick of his zipper filled the space.

And then he was pulling the sheet and blanket back, climbing in behind her and pressing his body to hers. His mouth brushed her neck as he buried his nose in her hair and inhaled. The oversized T-shirt she was wearing was pushed up as his hand moved under it, his palm on her belly.

"My girls," he whispered, his breath washing out across her skin.

At some point Harper had stopped counting her breaths and started counting the steady taps of her tears hitting the pillow.

Chapter Twenty-Two

I Don't Think I Believe
Everything You're Trying to Say to Me

It was the tiny popping against Liam's palm the next morning that woke him up. Sofia was kicking.

Harper shifted against him and stretched, her hand moving to the space next to his.

"Morning," he whispered in her ear.

"Morning." Her voice was rough, way more than it should be from just waking up. No, this was ravaged from her getting sick and hours of crying, most of that while he'd been lying right there next to her.

It made every part of him hurt. He'd known she'd been awake when he crawled in bed next to her. But she hadn't rolled over seeking his comfort, hadn't wanted him to know she was still up. It had taken her hours to finally fall sleep, and only then had Liam been able to do the same.

"How are you feeling?" he asked, trying his damnedest to keep his voice even.

"Okay," she said with absolutely no conviction.

He kissed her shoulder before he shifted, moving so he could gently pull her to her back. He needed to see her face, and when he did it was that much more painful. Her eyes were puffy and filled with a sadness that he hadn't seen since that morning in Jacksonville...before he told her he still wanted her.

"Honey, what happened?"

"I just...I just got a little overwhelmed at the concert. And I think whatever I ate at dinner didn't sit well...it all just kind of hit me at once."

"That's it?" he asked. "That's all that happened?"

"Yeah." She nodded, looking him straight in the eyes. *Lying* to him as she looked him straight in the eyes.

Well, that was new.

"Harper—"

"I'm fine," she cut him off. "And I need to use the bathroom." She pulled away from him, heading for the attached bathroom and disappearing behind the door before she closed it.

Liam rolled to his back, staring at the ceiling and the spinning fan above him. Why was she lying to him?

* * *

The rest of the day passed in an unsettlingly slow pace. It was like Liam was watching from the sidelines as Harper started to build up that wall again. Brick by brick. But what was he supposed to do? Push her for answers? Ask her why she was lying to him?

She'd just had an emotional breakdown and the truth of the matter was being with him was the root of it. This lifestyle wasn't easy, he knew that, but she hadn't known it when this had all started.

She hadn't been the only one hiding things in the beginning. When she hadn't known who he was at that bar all those months ago, he'd ran with it. And he'd kept running with it that entire weekend.

The thing was, when it was just the two of them, it was *just the two of them.* There weren't outside factors impacting what they had…at least not to this extent. Sure there'd been those stupid blog posts by that Bethelda woman, and that tabloid the week before. But in the end it was nothing to what they'd already worked through.

This though…this was different. This was Harper getting a taste of the life Liam had and the life they would have together.

Between what Celeste had told him when he'd gotten to the house the night before and the few things that Harper had told him, Liam knew that she'd gotten upset *before* anything that had to do with Kiki had happened. Whatever that woman had said had just been the icing on top of the shit cake.

And Harper wasn't revealing anything else.

They'd gone back to the cabin late that morning, leaving when Celeste was called in to the hospital for a patient who was having complications. Liam was with Harper the entire day, but she was only there physically. Mentally? She was somewhere else entirely. She took a long nap that afternoon, clearly wanting to be alone. She barely ate anything, picking at her food and moving it around her plate like he wouldn't notice.

After dinner, he cleaned up while she went to get a shower. The walls of the cabin were starting to make him feel claustrophobic, closing in on him as this beyond shitty day came to an end. So he poured himself a tumbler of whiskey before he headed outside to sit on the porch.

The sun was sitting low over the lake, and he grabbed one of the Adirondack chairs off to the side, putting his feet up on the banister that ran around the house.

He'd really thought coming up here would be good. They'd get a different ending than the last time they'd been in this cabin. He'd planned on proposing, that night in fact. He'd planned on recreating their first date…with a few minor alterations, like no gin and tonics.

Some things would've stayed the same, like the menu of food he'd made before. And he'd planned on singing "Forever" to her in the first place he'd ever performed it. But this time it would've been in its entirety and where she'd realized she'd fallen in love with him.

Love at first sound.

Yeah, none of that was going to happen.

Definitely not. Especially as he couldn't deny the feeling that she was running again. That she'd experienced something she wasn't sure she wanted.

And she wouldn't talk to him about it. That was the part that was really killing him. The part that made him want to down the rest of the amber liquid in the glass that his hand was currently wrapped around.

Instead he took another sip before he set it on the table next to him.

The door behind him opened and he looked over his shoulder as Harper stepped out. She was wearing one of his oversized T-shirts and a pair of cotton shorts, her wet hair pulled over her shoulder in a braid.

"Can I sit with you?"

"Never have to ask that." He pulled his feet from the banister as she crossed over to him. He held out his hand and she grabbed it, letting him help her as she settled into his lap. She rested her head on his shoulder, pressing her lips to his jaw.

They sat there for a good five minutes, Liam silently willing her to talk to him as he ran his hand up and down her back. His other hand rested on her thigh, tracing her knee in slow circles.

"I'm sorry we had to leave early yesterday," she finally said.

Both of his hands stilled and he moved the one from her leg to her face, pushing her chin up gently until he saw her eyes. "You don't need to apologize for that, Harper," he said as he shook his head.

"The first half was really good."

You mean the first half before something sent you into a panic attack so severe that you made yourself physically ill? Well, that's good to know. But he couldn't exactly say that now could he? So he just nodded.

"Sofia liked it. She was moving around more than ever when you were singing. She loves the sound of your voice."

For just a second he forgot everything besides the words that had just come out of her mouth. For just a second all he could think about was that his daughter had been moving around in Harper's belly while he'd been singing. For just a second all he could think about was that his daughter had been affected by the sound of his voice.

But only for just a second.

"Harper, what happened last night?"

Something flickered behind her violet eyes, and the small window that had been cracked for just a moment closed with a snap. "I told you. I just got overwhelmed. I—I'm fine now."

He really wanted to ask her if she promised…but there was a part of him that believed she wouldn't tell him the truth. He didn't think he could handle it. Didn't think he could survive her swearing on a lie.

And it killed him that he was pretty sure that was what was going to happen.

So he said nothing instead. He just nodded and did everything in his power to not lose it, because all he could think about was that he might be losing her. That he might be losing everything. Because in the end *she* was everything to him.

And it was that fact that he couldn't get out of his head when they went to sleep that night. That fact that he couldn't stop thinking about as he held Harper in his arms. That fact that he knew he had to fix.

Had to. There was no other option.

Now that he'd had her in his life there was no possibility of going back. Now that he'd tasted her lips, woken up with her in his arms, held her hand, felt their child move.

No going back…

At some point the thoughts of a life without her morphed into a nightmare. Him coming home to an empty house. Harper marrying another man. Them sharing custody of Sofia

God no.

* * *

Liam woke from his nightmare with a start and the second consciousness hit him, he knew he was alone. His arms were empty and even though the soft orange light from the pre-dawn glow of the sun was doing nothing besides showcasing the vacant side of the bed, he groped at the empty sheets.

Harper was gone.

No. No, that wasn't right. She wouldn't have left. There was no way.

He pulled the blankets from his body, forcing himself to wake up as he stumbled out of the room and down the hallway into the main part of the house.

Harper was on the opposite side of the kitchen, her back to him as she looked out the window at the lake. She had a glass of cranberry juice in her hand, and when she lifted it to her mouth it pulled the bottom of her T-shirt up, flashing just a glimpse of blue lace.

Liam stood there, staring at her as he repeatedly told himself she was here…in this cabin…not gone.

Not gone.

His heart was still pounding out of his chest and he hadn't caught his breath. Her eyes landed on his reflection in the glass and she jumped just slightly as she spun around.

"You scared me." She put her free hand over her heart. "Are you okay?" she asked as her eyes focused. She set the juice on the counter as she crossed the room, stopping in front of him.

He shook his head.

"Liam, what's wrong?" Her hands touched his chest as she looked up into his face. The warmth of her palms did nothing to combat the cold that had settled into his bones.

"I thought…I thought I could do this. I thought *we* could do this. That we were figuring this out. Moving forward."

Her hands stilled, her eyes going wide. "W-we are."

"No. We aren't. We're right back to where we started. I've been terrified to talk to you, terrified to push because all I can see is you running again. All I can think about is what it was like to wake up four months ago with you gone. And I swear to God, Harper, I woke up just now and I thought you'd left."

"I'm not running anymore."

"You aren't? Then why have you been lying to me since the concert?"

She took a step back, her hands falling from his chest at the same moment her eyes left his, her gaze moving off to the side.

"You're not going to deny it?" he asked.

She shook her head, a low sniffle filling the kitchen as she reached up and wiped at her face.

Her crying was breaking him…*everything* about this moment was breaking him.

"I asked you flat out what happened, and not once did you mention Kiki. I know that she was there. I know that she might not have been the catalyst for what upset you, but she was part of it. And whatever that catalyst was I think it was much more than you being *overwhelmed*. You don't think I see that you're scared, Harper? Because I do."

Her head came up and she looked at him again. That fear was right there at the center of her eyes, but it was surrounded by hurt and anger and confusion. "What do you want from me, Liam? It's scary, okay? It's scary that you're famous. Scary that you're only going to get *more* famous. That you get up on that stage and almost every woman in that audience wants you."

"I don't want them back."

"It doesn't change it. It still is what it is, and it's terrifying. It's terrifying to see a line of more than willing and able women."

"Don't you trust me? Don't you believe me when I tell you that you're all I want?"

"I do trust you, but that's not what this is about. It's about *not* being able to control…any of it."

"You don't think you have control?"

"No, I don't, Liam. I can't control those stupid tabloids and how seeing you linked with someone else makes every part of me hurt. Or this thing with Kiki, and her vendetta against you and now me. Or how much it hurts when you're gone for weeks on end and I don't get to see you. How much it hurts me when I wake up and you aren't in bed next to me. You're scared of me leaving? Well I'm scared of the same thing, and a life with you will always involve you leaving me."

And there it was. The truth.

"But I'm always going to come back." He took a step forward, reaching for her, one hand at her waist and the other palming her cheek. "I want *this* life with *you*. I want to build something with you. I want our daughter, and God willing more kids, running around a home that's ours."

"I want that, too…but…"

"But *what*?"

"Just because you want something doesn't mean you're going to get it."

His hands fell from her body and he took a step back. The

ground beneath his feet was unsteady, his world tilting on its axis. Here he was thinking that a life without her wasn't a possibility…where she was still trying to figure out if a life with him *was* a possibility.

How had he missed that one?

"Liam." She reached out for him, but he took another step away.

Her touch would surely break him. The hurt in her eyes was unmistakable, but the pain radiating through his body was more than he could overcome.

"What are you saying?" He somehow managed to get the words out.

"I just need more time to figure this all out. I still need to catch up. I thought that was what we were doing. Catching up."

A bitter laugh escaped his mouth as he shook his head. "I don't even know what the fuck catching up means anymore. I don't need time to figure anything out. You're what I want. What I've wanted from the start. And you're right, you don't always get everything you want in life. Especially when you aren't fighting for it."

"You don't think I'm fighting for this? For us?"

"No." He shook his head. "Because when it gets hard, you don't close in on yourself and shut the other person out. You don't try to *figure it out* on your own. You fight together. You tell each other the truth. You don't lie."

"I shouldn't have lied to you, I'm sorry."

"It's not the first time, Harper."

"That's not fair."

"None of this is fair. When it gets hard you run. That's why you were up here in the first place. You didn't want to be in Mirabelle the weekend that would've been your wedding. So you ran. You ran when you realized you were in love with me. You ran from the truth when you suspected you were pregnant. You're running now. And I don't know how long I can keep chasing you before it kills me."

She stared at him for a second, her shaky breaths filling the air. "So what are you saying?"

"I can fight for you for the rest of my life, but this is never going to work if you don't let me in."

"Where do we go from here?" She wiped at her face again; the constant stream of tears running down her cheeks hadn't let up for even a moment.

"I don't know."

"I don't, either," she sniffed before a sob broke free from her mouth. Her head bowed as she folded in on herself and lost it.

He couldn't take it anymore, couldn't just stand there and watch her break down. He crossed the few steps between them, wrapping his arms around her and pulling her in close. She pressed her face to his neck as she started to shake uncontrollably, each sob ripping through her one after the other.

His entire world was in his hands, and the only thing he could think about was he might lose it all.

Chapter Twenty-Three

It Was Always You

Harper's flight back to Mirabelle was that afternoon, and her leaving really couldn't have come at a worse time.

It would be a week and a half before she was going to see Liam again, and that fact had her stomach all tied up in knots. Yeah, she'd asked for more time, but time *apart* didn't feel like the answer.

But what was she supposed to do? She needed to get back home to her job…to her life. She'd already pushed the limits with so much time off. All she needed was to lose her job on top of everything else.

And while she was returning to Mirabelle, Liam would be spending a few more days in Nashville shooting the music video for "Forever." They were starting it that morning, and the plan had been for Harper to go with him and spend a couple of hours watching and hanging out before taking a car to the airport.

But the painful uncertainty between them was too much. There was a space that neither of them knew how to cross, and it was way more than she could handle. Add to that the fact that they were filming at the Second Hand Guitar? Yeah, there was no way in hell she'd make it out of that and not have a breakdown.

Who was she kidding? She lost it anyway when she said goodbye to him that morning. He was a mess, too, and she had no doubt he would've canceled that day's shoot if he could've. But he'd be rocking a boat that was already close to tipping.

He and his manager had fought pretty hard with the record label on what they were shooting. The label had wanted to tell the love story of the song with one couple in various stages of their relationship, Liam as the lead with some woman as his co-star.

He told them it wasn't going to happen. So instead they went with three different couples falling in love at the same show where Liam was performing. They'd already rented the space, hired the six actors, and got the extras to fill in the crowd at the bar.

Liam was going to have to get up on that stage and act his freaking heart out while singing the song he'd written about her. She knew it was going to kill him. She knew it and she couldn't fix it.

It made her hurt even more.

He'd kissed her before he walked out the door, his mouth moving over hers slowly as he held her close.

"No matter what I love you," he whispered.

"I know. I love you, too," she said as she pressed her face to his neck and inhaled.

But the unspoken words between them lingered in the air…*sometimes love wasn't always enough.*

It was Celeste who picked Harper up at the cabin that afternoon. The ride to the airport was not a chatty one. Unlike Delilah, her aunt wasn't pushy. It sometimes shocked Harper that they were related because they couldn't be less alike.

They said good-bye at the curb, Celeste giving Harper an extra-long hug before she headed inside. Because conversation or not, her aunt knew exactly what was going on.

The line at the baggage check was about ten deep, so Harper pulled her suitcase behind her and got in at the end. Her eyes wandered to the TV set up by the group of chairs off to the side and everything in her froze as she saw Liam's face on the screen.

Liam James Steps Out on Kiki Jean Carlow with Another Woman

A second later another picture popped up, this one of Harper and Liam outside Bourbon and Brine on Friday. His face was unmistakable, and Harper's long black hair and curves proved that she wasn't Kiki. Apparently those girls outside the restaurant weren't the only ones snapping shots.

"Another one bites the dust. Liam James isn't the good guy we all thought he was. This picture was taken just this weekend at a local Nashville restaurant." The volume was off, so the words of the E! news anchor were scrolling across the bottom of the screen in subtitles. *"And that is most definitely not Kiki Jean Carlow kissing Liam James."*

The screen switched to a clip of the "Beyond the Limits" music video. Even though it had been released the week before, Harper still hadn't watched it. Avoidance being the best policy and all, because obviously that was working out so well for her.

"It appeared that Liam and Kiki were hot and heavy for a moment there, but appearances can be deceiving," the anchor con-

tinued, switching to another photo of Harper from outside the concert on Saturday, this one with Kiki just a few feet away.

"But as the other woman in question looks to be more than a few months pregnant, it leaves people to wonder when the two ladies overlapped. And as you can see here, their first meeting isn't a pleasant one. Kiki left Nashville on Sunday morning, heartbroken over the betrayal." The last photo was a picture of Kiki at the airport, big sunglasses on her face as she avoided looking at the cameras.

"And now for the video. What do you guys think of these racy scenes between the former couple?"

The video for "Beyond the Limits" started to roll. The camera zoomed in on an old shack in the middle of the swamp, a hammock tied up between two trees. Isaac and a redhead with bright green eyes were wrapped up in each other's arms kissing as his hand moved up her thigh and under the skirt of her dress.

The next shot was of Hunter driving down a dirt road like a maniac with a massive grin on his face. A woman with caramel skin and black hair rode shotgun next to him while she hooted and cheered, throwing her arms up in the air. The shot panned out to the bed of the truck where Liam and Kiki were sitting. Bags surrounded them and she was holding a T-shirt to the cut above his forehead.

The video played on. The three couples doing various illegal deeds mixed in with steamy shots of them all over each other.

She'd really thought the ones with Liam would kill her, but they didn't. Because that look in his eyes when they were on Kiki? It was all an act. It was nothing, *nothing*, to how he looked at Harper.

She needed more time? More time for what? To figure out if

this was what she wanted? That Liam was what she wanted? He said they had to fight together, and she was walking away...no, running away. She was about to fly away from him when what she needed to be doing was proving that she was all in this.

All. In.

There was no dipping her toe into the shallow end of the water to adjust. Nope. She'd already jumped right on in to the deep end. Which had been more than shocking at first, but *that* was the reality. There was no getting out. No un-jumping.

This whole time she'd been trying to figure out how to adjust to having another man as her life raft. But Liam *wasn't* the life raft. He wasn't the thing keeping her from drowning. No, he was the person who was by her side learning to swim with her. Learning to survive it all. Together.

"What the hell am I doing?" she whispered to herself.

"Well, you could move forward." She jumped at the sound of the voice next to her.

She turned to the man in the suit, before she glanced back to the line that had shifted. Almost half of the people in front of her had been helped.

"You're right. I need to move forward. And there's no going back," she said as she grabbed her suitcase and walked out of the line, heading straight for the doors.

* * *

It was a damn good thing that none of these recordings of Liam singing "Forever" were going into the actual video. Because God help anyone who was forced to listen to that crap. He had a pretty good feeling that the extras out on that floor were in about as much pain as he was.

It was getting ridiculous.

But really, what in the world was to be expected? He was in the actual building where he'd met Harper, singing the song he'd written about her, and it was torture.

He shouldn't have let her leave like this. He should've fixed it. How? He had no idea, but he should've figured it out.

"Cut!" Jim the director shouted for what was probably the twentieth time. Liam had worked with the guy on a handful of other videos, and the two had actually become friends. Though, Jim looked like he wanted to throttle him at the moment.

"Can I get a minute?" Liam pulled the strap from his shoulder and set his guitar down, leaning it against the speaker.

"Sure, I'm getting a smoke," Jim said before he moved away from the cameras.

"Five minutes," the woman next to Jim shouted to the room.

As the crowd dispersed, Liam's manager Gary moved from where he'd been standing on the edge of the room and went up on the stage. "Man, you *really* need to not look like someone just killed your dog."

"I need a fucking shot."

A small smile turned up Gary's face. "You and me both. Whiskey?"

Normally that would be Liam's poison…but not now. "Tequila?" he asked, thinking about the last time he'd been in that room doing shots with Harper.

"Sure thing."

Both men jumped off the stage and headed for the bar. The

man behind it was actually one of the regular bartenders at the Second Hand Guitar. Everyone in the crowd got two free drinks. It was part of the ambience after all.

"Cheers." Gary held up his glass in the air when they got their shots.

Liam clinked it before they both tossed it back.

"What's going on with you?"

"Harper left today. And this stuff with Kiki is making her second-guess everything."

Gary knew *everything* about Harper. Liam had to tell him what was going on as the days around Sofia's due date were off limits to booking anything. There was also the fact that Liam wouldn't be in videos where he was acting out anything of the love variety with another woman. And last but certainly not least, the Kiki fiasco bullshit bomb that was about to explode.

That's what managers were for, right? Well, that and drinking a shot of tequila in the middle of the day. But it was five o'clock somewhere.

"You're pretty torn up about her, huh?" Gary asked.

"I love her more than I've loved anyone, but she doesn't know if she wants to spend the rest of her life with me."

"And you need to make her realize that she does." Not a question from Gary, but a statement of fact.

"Yes."

"You finish this shoot up today, you can be on a plane to her by tonight."

"Seriously?" Hope flared in Liam's chest.

"Most of this video has to do with the other three couples. They get all of the shots with you and you're done, my friend,"

Gary said as he reached for his pocket. His phone must've been vibrating because he picked it up and put it to his ear. "This is Gary."

The murmuring on the other end was barely audible as the crowd of people around Liam talked.

"What?" Gary asked, his eyes coming up and landing on Liam. "Okay, I'll be right out." He hung up, sliding his phone in his pocket. "I'll be right back." He reached out and grabbed Liam's shoulder. "You get up there and kill it. Understand?"

"Yeah." Liam nodded, taking a deep breath before he turned around and walked through the crowd.

He got back up on the stage, grabbing his guitar and pulling the strap over his head. He glanced up, catching Gary as he passed by Jim. The two men spoke for just a second. Gary probably telling the guy that Liam was going to pull his head out of his ass. Jim nodded before he headed back to the camera.

"You ready to get this shit done?" Jim asked as he settled in.

Liam took a deep breath and let it out. "Yeah."

"Then let's go."

His fingers strummed the chords of the guitar as the lights focused in on him. *"Love at first sight was something I'd never seen. But you walked in and became every one of my dreams…"*

It was at that moment that he saw her. The crowd disappeared and it was only Harper standing in the middle of that room and looking up at him.

"Violet eyes and the lips of a goddess. I knew I'd want more than just one kiss…"

Her mouth curved up in a smile as she watched him, and her

eyes closed for just a second as her body began to move to his voice.

"A day, a week, a month, a year. It would never be enough. I want forever, honey. Forever, honey…"

Her eyes opened and she looked up at him again. *"Forever with you,"* she sang along.

He kept going, Harper's mouth moving in sync with each and every word of the song until he got to the very end. *"I need forever, honey. Forever with you."*

The second his fingers strummed the last chord he was pulling the guitar from his body and jumping from the stage. The crowd parted and when he got to her he pulled her into his arms, his mouth coming down hard on hers as his fingers speared in her hair.

He tasted her mouth for a good minute before he pulled back and looked at her. "You didn't get on the plane."

"I didn't get on the plane." She shook her head. "I was wrong. I don't need any more time Liam. No more catching up. I want to spend the rest of my life with you. None of the other stuff matters. This is what matters." Her hand moved to his chest, her palm over his heart. "You and me."

"No more running?"

"I'm done running away from us. As long as you're next to me, I can handle anything."

"It's you and me, honey. From here on out." He leaned down, his mouth right against hers, their breath warm on each other's lips.

"From here on out," she agreed.

* * *

The second the front door of the cabin closed Harper found herself pushed up against the wall by the solid weight of her perfectly muscled, attractive as sin man.

Yeah, that was right. *Her man.*

"Haven't we done this before?" she asked as she looked up into his green-gold eyes. Eyes that had seen *her* from the very start. Eyes that didn't hide how much he loved her.

"I believe we have. But things have definitely changed since the last time we were here together."

"In so many ways."

"Buying you that beer is still the best decision I ever made." He grabbed her hands, pulling her arms up and pinning them to the wall above her head.

"Stole. You *stole* that beer."

"It was only fair. You stole my heart first." He grinned as he twined their fingers together.

"You're still using your lines on me. Apparently not everything has changed."

"Not a line." Liam shook his head, his lips brushing hers with the movement. "That's a fact."

"That so?"

"Yup. Want to know what else is a fact?" He skimmed his nose across her neck as he inhaled.

"What's that?"

"You smell incredible. You *always* smell incredible. Honey." He whispered the word, his warm breath hitting her skin before he pressed his lips to the spot just under her left ear. "My honey."

"Always yours." How had she ever doubted what they had? For even a second? Never again. Never, *ever,* again.

Liam's mouth left her skin as he pulled back, his eyes finding hers. "I'm going to kiss you now. So if you have any problems with that, you should speak now or forever hold your peace."

She couldn't stop herself from grinning at his words, the same words from their first night together. "No objections." She shook her head.

His mouth came down hard on hers, their tongues tangling together. It was a good long couple of moments before he pulled back. "Still no objections?"

"I'm objection-less."

"Thank God." He gave her a wicked grin before he let go of her hands and bent, sweeping her up in his arms.

"Liam!" she gasped, her arms going around his neck and holding on tight as he carried her through the house.

"I've got you, Harper."

"I know." Of that she had no doubt. She kissed his jaw, his beard rasping across her lips.

When they got to the bedroom he set her down gently. The second her feet were firmly stationed on the floor and she was standing up straight, his hands were on her hips and he was pulling her in close to his body.

"So I decided something," she said as she dropped her arms from where they were looped around his neck, running her palms down his chest.

"And what's that?" He took a step forward, moving her back through the room.

"I'm not going to let the lies in those stupid tabloids get to me. We'll make our own headlines."

"Yeah? Like what?"

"Well, the first one will say, '*Liam James and Harper Laurence Don't Care What Anyone Else Has to Say About Their Relationship, and Kiki Jean Carlow Is a Lying Piece of Work That Absolutely No One Should Listen To. Ever.*' Though that might be a little wordy?" The back of her legs hit the bed and they stopped moving.

"A little." He nodded. His hands had descended down and were now under the skirt of her dress.

"What about, '*Liam James and Harper Laurence Tell Everyone Else to Shove It*'? How does that sound?"

"Probably not the best for publicity." He grinned, palming her ass.

"Okay, '*Liam James and Harper Laurence Are Madly in Love*'?"

"No." He shook his head. "'*Liam and Harper James Are Madly in Love.*'"

She froze, as she looked up at him. "What?"

"Yeah, and the next will say, '*Liam and Harper James Settle into Their New Home in Mirabelle, Florida*' and after that '*Liam and Harper James Welcome Their Baby Girl into the World.*' I think I'm forgetting one though…" he trailed off, his eyes narrowing in thought as his mouth turned up at the sides. "Oh, the first one. '*Liam James and Harper Laurence, His Beautiful.*'" He kissed the side of her mouth. "'*Stunning.*'" He kissed the other side of her mouth. "'*Sexy as Hell Wife.*'" He pressed his lips to the center of hers. "'*Wed in a Small Beachside Wedding Surrounded by Friends and Family.*'"

"You want to marry me?"

His hands dropped from under the skirt of her dress, and her hands fell away from his chest as he reached over to the nightstand next to him and opened the top drawer. A second later he was holding up a little black velvet box, showing it to her before he flipped it open.

There, nestled in the white satin, was a cushion cut diamond, surrounded by a square of tiny diamonds that continued on to the band in two separate rows.

"Oh my God," she whispered as she looked down at the most stunning ring she'd ever seen in her life.

And okay, maybe she shouldn't be this shocked. Them heading toward marriage wasn't too much of a stretch. But he already had a ring. He'd already been planning to propose.

"I told you from the start, told you that the second I tasted you." He leaned forward and nipped at her bottom lip, pulling it into his mouth before he let go. "I'd want *everything*. But it happened before that first kiss, Harper. I wanted everything the second I found you. I've just been waiting for you to say yes."

She reached up again, her hands on his chest and moving over his shoulders. And then they were at the back of his head, her fingers in his hair as she brushed her lips across his. "You still haven't asked me the question."

"You're right. I haven't." He dropped to his knee in front of her. Both of her hands were still in his hair, and he grabbed the left and pulled it away to hold it in front of him. "It's always been you, Harper. You're it for me, have been from the very start. I didn't know something was missing from my life until I met you, and I never want to go back to how it was before you." He pulled the ring out, setting the empty box on the nightstand. "Will you marry me?"

"Yes."

He grinned up at her as he slid the ring onto her finger. Once it was firmly in place he was getting up off the floor, his arms wrapping around her waist as he kissed her.

"I love you, Liam James," she said against his mouth, her lips brushing his with every word that she spoke. "This is the life I want. The one with you in it. And it's the only one I will ever want."

"Promise?"

"I swear." And she sealed it with a kiss.

Epilogue

I Need Forever, Honey, Forever with You

November 2nd…one year and two months later

Liam adjusted the tie at his neck for what was probably the fortieth time that night. He still wasn't exactly what anyone would call a suit kind of guy even though he was wearing them a lot more lately.

He'd been sporting one this time last year when he and Harper had gotten married. They'd taken two months to plan it, the wedding happening that first weekend in November.

Harper had been six months pregnant and hadn't wanted to hide Sofia under layers of material. Adele designed the dress—obviously—and Harper's baby belly had been clearly outlined under the lace.

She was the most beautiful bride he'd ever seen in his life.

In fact, the gray tie he was currently wearing was the same he'd gotten married in. It was also the one he'd had on when he and Harper had found each other again in Jacksonville at the Stampede party.

He considered it his lucky tie. How could he not?

"Stop that," Harper whispered low in his ear as she reached up and grabbed his arm. "I haven't seen you this nervous since the day our daughter was born." She linked their fingers together as she pulled both of their hands into her lap.

"I wasn't nervous that day. I was terrified." Understatement.

But it was a thrilled terrified, if that made any sense. Their daughter had graced the world with her presence at eleven fifty-seven at night on January thirty-first. As it turned out she did have Harper's eyes and a full head of dark brown hair that matched Liam's.

There'd been nothing like holding Sofia in his arms for the first time. Nothing like her wrapping her tiny little hand around his finger as she slept. Nothing like hearing her sweet, perfect laugh.

Man did Sofia giggle like crazy. He loved that sound, loved it so freaking much.

She was ten months old now, a rambunctious little ball of mischief that didn't like to sit still for too long. She was very active, crawling around the house like it was her job, or playing with any number of her toys, Luna included.

The tiny dog was beyond gentle with the baby, and more often than not would be found sleeping somewhere in the vicinity, one ear cocked at all times and listening out for any threat. Not that there was anything that Luna could do besides bark, but it was the thought that counted.

Besides, threats were few and far between at their home. Liam's offer on the two-story beachside house had been accepted, and he'd had that thing baby proofed within an inch of its life before they'd even moved in. Harper had made the joke more than once that she was surprised he hadn't padded the walls.

He was a little surprised, too, actually.

But it wasn't just Sofia he wanted to keep safe. It was Harper, too. The woman currently sitting in the seat next to him was his *everything*. She'd given him the things that meant the most in this world.

In that moment, there were thousands of people sharing the same space as them, and she was still the most beautiful person in the room. Without a doubt. Her mouth was painted a bright red that matched her red dress, her hair curled and pinned up so that her neck was completely bared to him. She was wearing a long off-the-shoulder gown that wrapped around every one of her perfect curves. It was another one of Adele's impeccable designs.

"I'm really proud of you, you know. No matter what happens." Harper smiled as she leaned close, pressing her lips to his.

He moved his mouth from her lips to that cluster of freckles just under her left ear, kissing the spot before he whispered, "You're the reason I'm sitting here, Harper. You're the reason this is even happening." He pulled back so that he could look into her eyes.

It was then that the crowd of people around them broke out into applause. Liam pulled his gaze from Harper's and looked up as Isaac Dylan and Hunter Andrews came out onto the stage. They walked to the mike as the crowd quieted down.

"Song of the year is a category that is pretty near and dear to both of us," Isaac started.

Hunter leaned close to the mike to speak next. "It was this award that we were first up for seven years ago, and it was a launching point for our career. These are the nominees for CMA's song of the year."

Harper's hand tightened in Liam's and it only squeezed harder as Hunter and Isaac read through the list. The crowd cheered as they named each nominee, all the way through the last one: "Forever."

"And the winner for CMA's song of the year goes to." Isaac popped open the seal of the envelope and showed it to Hunter. Both of their mouths split into the biggest grins.

"'Forever' by Liam James," they said in unison.

Everything in him stilled. There was no way he'd heard that correctly. "Did that just happen?" He turned to look at Harper.

She grabbed his face, kissing him hard on the mouth before she pulled back. "Yeah it did. You won, baby."

He stood, pulling Harper to her feet and wrapping his arms around her as he kissed her again. When he pulled back there were tears in her eyes.

"I love you." He reached up and ran his thumbs under her eyes.

"I love you, too. Now go up there and get your award."

He kissed her one last time before he headed for the stage, the applause and cheers still ringing out loud around him. He mounted the steps and crossed over to where Isaac and Hunter waited.

They both gave him massive hugs, beaming hugely. They each said something. What? He had no clue. He couldn't hear over his pounding heart.

And then they were stepping away as the crowd quieted down, and Liam held the award in his shaking hands as he walked to the mike and looked out at the thousands of people in front of him.

"Isaac and Hunter presenting this award is pretty perfect as the beginning of my career has a lot to do with them bringing me out on the road during their tour." Holy hell, he was shocked his voice was steady as he spoke. "Thank you." He looked behind him and nodded at the two men before he faced the audience again.

"I want to thank my parents and brother and sister for their constant support. For years you all had to listen to me on my guitar and you never once complained. Then there is my manager Gary Kirkland, thank you for taking a chance on me. And finally, I have to thank the muse behind the song."

His eyes landed on Harper immediately, the radiating smile on her face making him feel like a fucking king.

"I saw her and I knew in an instant she was it for me. That night is the only time I've been more nervous than I am right now." A small rumble of laughter ran through the crowd.

"I asked for her name that night and told her I needed to know it so whenever I repeated this story, people would know the name of the most beautiful woman I'd ever met. I wrote 'Forever' within hours of meeting her and I'm sure a lot of you know about the stories that were around when it first came out. So tonight I'm going to set the record straight once and for all: Her name is Harper James. Not only is she my wife, she's the mother of my beautiful daughter Sofia. I've now experienced love at first sight twice in my life, and both of those women have the same violet eyes. This one's for you, honey."

He held the award up in the air, but as the crowd in front of him broke out into applause, all he could do was look at Harper.

She was still the only person in the room.

About the Author

Shannon Richard grew up in the Florida Panhandle as the baby sister of two overly protective but loving brothers. She was raised by a more than somewhat eccentric mother, a self-proclaimed vocabularist who showed her how to get lost in a book, and a father who passed on his love for coffee and really loud music. She graduated from Florida State University with a BA in English Literature and still lives in Tallahassee, where she battles everyday life with writing, reading, and a rant every once in a while. Okay, so the rants might happen on a regular basis. She's still waiting for her southern, scruffy, Mr. Darcy, and in the meantime writes love stories to indulge her overactive imagination. Oh, and she's a pretty big fan of the whimsy.

Learn more at:
ShannonRichard.net
Twitter, @Shan_Richard
Facebook.com/ShannonNRichard

Don't miss the next installment of
Shannon Richard's Country Roads series!

UNCONTROLLABLE

* * *

Available Spring 2016

CPSIA information can be obtained at www.ICGtesting.com
Printed in the USA
LVOW12s1306200116

470879LV00001B/2/P